crushed Violet

Tara Vanflower

CONTENTS

SUGGESTED MUSIC ACCOMPANIMENT:

- **Lycia** – Ionia, Estrella, A Day in the Stark Corner, Quiet Moments

- **Mike VanPortfleet** – Beyond the Horizon Line

- **Tara Vanflower** – my little fire~filled heart

- **Stone Breath** – The Silver Skein Unwound

- **Faith and the Muse** – Annwyn, Beneath the Waves, Vera Causa

- **World of Skin**

- **Swans** – Filth, Soundtracks for the Blind

- **Death in June** – Nada!

- **Current 93** – Swastikas for Noddy

- **Nitzer Ebb** – Showtime

- **Def Leppard** – Love Bites

- **Exploited** – Let's Start a War

- **The Cure** – Disintegration, Pornography, The Top

- **Soft Kill** – Let's Believe in Love

- **The Grinning Plowman** – I Play Jupiter

- **Bauhaus** – The Sky's Gone Out

- **Dark Muse** – Beyond the Silver Wheel

- **Type O Negative** – October Rust, World Coming Down, Bloody Kisses

- **Moth Masque** – Moth Masque

- **Queen Adreena** – Taxidermy

- **Arcana** – Dark Age of Reason

- **Minor Threat** – Out of Step

- **Fugazi** – Waiting Room

- **The Fall** – This Nation's Saving Grace

- **Nitzer Ebb** – Showtime

- **Cocteau Twins** – Garlands

- **Siouxsie & the Banshees** – Join Hands, Juju

- **Ministry** – The Mind is a Terrible Thing to Taste

- **Jane's Addiction** – Nothing's Shocking

- **Godflesh** – Streetcleaner

- **Black Happy Day** – In the Garden of Ghostflowers

- **White Lies** – Turn the Bells

- **Black Mare** – Field of the Host

- **Ides of Gemini** – Old World / New Wave

- **Catherine Wheel** – Fripp

- **The Soft Moon** – It Kills

I

CONTINUED FROM BEFORE

"The vampire? What vampire?" Roman asked, gripping her arms with his broken hands.

"I don't know. I couldn't see him. It was like I was inside of him, seeing through his eyes. He was old? Roman, maybe?"

Aquila? Aquila was gone. No one had seen or heard of him for eons. "What did you see, exactly?"

We were walking the streets, like old Roman streets. Or Greece? I don't know. Then we were in this beautiful home, and there was this woman, so beautiful, sleeping on a bed. He went to her, took her. He said we would be one, and that in 2000 years he would come for me. Roman, I felt what they feel when they feed..."

Roman looked at her for a long moment, their eyes locked. She looked terrified, but more than that, she looked overwhelmed. Exhilarated by fear.

Her description sounded like it must be Aquila and Ilya, but that made no sense. Aquila had been gone for several hundred years. And there had to be more than just two Roman vampires anyway. Since he couldn't see what she saw in her dreams, there was no way of knowing. *Fuck.* He would deal with figuring this vision out later. Right now he just needed to make sure she was alright.

5

"Are you feeling okay?" he asked, placing his hand against her cheek. She felt warm, but not fevered.

She took a deep breath as she assessed herself. "I feel fine physically. Fucked in the head, but fine. Make sense?"

Roman shook his head and exhaled. "Yes, it makes sense. Look, V, I don't know what your vision means, if it means anything. We'll worry about that another time. For now let me explain what I can."

He used his left hand to lift the photo album from the floor where he'd dropped it and set it in her lap. "There are volumes on the topic elsewhere, this is just an album of photos of my family."

It was intriguing to her that he kept a photo album with him. He didn't appear to be particularly sentimental that way. She looked over the photos. Some pictures were old and yellowed. Each picture held the images of men, women, and children with serious, straight faces. There were a couple photos of bodies in coffins, like the funeral photos she'd seen on those creepy shows they always play on TV around Halloween. Those images made her skin crawl, but she knew that had been "normal" during the time period.

"Centuries ago, one of my ancestors was attacked by a vampire. She was kept alive because they refused to believe there was anything wrong with her. One would assume, given the time period, that they would have at least thought she was possessed by demons. Instead, they just thought she had a breakdown, and that one day she would recover. It's ludicrous to think they were so ignorant, but apparently they were in denial. They fed her blood from the animals they butchered. It sounds barbaric, but that's what they did, and somehow justified it to themselves. They should have killed her. Not only was it wrong to keep her alive, but her life was nothing but misery, starving for blood and locked away like a prisoner for so many years. That is how the family became aware of vampires, denial or not."

Roman paused for a moment, thinking about how to proceed. There was so much to tell her, so much to try to explain, and he had never explained it to anyone prior. He looked into her eyes trying to gauge what she must be thinking. She looked confused, but not open.

"Everyone believes in legends and mythology to some degree. If they didn't we wouldn't have natural fears towards certain things. It's as though the side of our nature that hasn't evolved still recognizes the innate dangers of things like venomous snakes, spiders, etcetera. Our bodies know what our minds won't allow us to accept. We rationalize our fears away, when in reality, we should pay attention to them. So, needless to say, this was passed down from generation to generation. As the years went by, the family changed their stance on things and accepted what she was and she was put out of her misery."

"So, they killed her?" Violet asked, her brow deeply furrowed.

"It was a mercy killing."

"Was it though?" Violet asked. "Was she pure evil? Was she suffering outside of what was being done to her?"

Roman inhaled deeply. He had wondered the same his whole life but had just accepted that it was as he was told. He exhaled and looked away from her briefly.

"I don't have the answer to those questions since I wasn't there and neither were members of my family that I knew. I have decided to take the story as it was told. I can't judge their decision since I was not there." Violet nodded in response, satisfied with the answer. "After this is when they began seeking out vampires and killing them. I've been trained from birth to do this. I have known of their existence since I was old enough to be aware."

Violet didn't know what to make of what he was telling her. The rational side of her mind wanted to scoff at him, leave, and never look back. But she *knew* him, she knew he was telling the truth. His words resonated inside, perhaps with that dormant nature he spoke of now. It wasn't like him to waste words. He wasn't the type of person prone to fanciful ideas. This was all true. All horrifyingly true.

"This is my mother and father," he said, pointing to a picture.

His mother was beautiful, tall and strong looking in a quiet, dignified way. Her eyes shone with great wisdom, a depth that was almost tangible in the photos.

She was dressed in a white dress with red roses on it, crisp and clean, and the silver heart hung around her neck, resting in the middle of her stomach. She had a huge smile on her face, warm and sincere. His father looked almost exactly like Roman. He was tall and lean, with short black hair. There was darkness in the way he looked. Menacing. He looked lethal. Dangerous.

"She was pregnant with me in this picture," he said, his tone almost reverent.

Violet looked up at him for a moment, understanding the sadness in his voice. "That's why she's smiling," she said with kindness.

Roman looked at her briefly, and then back to the photos.

"Is that you?" she asked, pointing to a picture of a small chubby toddler. "Oh my God, how cute!"

"That is me," he said, as a hesitant smile came to his lips.

She took the photo album from him and held the picture closer. "So cute!" she repeated, and turned the pages, hoping to see more pictures of him. There were several more photos with his mom and dad. He and his mom were smiling in every picture but his dad was stoic and incredibly powerful looking, standing off from them as though his eyes were always searching the horizon.

"Was your dad a happy person?" she asked, going back to the beginning of the album and looking through the pictures again.

"Happy wouldn't be the way I'd describe him. He knew he had a job to do. He was a good and moral man, but distracted and distant."

She paused on the picture of him as a toddler again, and then closed the book, looking up at him intently. Her eyes focused on him with such intensity it was unnerving to him.

"I'm sorry for being angry earlier, Roman. I'm not sure why I had that re-action. I guess it just hurt to find out you were hiding so much from me. I mean, I've been pretty much as open as I could be with you." Her cheeks flushed pink. "Um, to an embarrassing degree, actually." Violet smirked nervously. "And I haven't really learned anything about you up until now. It just hurt me to find out just how much you've hidden. And I know I'm being stupid, because my first reaction is always anger. Honestly, your life isn't any of my business anyway. I shouldn't have been mad at you. I was just overwhelmed. I know you don't owe me anything."

"I have always kept everyone at arm's length. I didn't consider how that would affect you, because I had no intentions of getting you involved in any of this. But being attacked sort of changed that. "

"Yeah, I guess so," she said, turning towards him, "But I'm glad to know the truth, Roman. About you and about *them*." She rested her hand on his chest and looked intently into his eyes.

"I've always known there was something else out there in the world. I mean, I didn't know for sure, I guess, well, obviously. But I always just felt like I was missing something, unable to see something that was right in front of my face. I was blind and innocent before. Well, as innocent as I could be living the life I was living." She smirked briefly and looked away as if remembering something. Her eyes looked pained. "My parents died and that killed part of me. Now I feel like the rest of who I was is finally dead."

Her voice trailed off for a second, and her eyes lost focus, as though she was looking back over something again and examining it.

"Well, it's not like I've been exactly *innocent* for a long time. I just mean, parts of who I was have been dead for quite a while really, but tonight was the final nail in the coffin. Um, no pun intended." She snickered, looking up at him briefly, but he missed her joke being too focused on the seriousness of the situation. "And it's like I'm mourning the parts of myself that have been dead for a long time. Does that make sense?"

Roman furrowed his brow, looking over her sweet face. How could someone so young and so sweet be so tortured? It was hard to fathom. "It makes perfect sense. All you knew about vampires was the shit in movies and books. To find out they aren't just characters must be a mind fuck. I've been around this my whole life, it's never been anything but reality to me, so I can only imagine what it must be like for someone who didn't know any of it existed."

9

"But I think I did know they existed and I just pretended not to notice," she said, opening the book and looking through the pictures again. "Like you said, our bodies know, but our minds deny. None of this even feels shocking, weirdly enough. Just as part of me feels like it died, a whole different and separate part of me feels like it's waking up. I almost feel like the purpose in my life has just been revealed. Do you know what I mean?" She looked over at him. His face was serene, serene as she'd never seen it before. "It's sort of like the black sheep of the family finding out they're adopted. It just makes sense somehow."

"I think I understand."

"I want to do what you do, Roman," she said, resolved, putting her hands on his shoulders and staring into his eyes with determination.

He tilted his head slightly, looking at her with dark eyes. "Violet, I was born to this, you need to stay far away from the danger. My goal is to keep you safe."

"Why? Is there a reason you need to protect me specifically? And what better protection than to teach me how to protect myself? Stake through the heart? Decapitation? Garlic and holy water? Is that how it goes?"

He laughed. Her childlike curiosity was adorable to him. "You put a stake through anything's heart and it's going to die. Pretty much works for decapitation too." He laughed.

"Well, is that what you do?"

"Something like that." He smiled and shook his head. Her entire world was just turned upside down and now she wanted to learn how to kill vampires?

"I want to know what you know. I want you to train me. I'm strong enough, or at least I could be with your help. Maybe I was born for this too? There has to be a reason for my dreams all these years? I've had dreams about places I could never find in books. I've dreamt about people who were so real I was sad when I woke up to realize I didn't know them here. Some of those faces felt like family to me. Some of the places felt like home. Palaces and forests and black seas. Don't you think maybe I was born for this too? Maybe there's a reason we were brought together? Maybe you need my help as much as I need yours?"

Her eyes were alight with intensity, like two burning blue flames fueled by the wonder of it all. She looked almost inhuman. If he didn't know better, he would think she was a vampire, the way she seemed to command the room and maybe the elements themselves. He could feel her energy whirring around, raising the hair on his arms, almost compelling him to do exactly what she was asking.

"Roman, teach me!" she commanded.

They were perfectly still as they stared into each other's eyes. Waiting, searching.

"Okay." He finally surrendered, shrugging his shoulders.

"Cool!" she said, and flopped back down onto the bed beside him.

"No, it's really not cool, Violet," he warned her.

"I didn't mean cool like that, I'm satisfied, that's what I meant. So, what do I learn first?"

"First you're going to have to condition your body. We'll start running tomorrow."

"Ugh," she said, and settled back on the bed.

"You don't have to do any of this," he said, turning to look at her. He hoped she'd give up.

"No, I *will* do it!" she said with defiance, rising up on her elbows. She heard the familiar ring of her cell phone from her bag out in the living room.

"Why do you turn that thing up so damn loud?" he said, rolling his eyes and then standing up to go to the bathroom. His hand was throbbing, and he figured he ought to clean it out and assess the damage.

She ran out into the living room. Her mind was racing with fear, bewilderment, excitement, and clarity. "Hello?" she whispered, out of breath.

"Hello, angel." The voice was seductive, a lulling purr on the other end.

"Hey! Who are you?" she demanded.

"No need to worry about that. I assume you met my friends?"

"Who *is* this?" she asked again.

Roman walked out into the living room and over toward her. Violet was crouched on the floor beside her purse. He sat on the arm of the chair listening to the conversation.

"Is he there?" the woman asked.

"Yes," Violet answered, confused by the question.

"Good," the woman said, and hung up.

Violet turned the phone off and set it on the coffee table.

"What's going on?" Roman asked, with a look of concern on his face.

"It's that woman again. The one I told you about from the bonfire."

"And you don't know who it is? Think hard."

"I have no idea, Roman. She asked me if 'he' was here, I assumed she meant you, and I said yes, and she said 'good' and then hung up."

"I'm sure it's just someone fucking with you. Try not to worry," he said, hoping to assuage her fear. "Mark probably has someone harassing you." He wasn't sure he believed that himself, but he didn't want to add anymore bullshit to worry about at that moment. He could hunt down the mysterious caller later.

"You're probably right. But she asked me if I'd met her friends. Roman, you never answered me when I asked you if I had a specific reason to need protection." She sat down on the couch, looking up at him with wide eyes.

He had to tell her what he knew. "Lux sent me to protect you. That's all I know."

"Lux? How would he even know me?" Lux? What the fuck?

Roman chuckled. "He didn't know I was here to protect you when he sent me. He claims not to know what's going on, but with him you never get the whole story."

"And you still waited until *now* to tell me all this vampire shit?" She was annoyed with him again. He could see by the look on her face that he'd get another tongue lashing if he didn't just apologize straight away.

"Yes, it was a mistake. I'm sorry," he said. "But that's honestly all I know. He gave me no more information."

"Then we need to get him back here now. He's going to tell me what he knows, damnit. Something is obviously going on, Roman. What is going on?"

"I've been trying to get him on the phone, to no avail, and Mylori will tell me nothing"

"Of course she won't!" Violet said sarcastically.

"Well, she doesn't care. I know that sounds harsh, but that's the reality of who they are."

"Who they are?" Violet said, and then the light bulb went on. "They're vampires, aren't they?" Violet asked, slapping her legs with frustration and realization. She felt stupid for having gone on and on about him now. "Why don't you kill them?"

"Not everything is that black and white, V. They've helped me a thousand times. And besides, I thought you liked vampires? I seem to recall you saying that. So, now you want them all dead?" He teased her, knowing by the look on her face she was embarrassed.

His casual demeanor seemed to diffuse the tension to a degree. "Yeah, well that was when they seemed all romantic, or something. Now that I know they're real, it changes things a little."

"Yeah, reality has a way of changing things."

"But still, man, you must think I'm such an idiot! And how funny it must have seemed to *him*!" Violet was suddenly immensely embarrassed for having gone on about marriage and kids and oh-how-hot Lux was.

"Let it go." Roman smiled, knowing what she was thinking. "Besides, he's used to having women and men fawning all over him. It's nothing new to him. He has his powers of persuasion, and he enjoys the attention."

She covered her face with her hands, attempting to hide her blood-red cheeks from his view. There were a thousand and one questions to ask, and all she could think about right now was her humiliation.

"You have so much to learn about all of this. I had the advantage of growing up around it, so it's all second nature for me. I'll tell you anything you need to know. But right now, let's order pizza, eat it, and then go to bed." He stood up and walked to the telephone.

"I'm gonna call Amber and let her know I'm okay. I'm sure she's heard what happened at the store by now."

"You gonna tell her?" he asked, looking back at her.

"Not yet."

"See, the burden is heavy."

Violet looked up at him with a little more understanding now. She was still pissed he hadn't trusted her, but now she understood why he'd been reluctant.

The room was pitch black. Violet had borrowed one of his shirts to sleep in, the cool sheets felt good against her bare legs. Her mind was rolling with question after question, thought after thought. She fluctuated from dreadfully frightened to intensely curious. He knew that she must be reeling from all she'd seen and learned. She was bound to be freaking out.

"I can turn the bathroom light on if you want," he commented, leaning over on his elbow.

"No, the dark somehow seems more appropriate now." She hesitated.

He could hear the fear in her voice. "We're safe, sweetheart," he reassured her, pushing the hair back away from her face. "I'm the thing vampires fear."

The soft brushing of his hand across her cheek was comforting. It reminded her of how her mom used to comfort her when she wasn't feeling well or when she'd had a bad dream. Her eyes had adjusted to the dark, and she could see vague outlines of his face and eyes. They were wide open and looking at her.

"Roman?" she asked.

"Mm hmm?" he responded softly.

"Are you afraid of dying?" She felt the fear choking the words in her throat and she swallowed, trying to keep the panic down in her stomach where it couldn't erupt.

"No, we're all going to die sometime," he answered, and moved his arm over so it touched her. He thought it would make her feel better to have physical comfort without being smothered.

She considered his words. Yes, they were all going to die at some point. Terror shot through her. She didn't want to die. She didn't want him to die either. There had already been too much death, even metaphoric death. And besides, she didn't have the luxury of believing in what came next like her grandparents and parents had. They had always lived in peace, knowing that no matter what, they were going to be taken care of even in the afterlife.

"So, like, do you believe in God and Jesus, or whatever?" she asked with hesitation and slight embarrassment. This topic was one she never spoke about with anyone. She certainly had never talked about it with her friends, as most of them were adamantly opposed to any such thing. The idea of religion was idiotic to them.

"Of course," he answered, without any hesitation.

"Of course? Even after knowing these monsters exist?"

"If monsters exist then why not angels? If you can believe in one, why wouldn't you believe in the other? There are mysteries all over our world and elsewhere, and anyone who claims to know it all, knows nothing. I would never pretend I understand this world or the next, but I know what I've seen with my own eyes, and what I have experienced. There's a reason they held crosses up and cast demons out in the name of Jesus throughout history. And whatever came before him, I don't know. I'm not arrogant or delusional enough to think I have all the answers."

She had no more questions at that moment anyway. She was stunned by his answer. She rolled over and gripped his arm and cuddled against him. The thickness and warmth of his solid body was comforting. She stared blankly into the darkness of his small, cool room. She could feel by the slow, steady rise of his chest that he was now sleeping. God, he must be exhausted to fall asleep that quickly.

She couldn't understand how he'd been able to live this life. What even was his life? He literally lived in a different realm from the rest of them. She wondered if it finally felt good to have this secret off his chest, or if it would be a burden. She didn't want to be a burden to him.

Her thoughts shifted again to the phone call, to the fact that Lux and Mylori were vampires. *Roman slept with a vampire!* How insane was that? Were vampires like they are in books and movies? Or were they far more mundane and just like normal people? And what the fuck was going on with her life? It was officially fucked.

"Roman?" she asked quietly.

He stirred and opened his eyes. "You alright?" he asked, tilting his head and resting it against the top of hers.

"Yes."

"Good." He breathed deeply and closed his eyes again.

"Roman? Is it like in the movies and you're like some *chosen one* or something? Like some vampire killer from a movie?" She felt his mouth smiling against the top of her head.

"No. I'm just a guy who's good at killing things," he answered, his voice grumbly with sleep.

"Oh," she answered, full of a thousand more questions.

"Maybe you're chosen though. That remains to be seen," he muttered, drifting back off to sleep.

Her eyes widened, and she felt simultaneously petrified and enthralled. "Roman?" she asked again.

"Sleep, kitten, we'll answer questions tomorrow."

Violet felt her heart swell and contract, like the words he spoke were pure adrenalin. She pressed her body closer to his and closed her eyes, hoping she'd be able to sleep.

She fell back onto the bed, her hair splayed around her in thick black swathes. She was beautiful there. He could see her in the field, flowers hallowing her head and kissing her body. They bent towards her on their delicate green stems, pressing their yellow faces to her skin with reverence. Her children.

The silver moonlight dappled her flesh, like big perfect drops of rain speckling the surface of a still pool of cool water. How he wanted to wet his dry tongue in that water.

She would taste sweet. Like the nectar of those flowers.

He stood over her. A fortress. His hair so black and wavy, hanging down over his shoulders like vines. She wanted to wrap her wrists around those coiling vines and pull herself up the tower of his body. The white columns of his limbs like sculpted marble, like ivory. His mouth, the hidden temple. She wanted to explore and worship. And sacrifice.

His eyes looked different tonight. He looked at her like a man who wanted a woman. He had only ever been her protector, her big brother. But those weren't the eyes of a savior now.

Or maybe they were the same eyes that always looked at her but she had changed? Maybe she wanted to see a man who would want her, but really he was just her guard? Was she the ivory tower or was he?

Would he let her touch him? Would his soft flesh yield to her fingertips? Or would all the walls remain in place, impenetrable?

He bent over, his palms flat against the cool sheets as they slid towards her, one knee on the bed, then another. He climbed towards her, stalking, his eyes fixed on his prey.

She reached forward taking fistfuls of his hair in her hands, pulling him towards her. His lips met hers. So soft. Just as she had always imagined. He crushed himself against her, falling into the cradle of her body. Everything about this moment was perfection.

His tongue parted her lips, her fingers twisting like knots in his hair. Her arms snaked around his torso, holding him to her. Never leave.

Wake up.

2

PORCELAIN AND SWEAT

"Stop fretting," she said coolly, as she placed her long white leg across his lap.

He looked towards her, and then away from her to his friend who was slumped in the corner. He could see the faint rise and fall of the chest, the slow gurgling sighs escaping the mouth.

"He'll be dead soon," she mused, looking over her shoulder at the lump on the floor.

"Do me next!" Gwen chirped, rising to her knees and pressing her palms together as if she were praying to a living deity.

The woman smiled like a cat, wiped the red droplet from the corner of her mouth, and seductively placed the finger between her lips. "Ahh...little one, come to me." She sat up, opening her arms to the eager girl.

Gwen crawled on her knees towards her and fell into the woman's embrace, resting her face against her neck. "And you'll make me like you? You promise?" she begged, trembling all over with anticipation.

"Let us see what happens." She smiled seductively and wrapped her arms around Gwen, cuddling her like a loving mother, rubbing her back and cradling her head in her cold hands. She kissed the girl gently, soft as feather kisses, and then ripped into her throat, instantly severing the succulent artery. Blood flowed in a thick, hot river down her neck and onto her white silk gown. Gwen's eyes rolled to the back of her head and her mouth forced itself open, wailing deliriously. The woman gripped her for several moments, and then let the girl slide to the dirty floor in a heap.

He looked down at the lifeless body and then to the woman. She shrugged slightly and raised an eyebrow. "I didn't promise anything." She sniffed and stood up. "And she ruined my dress."

He looked back down at the dead girl. Her lifeless eyes dull and frozen. The cells of her body decomposing and expelling gasses too faint for most to smell, but he smelled it--fresh death. That sweet, delicious scent was intoxicating. He was already drunk on it. Already in love with the fragrance.

He stood up and followed the woman into the bathroom where she was running bath water. The steam rose in smoky wisps from the claw footed tub. She stood naked with her back towards him, her long brown hair hid the curve of her back from him, the silk dress torn and crumpled on the floor. She turned her head slightly, acknowledging his presence--her awareness of his eyes on her body--and then she stepped into the hot water and slid beneath the water's surface.

He walked towards the tub and went to his knees, waiting for her to resurface, watching as the bubbles of oxygen escaped through her nostrils to erupt at the still surface. Her body was milk white, bluish veins snaking just beneath the skin and seeming to rise as his eyes glided over them. The sight of her perfect breasts, her narrow hips and long sinewy limbs called to every cell of his body. She had the body of a dancer, lithe limbs long and lean, the neck of a swan. He admired the strong jutting of the collarbone and the sharpness of her hips. Just the kind of body he'd always wanted Violet to have.

Violet. Her name never seemed far from his mind.

He shook his thoughts, peering back at the woman before him. It was a bit intimidating, the way her eyes examined him through the cloudy hot water, knowingly, calculating. They bore into him, diffused by the milky hot water, but no less keen. Finally he reached into the water, urging her to surface, needing to touch her again, needing to break the spell.

She slid against the back of the tub as water spilled onto the floor in a loud splash, and then smoothed her hair back away from her face. The splattered blood was dripping in pale pink rivers down her chin in watercolor streams, back into the water where it swirled in spiraling ribbons. She licked her lips, then grasped the back of his head with her hand, beckoning him to come to her mouth. He obeyed. The taste of metallic water and saliva was a drug to him.

"Why didn't you keep her?" he asked quietly against her cleansing mouth.

"I don't like girls," she breathed into him, coolly.

"Wake up, sweetie," Roman said and yanked the blanket off of her. She was curled into a tight ball. He actually wanted to let her sleep, but there wasn't time if this is what she really wanted. And his brain was thinking too much about things his brain shouldn't be thinking about. His sleep had been less peaceful than usual. Not that he ever really slept well. "Come on, I'm making pancakes," he grabbed her foot and shook it.

He hoped he wasn't making a mistake. There was no way his family would have approved of bringing a stranger into all of this, of giving away secrets, but what did that matter now? They were all dead and buried. *His mother would have loved her.* The thought made him smile, and that made him shake his head. Violet cracked one eye open and stretched like a cat, contorting her body. He thought she looked cute, lying there in his oversized shirt, yawning like a tiny lioness. Or maybe more like a black panther.

"You're making pancakes?" she asked groggily, and rubbed her tired eyes.

"Yep, I went to the store," he explained, and walked out of the room.

"And you left me here alone?" she yelled, as she leapt out of the bed and ran towards the bathroom.

"Sunshine, sister, no need to worry about monsters in broad daylight," he yelled from the kitchen. "Well, not these ones anyway," he grumbled to himself.

She quickly shut the door and pulled her panties down and went to the bathroom. She could barely hold it, and wondered if she would have peed in his bed had he not woke her when he did. "That would have been embarrassing," she said out loud to herself. She finished and then washed her hands and face and trotted to the kitchen. She wanted to see these so-called pancakes.

"You need a lot of carbs if you're going to run today," he joked, walking a plate of pancakes to her. There was a pile of food he knew she wouldn't be able to consume. He also knew very well this wasn't a nutritious breakfast, but he'd never eaten nutritiously and he'd always been just fine.

She was sitting at the small dining room table, seemingly fascinated by the edge of the aluminum trim and gold flecked laminate top. The vinyl seats felt cold against her bare legs.

"I can't wait," she smiled, and rolled her eyes.

"It's going to be difficult," he walked back to the stove and picked up another stack of pancakes. "But you should get in shape fairly quickly. You're young and healthy, and not too terribly out of shape."

"Gee, thanks. Careful with the compliments. Wouldn't want my head to explode."

Roman just smirked and sat down across from her, took a knife and placed a heaping scoop of butter on his pancakes and spread it around, then poured syrup all over the plate, drowning the pancakes. She watched in amazement.

"Want some pancakes with your butter and syrup?" she teased him, with a feigned look of disgust on her face.

"Hey, I like sugar and butter. You already knew that about me," he said.

She smiled and took the syrup and did the same thing he did. The pancakes were large syrup sponges that tasted like heaven in her mouth. "Where'd you learn how to make pancakes?"

"My mom," he said, and took a bite.

Syrup oozed out of the pancakes and dripped onto his chin. She debated whether or not to tell him, as she thought it was pretty funny to see him with syrup on his face. She decided to keep it to herself. She smiled and remembered the dreams she'd had all night. Good dreams. And some bad ones. But it was hard to remember those as she looked at him now. She looked away to clear her thoughts and took another bite.

"So, how did your parents die?" she asked, completely changing the topic in her brain. She had a way of asking questions that were probably inappropriate, but Roman was unfazed.

"My mom died of cancer, and my dad was killed by vampires a few months later."

Violet dropped her fork to her plate, making a loud "ting" and looked at him, feeling aghast and sad for him. The way he said it so nonchalantly, as if he was talking about the weather, took her aback. And despite the strangeness of his life, he had once had a loving family just like her, just like most people have. It seemed odd to her. It seemed like he should have always been this age and this person. So big and serious. It was hard to imagine him as the child she saw in the pictures. She just couldn't rectify it in her mind.

"So, are they like in the movies? Like garlic, and holy water, and all that?" she asked, changing the topic again.

The subject change threw him for a second. Despite all that had happened the night before, it was still strange to be having this conversation with another person. "Sort of, in some ways, I guess. Garlic and holy water don't do anything. That's all just that kind of religious mythology stuff that people believed in a long time ago, and of course the vampires did nothing to dissuade them. I think the more mythological and fairytale-like they appear, the better it is for them. I prefer to chop their heads off."

Her mouth fell open, the brutality of what he said shot through her. Chopping someone's head off. That was harsh. It was so barbaric and ludicrous it almost made her laugh.

"Hey, it's the reality," he shrugged, noticing her reaction to the words.

"I know, it's just bizarre. I mean, *you cut people's heads off*," she said, looking at him with some kind of cross between admiration, fear, and pity.

"I don't *cut people's heads off*. I put down murderers." He set his own fork down, a bemused grin coming to his lips. "Doesn't this all sound so ridiculous? It sounds like some lame ass movie or something, and yet it's real. I never really got how fucking stupid this all sounds until just now. I've never explained this to anyone before. It is ridiculous." He smiled and took a big gulp of orange juice.

"It is ridiculous. I have all these questions in my head, and they all sound ludicrous. Like, I can't even bring myself to ask half of them because of the absurdity." She laughed and started eating again. "So, are there like a ton of them around, and eventually they will outnumber us or something?"

He laughed at her candor. "No, there are very few in comparison to how many of us there are. Most of them are pretty much loners to some degree, like lone wolves hunting on their own. But there are those that decide they want to people the earth with vampires. I guess they are my main concern. Honestly, whether someone dies from being bitten by a vampire or from cancer, what difference does it make? We're all going to die. But it's the crazy breeders I focus on. When vampires live together, trouble seems to follow. I guess that's why I was brought here." He still had no idea the full reason why Lux had sent him.

"There are breeders in this town? How fucking scary is that?" she asked, her mouth agape.

"Nothing I can't handle." He laughed again. God, this was so fucking strange.

"This blows my mind." She shook her head.

"I imagine it would. It blows mine too."

"What did you mean last night, when you said it remained to be seen whether or not I was chosen?"

"It means there might be more to you than I have figured out. Lux seemed pretty adamant that I would protect you the last time we spoke. You have to understand what that means. Lux doesn't care about human beings. So, it leads me to believe something more is going on here."

"Maybe he just thinks I'm cute?" She smirked at him, knowing how absurd the statement was.

"Violet, I guarantee he thinks you're cute." He smiled at her, wanting her to understand the truth of his statement, since she seemed to have some self-esteem issues. "But being cute means little more to him than just an extra tasty snack."

The reality of his declaration shot to the core of her being. Her face went still for a moment, and then her eyebrows knit together as the questions rose to the surface.

"Vampires view humans as nothing more than a food source for the most part. It's like the way we consider cows. Sometimes we may think they're cute, or even enjoy looking at them, or petting them, or taking care of them, but in the end, they're just a hamburger to most people."

"And you banged Mylori? So what does *that* mean?"

He choked on his food, not expecting her question. "Um, I guess she likes petting cows once in a while?" he reached for his juice and cleared his throat with a big swallow of the pulpy drink.

"Yeah, heavy petting cows." She laughed at him as his face contorted. "Well, what was that like? Weren't you afraid she'd, like, bite you or something?"

"I'm not discussing this." He shook his head and grinned at her.

"Come on! I want to know!"

"No. And if you're even getting *ideas* about Lux forget it."

She grinned at him and let the subject drop, though she would most definitely ask again at some point. "So, I guess this whole vampire thing changes everything," she said seriously.

"Yes, I suppose it does," he looked at her, a stillness coming over him. "You done?" he asked, breaking their gaze and standing up to walk his plate to the kitchen. He turned the water on and rinsed the syrup and butter off, then set the plate in the sink. She followed him and scraped the gluey contents of her plate into the trash, and then let him rinse it off.

"You ready?" he asked. He was looking forward to running with her. He'd never had anyone to run with before, at least not since his dad died. They used to run for miles and miles in silence, side by side. He remembered those quiet moments fondly. It was the only time they were really together. Just the two of them. It had taken all his strength to keep up. And the day it was no longer a struggle he'd known he was ready. His dad had treated him differently too. It was like a weight was lifted off his shoulders, well, partially. His father had never been burden free. And all that time spent running side by side with his dad was why he was so strong now.

She nodded her head and walked back to his room. She picked her clothes up from the dresser where she'd placed them and got dressed. Roman was in the bathroom, doing whatever it was he was doing. She walked to the closet, reached up for the album again, and leafed through it. The only people smiling in this whole book were Roman and his mother. She wanted him to smile again like this, he had to smile again like this.

"Hey, thanks for telling me I had syrup all over my face." He shoved her in the arm as he met her in his room.

"Sorry." She smiled, distracted by her thoughts. "Roman, are you ever going to get married and have a family?" She closed the book and handed it to him.

"No. I'm the last of this line." He put the album back in the closet and shut the door.

"But then, what will happen to all us helpless non-vampirey people when you're gone?"

He didn't say anything, but reached for his boots and pulled them on and began lacing them. She could see by the look on his face he didn't want to answer her question. She wouldn't pry... today.

"You're running in *that*?" She stared incredulous at him in his jeans and sweat-shirt as they walked down the hall to the living room.

"Sure. Vampires don't wait for you to go home and put on your work out gear." He held the door open for her, and locked it behind them.

"I guess they wouldn't, would they."

She hopped down the stairs and stood by his car waiting. "So, maybe I should start wearing tennis shoes all the time? It might be easier," she held up her leg and the three inch platform boots she was wearing.

He smirked and opened the car door for her. "We'll stop by your house so you can change. There's no use trying to get in shape in those. You'd probably break an ankle."

"So, what's the deal with vampires anyway? Can they like, turn into bats and all that junk too?"

Roman snorted and laughed out loud. "No."

"Hey! How would I know?" she whined with a pout, and pinched his arm. "I told you the questions were absurd."

"I know, I know, don't be so sensitive. It's just the thought of Lux as some blonde bat flying around cracks me up."

Violet snickered and asked, "Do they have any special powers?"

"Well, they're good at manipulating people. They can get in your mind and influence you. I'm sure you noticed the vibe around Lux and Mylori?"

"Yes, I just thought I was swooning cuz he's so fucking hot." She laughed.

"Oh man, if we're going to do this, you're going to have to stop that."

"Sorry, it's true," she said with a shrug. "Like you don't find *her* attractive."

He looked over at her for a moment, and then back at the road. "You really don't like her do you?"

"No. I really don't."

"Why?"

"I dunno, I just don't," she looked out the side window into the mirror, and watched the 4x4 truck riding up quickly behind them. "Stupid rednecks," she grumbled to herself.

Roman looked at her with a furrowed brow, wondering where that came from. They pulled into her driveway, and got out of the car and walked to the house. It was perfectly still and quiet.

"No one's home. That's a first," she said, tossing her bag down and walking into the kitchen. She noticed the rugs in the kitchen were messed up and there were muddy footprints on the linoleum. "I'm gonna call Amber and see what's going on." She looked at the notepad beside the phone and found Amber's work number and dialed.

"The Attic, Amber speaking. Can I help you?"

"Hey!" Violet smiled and leaned against the countertop.

Roman walked to the living room and sat down on the couch. He looked around the room at all the knick knacks and photos that adorned the shelves and the walls.

"Long time no see, Vi! When are you coming home?"

"Probably tonight, I'm not sure. Me and Roman are going to start running this morning."

"Running? What the fuck?" Amber laughed in question.

"Just trying to get in shape."

"Um, okay?" Amber said with skepticism.

"So, what's going on? There's mud all over the kitchen and the rugs are all messed up."

"Oh, Randy's helping Steve move out today. Can you believe that?"

"What? Why's he moving out?"

"He just said he wanted to move out."

"Come on, Amber, there's more to the story than that. Tell me."

"He just said he just wants to get out of your house. You know, it's all Mark. Don't take it personally, okay?"

"I'm actually glad he's leaving. I kind of want peace in the house, you know? I'm tired of all the chaos. And with Steve here the chance of Mark coming around is greater because Steve is a dumbfuck. Randy isn't stupid enough to invite that fuck over."

Amber laughed. "Now we can have romantic dinners, just the four of us." The smirk on her face was audible even through the phone.

"The four of us, who?"

"Really? You're not this dim. Me and Randall, and you and Roman, dork."

"Shut up!" Violet couldn't help her silly grin despite the embarrassment.

"So, did you guys do it yet?" Amber teased, but really did want to know.

"Oh my God, Amber!"

"Why are you so embarrassed? You used to tell me that stuff about Mark all the time. What's the big deal?"

"Because Roman's not Mark, and it's not like that between us, dick!"

"Okay, but you want it to be that way."

"What I want is irrelevant," Violet said, her tone noticeably dejected.

Roman's ears perked up at that, his brows drew together. He could vaguely hear the conversation in the other room and was curious about her statements, that last one in particular. The comment about Mark and him followed by the statement regarding what she might want sounded strange. And while he didn't know exactly what she was talking about, it somehow made him feel good in a way that alternately made him feel sick. He remembered the dream, his eyes going blurry as he pictured it. He shook his thoughts, his eyes drawn to the picture of her in the purple dress again. She would never be that happy again, he thought, especially not if he stuck around.

"Okay, I'm gonna go change," she said, bouncing into the room. "What are you staring at?" she asked, walking in front of him.

"I like that picture of you," he said in a monotone voice, standing up and walking over to her.

"That's me in kindergarten," she said, lifting the metal frame from the shelf. "That was my favorite dress. About three weeks after this picture I caught it on the swing set we used to have, and it tore to shreds." She looked at it for a moment and then handed it to him. "You can have it."

"I can't take this," he said, shoving it back towards her.

"Sure you can. I want you to have it," she said, stuffing it into his hand firmly. "Unless you don't want it?"

He smiled at her and took the picture from her and looked at it. "I'll take it."

"Okay, I'm gonna go get dressed," she said, and bounded out of the room and up the stairs.

He looked down at the photo and studied everything about the picture. He loved this picture. He wasn't even entirely sure why, he just did. After several minutes he heard her speeding back down the stairs.

"Okay, I'm ready," she said, walking up to him. She was wearing black sweatpants with a white thermal shirt with tiny yellow rosebuds on it, and tennis shoes. Her hair was in two long braids. This was a new look for her he'd never seen. He liked it.

"Let's go," he said, and stood up.

"Guess what?" she asked, grabbing his sleeve and holding onto it as she scooped her purse up from the couch. "Steve's moving out today. That leaves another empty room." She grinned at him with insinuation.

"Uh huh," he answered, opening the door and walking outside. He looked up at the sky. It was overcast and misty.

"Just saying, there's even more room for you." She let go of his arm and turned to lock the door.

"Duly noted," he said, looking down at her. He shoved the photo, which he'd removed from the frame, into the inside pocket of his jacket.

Her lungs felt like they were on fire. She wanted to puke them up in a scorched heap onto the track. The black cinders would stick to them and make them look like poppy seed muffins. She laughed to herself. Why the hell did imagery like this always come to her mind? She was weird. Duh, no kidding.

"You feeling alright?" he asked, barely winded.

"I'm okay. But I wish I had a nickel for every time someone asked me that." She panted as she wiped her runny nose with her sleeve, and bent over letting her arms hang towards the ground. She coughed a few times, trying to clear her lungs.

"We can stop anytime you want. We've already gone five miles," he said, raising his eyebrow at her. "Rome wasn't built in a day."

"But was Roman built in a day? That's the question," she said, and laughed. "Sorry, that was really really stupid!" She laughed at herself again.

"The answer is no. Roman was probably built in a couple minutes of drunken stupor." He shook his head and sped up.

"Sick!" she teased, and continued trying to catch her breath.

He wanted to test her strength. Would she be able to keep up with him, having already exhausted herself? "Come on, slow poke," he said, running backwards and taunting her.

She gritted her teeth and ran after him as fast as she could. Her legs were burning, her lungs bursting, but she continued to follow him as fast as she could go, until she finally stopped and threw her body over, letting her arms hang limply. She sucked down large lungful breaths hoping to get enough oxygen to slow her heart, which was exploding in her chest. She dragged herself over to the bleachers and pulled her tired carcass up the stairs and sat down, legs dangling over the edge. She watched him continue to sprint around the track for another lap at top speed until he'd finally made his way back around to where she sat, still gasping and wheezing. It was impressive, watching a giant with long black hair zipping around the track like an Olympian in black jeans and combat boots.

"I tried," she explained breathlessly.

"You did really well," he answered, finally breathing heavily as well. "Lift your arms over your head. You'll get more oxygen that way," he said, taking both of her hands and lifting them up, his own hands dwarfing hers. Roman placed them on the railing above her head, squeezing them before letting go. She held onto the bar, resting her head on one arm, as her breath slowly came back to her.

"I haven't run that much my whole life," she said, looking up at Roman, who was eye level with her now that she was in the stands.

"You did really well, seriously," he said, walking towards her and resting his hands on the bleacher where she sat.

Violet noticed his bruised hand, his knuckles still broken open, and frowned but said nothing.

"If you're really going to come into this world, you may have to run that fast someday over a distance, in order to save your life. You need to be ready for it," he said,

"Great," she said, and smiled at him.

"I wish you didn't know about any of this," he said, his tone very sober. He had already mostly caught his breath. He wished she was blissfully unaware of his world, but she wasn't, and knowing how to defend herself was good, regardless. At the very least, conditioning herself to run away was a good start.

She studied the forlorn look on his face, such sadness and depth in his eyes. His cheeks were flushed red, and his hair was curled from the sweat. Her breathing was finally slowing. She was exhausted, but felt alive like she'd really accomplished something, like her body was built for this, and it was happy to finally be doing what it was destined for.

"Try not to worry about me," she said, and hopped down off the stands.

He watched as she stretched her legs. She might be faster than him if she continued to run. The fact that this was the first time she'd run in years and had done so well was telling. She had kept up with him for a long time before burning out, even if he had run at a slower pace, it was still remarkable. He reasoned that if she took this seriously, she would be as fierce as he was, probably more so, because she was so emotionally driven and he was able to detach himself. Of course emotions were also the thing that caused a lot of people to be reckless.

"Come on. Take me home so I can take a shower," she said, starting towards the lone car in the parking lot.

He followed behind her and opened the door for her, then got in himself. "I'll just drop you off. I need to go home and get cleaned up too." He glanced over at her. She was resting her head against the headrest.

"Okay," she said, looking over at him. He looked gorgeous, all flushed and sweaty like he was. She wondered if that's how he looked after... She grinned.

"What?" he asked, looking at her with a funny expression on his face.

"Nothing." She rolled her eyes and smirked, then looked away.

He pulled off the side of the road in the back of her house and she hopped out of the car. "I assume I'll see you later?" she said, leaning down into the car.

"Sure," he answered, "give me a call."

"Okay. Bye dork," she said, and jogged to the back door.

Roman waited for her to get inside, and then drove away.

"Lux, tell me what's going on," Roman said, his voice a rumbling growl.

"Hello to you too," Lux said.

Roman could tell he'd have a smirk on his face if he could actually see him. "Just tell me what's going on. She knows everything." Roman leaned against the wall and blankly stared out his kitchen window, unaware of what he was even looking at.

"Interesting," Lux said musically. His voice was always so manipulative.

"We were attacked by two mongrels in a convenience store. What the fuck is going on?"

"I think you've forgotten that I don't serve you, Roman. I don't *have* to tell you anything. Why do you really care anyway?"

"You sent me here, asshole, and because I like her." The words stalled in his throat. He didn't like admitting that to himself, let alone this motherfucker. "She deserves the truth, whatever it is. Or at least I should know for her sake. So tell me why you sent me here."

Lux sighed, seemingly bored.

"You tell me now, Lux, or I leave."

"You won't do that," Lux said. "Your sense of duty is too strong. Is it annoying, playing the hero all the time?"

Roman was fuming. "Tell me why you sent me to her right-fucking-now."

"You need to come here. I'm not going to talk about all of this on the phone." Lux said, after a long pause. He was annoyed now. Normally he found Roman's anger entertaining. But he didn't owe the dickhead anything, and he especially wasn't going to tell him anything if it was a demand.

"Why do I need to come there? You sent me here to protect her but you're refusing to tell me why or from whom. Tell me what the fuck is going on now. Stop playing these games."

"It's not a game. I didn't think it would come to this but you've been careless and lazy, which I find interesting. I want to tell her to her face. Bring her to me." Lux hung up, not giving Roman time to say another word.

Roman slammed the phone down and walked to his bedroom, grumbling obscenities. What the fuck was Lux trying to pull? He got a change of clothes and went to take a shower. Cold water always cleared his head.

3

LOVE LETTERS

Violet sat down on the floor and grabbed the shoebox stuffed with old letters from the back of the closet. She had decided it would be a good thing to get the closet cleaned today. Who knew what she might find there, since it hadn't been cleaned in years. She started stuffing the papers into the garbage bag, stopping briefly to read a line or two here and there. The innocence and silliness of the notes made her smile. Life had been so much easier back then. She half wished she had taken some normal path instead of the one she'd taken. Life would have been easier if she had gone out for cheerleading or something instead of getting into punk music. Maybe.

She found a notebook from the sixth grade stuffed in the back of the closet beneath an old pair of shoes. It was pink, with hearts and flowers doodled all over the cover. She opened the book and found a letter she'd written to Amber that she'd never given to her for some reason. It went on and on about how cute Billy was and how she hoped she got paired with him for the square dance in gym class later in the day. She tore the letter out of the book and set it aside, figuring that Amber would get a huge kick out of it.

She continued stuffing the letters into the bag. All of these things were important to her at one time. All of these words had been life and death at one point, and now they were just meaningless words on paper that no longer affected her. It was as though they were written by someone else, a familiar character from a well loved book. Life, and what was important, had certainly taken on a whole new meaning these last several months.

She leaned back against the chest of drawers and let her thoughts drift off to all she'd been through the past few days. Her legs were sore, her back was sore, her head felt dizzy, and her stomach was in knots. She worried about Roman. She wondered where he was, and what he was up to right now. Her eyes focused again on the letters.

I love you so much. You're the prettiest girl in class. I hope you will be my girlfriend for a long time. Maybe we can go to the movies this weekend. My mom could pick you, Amber, and Josh up. I think it would be neat for all of us to hang out. I got some money from my Aunt for my birthday last week so I can pay. I love you. Billy (your boyfriend!)

Violet smiled and shoved the letter into the bag. As cheesy as his words had been, they had been real at one time.

She let her mind drift to Billy Myron for a moment. Her last day of school her senior year she had walked by Billy in the hall and he hadn't even acknowledged her. How had she gone from that little girl that he loved to the one he couldn't even bear to acknowledge? It hurt her, even if she had never allowed herself to feel it then. She had been rejected so many times in her life, never good enough for anyone. She hadn't been good enough for Mark, and she wasn't good enough for Roman to want either.

She shoved the rest of the letters in the bag along with all the old magazines and fanzines she'd been "collecting" for the last decade. She could actually see the nappy green carpet again.

She collected the stray papers and other trash from the floor and stuffed them into the bag, and then lugged it downstairs and out to the garage to the garbage can. She walked back to the front porch and looked out at the yard. The grass was wet and too long. Her father would have never let the grass get this long. She needed to nag Randy about cutting it before it got too late in the season. That was the deal. Her and Amber made food, he took care of the yard. He was neglecting his duties, though she hadn't been real good about hers either. If it was up to her they'd all starve.

Big black birds pecked at the stale bread Amber had tossed outside earlier. Violet remembered watching the birds from her mom's lap. She felt her heart ache for a moment before she pushed the thoughts aside. The small oak tree in the center of the yard had yellow leaves on it now. It was the first to truly turn in her yard. The leaves looked like delicate, lacey violins, hanging beautifully arranged from the snaky branches. She walked out to the tree and picked a couple leaves, then walked back inside. She set the leaves on the mantle and got back to her chores.

She went to the laundry room and retrieved the sweeper from beside the dryer and hauled it upstairs. She plugged the vacuum in and swept everywhere, minus Amber and Randy's boudoir, then took it back to the laundry room. Her stomach was burning, so she went to the fridge and grabbed an apple and a bottle of water. The apple tasted so sweet and juicy to her, like autumn candy. The scent was so fresh, it reminded her of going to the orchard with her grandparents, and buying bushels of apples, and drinking crisp apple cider straight from a barrel for a dime.

Since she started hanging out with Roman more, she'd been eating more and had noticed in the last week that she'd gained some weight. Her body wasn't quite as pointy, her ribs weren't quite as visible, and her clothes were actually fitting in lieu of hanging off of her. Mark would be appalled.

Looking around the room made her feel relieved. Of course there was still a little more cleaning to do, but she could actually see the floor. The carpet was lovely in its shaggy, outdated way. It looked like a beautiful green pasture, and she had played with her Barbie palomino many, many times on that floor pretending just that. There was no way she would ever get rid of this carpet, no matter how old and how bad of a dust trap it was. She could only imagine what all must be buried in that deep green grass.

Violet plopped down on her bed, staring up at the empty ceiling, feeling a sense of peace from order. The room was finally clean. Well, she still needed to go through her clothes and pare them down a bit. There were things she knew she'd never wear again. Like the ridiculous Lolita dress she'd saved money for months to buy, and had spent two hundred dollars on three years prior. Or the vinyl catsuit she thought was a good fashion statement at one point in her teenage years. She'd looked good in it, she guessed, but it no longer suited her. Maybe one of the little scary devil dolls would want these things? Maybe she'd just ditch everything and start from scratch.

She heard the door open downstairs in the kitchen and the rumble of male voices. She assumed it must be Randy and Steve returning to make another trip. She couldn't wait for Steve to be cleared out so she could deep clean his room and then use it for something else besides his sleeping quarters. Maybe she'd even convince Roman to move in eventually? That would be nice.

"Hey!" Randy said, peering into her room. She watched as Steve walked behind him, not even looking towards her room.

"Hi Randy," she said, lifting her head off the pillow and propping herself up on her elbows.

"You cool with this?" he asked, referring to the move.

"Absolutely." She smiled and sat up. "There's no hard feelings on this end."

"Good." He winked and closed her door, knowing she wouldn't want to be bothered with any potential weirdness. Because Steve was absolutely being weird.

She fell back on the bed and rolled over on her side. It was nice to be in a clean room again. Mostly clean, anyway. At least the floor was empty for the first time in years, and so was the closet, minus the extra clothes. Maybe she really would just take all of it and give it to Goodwill and start over. The thought was exciting to her.

The clock caught her eye, Amber should be home soon. Everything in her wanted to tell Amber what had transpired. She wanted to explain the whole story in detail, but how on earth could she? What would she even say? Roman had been right, there was no way to explain all this without sounding like an insane freak, or scaring the hell out of her. She would tell her the whole story, but not today. She needed to come to grips with all of this herself before she even tried to explain it to someone else.

Her eyes closed and she tried to go over the conversation in her head. How would one even start this sort of conversation!? *Hey, so guess what? Vampires are real!* Violet rolled her eyes and turned over on her stomach, pressing her face into the nice cool pillow. Ugh, she'd worry about all this later.

She heard a knock on the door. "Yeah?" she asked and rolled over onto her back. At some point during her *internal conversatin'* she had fallen asleep.

"It feels like I haven't seen you in a week!" Amber said, and sat down on the end of her bed. "So, what's going on? And don't tell me nothing, because that's obviously not true. Too much shit has gone on with Mark, and whatever else, for you to tell me nothing."

"I don't know, Amber. Mark just really scared me the other night. I have never seen him look that way before. I really thought he would kill me. I was afraid he'd follow me home and do something crazy, so I asked Roman if I could stay with him. I don't think Mark knows where he lives, and even if he figured it out, there's no way he could hurt me with Roman around. Plus it's been cool getting to know Roman better."

"And the jogging?" Amber asked with a confused smirk on her face.

"Roman's pretty influential in regards to physical fitness. I'm not sure you have noticed the man's body?"

"Well, gee, no, not at all," Amber said with a laugh and eyeroll. "I can imagine he must do a lot of exercise to maintain that godlike physique."

"Um, yeah... he is pretty, um, *hot*, huh?" she said awkwardly, her cheeks turning red. "Besides, I haven't ever really taken care of myself, and with everything that's happened, I guess I just figured working out is a good thing."

"I agree. You are already looking healthier."

"I think I gained some weight. I'm actually starting to look like a girl again and not a teenage boy."

"Shut up!" Amber said, and shoved her arm.

"It's true." Violet shrugged.

"Well, you were just *too* skinny, let's leave it at that. But you have never looked even remotely like a boy, dumbass. So, do you want to go out tonight?" Amber asked, changing the subject.

"I don't know," Violet said, looking away from her friend. The last thing she wanted to do was run into Mark, or worse, *vampires*. Vampires should probably always be top on the list of things she didn't want to fucking run into. She most certainly didn't want to be out at night without Roman to protect her, knowing what she knew now.

"Come on, it'll be fun. You never want to do anything anymore." Amber was getting sort of annoyed with Violet never wanting to hang out with her. She wasn't used to her not being around 24/7. It was selfish, but so what. She missed her BFF. "Roman is hogging you all to himself, and you're not even boning! So you say anyway." Amber smiled and wiggled her eyebrows.

"OMG, Amber! I just don't want to run into Mark. You didn't see the look in his eyes."

"Well what's he going to do even if we do see him? We'll be in public. If he shows up we'll just leave. We can get security to escort us to our car. What's the big deal? It's almost like you don't want to be a part of the group anymore."

"That's because I don't. What's so wrong with that? Can't you see through all the pretentious crap? They're all just a bunch of posers. Outside of you, Randy, and Roman I have zero desire to hang out with 'the group'," Violet said, trying to convince her it was a better idea to stay home.

"Of course I see through it, but what else is there to do around here? Sit and sulk? At least if we go out we can have a good laugh. Stop being so elitist."

"*You* are telling *me* not to be elitist? Um, isn't that like the pot calling the kettle black?"

Amber was trying to goad her into thinking it was best to go out and at least laugh at these people than do nothing at all, but Violet didn't see the point. And who was she to laugh at anyone anyway? She was starting to really see people for the pathetic sheep they were, but that didn't give her the right to criticize them. She'd made a thousand and one mistakes herself.

"I don't know," Violet said.

"Come on. Come for me. We never get to have any fun anymore. I haven't even seen much of you. You're always with your *booooooyfriend*," Amber said, as she rolled her eyes to tease Violet.

Violet sat quietly for a moment, looking into her friend's eyes. She felt bad for not having spent much time with her lately. "Alright, I'll go," she said, and stood up. "But if Mark shows up I'm leaving. And Roman is *not* my boyfriend, dick."

"Cool!" Amber said in triumph and stood up. "I'm gonna go take a shower. Let's go out to eat first too. I'm dying for something good. Papa Marianio's?"

"Ugh, damn you, temptress! You know I can't say no to The Papa's." Violet rolled her eyes and smiled. Her stomach growled just thinking about the garlic bread and all its ooey gooey buttery goodness.

"And, yes he is. Your boyfriend, that is. And we're going to have fun tonight, biatch," Amber added with a grin, and slipped through the door.

"Okay." Violet smiled, feeling a little hopeful inside. Maybe a good old fashioned night out with her friend was exactly what she needed? She just hoped to God no vampires or ex-boyfriends showed up. Roman wasn't her boyfriend. Was he? *NO!*

"Whatcha doin'?" Violet asked.

"Standing naked in the kitchen," Roman answered. "What are you doing?"

"Um, okaaaaay," she said, conjuring vivid images in her brain and then erasing them. *Good God*. "Nothing. I guess we're going out tonight. Want to come?"

He hesitated for a moment, not really wanting her to go out without his protection, but knowing he had some things he had to look into that couldn't wait. "I can't, Violet."

"But we're going out for Italian first," she said, trying to tempt him.

"I do like Italian, but I need to take care of some business."

"Like the *guys from the store* kind of business?"

"Exactly."

"Can I come?" she asked, with a bit of enthusiasm in her voice.

"No, princess, not yet." He couldn't help smiling. She really was pretty fearless.

Violet heard the smile in his voice, and it made her feel good. "Please?"

Hearing that word on her tongue in that tone made parts of him react he didn't care to acknowledge. "No, I want you to be careful tonight, though. Be aware of your surroundings at all times," he said firmly. "Call me if anything even remotely strange happens, okay?"

"You have a cellphone? Since when? And I don't even have the number! WTF?"

"I've always had it. Exactly one person has my number, guess who it is."

"Mylori?" Violet teased.

"Ha-ha," he said, and laughed for real. "No, her fuckhead brother. I'll send you a text message. Save my number."

"Good lord, you even know how to send a text message?"

"Yes, Violet. Lux and I share memes and inspirational quotes back and forth all the time," he said facetiously.

"Really?" Violet asked, amused but not getting that he was joking.

"No," he said and laughed again.

She rolled her eyes at herself for not automatically knowing he was kidding, but his tone had been so dry. "What about dick pics? You guys send each other dick pics?"

"Oh, fuck you," Roman said and laughed, the disgust at the thought was clear in his tone.

Violet laughed and really wished both of them would send her dick pics, ridiculous as it would be. "Oh wait, would vamp wang show up on film? Or, I guess it's not film, huh? Digital? Would vamp wang show up on digital?"

"Please shut up," Roman said, shaking his head with amusement. "Okay, seriously, be careful, and be on the lookout for anything abnormal. And call me, okay? I'm not happy you're going out tonight without me there to protect you."

Hearing those words made her stomach twinge. "Yeah, I know. I didn't even want to go, but I feel guilty for not spending more time with these guys lately. I miss Amber, and she is feeling neglected."

"I'm sorry you feel guilty, but, you know, if you really do make these changes in your life, you will likely spend less and less time with them. Knowing about all of this puts everyone you love in danger. And I would rather you feel guilty, and safe at home, than not guilty and in danger."

"I know," she said, sadness evident in her tone.

"You can go back to living a normal life. It's not too late to pretend you never met me, and know nothing about what you saw," he said, wanting her to understand she had plenty of options. "Violet, you're young, there's no reason you should give up your life. You should go to school, get married, have a family, do all that stuff."

He wanted that for her, even as he felt upset for saying it. He had grown far too used to being around her. He was going to be sad when he had to move on, and that freaked him right the fuck out.

"Roman, there's never going to be anything normal about my life. Even if I didn't know they exist."

There was nothing he could really say in response to that statement. He understood what she meant. She was referring to her family being gone. Being alone was one of the main things that kept him motivated to kill. If he had someone to care about he would be far less motivated to hunt Vampire. "If you have to go, then have fun tonight, and eat something good for me. Please, just be careful."

"I will and I'll try."

"Oh, and we're going to Chicago tomorrow."

"WHAT!?" she said, her reaction so loud he had to hold the phone back.

"Lux won't talk over the phone, so we're going to Chicago."

"Oh my God! And you were going to tell me this when? Oh my God! I can't wait!"

Roman laughed. He knew she'd be excited about the prospects of seeing Chicago. It was the reason he'd waited to tell her, savoring it like a prize. He loved her zeal. "We'll leave really early. Are you going to be ready?"

"Of course! I can't wait to see Chicago. I've wanted to go there for years. The scene is supposed to be really cool there," she panted, short of breath with excitement.

"Well, that will have to wait until after we see Lux."

"Of course," she agreed. Her heart was racing, and she was so excited it felt like her skin would burst. "Oh..." she said, suddenly dejected.

"What?" he asked, knowing what was coming next.

"Amber. She's going to be upset she's not going. And Randy too."

"I'm sorry," he said, not really feeling sorry. He didn't know her friends well enough to have remorse for them not being able to go, but he felt bad that she felt bad. "We can all go again soon," he reassured her, fully intending to keep the promise because he never made promises to anyone and he wouldn't break it. He had never had anyone to make promises to before.

"Okay," she said, still somewhat bummed.

"Violet, your happiness can't depend on the happiness of others. Be happy for yourself, and let others make their own happiness. You were excited about going, so don't let guilt rob you of that."

"You're right," she said. His words had lifted a burden. "Call me tonight, okay? Let me know you're alright."

"I'll be alright, V. This will be a walk in the park. Any sign of trouble on your end and you call me immediately. Hear me? Do not hesitate," he commanded, still concerned about her being out alone. He would have to try to get over there to do a swing by, just to make sure all was well at some point.

"Well, be careful. I can't bear the thought of..." She stopped herself, not wanting him to know just how panicked the idea of losing him made her feel.

"I'll be alright. I promise," he said, reassuring her. Another promise. "What time will you be home?"

"No later than three." She and her friends always stayed out late when they went out together.

"Wow, I guess you'll be sleeping in the car tomorrow."

"No, I've got enough excitement to get me through a whole week, I'm sure."

"I'll talk to you later," he said, with genuine affection.

"Bye."

4

ANGEL EYES AND THE PHANTOM

VIOLET WASN'T IN THE mood to go out AT ALL. The idea seemed almost offensive to her. She wanted to lie in bed, and watch old movies, and think about the trip to Chicago. She was afraid of seeing Lux again and hearing whatever it was he just had to tell her in person. What could be so bad he couldn't tell them over the phone? Her thoughts raced with the magnitude of the situation, and with ideas about what could be awaiting her. She had to stop herself when her imagination drifted to proclamations of undying love. Girl, *please*, she thought, and rolled her eyes. *Hel-lo, he's a vam-pire!*

She brushed the knots out of her hair. It was still damp from the shower she'd taken earlier. She stood in front of the mirror and studied her body. She was definitely filling out again, thanks to the recent consumption of fatty foods. She'd have to start eating healthy. The blood red lace bra and panties she wore looked vibrant against her white skin. She liked the way the colors contrasted. Mark had liked this ensemble. She felt vaguely sad for a moment, then shook off the feeling. That motherfucker deserved none of her sadness.

She pulled her hair back into a ponytail, then picked up the pink blush and applied it to her cheeks. She lined her eyes in black, then covered her long lashes with mascara. She dug through the floral print makeup bag for her favorite

46

blueberry flavored lip gloss, then applied it thickly. Her lips looked wet and smooth.

"Wow, you look nice," Randy said, walking into the bathroom.

His sudden presence startled her, and she jumped and instinctively covered herself. She expelled a thankful breath and smiled at him, then applied another layer of gloss.

"Um, thanks," she answered, and turned to face him.

"You are wearing clothes tonight?" He smirked at his nearly naked friend and BFF of his girlfriend.

"I suppose. It is sort of cold."

"Something like that," he said, leaning against the door frame. He'd seen her naked a thousand times, seeing her in her underwear didn't much phase him at this point—though the thought of *him, Amber, and Violet* had crossed his mind about ten thousand times. He'd even tried to convince them on more than one occasion. "So, you aren't mad about Steve taking off?"

"Nope, happy actually." She reached over and picked her leather pants up off the chair. They were so tight she struggled to get them up, and then she laced them as tight as she could stand. "I don't want anyone else here," she said, taking a deep breath and standing up straight. "Unless Roman moves in."

Randy raised an eyebrow at that.

"What?" she asked with a scowl.

"Nothing," he said, the corner of his lip lifting slightly. "I think it's sort of sad that everything seems to be changing."

"I know, Randy, it is, but what can I do? I think this is just a sad fact of life. People move in and out of our lives. I'm not still friends with Cassie, my best friend from middle school either. That was pretty devastating when it happened."

"I know you're right," he acquiesced, and changed the subject. "So, Amber says Roman is taking you to Chicago tomorrow?"

"Yeah, I'm pretty excited," she said, as she maneuvered her arms through the tight arm holes of the leather top. She zipped the snug shirt up and adjusted her breasts.

"So, why are you guys going--just for fun?"

"He's got some kind of family business stuff there. I'm just tagging along for moral support." She looked back in the mirror and pressed her shiny lips together. "I wish you guys could come, but Roman said next time we'll all go." She smiled, and brushed by him back into her bedroom.

He followed her, leaning against the door frame to her room. "He's a good guy, Violet."

"Yes, he really is," she said, as she started lacing up her boots. She stood up and pulled the hair tie from her hair and let it fall in loose straight swathes down her back and over her shoulders.

"You guys ready?" Amber said as she exited her and Randy's bedroom and leaned against Randy. He wrapped his arm around her and kissed her cheek lightly. She looked like a million bucks.

"I'm ready." Violet smiled, and scooped her bag off the floor and slipped it over her shoulder.

Roman knew from experience these two would be easy to track and dispose of quickly. He was hoping to kill them and make it over to The Cage to look in on Violet. The vamps had been clumsy and oafish and not good fighters. The fact that Violet had been able to fight one off herself was proof of that. More than likely, they had been turned very recently. And he assumed they'd be in the cemetery, as he was sure they'd adhere to all the stereotypes. They hadn't been very clever.

He tightened the laces of his boots, then strapped the blade on, and locked the house behind him. He took a deep breath, stretching his limbs, and cracking his neck, before sliding into his car. He drove about a mile from the cemetery and shut the car off. He wanted to walk up on them, as they would more than likely not be paying very close attention to their surroundings or for threats of violence. He knew from experience in dealing with idiots like this that they would think they were invincible, just as all newly turned vampires felt invincible. They hadn't been dead long enough to fear real death. And he imagined that they also hadn't had their brush with the Old Ones yet either. Roman snickered thinking how these two would fare against Lux--or worse yet--Mylori. There was no way either of them had faced anything so old or powerful, nor had they really faced him yet. They'd get their chance very soon.

The wet grass stuck to his boots as he moved with stealth on his way through the graves. The cemetery was situated on a rolling hill. The trees were tall and ancient, and the grass was long and emerald green by day. Everything was black now. Banks of dead flowers lined the perimeter of the grounds. The cemetery was old, containing crypts and headstones of the people who had founded this small town. He could already see the two morons in the distance, hanging around one of the decrepit mausoleums. He could hear them plainly, and he laughed to himself thinking that as loud as these two were, surely someone living adjacent to this graveyard would have eventually called the police on them, thinking they were rowdy teenagers.

"Idiots," Roman whispered to himself.

He stopped when he reached about seventy five yards from them and watched as they tossed back beer after beer and hooted and hollered like rednecks, and he thought how ridiculous it seemed that another vampire found these two worthy of bestowing the Dark Gift on them. It was a gift. Immortality, in any form, is a gift. And he found it preposterous that they were drinking alcohol when any good vampire would surely have had several victims under his belt by this time of night. Drinking beer would be pointless, a human habit that meant nothing post-death.

Roman shook his head and walked up to the two, deciding there was really no reason to even remain covert at this point. These vampires with their "superior strength" would be no match for him. He knew he was faster and stronger than either of them, Vampire or not.

"Well lookie here," the spiky haired one said to the other with his thick southern drawl. He could barely stand up straight. "You decide you want to die after all?"

"No, just here to kill you both," Roman said unemotionally to the wasted redneck. Vampires couldn't really get drunk, so the way the two were acting was purely based on remembered behavior, not reality.

They laughed and looked at each other. "I don't think so, son," said the greasy one who was sitting on a gravestone.

"Wow you two are pathetic. I've seen some really pathetic vampires in my day, but damn. You make them look like geniuses." Roman mocked them intentionally.

They sneered at him, baring their fangs.

"Oooo... scary," he said, with a wry grin. "Let's make quick work of this, shall we?" Roman removed the long, thin blade from the leather sling.

The long haired vampire leapt at him, throwing his hands towards Roman's neck. Roman sliced through the air with the blade, cutting through the torso of the lunging vampire. The heavy grating of the steel against bone and thick muscle was gratifying. The blade slicing smoothly through the body was like cutting through the carcass of a dead animal. There was a loud cracking of the bone as the spine was divided in two and a heavy thud as the body hit the ground. The split vampire writhed on the ground in separate parts looking wildly around, hands pulling desperately at the thick wet grass.

The other one was on Roman now, ripping through the flesh at his shoulder with his teeth. Roman pushed the greasy beast off of himself by shoving the heel of his hand against its chin and forcing it down on the ground. His injured hand ached as he did this, but he fought through the pain. His shoulder spasmed from the jolt the razor teeth made as they cut through his muscle. Fangs wedged between the bones of his joint, separating them with agony. The pain was immediate and thorough. Roman grabbed his shoulder and then looked at the blood on his hand that trembled from the shock. He wiped the blood across his chest and gripped the steel with both hands to steady himself. The vampire reeled on the wet grass beside his wailing friend and skittered across the ground until he had fumbled his way to his feet as he backed away from Roman.

"You may as well hold still," Roman said, his voice void of all emotion. He had done this a thousand times. All the feeling had gone out of this for him. Even the searing pain of his shoulder didn't faze him, now that the immediate shock of it had passed. He had suffered far worse; this was a simple flesh wound.

The vampire ran from him, and Roman shook his head once and followed. His footing was sure as he weaved between graves and leapt over them, closing the distance quickly. The vampire never gained more than a few yards on him, and then tripped on a headstone that had been knocked over a century ago and lay there face down in the muddy grass where it had fallen. The bewildered vampire rolled over, peering up at Roman through the darkness, trying against everything to use its power of persuasion on the killer that stalked it now.

"You were poorly made," Roman said, no inflection in his voice.

The vampire hissed and pulled itself backwards across the mud.

"You shouldn't have attacked us. You should have never touched her." Roman's eyes glowed now, making him look inhuman himself. He had gotten well beyond thinking he was any better than the things he hunted. He was a killer, every bit as much as they were killers.

He raised his hands and plunged the blade into the neck of the sniveling vampire, severing its spinal cord and detaching its head. He watched as the blood gurgled from the opened neck, oozing from arteries that had ceased to flow when the body had been reanimated in death. Then he pierced the chest cavity, waiting for the body to stop twitching. He walked back to where the other body was sprawled and cut through the neck of the beast as its black eyes peered up at him. He knew that once the sun rose in the morning these bodies would burn to nothing, there was no point in cleaning them up. The vampires were too new to sustain any amount of sunlight, and back here in this old part of the cemetery, no one would stumble upon them early enough.

He walked back to his car, pulling his cellphone from his inside pocket. No calls from Violet, just a text message that said *We're here!* He got in his car and drove home. Their deaths were usually anti-climactic. At least this time he felt some sort of pleasure killing the disgusting filth that had put their hands on Violet.

The club was only partially full. It was still fairly early and the regular crowd never appeared before ten-ish. Dory and Malinda ran over to meet Violet and her friends as they entered the building. Violet smiled cordially and hugged both of the girls. She told the two about the clothes and jewelry she was going to get rid of, and invited them over to sift through her old things. Violet noticed how strange the girls were acting. They were almost condescending towards her. Maybe she deserved their contempt? She had always acted this way towards nearly everyone, save the few she deemed "worthy". But she had always been cool with these two until recently. She wasn't the person that talked shit to people anymore. Something had changed in her--changed to her very core--these last few weeks. There was something about Roman's presence, and the way he called her on her bullshit, that had truly opened her eyes to a lot of things within herself. She wasn't perfect by any stretch of the imagination as the urge to be snarky was ever-present, but she had gotten better about it.

She looked over to the bar where Jim sat. He was drinking a beer and chatting with a new young girl she'd never seen. She almost felt pity for him now. She recalled the daydreams she'd had about him before, the giddy phone calls, and seductive across-the-room ogling she'd done to him previously, and now all she felt was pity. It made her feel like a jerk. Who was she to pity anyone?

"I'm gonna go get a drink," Amber said, leaning against her. She linked her arm through Violet's, and they pushed their way to the bar.

Violet turned her back and leaned against the counter, surveying the crowd. There were several people she'd never seen before. This wasn't too unusual, as sometimes people from outside the area or the universities came out to the club attempting to find some place new to hang out.

Amber leaned over, "You want something?" she asked.

"Diet Coke," Violet answered, not taking her eyes off the crowd. They got their drinks and made their way through the horde, trying to find Randy who'd already gotten lost in the sea of throbbing bodies.

"A lot of the regulars aren't here," Amber said to Violet as she bit into the cherry from her drink.

"Yeah, I noticed that," Violet answered. "Good, maybe that means Mark won't show up either."

"I hope that's the case," Amber said, as she rolled her eyes. "We should dance. Come on!" She took Violet by the arm and dragged her towards the dance floor.

They both half-heartedly danced to the industrial rhythms that thumped through the sound system. Malinda and Dory joined the girls. Violet was loosening up. Not seeing some of the usuals here made her feel more comfortable for some reason. The fear of Mark being here was subsiding. She was actually enjoying herself for once as she and Amber goofed around doing silly dances and laughing hysterically like they hadn't done in years. She was acting sixteen again. It almost felt like the good ol' days.

Randy came up behind Amber and stole her away. Violet continued dancing with Malinda and Dory for a little while longer, then excused herself to go to the restroom. There was a line as usual. Violet leaned against the wall. A sudden remembrance of the last time she'd leaned against this wall swept through her.

She could feel Mark's mouth on her neck, the hot breath sticking like humid air on her skin, and Roman's eyes peering through the dark room at her. She had wished it had been his lips on her neck in that moment. She shook her head and looked across the room to where he'd been standing. A woman was standing there now, looking directly at her with a faint smile touching her lips. The woman shifted, never breaking her gaze. Violet stared back at her intently. Something was off about this. She felt herself being pulled towards the woman. It was like she just *had* to know who she was.

"Hey, we're heading to the back, Violet," Amber said, shoving her friend.

Violet shook her head gently to break the gaze with the woman, and looked at her friend.

"What's wrong?" Amber asked, looking across the room at what Violet had been so transfixed by.

"Nothing's wrong," she answered, looking at her friend and then back to the woman. "Do you know who that is?" Violet asked, tipping her head.

"Uh, no, never seen her before, why?" Amber asked, looking at the woman and back to Violet.

"I don't know, just wondered," Violet answered, and focused her attention back on Amber. "I'll meet you guys back there. I gotta pee," Violet said, moving up in the line to the restroom.

"Okay, hurry up!" Amber smiled and turned and walked back towards the lounge.

Violet looked up at the woman and then walked into the bathroom. She peeled the hot leather off and sat down in the stall. She could hear the various conversations taking place in the ladies room. This was always amusing to her as she generally knew every person that was being talked about. Violet finished her business and pulled the tight pants up and laced them. She walked out and washed her hands in the dirty white ceramic sink. By the looks of the countertop and disgusting sink she was likely getting more germs by washing her hands and touching the sink as she would have by just leaving her hands dirty.

Violet rubbed her hands together to dry them as there were no paper towels and she wasn't about to touch the cloth hanging from the machine on the wall. As she walked back into the club, she noticed the woman leaning against the bar. She turned her head and looked at Violet again. Violet scowled, wondering what it was about her that had this woman so transfixed. She took a deep breath and walked over to her.

"Do I know you?" Violet asked, crossing her arms and tilting her head to the side. Violet wasn't going to allow anyone to make her feel uncomfortable.

"Hello, angel," the woman cooed.

Violet felt her skin crawl. The hair on the back of her neck stood up. This was the woman who'd been calling her. "It's you!" she accused.

The woman smiled and licked her red lips. "Yes, nice to finally meet me." She took a drag from her cigarette and blew the smoke above her head in a long thin stream. Her face was gaunt and white as bleached bone.

Violet felt her blood swirling in her body. She felt dizzy and light headed suddenly and she remembered what Roman had told her about Lux and Mylori. She steadied herself and cleared her head. "Who *are* you?" Violet asked in anger.

"Oh, I am your friend, sweet girl. Take it down a notch." She smiled, and reached out to touch Violet. As the woman dragged her finger across Violet's bare chest, chasing the rise and fall of her breasts and the blood red lace peeking above the leather, Violet felt her head spin again. The trail the finger left tingled with electricity as the cool pad smoothed over her flesh.

Violet pulled herself away from the woman, feeling her blood rise to the surface of her skin where her fingers had touched. "What's your name?" Violet asked, planting her feet firmly on the ground. Her knees were wobbling and her legs felt on the verge of collapse. But she would not crumble.

"Cecelia," she answered, smiling like a she-devil.

"What do you want?"

"Well, *you*, of course." She grinned, and took another drag from the cigarette. "Come back to my home." She smiled, taking Violet's hair between her fingers and curling it around them, again and again.

"No," Violet said, and backed away from the woman never breaking eye contact.

"Tell *The Killer* I said hello," she purred.

Violet finally mustered the strength to turn away, leaving the woman with a satisfied grin on her face. She hastily retreated to the lounge and found Randy and Amber seated at their usual booth. Her heart was pounding. Knowing what this woman was, feeling that power, and knowing why it was there, terrified her. She questioned her eagerness for learning Roman's job at this moment. How the hell did he face them with seemingly no fear whatsoever? He was so flippant and nonplussed about the whole thing. He had been doing this his whole life. How?

"We have to go," she said, slipping in beside Amber, her words expelling in short bursts.

"Is Mark here?" Amber asked, leaning into her friend.

"No, we just need to leave. Now," Violet said, near panic. She was scared to death.

"What's going on?" Amber asked, grabbing her friend's arm to steady her.

"Just please come on!" Violet said, standing up and tugging on Amber's arm.

Amber shrugged her shoulders, looking back at Randy, who was quickly following. Violet scurried towards the door, not stopping to say goodbye to anyone with Amber and Randy on her heels. They were completely confused.

"What's going on, Violet?" Amber said, pulling the passenger side door open and sitting down. Violet already had the car started.

"Remember that woman I asked you if you knew?" Violet asked, backing out, Randy barely getting into the back in time.

"Yeah, what about her?" Amber said.

"It's that bitch I was getting calls from a while back. We assumed she had something to do with Mark. Remember?"

Amber thought for a moment. It was obvious by the look on her face when she remembered. "Oh yeah, I remember. So that's her? What the fuck? Who is she and how does she even know you?"

"I have no idea," Violet said, really meaning that. She had no clue how this woman knew her, or why she would be calling her.

"She threatened me." Violet didn't want to tell the whole story. She wanted to get this all figured out before she sent their lives into upheaval.

"That's it? Some prank calls and some bullshit threat? Since when are you scared of some stupid chick? You usually thrive on that kind of crap drama. Besides, you could have told the bouncers and had her kicked out," Amber said, confused by Violet's sudden fear. She had never been one to back down from anyone.

"She just scares me," Violet said, looking over at her friend and then back at the road.

"You're talking about that woman with the long brown hair? She was weird," Randy said, leaning forward from the back seat.

"Yeah, her," Violet said, looking at him in the rearview mirror.

"She was creepy. I can see why you'd be freaked out by her. She asked me to come over to her house, and to bring my girlfriend, and I said no fucking way."

Amber laughed and turned sideways in the seat to look at him. "What did she say to that?"

"Something like, 'I'll see you around', something stupid like that. She thinks she's uber cool or something. I didn't pay a whole lot of attention to her. But she def seemed off."

"Stay away from her!" Violet ordered, looking at them both now. "Don't go near her."

Amber looked at her with concern in her eyes. Why was Violet reacting like this? This was the girl who'd spit on skinheads three times her size and who had started fights with punk girls at shows just for looking at her funny or for saying hello to Mark. There had to be more to all this. Her sudden change in personality was enough to make Amber worry.

"What's going on?" Amber asked, reaching over and touching Violet's arm to get her to look at her.

"Nothing, Amber," she answered, trying to reassure her friend.

"*Something* is going on," Amber grumbled under her breath, and looked out the side window.

"You know, there is something going on, and I promise I'll tell you both as soon as I have my head together. Okay? Just promise me you'll stay far away from that woman," Violet said with vehemence.

Randy and Amber were definitely worried now. Amber wondered if Violet had gotten into something bad with Roman, but she knew her friend, she wouldn't do anything too terrible. She was smarter than that. But even the smartest woman could get sucked into bad shit over a man. Roman didn't seem like a bad guy, but what did she really know about him? No, it couldn't be either of them. Violet wasn't stupid. She'd tell Roman to fuck off before she'd go along with anything illegal. And besides that, Violet had seemed so much more at peace lately and Roman seemed to be a good influence.

"Promise me," Violet said, looking at her friend.

"Okay!" Amber said in aggravation. "Does this have something to do with Roman and why you're going to Chicago tomorrow? Violet, you better not be into something dangerous!"

"Ooo... Is he Mafioso?" Randy said with wide eyes. "I could see him being a mobster." He looked at Amber, sharing a look of satisfaction for having figured out the big secret.

"No! Don't be a fucking moron, Randy," Violet said, as if even the thought was ridiculous, which it was, well, sort of. But honestly, that would make more sense than vampires. "It has nothing to do with him or Chicago. I'll fill you in when I get back, okay? I swear. Just trust me."

"Geez, bite my head off," Randy grumbled, and sat back.

Violet looked at him in the mirror, feeling genuinely remorseful. The truth was that what Roman did with his life really wasn't too terribly different from dealing with some organized crime syndicate. She thought about it and realized Randy's guess had been closer to the truth than not.

"Sorry, Randall, I'm just stressed out," Violet said in the most sincere tone she could muster. She hated bumming him out. It was like making a puppy sad, and who would want to do that?

"It's all good," he said, smiling for her.

"Alright, fine," Amber said, crossing her arms and looking back out the window. "Don't tell me what's going on. I mean, I'm only your best friend and we've never had secrets before. But whatever. I guess you can tell your new best friend everything and leave me in the dark." She was hurt that Violet was hiding something from her. She was angry that Roman was Violet's new confidant. She'd never been on the outside with her before.

"Don't be like that, Amber. I promise you, I'm doing what's best. Trust me. *You have to trust me on this*," Violet said, hoping Amber would understand.

"I trust you," Randy said with a shrug, accepting Violet's word, and then leaning forward to put his hand on her shoulder.

"Hello?" she said, her voice barely a whisper. She looked at the clock. It was exactly 3 AM.

"You sleeping?" he asked. His voice was quiet and smooth.

"Dozing a little," she answered, suddenly very awake. "Hey, did you get them?"

"Yeah, piece of cake. I told you it would be. Did you have fun?"

Roman's casual confidence always reassured her. "Funny you should ask."

"Huh oh, what happened?"

"I met the woman who's been calling me. She's one of them."

"What happened?" His tone was suddenly dry and serious and all business. She knew that he'd be sitting upright now, hands clenched, eyes fixed on the floor.

"She was at the club. Her name's Cecelia."

"Cecelia? Doesn't ring a bell. What did she say to you?"

"She said she wanted me and then told me to tell *The Killer* she said hello. I assume she meant you."

"Fucking idiots. She didn't try to hurt you, did she?"

"No, Roman, she didn't do anything to me. She did invite us to her house. She asked Randy to bring Amber. And she asked me separately. He said no and so did I, obviously. What can we do? We need to get her before she hurts someone."

"Did she tell you where her house is located?"

"No."

Roman paused for a moment as he put his thoughts together. He could hunt the vampire down easily enough, although it may take a few days. She could be anywhere in Northeast Ohio. But more than likely he could find her tonight just by calling everyone Violet knew, and seeing who had been invited. Surely someone would have accepted the offer. Though whether or not they would still be living, or allowed to leave without being turned, would be unlikely.

But then he decided it was wiser just to continue with the plan and get to Chicago. The more he knew about the situation the better. There were only a few hours before they were planning to leave, anyway. Besides that, his arm was hurting where the fangs had separated the bone and cut through the muscle in his shoulder. Since he didn't know Cecelia he didn't know her age or strengths, though likely the fact that he didn't know her meant she was young. He would go to Chicago, see Lux, and get answers, then come back and deal with the vampire.

"We need to get to Lux. Obviously there's more to this story if Lux won't tell me over the telephone, and he sent me here to protect you without even telling me that's why I was coming. That is weird even for him. Without all the facts I'd just be operating with blinders on, and I'm not going to risk your safety by doing that. It's not like hunting some random lone vampire. She has obviously come here for a specific reason. Man, I'd like to track her down tonight, but there's no time. She could have dozens of others with her for all we know. We already ran into two. It's just going to have to wait until we get back. Did you tell Amber and Randy to stay away from her?"

"Yes, and I made them promise."

"Will they really listen?" Roman asked, unsure that her friends would be safe.

"Yes, I think so," Violet said. "I was adamant about it, and Randy already thought she seemed weird and wanted nothing to do with her."

"Good boy," Roman said, somewhat relieved. "I want you to reiterate the importance of not being around her. In fact, tell them to stay in the house as much as possible. I wish I had a clone who could stay behind and protect them too, but I do not."

"Two of you? That would be quite..."

Are you ready to go?" Roman asked with a chuckle, cutting her off.

"Just about," Violet said. She'd already packed most of her things earlier in the evening.

"Good. I'm going to come over. We'll get a couple hours of sleep and hit the road a little earlier than I'd planned."

"Why not now? What's the point of waiting around?"

"Because we won't see Lux until early evening tomorrow anyway, and we may as well try to get a few hours of sleep. It's about an eight hour drive there. We'll leave around six. I'll be over soon." He hung up the phone.

She sat the phone down and slid back on the bed. She heard Amber and Randy across the hall. They were still awake and obviously wrestling around, and doing whatever else. They had each other. Hearing them made her feel so lonely. She so wanted to have someone to help take her grief and sadness from her. She wished she had someone to share all this with, someone she could be intimate with, the way lovers are intimate. She wanted someone to hold her and look into her eyes knowing what she was thinking before she ever spoke a word. It would be nice to have someone who made her feel whole, who took away her self-doubt and made her want to be a better person. It was unrealistic, and she knew it. It wasn't any human's job to heal another, only to comfort them on the journey. But she so wanted to feel loved again.

Roman certainly filled part of that position. He was the closest she had to a confidant at the moment. But it wasn't the same. There was still an element missing. She was lonely in a way she'd never been lonely before. She hadn't realized just how much was missing from her relationship with Mark before she met Roman. Why couldn't she find someone like him who wanted her? Roman didn't want her like she wanted him.

And where the fuck did all that come from?

She rolled over on her stomach and closed her eyes, burying her face in her pillow as hot, silent tears fell. All of this was so scary and confusing and she wanted her mom.

"She certainly is fetching," the woman said, slipping the black satin dress to the floor. She was fond of the slippery way the material slid over her skin. She rubbed her hands together, warming their surface, and then followed the hard muscle of his stomach to his groin. He leaned his head back for her as she bent over him, hovering like a black shadow, and taking his neck between her teeth. He wrapped his arms around her, pulling her down on top of his muscular body.

"Fetching, that's funny. She is a bitch," he said, snarling as the woman pierced the skin and ferociously drew the blood to the surface.

"Ahh...don't be so bitter, baby," she said, releasing his neck, blood spurting from the open wound onto her face.

He licked the glistening drops away, his own blood tasted rich and full of her flavor. He looked at the woman, studied her perfectly angled Germanic features, and pictured her in military apparel, a slow smile creeping across his lips. He liked the idea of that and smiled at her.

"You did love her once," she smiled at him, expecting to infuriate him. She so loved an angry fuck.

"No, she was just a girl," he replied, and buried his face in her breasts. "You, I love."

She saw the lights move across her wall and hopped up, then jogged down the stairs to meet him at the front door. She was spooked about the woman and hadn't realized just how much until he arrived. She'd been holding her breath the whole time, though trying to convince herself otherwise. Now, with him here, she could relax and focus. They were going to Chicago! And she was excited, even though she had no idea what was ahead with Lux.

"I thought you'd be asleep and I would have to pound on the door," he said, walking through the door and around her.

"No, I can't sleep," she said, taking the bag from his hand and leading him upstairs.

He followed behind watching as the muscles in her arms flexed from the weight of the bag. She wasn't the frail creature he'd once thought she was. The tight leather pants she was wearing adhered to her body like a second skin, and subsequently drew his eyes away from the taut muscles of her arms and shoulders. The lacing up her legs was begging to be unlaced. He caught himself thinking too hard about that and looked away.

"You thirsty?" she asked, setting the bag down beside her dresser and picking up the half empty bottle of water.

"No, I'm fine," he answered, and took his jacket off. He folded it and placed it on top of his bag. "We should try to get a little bit of sleep. Tomorrow's going to be a long day. I did call and reserve a room, so if we get there early enough we can take a nap before meeting Lux."

His hair was pulled back away from his face. Since she'd last seen him, he had neatly trimmed his sideburns. *My God, he looks hot with sideburns!* Violet looked away and grinned and looked back. His body was distracting, a tight black t-shirt hiding absolutely nothing of his muscular build. The combination of his pitch black hair and eyebrows and pale white skin made the green of his eyes vibrant. He was stunning.

Roman stood with his hands clasped, waiting for her to make some sort of move to let him know what he should be doing. Should he be sitting on the bed or preparing to sleep on the floor? He had no idea how to read this girl, even after all the time they'd spent together, and he would never assume anything just because they had shared a bed prior.

She felt awkward and a little shy for some reason, and was disgusted with herself for feeling that way, considering the situation. Everything about her life was in complete upheaval, for all she knew her world was about to come crashing down all around her again, and yet she was sitting here like an immature schoolgirl. It was stupid.

"I should put some pajamas on," she said, pulling the top dresser drawer open. She looked over at him, still standing there uncomfortably. "Sit down and stay a while." She grinned at him awkwardly, then rolled her eyes at herself.

He sat on the end of the bed and started unlacing his boots, then pulled them off and placed them next to the door that she had closed behind them. The room glowed softly from her trusty nightlight, which she'd been sleeping without recently, but was now plugged back into the outlet. She turned her back toward him, unzipped the leather top she'd been wearing, and hung it back in the closet. Her bone white back was in stark contrast to the red of her bra. He looked away from her and leaned back onto the bed, his feet still placed on the floor. *He needed to stop looking at her like that.*

"Can I use your restroom?" he asked, sitting up.

"Of course," she said, turning briefly and covering her breasts with her hands. "Feel free."

He stood up and walked across the hall, hoping she'd be finished changing by the time he returned. She may not have a problem being nude in front of people, but it made him uncomfortable. He turned the faucet on and splashed his face with the nice cool water. It felt good on his tired eyes. He dried his face on the hand towel and peeled his shirt back, looking at the puncture mark on his shoulder. The wound looked a little crusty, he hadn't cleaned it very well earlier, but it was already starting to heal. Vampire saliva actually caused wounds to heal more quickly. He'd learned that lesson from Mylori when she'd healed some rather nasty wounds by licking them clean. Roman growled and washed his hands again, stalling for a few more moments, and then walked back to her room. She was sitting on the bed adjusting her clock, wearing a small black t-shirt and underwear. Her hair hung over her body, nearly covering her small frame. Not a good image to see for keeping his thoughts pure.

"You want to leave at six, right?" she asked, looking up at him.

"Yeah, around six," he said, sitting back down on the end of her bed.

"I'm gonna set the clock for five thirty so I can take a shower before we go. How long are we staying? Maybe I should pack some more stuff?" she asked, looking at him, now concerned.

"Just the day probably," he muttered, and leaned back against the wall.

She finished adjusting the clock and leaned back on the bed. She looked over at him as he sat uncomfortably against the wall and laughed. "Come on already. Take your clothes off," she playfully scolded him. "Sleepy time's a wastin'."

She rolled over with her back towards him and closed her eyes trying to force sleep to come. The bed rose as he stood up. *Holy crap, he's really going to take his clothes off?* Violet opened her eyes wide, staring at the wall across the room.

"Nah, I'm gonna sleep in this," he said, not wanting her to see his wounded shoulder. He didn't need her worrying more than she already did. And besides, he felt awkward being nearly naked around her now. "Hey, you cleaned your room," he mused, finally noticing and conveniently changing the subject.

"Yep." She smiled, looking back over her shoulder at him.

"I didn't even know you had carpet," he teased, and slid down on his stomach beside her. He pushed his hands beneath the pillow, relishing the cool cotton fabric on his face and arms. His shoulder throbbed as it adjusted to the position. Her bed still smelled fresh as it had the last time he'd been here.

"Roman, you killed someone today," she said matter-of-factly.

"Not someone, *something*. Two of them actually." He closed his eyes and inhaled deeply, taking in the sweet smell of her pillow.

"What does it feel like?" She rolled over on her back and looked at his closed eyes. He looked serene resting there with his eyes closed and his face buried in her pillow. She wanted to take her finger and gently trace his eyebrows, his jaw and nose, and that soft mouth...

"I don't know how to answer that. It's all I've ever known and have never defined it before," he answered, cracking open an eye.

"Try. What does it feel like?"

"Ever rip the drumstick off a turkey at Thanksgiving and it cracks and rips as it comes apart? It feels sort of like that. Or like chopping through a huge roast with a sharp knife."

"Sick. Oh my god, gross, Roman." He shrugged in response. "Doesn't that freak you out? I mean, they talk to you and everything, so isn't it weird killing them? They're just like humans. They *were* humans."

She had a look of fear and shock in her eyes. He couldn't feel absolutely nothing when he killed them. He couldn't possibly be that unfeeling. The thought of him being that cold scared her.

Roman sighed and looked at her, opening both eyes and measuring his own thoughts on the matter. "It can be difficult at times. I try to be quick about it. I don't want to know them. It's my job, V. I've been doing this since I was very young. All I can compare it to is someone who grows up on a farm and is used to slaughtering pigs. It's not pleasant, but you grow accustomed to the feel and sound of it."

Violet was satisfied with the answer, though the reality of his life was terrifying. "You said you mostly go after the breeders, right?" she asked, closing her eyes again.

"Uh huh," he muttered, with his eyes closed. He was quickly drifting off.

"Well, why'd you go after the two from the store? They weren't breeders, were they?"

His eyes opened again and found hers. "No, but they tried to hurt you, and I'm here to protect you. I will never let anyone hurt you." He lifted his hand and rubbed his thumb across her warm, plump cheek, then took his hand back and closed his eyes. "Besides, I take care of strays when I can. And I didn't like them."

Violet let her hand do what it had wanted to do when he'd first slid down beside her. She traced the line of his brow and followed the sharp cut of his cheekbone and the black hair of his sideburn, then let her hand rest back on the bed against his side as her eyes closed of their own volition.

"Roman?" she asked, barely getting the word to form. She was so tired, so emotionally, and physically, exhausted.

"Yes?" he asked, equally as fatigued and trying like hell not to enjoy the feel of her touching him.

"I'm scared."

He opened his eyes and looked at her intently, trying to draw the fear from her. She looked like she had every day since he'd known her. Small and sad and delicate. He rolled onto his side and pulled her close, wrapping his arm around her. She snuggled against him, tucking her head against his shoulder as he rolled onto his back and held her in loose, but consoling arms. She inhaled deeply, filling her lungs with his comforting scent.

"Go to sleep, kitten."

He closed his eyes and nuzzled her hair with his nose and mouth. She shut her eyes, feeling warm and protected. And they both fell asleep.

She walked across the field. Her hair was entwined with ivy and coiling all around her. Her skin was nearly iridescent as it absorbed the moonlight. He could see the faint blue veins just beneath the surface of her skin, rising to the surface like eager fish to meet him beneath ice blue water. She stopped and looked up at the great face in the sky, her arms rising; she held the glowing orb in her hands and pressed it to her cheek. Her eyes closed, embraced by the heavenly light. She opened her eyes and looked at him now directly. A sliver of a smile, like the crescent moon, peeled across her face, not disturbing the openness of her eyes. She fell back into the tall wheat, losing him in the golden feathery arms of grain. He could see the empty space in the dancing blades where she rested. An anomaly she'd created in the sea of waving grain.

Slowly he walked toward her, drawn by the vibration of her body, a soft electric hum just below the sound of bristling grass and summer night breeze. He felt as though he'd never reach the spot where she nested. As he got closer, he could feel the humming of her body, vibrating in tandem with his own body's lulling rhythm. He bent over her, her eyes closed, the eyelashes curling like tiny honeysuckle vines shooting up from the ground and haloing those huge blue pools. Her lips were slightly parted and dewy, as if she'd just taken a sip of water. Her back was slightly arched as she lay against the prickly flora, her arms placed neatly at her sides, hands clasped against the soft roundness of her belly.

He looked at her navel, the only proof she'd been born into this human world. The swirling scar the umbilical cord had made, like a snail's shell, swirled and perfectly formed. The sacred geometry of her body. Perfect. Divine. He needed this proof, this sign that she was human, because she seemed so otherworldly, better than human, better than himself. Her delicate hands looked like a doll's, intricately carved by someone's tools. The slight outline of each rib, the soft plumpness of her breasts, the beautiful pale pink rose of her nipples, and the sculpted muscle of her lean legs... he fell to his knees beside her, feeling the veil of tears covering his eyes now. She was just so beautiful. So perfect. Too perfect for their world.

He should cover her with the protective grass and leave her here to sleep beneath the cold moon. Let the wolves circle her and keep her. Or he should cut his heart out and leave it bleeding and swollen in the center of her belly. Plucked from the hole in his chest and held like a fragile egg between her caressing palms above the symbol of her life. His life, for hers.

He reached out to feel the beating jolt of blood running through her. He could hear the faint swish as the vena cava moved in time with his own pounding.

She was alive...so very alive.

He leaned forward, resting his head on her soft breast. He felt the petal soft flesh against his cheek, warm and heating to his touch. The rose hued nipple inviting him to sup. Her moist honey breath fell against his face.

He closed his eyes as her fingers snaked into his hair.

Roman rolled his head and slowly opened his tired eyes. She was still sleeping there against him. He looked away from her towards the clock which read five ten. Slowly he pulled himself up and grabbed his boots. He walked across the hall, hoping not to wake anyone. He turned the water on and rinsed his face. The cold water was shocking against his sleep-warmed skin. He cupped his hand and scooped a handful of water into his mouth and swooshed it around and spit it out, then leaned against the counter and looked at himself in the mirror.

He remembered the dream in vivid detail, like it was a photograph in his head. It wasn't a dream, he knew that. They were there together. Somehow. He could still feel her skin, still taste her on his tongue.

He dried his face on the hand towel and then sat down on the edge of the bathtub to put on his boots. He finished up and then went back to her room.

She had rolled over onto her back. Her left arm had fallen to her side; her hand slightly cupped, facing upward. She looked so sweet lying there. He wished the alarm wasn't going to scream her awake in just a few short minutes. It would be for the best if she just slept. Actually, it would have been best if she'd never met him or been put in this situation. The imagery flashed in his head again. He could still taste her, feel her. He swallowed the memory.

He looked away from her and sat down on the edge of the bed and thought through the day's plans. They would get to Chicago, go to the room and rest, then call Lux and go to meet him. He was worried about this situation. What could Lux possibly have to say? No, he shouldn't worry, this all could be nothing. Lux could just be screwing with him. Right, because that made perfect sense. Nothing Lux would say would be good. Period.

He looked up at the clock. It was five twenty five now. He wanted to crawl back into her warm bed and sleep the day away, and let someone else take care of this crap for once. His arm ached, reminding him of the fight earlier with the vampires. He was so tired of it all. How long would it be before he messed up and got himself killed? How old would he be when his skills would begin to wane and he too would be slaughtered like his father had been? There was no one to take his place. This was it.

He could just give it all up.

The alarm went off, rousing him from his thoughts. She stirred and rubbed her eyes, rolling onto her side and flipping the switch off. She lay there completely still for a few moments, and then sat up and looked over at him and smiled.

"Good morning," his voice lulled. It was a deep and sleepy sound that reverberated in her chest.

"Morning," she said, stretching her arms and yawning. "Why are you awake?" she asked groggily, standing up and walking to her closet.

"I woke up a few minutes ago."

"Why don't you lie back down while I take a shower?" she asked, rummaging through her dresser for clean socks and undergarments.

"Cuz I won't get back up."

"Yeah, I get that," she said, and walked towards the door. She stopped in front of him and turned back, looking down at him with a curious expression on her face. "I just had the strangest dream."

Unconsciously she bit her bottom lip, her tongue moistening it as she pulled it between her teeth. She looked shy all of the sudden, filled with something he hadn't seen before. Roman took a deep, slow, breath, looking directly into her eyes as though he shared the memory. She leaned into him, urging him to give her a hug. He wrapped his arms around her hips, allowing her to fall against him. She rested her forehead against his briefly, then kissed the top of his head and left the room. He leaned back against the wall and closed his eyes. *Fuck.*

5

3I5

VIOLET FINISHED WRITING THE note to Amber and placed it on the kitchen table. She reminded her about avoiding Cecelia and that she could always reach her on "the damn cell phone"--and "P.S. Roman looks hot with sideburns."

Roman was in the car already. He had it warming for her and hoped said warmth wouldn't put him to sleep. He would stop and fill up the car, and get a large coffee and whatever she desired. He wanted her to sleep some during the drive. This day could be potentially difficult for her. Not only was she going to be excited about going to Chicago, but there was the impending drama of also seeing Lux (and probably Mylori) and who knows what the asshole had to tell her.

Roman had decided he would have to take her to Navy Pier while they were there, maybe on the way out of town. She would like that. She'd get the cotton candy she'd missed out on at the Ox Roast. He watched as she walked to the car. Her hair was sopping wet and pulled back in several braids. She had on a hooded sweatshirt and black leggings and the prerequisite boots that seem to dwarf her with their size. She was so damn cute.

"Okay," she said, as she fell into the seat. She heaved her bag into the back and pulled the seatbelt across her lap and latched it. Roman looked over at her and laughed. "What?" she asked, pouting.

"Bring enough stuff?" he asked, pulling down the driveway.

"Hey, you think I'm gonna go meet Lux in this?" She grinned, sinking down into the seat.

"Even knowing what he is, you still have the hots for him." He shook his head.

"I don't have *the hots*--I just don't want to look like a slob is all."

"Okay," Roman said, content to drop the subject.

They drove to the gas station and she waited while he pumped the gas in the car. He rubbed his shoulder. The muscles were stiff and achy beneath the pressure of his fingers. The puncture wounds the vampire's teeth had made felt deep as he dug his fingers into them. Driving all day was going to make it stiffen up even more. A shoulder rub would feel good, but he wouldn't ask Violet to do that. It would be too personal, and besides, she would feel the wound if she did. It would be unavoidable.

She was anxious to get on the road, not having been on a road trip in several years. The last trip she'd made was to Niagara Falls with her parents. She'd enjoyed Maple Leaf Village and the Houdini Museum. She had vowed to return again someday. She remembered the sweet sugary maple candy and how it melted on her tongue but hurt her teeth when she bit into it. The texture was off putting. Maybe she could convince Roman to go after the Falls had frozen. She wanted to see that.

"You want something?" he asked through the closed window.

She nodded her head and climbed out of the car and followed him.

It was still dark out and quiet like it can only be quiet early in the morning in a small town. They went to the coffee and each created their own distinct sugary mix and then walked to the counter to pay. Violet picked up a magazine from the rack beside the cash register and begged Roman with her eyes to pay for it. He smirked at her, paid for everything, and then they went to the car.

"You know you want to know all the latest Hollywood gossip." She teased him with a shove and a side eye.

He grabbed her hood and pushed it down over her head. They got in the car and sped down the street towards the turnpike.

The sun had risen and was hovering above the tree line like a smiling face. She had been asleep for forty minutes. He looked over at her sporadically. Her mouth moved gently into sleeping smiles occasionally. Her eyes looked swollen and tightly closed like a newborn baby. She would probably have a sore neck when she woke up, based on the precarious position of her head.

He turned the dial on the radio. The only thing this old stereo could get was AM for some reason. He settled on a random local station with some old man talking about the local farming community. The inane, unfamiliar banter was somehow comforting in some strange way. He drank the last of his cold coffee. It left a bitter sugar-rot taste in his mouth. His tongue felt thick and furry as he raked it against his teeth. He wanted to put the windows down, to feel the cool air on his face, but he'd wait until she woke up.

She found the edge of the woods. Her feet cracked out sounds like bone as she walked around the roots and acorns beneath the tall oak. She walked out into the clearing. The moon sang to her, its dazzling face shining like silver against the cobalt sky. She followed the call out into the field. The wheat felt like stiff feathers against her bare flesh. She could feel the tickle of the grain and the sweetness of summer dew as she moved through the golden sea. The scent of earth and air left a thin film on the surface of her skin, adhering to the moisture of the night kissed vegetation. Her eyes glowed in the sight of the satellite. She raised her hands to capture the face and brought it to her lips. She let the light-being go and peered out across the field.

He was there. Alone. Magnificent.

She wanted to go to him and worship at his feet. She wanted to offer herself as a sacrifice to him.

He needed no sacrifice. It was an insult to think he would.

She felt the heaviness of sleep taking her. Her limbs were numbing, warmed by the sweet night air and succulent breeze. She wanted to run towards him even as she fell back into the lush grain.

Her eyes closed. Her body, asleep and blissful. She hadn't slept this sleep for a thousand years.

She felt the thickness of the earth beneath her. It pulsed under her body, lava sweeping with the ebb and flow of her whispering heart. She could feel his footsteps in time with them, his body echoing the tide of the ocean of blood and salt and Moon. She watched in her mind's eye as his muscles moved beneath his white skin. So like a panther he moved and stalked.

He was The Hunter. Orion.

She felt the heat of his body as it hovered over hers-- she was unable to open her eyes to gaze upon his splendor--so taken with sleep. So taken with dream.

She felt the cells of her body bend towards him, leaning towards the light of his eyes as they passed over, warmed by the touch of his green eyes.

She willed him closer, beckoning him to join her here in the deep golden sea, in deep golden dawn. The earth trembled as his body fell to it, his body electrically charged and static as he knelt beside her. She could feel the radiant warmth emanating from his organs, hear the faint churning of the fluid and blood, the dividing of cells regenerating his perfection.

His cheek pressed against her breasts, the strong bone of his jaw furrowing rows into the pink fertile soil of her body. He would plant strength and power into her cells. His breath inhaling and exhaling, cooling and warming her dew covered skin, divine and dancing across the surface. Their hair entwined and coiled together in a mass of black fur; white animals with glistening black fur.

Her eyes opened as the Moon made its path above them. The face smiling and smiling and smiling.

She felt the velvet of his red lips against her now, soft and intimate and suckling.

Her body jumped, waking her from the dream. She straightened up in the seat, looking at the floor and pulling the hood off her head. A repeat dream? Right down to the last moment.

"Bad dream?" he asked, looking over at her.

"Uh, no, good actually." She grinned sheepishly and took a drink of her nearly full, but ice cold, coffee. "How long was I sleeping?"

"Not long."

"I have to pee."

"There should be a rest stop coming up shortly."

"Good," she said, uncomfortably shifting her body to try and relieve the pressure on her bladder. *Or maybe her body just ached from the memory of his touch.*

"So, what was your dream about?"

"I don't know, walking in a field at night, nothing much." She wondered if her face was as red as it felt. She was trying to play it cool.

Roman didn't say anything.

Change of subject time. "So, vampires are like what? Like where did they come from and what are they?"

Her question threw him off. He hadn't expected the drastic subject change. "I don't know where they originate really. I mean, I think there are some who have always been, and others who were made. My uncle had all the books and whatnot regarding the history. I was never completely interested in the history. I did read a lot, but I was young and didn't really care much. I was more interested in killing them. Typical male aggression, I guess."

Violet chuckled and then blanched, thinking about what he'd just said. She looked over at him and remembered the dream she'd just had. It was so fresh and real to her, she could picture his mouth now tracing the curve of her neck and jawline.

"What are you staring at?" he asked, not looking at her.

"Nothing," she said with hesitation. "I mean, you, I guess."

"Why?" he grimaced, and laughed at her.

"Stop being stupid," she said, slouching down in the seat and pulling the hood back over her head. "Let me know when we stop." She closed her eyes and tucked her hands between her knees, embarrassed that he'd caught her staring at him. She wouldn't be surprised if she had drool dripping from her mouth.

She walked out of the restroom and dried her hands on her pants, then pulled the sweatshirt off and tied it around her waist. She was wearing the t-shirt she'd slept in the night before. The sleeves were short, revealing the toned muscles of her arm. He watched as she walked to the snack bar and bought a drumstick from the ice cream machine. A youngish man walked by her and stopped to talk. It was obvious by his body language he was somewhat taken with her. She looked exceptionally girly, standing there twirling her hair with one hand and clutching the ice cream with the other. For some reason it was unnerving. It was strange to see her in this context. The time they had spent together he'd never seen her as "a girl" in this way. She had only been someone to protect, and a friend. But seeing her standing there with another guy, even if he was a pipsqueak that Roman could crush with one hand--*whoa, where did that come from?*—was strange to witness. He looked away briefly, then back as she walked away from the kid, turning back to say "Nice to meet you", and then skipping towards him.

"You know we're going to burn to a crisp?" she said, biting the chocolate and nuts from the top of the treat as she referred to the missing top of the car.

"We won't leave it down all day." He smiled at her with a teasing grin.

"What now?" she asked, jutting her hip out and putting her hand on it dramatically.

"You're such a flirt." He shook his head and walked around to the driver's side and climbed inside.

"No I'm not!" she said, acting as though she'd been insulted.

"Oh, come on," he laughed at her.

"Okay, I guess I am a little flirty," she admitted with a smirk.

"Yeah, *a little*," he scoffed.

"Shut up!" she said, shoving his arm.

They rode quietly for miles, listening to harvest reports, and local weather, and traffic advisories. The soft autumn sun felt warm and soothing. Her skin felt tight against her face. The smell of the air, furrowed fields and dried leaves, the remnants of last night's smoking chimneys, the warm butter sun and cotton ball clouds...she loved it all so much and never wanted it to end. She wished they could drive and drive forever, forgetting all that lay behind and ahead.

Her eyes lit up as she saw the Chicago city limits sign. Autumn scented air was choked out by the smells of the city. The buildings grew around them engulfing the sky. The freedom she felt earlier was faded now, and she'd moved from excitement to fear, which sat heavy in her belly, groaning and churnin. She ignored it. Whatever happened later would happen. She wanted this moment of exhilarating excitement and she refused to allow the darkness to seep into it.

She had been to big cities before, it wasn't as though she was overwhelmed, or some little country mouse, nothing so ignorant as that, but she'd never been *here* and that was thrilling to her. She'd corresponded with people from Chicago in the past. She wondered if her old friends still lived here somewhere in this miasma of concrete.

The traffic was busy, as the traffic is always busy heading into town. They wrapped around the loop, passing the Aquarium and various other landmarks. The bright blue of Lake Michigan was overwhelming to her. Lake Erie was murky grey-green, and that was the only one of the Great Lakes she'd ever seen. The choppy water looked endless. She watched the cyclists and rollerbladers snake their way down the paths, magically missing each other somehow. For a moment she imagined what it would be like to live here. She could do it. This could be her home. There was nothing keeping her from leaving Mantua now.

"I like it here," she said, beaming as she looked over at Roman and putting her hand on his leg without thought. He let go of the steering wheel and held her hand, not letting her take it back. He smiled at her and kept quiet, content to watch her soak up the place and listen to her rattle on about everything she saw that drew her attention. The thought that he liked her way too much entered his mind, only to be squelched by yet another gleeful observation.

They turned down several busy streets, making their way to Clark. Violet saw a handful of stores she wanted to visit before she left. It was hard to imagine having so many places so accessible at any given moment. People of all walks of life walked down the street, none giving any notice to the other. This seemed strange to her, coming from such a small town where nothing went unnoticed.

"Here's the hotel," he said, pulling into a parking garage. They found a spot and locked the car up. Violet hoisted her bag over her shoulder and reached out for his hand, grasping his pinky. Her eyes scanned over everything, she was like a sponge, absorbing the sights and sounds,

Roman walked up to the counter and got the key to their room. She watched as he smiled politely to the woman behind the counter. Yeah, and Roman thought *she* was a flirt?

She looked around the lobby. Floral patterns festooned the dark green carpet, beige and gray striped wallpaper plastered the walls. The hotel was older, but clean and bright. She could tell by the other guests--most of whom wore business attire--that this was not a cheap place to stay. She was used to motor lodges and chain budget hotels. This was not that sort of place.

He waved off a bellhop, tipping him anyway, and then walked over to her. He looked down at Violet and placed his hand on her back, urging her towards the elevator. "Room 315," he said, and pushed the button.

The doors closed and they ascended to the third floor. The doors opened and they made their way past the oncoming guests and followed the well-lit signs to their room. He unlocked the door and let her in first.

She set her bag down on one of the beds and immediately went to the window, opening the curtains so she could look down on the street below.

"I love it here." She smiled and sat down on the edge of the bed, bouncing herself a couple times and laying back on the floral print bedspread.

Roman set his bag down on the dresser and turned to her. *Shit, maybe he should have gotten two rooms? It hadn't crossed his mind, but isn't that what normal, non-couples who weren't related would do?*

"I can get you your own room if you want? I didn't even think about it," he said, walking towards her as she bounced up and down on the bed. The remark ceased her bouncing.

"Don't be fucking stupid. Well, I mean, unless you want your own room? Like, why would I want to stay alone when you're here to fuck around with? I mean... not literally fuck around with... but, oh you know what I mean." Her cheeks turned pink as she rolled her eyes at her bumbling.

Roman snickered and rustled her hair playfully. "Yeah, no, I'm fine sharing."

He squeezed his eyes shut briefly, trying really hard not to think about fucking around with her. *Get it together. You've got a job to do.*

He turned away from her so he could stop thinking about it. He would take a shower and try to get some rest, but if she wanted to go out he would take her.

He turned back to her, finding she had resumed bouncing on the bed. "So, do you want to go out, or stay here?" he asked, peeling his shirt off and folding it, forgetting about the wound on his shoulder.

Violet was suddenly surprised by his actions and looked away. Maybe he did actually want to *fuck around*? She could feel her face turning red. He had a perplexed look on his face and sat on the other bed then began unlacing his boots.

"Well, I want to go see stuff, but you've been driving all day, so if you want to rest that's fine with me too." She reached over and grabbed the remote control off the nightstand and began surfing through the channels, stopping on a local news show, mystified by the different anchors and the strangeness of their delivery. It was always weird watching the news in an unfamiliar town. *Nice distraction from Roman's naked torso.*

"I want to take a shower and maybe take a short nap. Lux won't be up and around for another five hours give or take, so there's plenty of time to do something before we go over there."

Violet felt a sudden panic sweep through her. She'd been able to forget the magnitude of this visit all day, but here it was again. Inescapable and inevitable.

"Hey?" he asked, standing up and walking over towards her. "You alright?" He had perceived the sudden dread.

"I just keep forgetting the reality of all this, and then it smacks me in the face," she said, looking up at him and noticing the red holes and dark bruising in the muscle of his shoulder. She winced and looked away.

"I can't imagine how scary this must be for you. You're a very brave little girl." He reached over and put his hand on the top of her head and patted her. He internally cringed at what he'd just said, knowing how inaccurate at least part of it was. She was not a little girl.

"I'm not a brave *little girl*. I'm terrified," she said, staring blankly at the television. His words could cut her to the quick. She wasn't a *little girl*, she was a fucking woman.

"You'd be foolish not to be. Most people would probably go insane knowing what you know. And given the reason for your being here, I wouldn't blame you if you wanted to go back home and pretend you never met me and never knew anything about any of this. In fact, that would probably be the smartest thing you could do."

The offense was evident in her tone as she reacted to him calling her a little girl, but he had to keep repeating it to himself, because lately he was feeling way too much for her. If he could just view her as a girl that was too young for him, as nothing more than this girl to protect, a job and nothing more, then once she was safe he could move on, thus protecting her further. The problem was, he didn't really see her as too young anymore, she wasn't too young, and the words felt sick even coming from his mouth. She most definitely was not a little girl. And his idiotic behavior over this whole situation was getting on his own nerves. He could only imagine how annoying it was to her.

"Don't ever say that," she said, standing up and walking to him. A flash of brilliant anger seared him, shooting through her eyes to his as if an arc of electricity had leapt across the room. She went to him, wrapping her arms around him and holding him as close as she could, as though he would slip away if she let go.

The sudden shock and force of her grip almost knocked him over. His shoulder, wracked with pain, throbbed at taking the fullness of her weight. He reached around her, hugging her tightly and lifting her off the ground. He ignored the burning of his shoulder as he held her. It had been so thoughtless of him taking his shirt off in front of her. Even more thoughtless to be holding her so closely in a hotel room where they were alone. How was he supposed to react to her or this situation? He still wasn't used to all this human emotion/friendship nonsense. There was no doubt she was terrified, and now she'd seen the injury on top of being put in this situation.

"Sorry," he said, squeezing her and setting her feet on the ground, then backed away a step. "I'm going to take a shower," he said, leaving her there alone. He could feel the blood seeping from the wound. He took his duffle bag and shut the door behind him.

She heard the water running. *Little girl! Pfffft. You weren't thinking that in my dream, you dick. And you sure as hell weren't thinking it right now.*

"This show is so stupid," she said, looking over at Roman.

He was asleep, curled up on his side with his hands tucked beneath a pillow. The road atlas he'd been reading still sat open to the last map he'd studied. He had a thing for maps, which was good because she couldn't read one, and couldn't even tell north from south if someone asked her. She had a cellphone to help with directions. When did she ever need directions though? She lived in the place she'd grown up and never left. She knew where everything was she ever needed to go. Her focus went back to him. Right now was the perfect opportunity to study his physique, since she knew he would be none the wiser.

He'd pulled his wet hair back into a ponytail. The pointed line of black sideburn across his cheek made him look like a pirate. She smiled, picturing him with a patch over his eye. He was still shirtless. The rounded muscle of his shoulder and the chiseled form of his biceps was appealing. Duh, of course it was. His body was perfect. Every freaking inch of it that she'd seen was perfect. And she imagined those she hadn't seen were as well. She rolled her eyes at herself, and then she thought of biting into that yummy looking arm muscle. The idea of it made her lower half warm and achy. She could feel it in her mouth, picture it perfectly. All thick and solid as her teeth sank into his pliable skin. The vision made her mouth fall open slightly, her eyes blurring as she daydreamed. Then the red, purple, and black wound glared at her. A chill ran through her body as she realized what had caused those angry looking holes.

Stop being morbid. Stop wasting this opportunity on scary stuff. Gaze at his splendor, you dummy. She scolded herself and shook her head, letting her eyes travel away from those angry looking bite marks to appreciate the rest of him. She liked the thick, strong bones of his wrists and the way the veins rose to the surface of his forearms and hands. Faint scar tissue criss crossed from his fingers up his arms, marring the otherwise perfect skin. An even fainter trail of whiter flesh scarred his side, stretching over his ribs. She could only imagine the wounds that had been inflicted over his body. What the hell had he suffered?

His stomach was flat except for the slightest little pudge right around the waistband of his pants. It was barely enough to pinch, or bite. *Again with the biting.* Seeing as how she was freaked out by the marks on his shoulder, biting shouldn't be a thought she preoccupied herself with, but there she was again.

Her mouth watered thinking about it, her teeth almost aching at the vision in her mind.

I will attempt that one day. She smirked and licked her bottom lip.

She stared at the soft dark hair that trailed lightly over his strong chest and picked up again beneath his navel, disappearing into the waistband of his jeans. All the men she'd seen naked before were hairless. Randy couldn't grow a beard, or a chest hair. Yes, *a* chest hair, singular. Let alone a patch of it. And Mark had been hairless. Even his arms and legs barely had any hair on them. Roman looked like a real man, not a boy.

Ugh, she wasn't normally one to ogle someone like this, but dang. What a lovely thing it would be to touch him, to tickle his skin with her fingers, just lightly enough to raise goose bumps. To feel the softness of his skin beneath her palms, with her lips...

She shook her head and looked away from his stomach. His long legs stretched out over the end of the bed, his bare feet dangling off the edge. His toes were long and straight and well kept, of course he would be as meticulous in his grooming, she assumed, as he was in his housekeeping. Never once had she seen anything out of place at his apartment, so naturally he would care for himself in the same manner. His feet were white as milk. She figured they had probably never seen sunlight a single day of his life. His body was perfectly sculpted. The embodiment of masculinity. But it was his beautiful face that caught her most of all. *He is so beautiful.* It actually hurt to look at him. It made her want to cry for some reason.

Man, she had to get out of here or she was going to jump him. She tore her eyes away. She was much too excited to be in this city to sit here any longer anyway. She got up and walked over to the notepad that was sitting beside the phone and wrote a note for Roman so that he wouldn't worry. There were a bunch of little shops she wanted to visit along the street outside that she'd seen on the drive to the hotel. Plus she wanted to buy Amber and Randy a little gift, and maybe buy herself a new outfit too.

It was chilly out, so she tied her sweatshirt around her waist again in case she needed it, then sat down on the floor to put her boots on and scooped up one of the keys off the nightstand. She set the remote on the bed next to Roman and stopped to look at him briefly again. Her desire was to bend over and plant a kiss on his cheek, or maybe lick that soft little pudge of fat right along his waist and then... but she didn't. She swung her bag over her shoulder and left the room.

The sun was getting lower in the sky, reminding her that in a few hours she would be faced with something completely insane. There was a good chance that she may learn some terrible truth about herself. What that could be, she had no idea. What the hell could it be? What could Lux possibly know about her? It had to be horrible, whatever it was. Fuck, there was always some horrible truth lately. Life was completely insane enough without whatever Lux was going to divulge.

She also might find out nothing, there was that possibility, but yeah right. Why would a vampire call her here for nothing? The fact that she was sort of excited to see Lux again made her feel conflicted. There was nothing about this situation that ought to be exciting. She *should* be terrified. Then her stupid brain recalled the kiss he'd given her. His mouth had felt electric against hers, and not in some romantic notion kind of way. It literally felt electric. Like all her nerve endings were firing simultaneously. Like some little electric cells were traveling to meet his lips and zapping her to get to his touch. *God.* Even knowing what he was, she still fought the intriguing nature of it. She couldn't help it with all the fairytale romanticizing she'd done in her head about vampires through the years, and he was the physical embodiment of all those fairytales. And she felt guilty, stupid, and pathetic for thinking these thoughts.

She walked by several shops that looked interesting. The streets were filled with city people, the kind of folks that were so different from those she'd grown up with, or maybe they weren't. Yes, they were. But somehow this city felt homey to her, like she'd been there before. If she ever did decide to move, this might be the place. She had liked Toronto that time she'd visited too though. There were a lot of places she wanted to visit.

She noticed the jack-o-lanterns and black cats lining the windows and it dawned on her, today was Halloween and she'd forgotten all about it. Right now her friends were probably getting ready to go down to KSU to wander the streets in costume with all the drunken college kids. How could she have forgotten? Duh, she had forgotten because her life was now the literal embodiment of Halloween. Oh and yes, she was going to talk to *a vampire* on Halloween, how apropos. Seriously? The thought made her laugh out loud like a crazy woman.

Her grin faded, and she saw a store across the street with punk looking clothes in the window. This caught her eye and drew her from her thoughts. She got to the next intersection and crossed the street, doubling back to the store. The smell of nag champa incense hit her the moment she stepped through the door. She loved the smell, but it made her eyes burn. Lush ambient strings and tribal rhythms poured through the store's sound system. She looked around the shop, eyeing a million things she wanted to buy, but she would restrain herself. Not because she didn't have the money, but because it was silly to go overboard on things she didn't need.

She saw a black fuzzy purse with a pink vinyl cat on it and knew this was the gift for Amber. Her friend collected purses and had twelve thousand or so unique purses in her collection. Of course that was an exaggeration, but Amber loved her bags. She carried the purse and began looking for something for Randy. Across the room she spied a black baseball cap with a red, white, and blue patch on it that said "proud white trash". This was perfect for him because it tied to a common joke amongst his friends. They were all used to being called white trash, or some variation thereof. Even Mosely, who clearly wasn't white trash. This was Randy's gift, she knew he'd like it, so she placed the cap on her own head and kept looking.

There were so many different shirts and dresses she wanted, but when she saw *The One* she knew it. It was a baby pink and black pleated skirt and a black leather corset top with pink ribbon ties. She went to the rack and looked for her size, so excited and afraid they wouldn't have one to fit her. A sigh of relief escaped her when she found her size. She decided to try it on just in case, because she didn't want to be bummed out if it was too big or looked weird on her body.

There was a death rock girl behind the counter that she asked for assistance. The girl seemed fairly uneager to help, but did so anyway, showing Violet to the fitting room in the rear of the store. Violet thanked her, realizing that this girl would have probably been the coolest person in their town had she lived there, and that she herself would be just another face in the scene here in Chicago. She almost envied the idea of being anonymous.

It was strange to her that all these "cool" items were so easily accessible and that the people where she lived had to work so hard to find things even half as "cool" as what was probably offered in at least a dozen stores right in this general area of town. Most of the time they were stuck making their own clothes by altering fairly mundane articles of clothing into something fashionable. Maybe that made them *more* genuine than these people? Anyone could walk into a store and purchase the goth "costume". They had a word for those people. Posers.

She stripped her clothes off and pulled the garb on with excitement. She laced the corset tightly, and turned around, looking at her body from all angles. She loved it. She loved pleated skirts and figured it was probably due to her unrequited desire as a young girl to be a cheerleader. Yeah, like they would have welcomed her onto the squad? Pffft, not likely.

She smiled and took the clothes off, got dressed, and walked back into the store. She took another turn around the store, thinking she may find something better, but knowing that this was it for her. She meandered through the racks and the meager men's section, which took up only a quarter of the store's space. This place was definitely geared towards women. A black t-shirt with the word "killer" in classic white velvet iron on letters called out to her. She thought of Roman and knew that he probably would never wear the thing, but decided to buy it anyway because it was funny. *Wow, since when is being a killer funny?* Well, he would at least get a chuckle out of it, *maybe.* She remembered from borrowing his shirt that he wore a snug extra-large and sifted through the rack and found the last one available. She walked to the counter and purchased the clothes, the clerk never muttering more than the amount and a feigned "Thank you" after she'd paid.

Violet walked outside, content with having found some cool things. She stopped in the sandwich shop by the hotel and ordered two meatball subs and a couple bottled waters. Her arms were full as she entered the lobby and made her way back to room 315.

6

DRACULA'S DAUGHTER

ROMAN WAS SITTING ON the end of the bed watching the news when she walked in the door. He looked over at her as she fumbled with the door, and the various bags she carried, and hopped up to help her.

"I'm glad you brought food. I am starving," he said, taking the sandwiches from her and setting them on the bed. "Did you have fun?" he asked, opening one of the waters and taking a big gulp.

"Yes," she said, walking to the other bed and setting all the stuff down. "I got you something." She rummaged through the bags with excitement

He leaned back on the palms of his hands, watching as she sifted through her things. It was nice to see that look of excitement on her face again.

"Now, you will probably think this is stupid, but I saw it and it reminded me of you, and if you don't like it you can at least wear it to sleep in, or use it as a dishrag, or something."

"I'm sure I'll like it." He laughed at her. Every single time she felt awkward about something, she qualified it with some rambling self-deprecating statement or apology.

She found the black shirt and pulled it out and held it up against her body and smiled as she looked at him. "It says killer! Isn't that funny?" she asked, tossing the shirt to him. She stopped talking and flittering about, noticing the wound on his shoulder again. It was bruised, black, and dark blue around the massive puncture wounds. How was she supposed to react to that thing? Should she mention it, or pretend not to notice? Looking away, she went back to her bag of things.

He held the shirt out and read it himself. "That is funny," he said, holding it up to his chest. This was not something he'd ordinarily wear. "It would probably look better on you though, you're the killer."

"What?" she asked, crinkling her nose and continuing to survey her plunder. "You're the killer, *Killer*. Look what I got for Randy and Amber." She held the articles up, expecting him to be as excited as she was. He calmly looked at them and smiled and picked up the bottle of water and took another sip. "Oh! And you know what I realized?"

"What?"

"Today is Halloween. How dumb is that?"

"Dumb?"

"Well, yeah, I mean, I'm going to talk to a *vampire* on Halloween. That's pretty fucking dumb."

"Seems sort of appropriate to me actually," he said, shrugging his shoulders and grinning. "Come on, let's eat. I'm starving." He picked up a sandwich and looked at her for permission to eat.

"Go ahead," she said, somewhat let down by his lack of enthusiasm for her presents and the ironic realization. Perhaps he didn't quite understand how important these things were to her? Maybe he didn't quite get how insanely overboard her and her friends went for Halloween. And dammit, he should be thrilled to look at these gifts she'd bought her friends. What was wrong with him? She internally groaned at herself for being ridiculous.

He could read the expression on her face and realized he hadn't given her the reaction she'd hoped for. He felt bad, but he was a guy and didn't really care about goofy stuff like this. Although, he was excited that she was excited, and was happy about that. "So what'd you get for yourself?" He threw her a bone as he unwrapped the sandwich.

She perked back up, and held up the skirt and corset against her body. "Cool huh?" she asked, swinging her hips back and forth and looking down to watch the skirt swoosh.

"Nice," he smiled, attempting to hide the thoughts he was having. Vague reflections of that dream he'd had periodically surfaced, and this outfit she was holding up didn't help matters. "Are you wearing that tonight?" he asked, taking a bite of the sub.

"I don't know," she said, setting the clothes down and reaching over for her food and water. "I don't want to look like some douchey gothy vampire girl when I go over there." A smirk came to her lips as she sat back on the bed.

"Trust me, that won't be a problem," he said, turning his attention back to the news on the television.

"What do you mean?" she asked, unwrapping her own sandwich and tearing off some bread.

"What I mean is that I don't think Lux would think that even if you showed up in a cape and black lipstick."

"What? Why would you say that?"

"Because it wouldn't matter to him if you were in a tutu or a hockey mask, he'd still be enthralled."

She considered his statement and hid her smile behind her sandwich. Though now she wondered if he'd meant Lux was enthralled with her specifically, or with women in general. Or maybe just anyone with blood? She refrained from asking him anything more to avoid the risk of embarrassment with any of the stupid girlie questions she wanted to ask.

Roman stopped eating and looked at her. "You do know that if I wasn't around, he would have taken you by now?"

She stopped chewing and looked at him, not fully understanding what he meant. His eyes were serious, his mouth firm and straight.

"I mean he would have killed you, Violet," he said, clarifying himself.

His words cut to the core of her, the reality hitting her again hard in the face. She set the sandwich down and picked the water up and took a swig. Her eyes began to tear up, and she didn't want to be reduced to a sniveling baby again. She was tired of him having to ask if she was "okay". She wanted to be strong like him. She wanted to be emotionless.

"I didn't say that to hurt you, that's just the reality of what he is. And if he didn't get you, Mylori surely would have."

"How do you stand this?" she asked, now fighting the well of tears that threatened to spill down her cheeks.

"It just is what it is. It's all I've ever known."

"Why don't you kill them then?" she asked, wiping her eyes with her fingers in shame for crying again. "If they're so horrible and evil, then why not kill them?"

"As I said before, it's not so black and white. I am only one man," he said. He hated being the cause of so much pain for her, even if it was indirectly.

"I hate this," she said, resting her face in her hands and leaning over onto her elbows. "I liked it better when I didn't know they were real."

"I'm sorry," he said, standing up and walking over to sit down beside her. He put his arm around her shoulder. This is what he needed to remember. She was a frail girl incapable of doing the kinds of things he was capable of doing. She would never be able to shut herself down like he could. And she would never be able to live with herself if she did things he'd been forced to do. He would protect her for as long as he could, hoping she would be able to go back to a normal life once he was gone. "Don't cry," he said, painfully soft.

His words forced the sadness to the surface even more. She seemed to be able to handle cruelty far better than kindness. She leaned into him, embarrassed yet again by her inability to control her emotions.

"Leave it to me to wreck your fun," he said, disgusted with himself.

There'd been no reason to mention Lux at this moment. She didn't need to know the full extent of reality every given second of the day. She didn't need to know any of it, really. And he was an idiot, because he was taking her to see the asshole. Did she really need to be worried about Lux killing her on top of whatever else that dick might have to say? *Stupid.* He should have kept his mouth shut. He could protect her even if she was completely in the dark about all of it. But that wasn't completely true, was it? She needed to be aware of everything around her now. The threat was too close and too real. The fact that she was attracted to Lux in the first place would have been enough to get her killed. Lux would have worked her like he'd seen him work a hundred women before, and she'd be nothing but a memory now.

But then, why had Lux sent him to protect her in the first place? None of this shit made sense. But he was going to keep her safe. Lux wasn't going to get his hands on her. He would kill Lux before he'd allow that. But Lux wasn't the problem. Something else was.

He could hear her splashing in the bathtub and hoped it would relax her some. She was singing to herself and the sound echoed against white ceramic tile and into the rest of the room. The shirt she'd bought for him caught his attention, so he picked it up and looked at it again.

Killer. At one time that word was repugnant to him, now he just understood that it was who and what he was, and would always be, until the day Death caught up to him.

He picked up the phone and dialed Lux's flat. He spoke to him briefly, letting him know they were in town and would be over in a few hours. He also made it more than clear he wasn't in the mood for bullshit. The sound of her singing lulled him so he slid back on the bed, closing his eyes, and enjoying the sweetness of her voice through the wall.

She unbraided her hair and raked through it with her fingers, loosening the wavy tresses. She put powder on her face and lined her eyes with black liquid eyeliner, curving it up slightly at the edge of her eye. Then she dusted the lower lid with black eyeshadow, smudged it with her finger, and then put on mascara. She brushed her cheeks lightly with baby pink blush and then applied raspberry lip gloss to her lips.

She looked at her ghostly white naked body in the mirror for several long moments. Her stomach was churning with fear and apprehension. Theoretically, she could still walk away from all of this. She knew Roman wanted that for her. But she had to understand all of it now. She needed answers. And she knew she could never go back to the way things were anyway. Her life, as it had been, was dead. Just like her family.

She looked at the new clothes that were sitting on the vanity, loving them. Simple things gave her something normal to appreciate in the midst of all the chaos. But then she thought again about the purpose of her visit with Lux, and decided it was inappropriate to dress as though she were going clubbing. She put the pale pink bra and matching panties on and opened the door and walked to the bed where she'd piled the rest of the clothes she brought with her.

Roman opened his eyes and watched her as she rifled through the pile. She never looked at him or acknowledged his presence, too busy rifling through her things. He wondered how he'd read her so wrong in the beginning, thinking she was some shy girl that would be embarrassed by her nakedness around him. Maybe he viewed women from some archaic angle? Like they were all virginal, blushing brides or something. He certainly hadn't viewed *all* women from that angle, maybe only her? Maybe he had to view her that way to make sense of shit in his head? It made his brain hurt. She had no apprehension when it came to her body. It was strange to him, because in so many other ways she was completely insecure. She was comfortable in her own skin, or maybe she wasn't. He had no idea who this girl was. He wouldn't allow himself to know her that well. Or maybe he was in denial.

She gathered some clothes and walked back to the bathroom. It was a good thing she'd decided to bring something a little less revealing with her. She put a tight, black, long sleeved button down blouse on and smoothed it, running her fingers down the sleeves and tugging. It was wrinkled, but that didn't matter to her. It was more hip somehow that way or something. Casual. Yeah. She adjusted the collar and cuffs and then put on the black and pink pleated skirt. The thought that this seemed only slightly more appropriate for the occasion crossed her mind, but then, what would really be appropriate for a meeting with a vampire? She pulled the black thigh high hose up and then walked back into the bedroom.

Roman sat up and leaned back on his elbows. "Not wearing the new shirt thing you bought?" he asked, checking her out, somewhat relieved and also somewhat let down.

Violet smirked in response to his not knowing it was called a corset. "No, it didn't seem appropriate," she said, and sat down beside him. "But what would be appropriate?" she asked, leaning back against him and rested her head against his chest.

"I don't know," he said, taking his hand and smoothing her hair away from her face. "A shirt with a cross on it and a necklace made of garlic?" he laughed, and could feel her smile against his chest. "You look nice."

"Thanks," she said, feeling nothing but emptiness.

"Don't be scared," he comforted, lying back down all the way. He rested his arm across her chest and she picked up his hand, playing with his fingers nervously.

"You say that, but there's no way I can be anything but scared."

"You're right. I hate that you're in this position."

"I know," she replied, holding his hand tightly and closing her eyes. "Roman?"

"Yeah?"

"Does your shoulder hurt?" she asked, her voice a timid whisper.

"Only when I move it," he joked, trying to lessen her concern.

"Funny," she said dryly. "When are we going?"

"Soon," he said, closing his own eyes.

Violet went to the bathroom for the third time in thirty minutes. She was nervous and her bladder was proving that fact.

"You ready to go?" he asked, picking up his jacket and stuffing his arms into the sleeves.

"I suppose." She looked at him with trepidation, eyes wide and glossy.

"If it gets too crazy we'll just leave. Try not to worry. Nothing's going to happen. I would kill Lux before I let him fuck with you. Actually, it would give me an excuse to finally get rid of the asshole."

"You sure about that? Are you bringing a sword, or whatever it is you use to kill them?"

He snickered and put his hand on her back, guiding her out the door. "No need for all that," he said, pulling the door shut. "Trust me, he'll be on his best behavior. We can walk or drive."

Her eyes widened. She hadn't realized Lux lived so close to the hotel. How strange that all these people were bustling about in the streets and a freaking vampire lived in their midst. Weird. "Drive," she said, pointing to her high heels.

They walked down to the lobby and out to the parking garage.

"So, they just have a regular house or whatever?" she asked, waiting for him to unlock the door.

"Basically," he answered, opening the door for her. "I've never been to their Chicago place."

"How bizarre."

"Yeah, I guess it is." He started the car and pulled out of the garage. "I'll take the scenic route so you can calm your nerves a little, okay?"

"Sure." She smiled and took a deep breath. Her thoughts went to her mom and how she wished her mom was here with her now. Her mother had always known how to calm her nerves. She remembered the time she'd fallen and broken her arm, and how terrified she'd been before the doctor was about to set the bone. The softness in her mother's voice as she had rubbed her back the entire time had soothed her fears and given her the strength to put on a brave face. Violet had never shed a tear during that whole procedure. She tried to imagine her mother here with her now. It helped a little.

They drove for fifteen minutes or so, and finally pulled up in front of a retired factory. It was an old brick building, which the vampires had apparently bought and converted. Roman parked the car on a side street and looked over at the nervous girl. He felt anxious for her. They got out of the car and Violet circled in front to meet up with him. She took his pinkie finger in her hand and followed him timidly to the door on the side of the building. Roman knocked quietly once on the door and then twisted the knob. It was already open, of course it would be. Vampires would probably welcome random humans stumbling into their home. He pushed the door and peered into the building and saw light coming from the top of the tall, wide staircase directly in front of them. Violet looked around, noticing the bottom level was completely empty and dark except for a few crates and odds and ends pieces of furniture sitting about somewhat randomly like it was storage.

"You okay?" he asked, looking down at her.

"Uh huh." She breathed deeply, looking up at him.

Her eyes left his and drifted to the top of the stairs where she saw Lux appear, looking down at them. He was backlit with soft orange light. His hair haloed around his head in a pale yellow tousled crown. He was so tall and lean. She could see his glistening eyes penetrating the darkness. He was looking directly at her, and subsequently her heart sped up. Roman squeezed her hand quickly and urged her forward. They walked up the stairs, standing side by side. Roman spoke casually to Lux, who greeted them warmly. Violet was silent and terrified. They reached the top of the stairs and Lux waved them into the room.

It was meticulously decorated. The walls were covered in some kind of rich metallic gold wallpaper that looked opulent, and the floors were black marble with golden veins weaving through that glittered as they caught the light. She was utterly astonished by her surroundings. It was almost like some palace, or a set from a movie. The furniture and accessories were all very lush and expensive looking. Black leather furniture, metal tables, and old pieces of art dotted the huge room. Thick crimson velvet drapes hung partially open from the massive industrial windows and puddled onto the floor beneath in red pools. Thick fur rugs covered the shiny black floor here and there. She was amazed by this place.

"Nice," Roman said, squeezing Violet's hand and letting go before walking across the room and slouching down in a massive tufted leather chair. He threw his feet up on the ottoman.

Lux smiled and guided Violet to sit on the couch. She timidly made her way to the sofa, avoiding eye contact with the man.

Thickly scented candles of some sort of flower burned on the marble mantle. The fragrance was so intoxicating, transporting.

"Mimosa," Lux said, noticing the subtle intake of air as her eyes found the candles.

Violet had never smelled mimosa before.

There was a fire smoldering in a huge fireplace, giving the room a soft warm glow. Roman looked at her and smiled with reassurance. A wary smile came to her lips, she was so uneasy with the situation. Lux sat on the end of the couch beside Violet, crossing his legs and resting his hands in his lap. She could feel his eyes on her, so she focused on her surroundings, occasionally looking to Roman for support. There was a substantial oil painting above the fireplace of Mylori. Her eyes were silver-blue and shining, just as they were in real life. The artist had captured her likeness perfectly, and Violet had to look away as the face was too real, the eyes too piercing.

Roman made small talk with Lux, trying to defuse the situation. He wanted her to have a chance to calm down before diving into whatever she was there to learn. If he went all aggro with the questions and demands for answers all it would do is make her a nervous wreck or end with them getting nothing. So, he made small talk. It wasn't as if he didn't somewhat like Lux, he just hated the games.

Lux sat perfectly still, speaking with his smooth honeyed voice about weather, and their trip, and the current state of the local economy. She wondered why he would even bother to notice such things.

He turned to Violet finally, who had effectively avoided making any eye contact with him since she'd first come into his home. He started to speak and then stopped and stood up. He walked to the carved mahogany bar across the room. She felt free to watch him now that his back was to the room. And that was his purpose in getting up, though she didn't know it. He wore a finely tailored silk suit of dark gray and some expensive looking leather shoes that probably cost more than some people's cars. This was not the rock God she'd seen back at home. This was the businessman. *Or the freaking supermodel.* She watched as he walked behind the bar, and then looked up at the two seated across the room. He raised a bottle of wine and offered it to them. Roman agreed to a glass and Violet declined, the words stuck in her dry throat.

"Water then?" he asked, flashing a captivating smile.

Violet nodded her head and looked back at Roman, who gave her a knowing look, hoping to calm her down. She needed to know she was alright.

"Come here, Violet," Lux said, his tone soothing as he looked up from pouring the wine.

She looked at Roman quickly with a sudden jolt of fear piercing through her body. Roman nodded his head at her and stood up. He would go with her so she wouldn't be so afraid. She stood up and walked towards Lux with hesitation. He was grinning at her now.

"Don't be afraid, little one." He smiled at her as he held out the glass of wine to his friend. Roman sat down on a leather bar stool, taking a slow drink. Lux picked up a heavy crystal glass and filled it with ice from the freezer below the bar. He twisted the cap off the bottle of sparkling water and poured it for her then handed her the glass. She took a sip and thanked him.

"See this painting?" he asked her, motioning towards an oil canvas hanging on the wall behind him. It was of a large thin dog lying in a field with a dead rabbit between its paws. Its ears were erect and pointed and it had a regal look about it. The dog appeared sculpted of marble, perfect muscular body and bone structure. "This was my dog," he said, looking back at her.

She noticed the cracked aging of the paint and wondered just how old it was, how old *he* was. Her knees went wobbly just thinking about it. Damn her for wearing clumsy heels. She leaned against the bar looking past Lux to the painting again.

"His name was Rex," Lux said, looking back at the painting, seeming deep in thought.

Roman watched the scenario curiously. He had never seen this side of Lux and wondered what all went on in the man's mind. What had he experienced in his long life? Roman knew some of the stories, of course, but not the small details, like this dog for instance. Lux clearly had a fondness for the memory. It was interesting, and even more interesting that he was sharing this with Violet. Perhaps he was trying to make her feel comfortable, diffusing the situation.

"He was my only friend," Lux said, his voice quiet, thoughtful.

"Besides me, *brother*." Her voice was low and echoed from across the open room.

Violet jumped slightly and looked in the direction the voice had come. Mylori stood halfway in the room, wrapped around the entryway leading to elsewhere in the flat. She slinked around the corner, not taking her eyes from Roman. She was wearing a tightly fitted red dress. Her hair was twisted up in a chignon held in place with long thin silver needles with teardrop shaped pearl heads. She looked elegant and model-like again. Violet felt her skin crawl as the woman made her way towards them.

"Well, you are *man's best friend*," Lux teased his sister.

Mylori rolled her eyes and walked up behind Roman and snaked her hands around his torso onto his chest beneath his jacket. "You're injured," she purred, pressing her lips to his shoulder as she leaned in to smell him.

Roman moved away from her and took a swallow of wine.

Violet looked down at her glass of water and took another drink. Lux noticed her awkwardness, and set about wiping the counter up behind the bar, placing the bottle of water back in the refrigerator. Violet made him nervous in some ways, which was so strange. He wasn't nervous around anyone, though she wasn't just anyone. Roman shifted in his chair, uncomfortable with the situation. He wanted Mylori to go away. This wasn't the time for all of this. The vampire leaned in and kissed his cheek, running her fingers against his facial hair. Roman moved away from her.

"Infected," she hissed, and took a step back.

Lux laughed and Violet looked up, curious about her reaction to Roman. Mylori smiled at her coolly, long thin fangs catching the light.

"Be nice, Mylori," Lux warned his sister.

She looked at him, her eyes blazing. "I'm leaving this place," she said, acting disinterested with their company, or maybe trying to get away.

"Yes, please leave, *bikkja*," Lux laughed and walked around the bar and shoved his sister playfully. Mylori scowled at Lux and looked back at the two guests, then continued walking. Violet listened to the click of her heels as the woman made her way across the room. She stood in front of the fireplace staring into the flames, but didn't leave.

"Come over here where it's comfortable again," Lux said, sitting back down on the couch.

Roman looked at Violet, almost half ashamed by what had happened. Mylori and he had unresolved business that he had just planned on never dealing with, assuming his lack of response to her would be enough. Apparently the woman still had ideas. He stepped down off the stool, and he and Violet walked back towards Lux. Roman sank back into the chair and took another sip of wine, deciding it was time to get to business. Violet sat on the end of the couch Lux was reclined on, his feet propped up on the coffee table.

"There is a vampire named Cecelia who is threatening Violet," Roman said.

Mylori laughed deep in her throat. Violet looked across the room at the woman, who had turned and was looking at her directly now, candle in her hand as the flames lit her face. "That little cunt is barely fifty years old."

"I thought you said you were leaving?" Roman seethed, turning his head to the side, directing his voice at Mylori

Lux laughed out loud and clapped his hands together. Violet was startled by the sudden loud noise and jumped. Mylori's eyes fixed on Roman, and she walked towards the group, quickly passing them on her way towards the stairs. Her heels were loud as they clicked across the marble floor, her eyes never leaving Roman. Violet listened to the staccato clack of her stilettos as she moved down the stairs and out the door.

"Guess he told her," Lux said, and laughed as he tapped Violet's arm. Violet smirked at him. "Ah, there's that smile," he said, seeming to beam. She couldn't help but fully smile then. "Cecelia's just an old whore," he said, finally responding to Roman's comment with a flippant wave of his hand.

"What do you mean?" Roman asked, wanting a direct answer.

"I mean, literally, she's an old whore. And she's a little mad at me for spurning her."

"What? You didn't pay her on the way out?" Roman asked with an annoyed tone.

"Ha-ha," Lux laughed sardonically, "As if I would ever have to pay for sex. No, I turned her and left her after a couple of months. She was a total bore. A bore of a whore," Lux laughed to himself. "And yes, she's only fifty-three years young, an easy kill for you, Roman."

"If she's only fifty she's not the woman from the vision, Roman," Violet said, remembering the vision she'd had after she first found out about vampires.

Roman looked at her and nodded.

"Vision?" Lux asked.

"She had a vision," Roman said.

"About?" Lux asked, intrigued.

"About some ancient Romans," Violet responded. "I couldn't see the man. I was inside of him somehow. And he could talk to me in my mind. It was like I was inside of his body, seeing everything he saw, and he could talk to me in my mind. But there was a beautiful woman with black hair. The male bit her and told me he would be back for me in two thousand years."

"Hmmm..." Lux pondered. "That would not be Cecelia."

"No shit. So what does this bitch have to do with Violet?" Roman asked, getting increasingly agitated by Lux's flippant tone of voice.

"Yes, well that is the point of your visit, now isn't it?" he said, looking at the girl. "God, you've grown into such a beautiful woman," he said, voice filled with wonder as he smiled at her. Violet was startled by the comment. She felt her face turn red and her heart began to race. No one besides her grandma had ever told her such a thing. Maybe her aunt. But it was weird to hear from him.

Roman looked at the way Lux's gaze slid over her body, he had seen Lux seduce a number of girls, but this is not what he was doing with her. He seemed legitimately in awe.

"You were this tiny little angel and now look at you," he said like a proud father.

Violet's eyebrows creased with questions. Roman was eyeing the vampire, wondering where this was going.

"It was you," she said, finally connecting the dots. Her eyes lit up with sudden revelation.

Lux smiled, impressed by her intelligence. But then, he knew she'd be intelligent. *Just like her mother and father.*

Roman remembered the dream she'd told him about the vampire in her room when she was a child, and he knew this must be what she was referring to now.

"Yes," he answered, and reached over and felt her hair. "I was there with you." The way she looked enamored him; the black crimped hair, the black around her eyes. "You could be Cleopatra's resurrection." He smiled as the silken black tresses wound around his fingers.

"Great, now you're telling me I am reincarnated?" Violet looked at him funny with the most seriously irritated expression he had ever seen. And that was amazing considering how annoyed his sister could get. It made him laugh.

"Not really, Violet, this has nothing to do with her." He smiled at her, leaning forward and touching her arm.

"Did you know Cleopatra?" Violet's eyes were wide.

Lux smiled with amusement. "No, I did not." *Although he hadn't been far removed, but she didn't need to know that.*

She smiled nervously and leaned back into the soft warm cushions. "Well, who the fuck knows, considering vampires, and God knows what else, exist. For all I know you're really Julius Caesar." She turned sideways, resting her leg on the couch and never taking her eyes from his.

Lux smirked, completely amused by her. "No, I am not Julius." He chuckled at the thought. "You could be immortal, you know? Just say the word," he whispered, leaning his head forward slightly. His tousled blonde hair and youthful face were deceptive. God he was so beautiful, too beautiful, to be evil.

"No," Roman interjected, sitting forward in the chair, ready to rip Lux's heart from his chest.

"Relax, Roman." Lux grinned and rolled his eyes.

"Why were you there?" she asked him. Now she really wanted answers. She wanted to know how he'd gotten into her house, how he'd found her. Had it been planned? Or was it random?

"I slipped into your room. I was standing over you watching your eyelids twitch as you dreamed your baby dreams. Your cheeks were so pink and your hair so dark against your skin. I loved your smell. The smell of your silken hair, and your sweet lotioned skin. I loved your plump little arms, and the way your tiny fingers clutched the edge of your blanket."

Roman was engrossed by this. He noticed how Lux talked to her in a way he'd never seen him talk to anyone. It was intimate and almost fatherly, but it was more than that. Lux admired her. *Lux* admired *her*. He seemed awed. Roman looked at Violet's eyes as Lux spoke, watched as her chest rose and fell with each deep breath. She wasn't afraid any longer, and that scared him.

"Then you opened your eyes. You looked into me with such utter depth that it shamed me to my very core. I saw your soul. I saw your mother, your father, and your ancestors. I saw into you."

"You were going to kill me," she said, matter-of-factly.

"Yes, Violet, I was going to kill you." He seemed remorseful and disgusted by the words he spoke.

Roman was shocked by Lux's demeanor. Never in all his years of knowing the vampire had he seen him care in any way towards a human. He knew that if Lux could, he'd rip out his throat. And yet here he was, taken with Violet. Perhaps this was how he was with Ilya, all those centuries ago? Or maybe it was all an act. Roman detected no hint of deception in his body language, but Lux had many years to hone the art.

"But you didn't," she said, her eyes softening.

"I couldn't. You were more powerful at age seven than I will ever be. You killed a part of me when you looked into me like that."

"I don't understand. I am not anything special. This is ridiculous," she said crossly, as she rolled her eyes and scoffed

Lux and Roman were both shocked by her sudden annoyance.

"You're wrong," Lux answered.

"So, does she have some supernatural power or something?" Roman interrupted.

Lux looked at Roman, understanding his impatience. "No, nothing *supernatural* really, but you of all people understand what I mean, don't you?" Lux leaned back into the couch and crossed his legs.

"Well, *I* don't understand what you mean. So, explain it to me," Violet snapped, and stood up.

She walked around the polished metal table and stood across from him. It still blew her mind that it had been Lux all those years ago, and that what she'd thought was only a dream had really happened. But she wasn't buying this bullshit about her being some sweet innocent kid that somehow captivated him. He was some ridiculously old vampire. She didn't know how old, but whatever. He_was_a_vampire. What the fuck reason would he have for giving a shit about some seven year old girl, out in the middle of nowhere?

Roman understood what Lux meant. There was power there in that tiny little woman. She had captivated him from the moment he had met her.

"You were going to just be another death to me, but I couldn't do it, Violet. You, with your quiet knowing eyes, stopped me. Me, who had killed thousands before you. I felt in that moment the reality of your world and the fact that I will destroy reality for thousands upon thousands. You made me feel guilty for a brief moment, and I couldn't kill you after that."

Violet pushed her hands down on her hips, her leg cocking out to the side. "So, basically what you're saying is that I made you feel human, even though on my end of things I just saw Dracula standing in front of me? There was nothing wondrous or deep about any of it, Lux. I fooled you. A dopey little seven year old fooled you." Violet smirked at him. *Completely ridiculous.*

Roman looked at her with curiosity, completely surprised by her reaction, and the strength she now seemed to possess. She stood up straight, in command of herself like he'd never seen her since they'd met. He smiled at her, and then looked at Lux, who seemed somewhat mystified by her statement.

"You said it yourself, there's nothing supernatural about me. I was a little kid--you felt that guilt all on your own. It had nothing to do with me."

"No, there was more to it than that," he said, placing his hand to his mouth and looking away from her. Maybe a part of her statement was true, but there had to be more to it than that. She had made him feel guilty because of who she was.

"What does this have to do with Cecelia?" Roman asked Lux, and then looked up at Violet.

"Yeah, what does this have to do with her?" Violet said, and walked over to Roman and leaned against him.

Lux looked up at her and back to the ground. He was still reeling from her comment. Had he really applied such importance to this experience? It had been an integral part of who he'd become. That night had changed him, had it really all just been his own conscience playing tricks on him? No. Of course not. It was who she was. Who her parents were. Was there anything supernatural about her? Maybe not at present. But there would be.

He had started visiting her mother again after that night. To know the woman who changed everything. He had wanted to be close to her, to watch Violet grow. And he wanted to reconnect with the human who had caught his interest all those years prior, when she was still so young. A marvel herself. Violet's mom would meet him once a year by the river, and he would talk to her until the sun rose. And he understood her appeal to his core. But she had been off limits.

"I came to visit you throughout the years. I watched you grow," Lux said, looking back into his memories as if watching a movie.

"But how? I don't remember ever seeing you again after that night?" Violet asked, and sat down on the arm of the chair where Roman was seated. The supple hide felt buttery soft against her bare legs. Roman wrapped his arm around her waist. He noticed the subtle look that crossed Lux's face. Jealousy? Regret?

"Mylori and I were chosen for our abilities," he explained. "You would call it astral projection," he said despondently.

"But why did you care? Just because you thought I made you feel something?" Astral projection? She had these abilities herself, although she'd never really known the words for it. She had always taken herself places, even in her dreams, to the same places over and over. And now Roman was there too? The presence in the woods, had that been Lux?

"There was more to it than that. Stop being so dismissive about all of this." Lux stood up, obviously angered by her tone of voice.

"You are in love with her," Roman said with sudden revelation.

"What?" Lux said, looking back at him with fire in his eyes.

"That's what this is about, Lux," Roman answered, looking at the man, hoping he'd understand.

"No," Lux said, sitting back down on the couch. "That's not possible."

Well, that was a turn she hadn't expected. Lux, in love with her? *No fucking way*. Her stomach lurched in sickness. What the hell was going on?

"Why is Cecelia after Violet?" Roman asked, trying to hone in on an answer.

"Because she's angry with me and..."

"And wants to hurt the one you love." Roman said, cautiously.

Lux looked up at Roman, realizing he had figured out something he himself had never even considered. He glanced at Violet, who stared at the ground looking very uncomfortable.

"You knew I wouldn't normally go to do such a small job. I wondered why you were so adamant about me going. Now I know why, because you had a personal interest." Roman had been confused as to why Lux had made his going to Mantua so urgent. It hadn't made sense, until finding out how much Lux had invested in Violet.

"Yes, and because I wanted her to know about us. She needs to know who she is."

"Why didn't you just come to me yourself?" Violet asked, very sad for him. He seemed to be struggling with all of this. It must be confusing not knowing your own feelings, she could sympathize.

He looked up at her. She was truly human in every way, something he had never allowed himself to see. Somehow he had built her up through the years into some mythical being. The Great One who had made him feel empathy. But she was just another human. No, not just another human, she was *the* human to him. But she wasn't, was she? And maybe that was also the appeal. "I don't know why?" he said calmly. "Wow, I really am pathetic," he said, laughing at himself.

"No you aren't," Violet said, smiling at him. "But you should have just come to me yourself. Then you would have realized how pathetic *I* am, and you could have saved yourself a lot of time and energy."

"What is time to me?" He grinned, the weight of those words sinking into Violet.

"So, what about this Cecelia woman, Lux?" Roman asked, annoyed by the turn the conversation had taken as the two of them were far too comfortable with one another.

Lux looked at him dismissively and then shrugged his shoulders. "Kill her. What do I care?" He leaned back into the couch, eyes gleaming again. That frightening brilliant gleam she'd seen earlier, lustrous, alive.

He is still a vampire, she reminded herself. "Why did you want me to know about you?" she asked, thinking she already knew the answer.

"Why do you think?" he asked with a sly grin.

"Okay, time to go now," Roman said, standing up and swallowing the last of his wine. He walked over to the bar and sat the empty glass down. There was no way he was going to sit around watching this devolve to mutual teenage googly eyes and awkward grins. Besides, she was his. *What?* Roman furrowed his brow and clenched his jaw.

Violet and Lux stood up and followed him. She drank another sip of the water and set the drink down on the bar as well. Lux still couldn't take his eyes off of her. *There is more to it than that.*

"Thanks for the information," Roman said, reaching his hand out to Lux. "Though you should have just told me from the beginning."

"Which would have resulted in you never stepping foot in that town." Lux smirked, and picked up the wine bottle, taking a long swig.

Roman smiled at him, knowing that would have been the case. "And don't get any ideas." Roman poked Lux in the chest with his finger, pushing him backward.

Lux smiled briefly and then turned his attention back toward Violet.

She smiled at Lux, her cheeks pink with shyness. It felt strange knowing this being had devoted his time to her through all these years, and she had only known him as a fleeting childhood dream. It was flattering, intriguing, and utterly frightening to realize she could have been dead all those years ago if *something* hadn't awakened her from sleep and kept her calm enough to not cry but to just stare into the eyes of her dream.

"See you again," he said sweetly, and brushed his hand across her cheek. He reached out and wrapped his arms around her, pulling her close. Roman started to intervene but Lux looked at him in warning. There was something so lost about the look in the man's eyes that it stopped Roman in his tracks.

Lux closed his eyes tightly, the memory of Violet's mother coming to life as he held the young woman. He kissed the side of her head and released her. She would be safe now.

Violet's heart was pounding as Lux took her in his arms and held her so tightly against his chest. Was he going to kill her? Why wasn't Roman stopping it? And then a wave of comfort engulfed her, and she sighed against him, enveloped completely. He was so powerful, it burned into her. And then he released her. She looked into his eyes for a long moment, remembering his words *You could be immortal.*

"See you." She smiled and followed Roman, who was already heading for the staircase.

Lux watched as they descended the stairs and walked out into the street.

"And you thought *you* were too old for me?" she laughed, and elbowed Roman's side. Roman shook his head and opened the door for her.

"Hey. Are you having fun?" Amber asked.

"Yeah, we're having fun, I guess," Violet answered, looking over at Roman who was staring blankly at some late night horror movie. He had taken his shirt off and the wound was glaring at her from across the room.

"Sorry to call so late. I just figured you'd still be out partying or something."

"No, no partying, but we're still awake."

"I'm not *disturbing* you, am I?" Amber teased.

"Shut up!" Violet said, leaning back into the pillows.

Roman looked over at her briefly, then back to the screen. He was emotionally and physically drained. All of this evening's revelations were weighing heavily on him.

"When are you guys coming home?" Amber asked.

"Probably tomorrow. I got you something cool!" Violet said with enthusiasm.

"You didn't have to do that, but thanks. You know I love getting gifts." Amber chuckled.

"I know. Ain't no shame in your game. I love getting gifts too. At least we also both love giving them."

"True. Speaking of gift giving, if a cheesecake was worth a BJ what's a trip to Chicago worth?"

"Dude, you never stop." Violet laughed and shook her head, though her cheeks were warm at the thought.

"I won't be content until you're an official couple." Amber chuckled.

Violet looked over at Roman and felt her heart swoon and then sink. "I don't see that happening," she said with a sigh.

"Make it happen. I know that's what you want, Vi."

Violet sighed again and turned away from Roman. "I told you before that it doesn't matter what I want."

Roman looked away from the movie to look at her. She looked sad, she sounded sad, and it gutted him. He wasn't sure what she was talking about with Amber, but he had a feeling what it was, and he was the cause of that sound in her voice. He looked away from her and back to the lovesick teens being hacked to death on the television. Appropriate. He shut his eyes.

Amber proceeded to tell Violet all about her and Randy's day, their "home alone" date, and the horror movie marathon after getting home from the halloween festivities in Kent, and how it hadn't been the same this year. Violet looked over to see that Roman was sleeping. He looked perfectly serene, hands folded across his stomach, lips slightly parted. She could hear the raspy breaths falling rhythmically from his mouth in even intervals. She smiled, but it was touched with sadness, thinking about all that he must have been through in his life and how happy she was to now have him in hers. Even if things would never be what she wanted. What did she want? Him? *That* way? Yes. Her eyes pricked with tears.

"I'm gonna go, Amber. I'm tired," she said quietly. "I'll see you tomorrow evening."

They said their goodbyes and Violet hung up the phone, setting it down on the nightstand. She looked at Roman, hesitating, and then went to the bathroom and washed the makeup from her face. She replayed Lux's words as she changed into what qualified as her pajamas, a black t-shirt and her underwear, and pulled her hair up away from her face. After finishing up she walked over to Roman and took the remote from his hand, turning the volume down, and then slid down on the other bed, crawling beneath the covers and kicking her pile of clothes out of the way. She rolled over onto her side and watched Roman sleep, the blue light of the television flickering on his skin. As she admired him, her thoughts drifted to the meeting earlier.

There was no way Lux was in love with her. He was in love with the *idea* of her, maybe. But she had never been anything special and she wasn't "chosen", whatever that meant. She was a plain, ordinary human being that should have been dead all those years ago, but because of some *divine intervention* he had spared her life. What if there was more to it? There were some things he'd said that sounded weird, but she couldn't remember now.

Mylori's searing eyes suddenly flashed before her. The wicked way she'd hissed "infected" at Roman. What had she meant by that? *Whoa, maybe his wound is infected? No, it didn't sound like that.* And what had stopped Mylori from jumping on her and killing her? It was more than obvious Mylori didn't like her, but of course she knew Roman wouldn't let Mylori hurt her, and Lux might not have either. What was the deal with the way Mylori had clung to Roman? It was as if that had maybe been normal behavior for her to do so, but Roman had stiffened noticeably. How strange. But then it wasn't strange, was it, given the fact that they had been lovers. Maybe there was more to their relationship than Roman had admitted to previously?

She focused her eyes on Roman again, wishing she was over there snuggled up against him. She wanted his arm wrapped around her waist, his face nestled in against her neck. But she wouldn't invade his space, or assume she was welcome there. He had been very quiet since they'd left Lux, more so than he usually was, which was confusing and disheartening. When they first left he seemed fine, but since then he'd been pensive and quiet. It was a mystery what was going on in his mind, and she was too afraid to ask. Sleep was claiming her, trying as she did to fight it, and her eyes closed.

She walked up the black stairs and into the warm orange glow above. He smiled down at her, arms extended and inviting. She took his white hand. It was colder than anything she'd ever felt. No, not colder than anything, her mom and dad's hands had felt this cold in their coffins. She shuddered at the recognition. He squeezed her hand, letting go as if knowing her thoughts. Placing his hand to the small of her back, he led her through the large room, passing by the painting of the dog, beyond the smoldering fireplace, and through the doorway to the rest of the house. The floors were dark mahogany here, not the gleaming marble from the other room. The wood felt warm and soft against her bare feet and made each step silent.

There were dozens of rooms, some with open doors that she peered into, some closed, which made her wonder what lay beyond. Every room was lushly decorated and filled with interesting things she wished she had more time to explore.

Lux looked down at her, pleased by her reaction. He'd expected her to be frightened knowing what she knew now. But apparently she was a brave woman, the kind of woman who would make the perfect partner in immortality.

He breathed in deeply, relishing her scent, which wafted around her heavy like the perfume of flowers on a balmy summer night. She had no idea the power she possessed. It had been the look behind her eyes that had stolen the death from him all those years ago. He had known then what she would become one day and had never forgotten. She was everything her mother had been afraid to be. No. They were vastly different. He'd watched as Violet had grown from plump child, to awkward teenager, to strong young woman. He had seen her suffer the cruelty of adolescence, and witnessed the bitter sweetness of her loss of innocence, all the while wishing he'd been human for just one day of it. But she wasn't what she seemed.

Had he been a human, he would have been the one to take that innocence from her. He would've loved her and given her anything a human boy could give.

But he was Vampire, not human, and there were things he could give her now that were far more long lasting than making love for the first time.

The subtle changes she had gone through had been fascinating. There had never been a time that he had cared for a human, not really, not beyond a child's obsession with a favorite toy. The one which eventually finds the back of the closet, or gets abandoned at the dump. But she had been different. A princess. The princess. He had never been able to forget her. She had been fascinating in ways he didn't understand beyond the obvious. He still didn't understand. What was it about her that clung to him so? She was a princess. The princess.

And she had made him regret immortality.

Yes, Violet, there had been more to it.

Finally he led her to a room, stopping and waiting for her to enter first. She looked around curiously. Dark blue walls with black crown molding and black velvet curtains and bedding made the room look so grand and stately. She studied the painting above the large four poster bed. It was of Lux, looking the same as he did now, the only difference was the style of clothes he was wearing. She didn't want to take her eyes off it.

"What do you want?" she asked, finally turning towards him and looking into his eyes.

"Something I can't have." He smiled.

Violet walked around the room. There were volumes upon volumes of books piled on shelves which climbed to the ceiling, and photographs in stacks strewn on a massive desk. She sifted through them, wondering who these people were. She held up a photo of a black haired baby. "This is Roman," she said, turning to look at him.

Lux smiled and moved over to the bed and fell back into the billowy comforter and stared at the silver leafed ceiling.

She continued looking through the photos and then walked over to Lux, clutching the photo in her hand. "Why do you have this?"

"Know your enemies," he said, lifting his head to look at her.

The bed was tall, nearly to her chest. "Why did you bring me here?" she asked.

"Because I can."

"But why?"

"Because nothing will ever be the same, and I wanted you to myself one last time."

"What are you talking about, Lux?" she said, leaning against the bed and resting her chin on her hands.

"It's so strange to hear my name coming from your mouth."

"Why are you being so morose?" she asked, confused and dismayed by his tone.

"Kind of a funny question to ask a vampire isn't it? Aren't we supposed to be all deep and sullen?" He grinned at her as he rolled over and propped his head up with his bent arm. He watched the sudden jolt of his words pierce through her, as though he'd delivered an invisible blow. It hurt him to see the distrustful look in her eyes. This human girl hurt him. What a curious anomaly. She was more than that though.

"Vampires should be happy," she said, the word 'vampire' feeling queer on her tongue.

"And why is that?"

"Because you'll never grow old, and you'll never die."

Lux nodded his head once, a reasonable explanation for a human. What she didn't know was that "never" was a long time and things continuously died all around him. Friends, lovers, cultures, even language. Death was everywhere and everything.

"What is it you want from me?" Her eyes on him never wavered. He sensed no fear from her then. This was perhaps the thing that hurt him the most. Knowing that she was the one with the power between them.

"What I want is for you to ask me for immortality. Even if it means running forever from Roman, who would undoubtedly track me down to the ends of the earth and kill me. But you won't do that. No," he said with a pause, considering what to reveal to her. "What I want is to be the human I was before, just for a day, so that I could know what it is to feel what you feel. It has been so long that I no longer remember what it is to feel human."

She felt sad for him. Lux saw the pity in her eyes and regretted revealing his wayward thoughts.

"I love being what I am, Violet. I've never looked back. I love the taste of death in my mouth. I love the power it gives me. I love the control I have over everything and everyone. I love being Vampire. And you stole that from me and I've been cut in half since that day."

"I don't know what to tell you," she said, shrugging her shoulders.

He smiled at her. She was too honest in her innocence. She truly didn't know what to say, and didn't pretend to have answers. He loved that. "Just come here and pretend for a little while... and then I'll let you go," he said, reaching his hands towards her.

She took his hand and pulled herself up onto the sumptuous bed and settled on her back beside him, staring up at the ceiling.

"I would have liked to have known you," he said, looking over at her, their faces inches apart.

His eyes gleamed, so brilliant and sparkling. There was a hint of teasing, of depth she couldn't fathom. Grief, love, loss, wisdom. Time.

"Lux, I..."

Violet felt her body sinking back into itself. She jumped as she felt her spine put back in place, and at the tug of her organs as they rested against the inner layer of her skin. She gasped, waking herself, reaching for her chest as she sat up. It took a moment for her to regain her composure as terror shot through her body. She pressed her hands against her face and could smell the faint floral candle scent on her skin. She looked over at Roman who was now sitting up and looking at her. It was strange, him sitting there so still, and then he smiled at her.

"Hey," he said, tossing his feet to the floor. "I'm fucking starving."

Violet smiled and sat on the edge of the bed. There was no way she would tell him what had happened. Roman would be infuriated even though Lux had meant no harm. At least she didn't think he had meant any, but what did she really know about him or his motives?

"Are you hungry?" he asked.

"Kind of, yeah," she said, as she rubbed her eyes.

"There's a little diner about a block down the street. Want to go?"

"Isn't it like four o'clock?" she asked as she grinned at him.

"So?"

"Alright. I want french toast and blueberries," she said, standing up.

He watched her walk to the bathroom. The sight of her underwear riding up her ass cracked him up, then she tugged on them and turned to look at him with a perceptive grin. She should probably start wearing bottoms around him, cuz yeah, maybe that hadn't actually been as *funny* as he'd made it out. He shrugged his shoulders, then stood up and walked to his bag and grabbed the shirt she'd bought him and pulled it on over his head. It was snug across his chest and around his arms, probably too tight. He felt silly wearing the shirt, but knew it would make her happy, and she deserved to feel some happiness right about now considering the earlier revelations.

She washed the sleep from her eyes, stopping for a moment to recount what had just happened. That had to have been a dream? Yes, it was a dream, she convinced herself. But she knew the truth deep down inside. Every bit of it had happened. *Could Lux just feasibly come and get her whenever he wanted? And what if he didn't allow her to come back? What of her body? Her soul? Maybe that's what happens to people in comas?* She felt panicked for a moment, her breath coming too quickly, but refused to allow it to sink in and just shrugged it off to imagination. *None of it was real. It was all just a dream.*

She picked up the skirt from the floor, and walked back into the bedroom. She scanned the floor for her socks, pulling them on, and then put on her boots. She dug through the clothes she'd brought and found her favorite hoodie with the pink skull and crossbones on the front and zipped it up. Her hair was tucked into the shirt

"Hey! You're wearing my shirt," she said, shoving him in the chest.

"I told you I would," he said, taking the force of her blow.

Roman picked up the key and they left the room, making sure it was locked behind them. They rode the elevator. Violet had that sick to her stomach feeling she always got when she was overly tired, and hoped the food would settle it.

"Let's sleep in tomorrow, okay?" she said, looking up at him.

"Yeah, I want to sleep late. I'm just going to take the room for another night so we don't have to be so rushed tomorrow. Besides, there's going to be a lot of work to do when we get back to your house. We may as well rest while we can."

She didn't exactly know what he meant by "a lot of work", but was too tired to give it much thought. They exited the elevator and Roman walked over to the counter and told the woman to reserve the room for another night. Violet looked around the lobby as she yawned, deciding that she hated the brassy gold finish of all the light fixtures. They were too shiny and too gold.

"All set," Roman said, as he put his hand on her back and led her outside.

She was surprised by the amount of cars and people still out and about. Her town closed down at 8 PM.

"Roman, what do you think about the vision I had? I don't see how this could relate to Cecelia?"

"I have no clue, V. I don't see how it is related either. Maybe it was just some random thing your brain created to deal with what had just happened? Fuck, I don't know."

"It was so real though. I was there. If I saw her, I would know her."

"Let's just hope we don't see her. Two thousand year old vampires are... powerful."

Violet shuddered. "But nothing you can't handle?"

He looked down at her and smiled for reassurance. "Nothing I can't handle." Fuck, he really hoped it wasn't Ilya she had seen.

She looped her hand through his arm as they walked towards the Tucson Truck Stop.

"Tucson Truck Stop?" Violet grimaced.

"Who knows," he said, and opened the door for her.

A gaggle of goth kids seated in the back of the restaurant drew her attention. Obviously this ritual of hanging in greasy spoon restaurants was national. Or at least regional. Besides the goths, there were stray people scattered about, few and far between. Roman and Violet waited to be seated. The waitress brought a pot of coffee and offered the two a mug.

"No thanks, just water," Roman said, putting his hand over the cup. "I'm going to bed as soon as we're done eating." He smiled at the woman, who gave him a look that said she was thinking he was going to bed, but not for sleeping.

"None for me, thanks," Violet said and smiled at her too. The woman gave her the once over and handed them both sticky plastic menus. Which were also universal in these kinds of establishments.

"Why do waitresses always hate me?" Violet asked, and wrinkled her nose.

"Jealous?"

"You sound like my mom. Anytime anyone didn't like me they were automatically jealous." Violet snickered and leafed through the menu.

"It's probably true." Roman looked up with a smirk on his face.

"Doubtful. More like this one doesn't see why you would be with the likes of me."

"Doubtful," Roman replied, and looked back at the menu.

"Whatever, you know it's true," she said, and shook her head with a grin. She set the menu back on the table, having decided what she wanted.

They ordered their food. Roman noticed the goth kids intermittently looking in their direction. Apparently they found their presence interesting for one reason or another. Violet turned to see what he was looking at and caught the gaze of one of the girls. She smiled at her, recognizing her from the boutique she'd visited earlier in the day. The girl looked away and laughed to her friend. Violet made a face at the group and then thought about how her friends treated people with the exact same disdain. Well, at least she and Amber had at times. The boys didn't much care about anyone.

"I saw that girl at the store," Violet said, turning to look at Roman who was now downing his glass of ice water.

He nodded his head at her and finished swallowing, looking at her with a sly smile on his face.

"What?" she asked, kicking him under the table.

"So, Lux is in love with you," he teased, completely changing the subject.

"I don't think so," she answered, feeling her cheeks flush. "I think he's in love with *the idea* of me. He doesn't know me, Roman."

"He does know you," Roman replied, changing his tone to a more serious one. He had watched the way Lux had reacted and spoke to her. He saw her as a woman. Lux, being thousands of years old, saw Violet as a *woman,* when he had convinced himself she was way too young.

"It doesn't matter," she answered as she unzipped her sweatshirt and pulled her still crimped hair out of her shirt. It fell over her shoulders and breasts and pooled onto her lap. She licked her parched lips and took a sip of water.

Roman watched as her eyes moistened and blinked, the gray smudge of old makeup making the blue more vivid. She turned her head--the arteries of her neck in long straight columns--and she watched the waitress straightening the table beside them. He could see how Lux would want to taste this neck. Perfect, delicate. He had been trying to convince himself she was just too young because it was the easiest way to deal with her. All he needed to do was take care of her, protect her, and then he'd be moving on to the next stop. It was essential that he not get too emotionally attached. There couldn't be any strange emotions involved. She was his responsibility. Nothing more. He'd have to move on once this job was finished, and he had no room for attachments.

But it had already grown far beyond that, hadn't it? She wasn't some stranger he was doing a good deed for now. He *missed* her when she wasn't around. He loved the sound of her voice when she picked up the phone. He even loved it when she was angry and rude towards him. But if Lux could see her as a woman, then he was just lying to himself every time he'd tried to convince himself otherwise.

"That looks so good!" she said, referring to the omelet the waitress sat down before him.

He blinked his eyes and cleared his thoughts. "*That* looks good," he responded, looking at her plate of blueberry slathered french toast.

"You can have some if you let me have some of yours."

"Deal," he said, lifting his plate and scraping some of his food onto her plate.

"Mmm...blueberry eggs," she said and laughed and did the same to him.

They ate their food and made small talk about what they might do the following day when they finally got up in the morning. The table of goths walked by as they left and stared at the two of them who were busily stuffing their faces and laughing.

"What was that all about?" Roman asked, creasing his brow.

"Who knows? Fucking elitist snobs." Violet shrugged and scooped another slab of toast into her mouth.

"Aren't you one of those?" He looked down his nose at her with a crooked grin on his face.

"I guess I was." She laughed and shoved her plate away. "I can't eat anymore. I think my stomach's going to burst."

Roman finished his food and then ate the rest of hers. She was amazed by his capacity to eat. They paid their bill and walked back to the hotel. Roman laughed as Violet told him various stories of her and her friends' exploits. This was the first time she'd really shared any of these things with him. He was envious that he'd been robbed of a normal life. They talked for a while and then made their way back to the hotel.

They got to their room and Violet went straight to the restroom where she washed her face again and took her clothes off and went back into the bedroom. Roman was lying on his side beneath the covers. *Lost in Space* was playing on the television and he was watching through half closed eyes. She sat down on the other bed and put her hair up and reached over and flipped the side table lamp off and pulled the blankets back.

Roman lifted his head and looked over at her. "Come over here," he said.

She looked at him with curious confusion. Something had changed about his demeanor, like the hardness of his exterior had softened. His defenses were lowered. It was a subtle change, but a change nonetheless. She climbed out of the bed and lay down beside him, resting her head on his arm. He wrapped his arms around her and pressed his face against her soft hair.

"Goodnight," he said, half asleep against her neck. The warmth of his blueberry scented breath on her neck felt comforting.

"Night," she said, settling in against him, her heart racing, feeling all warm and comfortable. God, she just wanted him to kiss her. One move, one acquiescence, and she would give herself to him. But instead he went to sleep.

7

FLASHBACK: HOW THEY MET

ROMAN RAN THROUGH THE alley, pitch black night surrounding him. He cursed his human vision, perfect as it was, it still didn't compare. He could be surrounded right now and he wouldn't know. Yes, he would know. He always knew somehow. But it still sucked to have the visual disadvantage.

He turned the corner, hugging the side of the brick building, and then watched as a heavy gray door slid shut. Gripping the blade tightly in his hand, he inched towards the door and then took a deep breath and walked inside. The room was dark, a dim light emanating from somewhere. The concrete beneath his boots scraped as he walked forward towards the beckoning light.

They were here.

He peered through the faint light, trying to decide which direction to go next. His heart pounded in his chest, knowing they'd be able to smell his adrenalin rising. Taking a deep breath to settle his nerves and regaining his composure, he crept forward.

"Roman..." he heard the voice singing, "we're here."

He walked forward with caution, keeping an eye on the room around him. He didn't want to be ambushed.

"Don't be silly, Roman. There's no one here but us. You know that."

"I can't trust that," Roman said, continuing his forward motion.

"You'd be wise not to, but it's the truth."

Roman walked around a wall and saw the blonde man sitting in a leather chair. His leg was slung over the arm and he was settled down into the chair, leafing through a book.

"Have a seat," he said, motioning towards the other chair.

"Where is she?" Roman asked, standing to his full height and looking down at the vampire.

"She's around somewhere," the vampire said, dismissively. "You've really no need to worry." He looked up over the top of the book at Roman.

"*You* have reason to worry," Roman said, leaning against the back of the chair opposite the man. He sat the sword down in front of him.

"I know we have reason to worry, Roman, that's why I'm not running any-more. You've been chasing us for nearly a year now, and I've decided this will end badly if I don't do something now, while you have us cornered."

Roman was puzzled by his words. He was used to hearing pleas and threats, but this man's tone was different. "Go on."

"You need my help and I'm tired of this annoying chase. There's a deal in the making," he said, shutting the book and tossing it to the floor.

"I need no one," Roman said, looking the vampire in the eye.

"Well, maybe not *need*, per se, but I could be a great ally to you and your cause." He put his foot on the floor and sat up straight in the chair. "You see, I don't want to die, and I'm tired of you chasing us simply because I'm old. We could kill you, of that I have no doubt. But there's also a slim chance you could kill us. I've seen what you're capable of, and I knew the strengths of your father and the wisdom of your uncle. And you are well aware of our considerable abilities. We are legendary even amongst immortals. We are the Old Ones. You've read all about us in your books."

Roman scoffed, causing Lux's eyes to narrow.

"I can smell your fear, Roman. I heard it pounding in your chest as you walked through my door. You aren't certain you can take either of us, let alone both. You've never been around beings as old as we are. You've never encountered creatures as adept or as brilliant. You know this is true. Do you really want to die?" His voice was focused and pure in tone, the timbre thick and resonant in Roman's ears. The vampire's eyes gleamed and honed in on Roman's as if to burn a hole straight through his head.

"You obviously don't know for sure that you're capable of killing me, or you would have already done it, *vampire*." Roman said, looking at the creature, never wavering from his firm gaze. There was no fear in him, only caution and skepticism.

"You're right, I already mentioned that, *human*, hence my proposal to you."

"Which is?" Roman asked, interested in what this vampire would suggest. He had no doubt this was some sort of trick.

"My pledge to you is that I will help you root out the covens. I will tell you where they are, and allow you to destroy them. In return you leave me and my sister alone, and in the process destroy all the vampire trash who seek to pollute the earth with our kind."

Roman stood up straight, tilting his head to the side and furrowing his brow. "As if it's not your own goal to populate the earth with *your kind*."

"No, it's really not, the more bloodthirsty idiots running around the bigger the threat of being exposed. It may sound silly to you, but why would I want the governments of the world deciding they need to unite their forces and focus their militaries on us? I'd rather be left in peace and live in anonymity. Come now, Roman, you've wasted all this time hunting us, for what? To kill a few measly vampire *morons* my sister created out of sheer boredom? I will keep her busy and inform you of the whereabouts of the real threat to your mortal society, so long as you leave us alone."

"And why wouldn't I just kill you both, and then worry about the rest later?"

The vampire smiled and lifted his elbows onto the tufted leather armrests and folded his hands in front of his chest. "Because, remember, you're not sure you can take both, or either, of us. I can tell you where they are far easier than you can find them on your own or through your little network. Think of me as your mob connection." He smirked and rested his hands against his mouth. "And besides, if I renege you can always hunt us and kill us then, right?"

"And how would you get in touch with me?"

"How quickly you forget our considerable abilities. And those handy dandy things called telephones."

Roman heard feet shuffling behind him. He turned to see her seemingly float across the floor. Hair like silk, long and straight and flowing, just like the other vampire's. Her body was wrapped in dark purple satin. He couldn't help but be taken by the sight of the woman.

"And this is The Killer?" she cooed, looking lovingly at her brother.

"Yes Mylori, this is the one who's been tracking us."

She came up behind him, taking in a deep breath. "Can I have him?" she asked, as she slid her finger along his shoulder blade.

Roman turned and looked the woman in the eye.

"Careful sister, remember who he is. And besides, he's our *friend* now."

"Goody," she said without emotion, and walked around Roman and sat in the chair. "I like being friends," she said and smiled, staring at her brother and crossing her long legs.

"We will never be friends. I will use you until I don't need you anymore, and then I'll kill you," Roman said matter-of-factly, picking the blade up and slipping it back into the leather sling.

"No need to puff out your chest, Roman. We understand your strengths," Lux said with a smirk.

The woman turned her head slightly, showing him the smile on her face. "You have no idea who we once were, human." She said the word as if it were toxic.

"History is always forgotten," Lux said to his sister. "Who we were means nothing to no one."

"Big, scary vampires. I know," Roman said, his tone bored.

Lux looked at Roman for so long it became uncomfortable. He smiled. "Now then, about our business. There's a group beneath the bridge on 38th Street. That is my gift to you. If I'm lying, come back and cut my head off. If I'm not, then go in peace and wait for my next gift," Lux said with a shrug and a no facial expression.

Roman backed away from them, convinced he was making a mistake. The night was alive outside. Horns beeping, sirens blaring. He ran from the building, heading for that bridge.

8

LAKE MICHIGAN

HE SLIPPED HIS ARM from beneath her neck and walked to the bathroom, looking down at his watch. It was eleven thirty five. He was glad he'd taken the room another night, otherwise they'd be in a hurry right now. He got in the shower. The cold burst of water woke him immediately. It nearly made him jump out of his skin. He took the tiny bar of soap and washed his face and body, then washed his hair and stood in the cold water for a long moment and thought about the prior evening.

Lux had spoken to her so intimately. The tone of his voice and his body language had infuriated him. Seeing the vampire speak to her almost as if he was desperate had opened Roman's eyes. His emotions had been something he'd been hiding from since the first day he'd seen her, knowing that he would have to leave her. There was no point in having feelings for her or anyone. A relationship was something he'd never had and would never allow.

Housekeeping was knocking on the door and it pulled him from his thoughts. He didn't want Violet to be awakened, so he hurriedly turned the water off and grabbed a towel, wrapping it around his waist. He opened the door and stuck his wet head out.

"Do you need maid service, sir?" the older woman asked.

"No, just towels maybe?" he said, wanting to get back in the room, his wet body was dripping all over the floor.

She handed him clean towels with a smile, and then pushed her cart to the next room.

"Thanks," Roman said, slipping his head a little further into the hallway and then shutting the door.

He ducked back into the bathroom and sat the towels on the counter. He dried himself off and rubbed his hair with the towel. His hair was a mass of knots, so he found his comb and raked it through, then pulled it back at the base of his neck. As he was shaving the wound on his shoulder drew his attention. It was healing nicely. It barely even ached now. He put his jeans and socks on and walked back to the bedroom. She was still sleeping, so he sat down on the other bed and watched her. She looked content. Her delicate arms and hands looked like they had been sculpted from marble as she slept there with them tucked beneath her face. Her long black hair fell in crumpled waves around her face and over her shoulders. Her lips looked full and rosy, her nose small and straight. He thought her face looked so kind in sleep. She was capable of such sweetness and also had a terrible temper. Violet had kicked the blanket off as usual. Her milky legs lay bent together, his mother's necklace lying against her soft belly. He couldn't see the bones of her ribs or hips jutting through her skin anymore. For the first time she looked like a woman to him. Something had changed. Maybe it was seeing that Lux wanted her so badly? It made him uncomfortable, and yet at the same time he craved the feeling. There was an ache inside as he looked at her, a pain he had never, ever felt. It was unsettling, and addictive.

He really needed to clear his head.

He stood up and pulled a shirt on and tucked the room key into his pocket. He closed the door behind him and walked down to the lobby, going over to peruse the buffet table. There was tons of fruit and pastries, little boxes of cereal, bagels, hard boiled eggs, and a variety of yogurts. He grabbed two cartons of chocolate milk, some water, two muffins, and some granola bars from the picked over table and went back to the room, realizing he'd walked down without even putting shoes on his feet. So much had changed about him. Not only had he gotten lazy with his duties, but there was zero chance he would have ever walked barefoot anywhere before meeting her.

He set the food down on the small round table in the corner of the room and picked up his atlas and began looking at the map of Illinois. She rearranged herself on the bed. He looked up and watched as she stretched her body across the bed like a cat. He drank the milk and ate a muffin, watching her as she slept. *Damn*. After he finished eating, he settled back down beside her and went back to sleep.

"Wake up," she said, hovering over his face. She was on her knees and tickling his nose with her hair.

He reached for his face and opened his eyes, startled by her closeness. She tickled his nose again and laughed when he batted her hand away as she moved out of his reach and sat back on the bed.

"What time is it?" He yawned and checked his watch. It was around one in the afternoon. "Holy fuck," he said, and sat up. "When did you wake up?"

"Just like twenty minutes ago," she said, standing up and finishing the water she'd opened. "Thanks for the breakfast, I assume you went and got it, right?"

"Yeah," he said, and stood up, stretching his long limbs. She watched as his muscles pulled over the bones. His stomach caved in as he sucked in a deep breath. "I hope you didn't drink the milk." A smirk teased his lips.

"No, I thought better of that," she said, with a grin. "So, where are we going today?"

"I thought I'd take you to Navy Pier."

"Cool!" She jumped up and looked for her boots, which she'd kicked off in haste the night before. Since she'd already showered before waking him, she was pretty much amped and ready to go. One of her boots she found up under the bed, and another against the wall behind the door.

"I guess you're anxious to go?" He smiled and reached for his own boots.

"Um, yeah, kinda. We've already wasted enough time sleeping."

"That was not a waste," he said, looking at her.

"Yeah, you're right. That was the best night's sleep I've had in ages."

"Me too. Make sure you bring a jacket or something. I saw on the news yesterday it's only supposed to be forty five degrees, and it'll be windy by the lake."

She stood up and found the skull hoodie and pulled it on over her overalls.

"How many outfits did you bring?" he said, noticing she was wearing yet another.

"Only three," she said, defensively.

Roman laughed and put his hand on the top of her head, ushering her out the door.

The water was choppy and sapphire blue. She had been to Lake Erie a bazillion times and it never looked this pretty or vast. Lake Erie was either greenish or grey, depending on the weather, and had that sort of monster-in-the-lake look when the weather was gloomy. Lake Michigan seemed like the ocean to her. It was vast and endless.

He pulled into a parking spot. As he came to a stop, she jumped out of the car and waited impatiently for him to follow, which he found highly amusing, so he slowed himself down on purpose, just to tease her some more.

"Hurry up," she demanded, bending at the knees as if trying to keep herself from stomping her feet.

The wind picked up her hair, whipping it against her neck and stinging her with its lash. The sky was gray and blue, the puffy white clouds being taken over by the darker ones. She reached out for his hand and pulled him up the street towards the Pier. The Ferris Wheel was the first obvious thing she noticed, but it was the carousel that caught her eye. With rabbits and ducks and cats all intricately carved and bejeweled. Her mind raced back to dreams she'd had as a child and books her mother had read to her of magical lands where animals spoke and lived as humans. She had always wanted to find that place and she figured this might be the closest to that ever existing.

"You know we're riding that, right?" she said, tugging Roman's hand and pulling him towards the ride.

Roman reluctantly followed, knowing he could not begrudge her request. They waited in line and he listened to her as she changed her mind from cat, to dog, to rabbit, about which she'd choose to sit. He would ride the chair *obviously*. Or better yet, stand beside her.

"No, I think you should ride the frog," she said, looking at him slyly, knowing exactly what he was thinking. "It's beside the rabbit. Okay, so it's rabbit and frog. Now make sure to run once they let us up there."

"Should I push children out of my way if they get in front of me?"

"Well, duh, of course." She laughed and slugged him playfully.

Their turn came, and he walked behind her as she made a beeline to the rabbit. He strolled to the frog and sat on it, looking very uncomfortable in his leather jacket and long messy wind-whipped hair. She looked at him and laughed, and he just shook his head and waited for the ride to start and end as quickly as possible. As cute as it was to see her all smiles and giggling, this was not his favorite thing in the world, and would much prefer slicing the head off the living dead. Still, she was adorable.

They walked to the end of the Pier. The dark blue and grey clouds were swelling and rolling across the lake. It always amazed her to see virga. It fell halfway to the lake in pale white sheets. She felt the faint mist of crashing waves against the concrete piles as she leaned into the wooden rails. Roman seemed deep in thought, a million miles away, when she looked over at him. His hands were pressed against the wood, dry and worn. His fingers were bent up, clearly broken numerous times. She wondered to what extent his body had been tortured. His father had died doing what he does, after all. Her gut knotted up, and a sudden chill went through her body. Her arms wrapped around herself, suddenly frozen to the bone.

"You cold?" he asked, looking down at her.

"A little," she answered, knowing that he would want to leave, but she didn't want this time to end. It was really the first time since she'd known him that they had been able to just exist. There was no drama at this moment. Just the two of them, together, like any other tourists. It was the first time she was able to just let go of most of the stuff she'd been dealing with since her parents' death. Hell, she hadn't even thought of Mark for days now. And the fear of what Lux might tell her was gone now too. She hadn't even bothered to consider the threats that waited for her at home.

"You ready?" he asked.

She let out a deep sigh. "Yeah, I'm ready," she said, and turned around, feeling the lake pushing against her back with its blustery wind. Her hair flew in swathes around her face, shielding it from the cold air. He put his hand on her shoulder and patted her back as they walked back towards the carousel. She looked at it again. This would be a good memory.

"Hey, cotton candy," he said, stopping and pointing to the stand.

"Let's get some," she said, and smiled at him.

They walked back to his car, Violet soaking up every bit of the atmosphere she could to take with her back home. She loved this city, loved the smell in the air, the coolness of the overcast sky, and the magic of being somewhere else. This would be a magical day she would reflect upon forever.

"Are we going to go home now?" she asked, wrapping her tangled hair up on the top of her head with a hairband she'd slipped from her wrist.

"It depends," he said, watching her open the bag of blue sugary perfection and shoving a large pinch into her mouth. "Are you ready, or do you want to stay another night?"

She pondered the question. "I'm ready, I suppose, but I want to stay another night." She grinned with blue lips.

"Good, so now what do you want to do?"

"Maybe I'll buy myself some more stuff I don't need. Plus, I'm hungry for real food. And then, maybe we can find some stupid club to go to tonight just so I can say I checked it out."

"Whatever you want to do is fine with me."

"Will you see Lux again before we go?" she asked, shoving another bunch of blue melty goodness into her mouth.

"No. We're not friends, Violet," he said, looking over at her with a slight grimace on his face.

"You're not enemies either," she said, returning his grimace.

"Well, the answer is no. Seeing him two days in a row is a little much for me."

"Okay, big baby," she said, and pulled off a bunch of cotton candy and fed it to him. "Let's eat pizza for dinner," she said, slouching down in the seat and resting her knees on the dashboard. "Always wanted to try pizza in Chicago."

"Real food, huh?"

"It's got all the food groups,"

"You know, I could take you to a real restaurant. The kind of place where fancy people pay a lot of money to be seen." Roman smirked and started the car. As gruff as he appeared, he was actually cultured. He'd been all over the world, in all kinds of situations. The guy knew how to operate in high society and the gutters alike.

The idea was a bit intriguing. "Nah, I'm not up for putting on a charade."

"Suit yourself."

9
MOON IN YOUR EYE

THEY SPENT SEVERAL HOURS walking around the neighborhood by the hotel. Violet purchased more clothes, a pair of flat soled boots, and a few old children's books she'd found in a used book store. She felt sympathy for Roman, having had to endure her perusing. He had waited patiently for her as she rummaged, and tried on, and compared. At least she hadn't made him hold her purse or something like that.

"You poor thing," Violet said, meeting him on the sidewalk in front of the store.

"I'm alright," he said, shrugging his shoulders and walking. "Though, I think it's time to eat something, I'm starving."

"Yeah, me too actually. Remember there was that pizza place not far from the hotel?"

"I don't care where we go at this point. I'd settle for an alley and a dumpster."

"Aw, like *Lady and the Tramp*,"

Roman looked at her oddly and shook his head.

They walked back to the hotel and dropped her bags off in the room. Roman went to the bathroom and she called Amber and let her know they'd be back the following day. She was still chatting when Roman walked over to her and tapped her on the shoulder.

"Come on, I'm hungry," he complained, as he held his stomach.

He never complained, so she knew this was serious business. A grin came to her lips as she nodded her head and said goodbye. "Amber saw Mose yesterday."

"Oh yeah?" he said, standing by the door impatiently waiting for her. "Will you hurry up? You can tell me on the way." His tone was playfully annoyed.

She stopped looking through her new stuff and snarled at him in jest. Pushing her pile of goodies off her lap, she walked over to the door, not saying anything.

"Hey, maybe you can go without eating but I need food," he teased her and opened the door, holding it open. She walked under his arm and waited for him to close the door.

"So, anyway, she said he was acting really weird. None of us have talked to him in weeks, and she said he was just weird and evasive. I guess he and Steve are sharing some old RV or something at that trailer park over by the diner. Gross, huh?"

"Whatever floats your boat, I guess. I think I'd rather live at your house with a toilet that doesn't require emptying, but whatever."

"Hey, you know you can? I have one bedroom and a whole basement open now," she said, walking backwards with a huge smile on her face.

He smiled at her reluctantly, reminded again that he'd be leaving very soon. He liked the idea of settling in with them, but it wasn't reality. He would kill Cecelia and have to move onto whatever bullshit was next. That was just the reality of his life. There had been rumblings of something going on in Germany the last time he was on-line, but that had been months prior. God only knew how out of hand that situation was now. Eh, there were others who could worry about it for once.

"No answer?" she said, looking very dejected.

"I don't want to talk about it, okay?" He tried to keep his tone as even as possible.

"Okay," she said.

"It's not that I think it's a bad idea, I'm just not sure where I'll be, and I don't want to think that far out right now. Don't get hurt feelings."

"Just know the offer stands," she told him as she grabbed his arm and looped it through hers.

He smiled at her. The restaurant was only another block up the street. Roman held the door and Violet dipped in under his arm.

"Two?" the petite girl asked. They nodded and she took them to a booth towards the back of the room.

The restaurant looked like a pizza place should look with its dark red linen tablecloths and creamy plastered walls. The room was dimly lit with dark wooden booths and candles on every table. Dean Martin sang softly over the noise of the bar. And the place was vibrant with laughter. It was a cliché, but it was a good cliché. Roman thanked the hostess and slid into the booth, nearly knocking his head on the stained glass lamp that hung over the center of the table. Violet laughed at him and sat down on the opposite side of the booth.

"I'm so hungry," she said, opening the paper scroll-like menu. She unzipped her hoodie and slipped her arms out of the sleeves. The room was warm due to the large wood-fire ovens and the amount of people. "What do you like?"

"Pretty much anything edible," he said, not opening the menu.

"Okay, what *don't* you like?"

"Green peppers."

"What is wrong with you? They totally make the pizza."

He looked at her with a smirk. "Well, what don't you like?"

"Onions,"

"See, that's just wrong," he teased.

"Ugh, they're sick! Like nasty tapeworms."

"Oh, that's really appetizing. Now that's all I'll think about from here on out." He laughed and shook his head.

"Good, then I've sufficiently wrecked them for you too. Now I'll never have to worry about picking them off our pizza." She looked back at the menu.

He watched her as she read. Her cheeks were bright pink, flushed from the cold outside and the sudden warmth indoors. Her hair was tousled and haphazardly arranged. She looked perfectly windswept, and for a brief moment before he caught himself, he pictured messing her hair up in bed. He really needed to stop this. Nothing good would come from entertaining these thoughts.

"Okay, so I guess we want a large pizza with everything but stupid onions and green peppers?" Violet looked up to confirm with eye contact.

"That's fine," he responded with a distracted grin, and sat the menu back down, never having looked at it. It automatically rolled back up when he let go of it.

Violet found this somewhat entertaining and opened and watched hers close two or three times. She noticed him watching her with a peculiar expression on his face. "Hey, I'm easily amused, what can I say?"

Roman just shook his head and smiled.

The waitress brought them a bowl of garlic bread and took their order. They gobbled down several pieces of warm, gooey bread as they made small talk, and Violet looked around the room, taking in the atmosphere. As Roman talked, it dawned on her just how much his personality seemed to have changed these last few days. She couldn't quite put her finger on it completely, but he was in some ways more relaxed, and in other ways more guarded. The desire to ask him what was going on was killing her, but she didn't quite know how to delve into it.

God, she wanted to know everything about him. Every minute detail about his life, his past, his thoughts on everything from religion, to politics, to his favorite movies. Everything. Then his eyes caught the light, illuminating the lustrous green, and her brain stopped working and she just started admiring him again. Ugh, it was so hot the way his jawbone moved as he chewed, making the muscles in his face and neck tense and relax. His mouth was beautiful, those perfectly lush lips, the pointed arches on top, the plump bottom lip... his eyes all vibrant green and shining...

"What?" he asked, wondering why she was staring so intently.

"Um, nothing," she said with a snicker and took a drink from her soda.

Roman scowled and shook his head. She looked small, placed between the high back of the booth and the tall table, which came mid-chest on her. He had to lean forward in order to see her entirely, as the lamp was so low above the table and he was so tall.

"Scoot over against the wall so I can see you," he said, leaning forward. "Please?"

The request somehow made her ache inside. Violet complied, sliding over and slouching against the wall as she pulled her leg up resting her foot on the bench and her knee against the table.

"This is good," she said with a smile, taking another bite of bread. He nodded as he finished his third piece. "Roman, tell me about your family."

The question threw him off a little, but he hid that fact and swallowed the mouthful of bread. "What do you want to know?"

"I want to know what they were like, what happened, you know, I guess everything."

He took a drink from the bottle of Miller High Life he was nursing and gathered his thoughts, trying to ascertain how to start. Violet wrinkled her nose.

"What?" he asked, amused by her expression.

"How do you drink that?"

"It's the champagne of beers. Says so right here on the label."

"You goof, I meant beer in general." His explanation made her laugh. She hated beer.

"Drank it with my dad," he said with a shrug.

"Weren't you kinda young?" She snickered as her eyebrows rose.

Roman thought about it for a second, yeah, he had been. Dad had given him his first beer when he was nine years old after he'd witnessed his first slaughter. The memory of seeing that family disemboweled, and the subsequent vampire massacre by his father, brought bile to his throat.

"I was young. I was forced to grow up a lot younger than most. There's a story behind it, but I'd rather not discuss it at the moment." There was no use in ruining their evening with horrific tales of yesteryear.

It was strange enough having someone in his life, even more odd that she wanted to know anything about him or his history. The only person he had ever talked about these things with had been Lux and Mylori. And even then he hadn't gone too far into detail.

"Sorry to pry. You don't have to talk about anything," Violet said, interrupting his thoughts.

"No, it's okay. I just, I have no clue where to begin."

Roman thought back on his life, flipping back through random memories, things he hadn't thought about, hadn't allowed himself to think about. What would be the point of sharing all this brutality with her? Too much grief. Too much violence. He was a monster. Not because he wanted to be, because he had to be. She didn't need to know about all this bullshit. It would do him good not to know about it all himself.

He took another swig from his bottle and started, "My mom was happy and gentle. She was a good mom, especially considering the circumstances. Life wasn't easy, and no doubt she wished there was another way. But she tried really hard to make my life as normal as possible, though it wasn't at all normal when I look back now. We lived with my uncle on my dad's side because of my dad being gone most of the time. My uncle took care of me after she died."

"What was he like?"

"Typical older man, I guess. All my training and schooling I owe to him. He was the family historian, and at one time, a hell of a fighter. He could be strict, but mostly he was just relaxed. Amazing considering all he'd endured."

"So, what happened with your mom? You said she died from cancer, right?"

"Yeah." He looked down at the table briefly, remembering the look of peace on her face when she had taken her last breath. "She was perfectly healthy, and then got cancer and died a year later. I helped take care of her and everything. Towards the end we just prayed she'd go. It was a relief when it finally happened. I know that must sound terrible, but she was ready, and she was at peace."

"I'm sorry," Violet said.

"Yeah, it was rough, but it's part of life, unfortunately. You'd think I'd be used to seeing things die."

"But she wasn't a *thing*, she was your mom." She felt her eyes swelling with tears as she spoke, understanding too well what he felt because it was the same thing she felt herself.

"Don't get all weepy on me," he said, trying to crack a smile. He reached across the table and took her hand. He felt his own eyes blurring, and that was some sort of miracle. He hadn't felt much of anything for a long time, let alone the desire to cry.

"Sorry." She laughed nervously and wiped her eyes with her free hand. "What about your dad?" She laced her fingers through his, relishing the feel of his hand against hers.

"My dad was very reserved, strong, strict, and probably the most moral human being I've ever known. He expected that from me. He taught that to me, though I'm sure I've failed. He'd probably be disappointed with a lot of the decisions I've made."

"But it's your life and you have to do what's right for you."

"Yeah, well I haven't always done what's been right for me. I know you're right, but you know it's that guilt thing that hangs over your head that only a parent can make you feel."

"Yeah, it's one of the things that still haunts me. I know if my mom had known all I've done, it would have killed her."

"Live and learn, right?" he said, taking another drink. He took his hand back awkwardly.

"I guess so," she shrugged, feeling bereft. "So, tell me about what happened to him."

"I was fifteen when my mom died. I think my dad lost his focus after that. He died about a year later. I had seen him take on small armies, there was no way only one vampire could have killed him. I think he just gave up. I've always thought it was a passive suicide." His eyes trailed off briefly, contemplating what had happened and how they'd found his body mutilated. There hadn't been much left to bury. A clear statement.

"That's not right, Roman. He still had a child to think about." The idea that his dad would leave him to fend for himself pissed her off.

"I wasn't a child," Roman corrected her.

He hadn't really been a child since he was nine years old, after seeing what he'd seen and having been expected to take on these responsibilities. He thought about all that had been required of him, and all the shit he'd seen that no one, especially not anyone that young, should've been subjected to. Hence the early introduction to alcohol and the glory of "forgetting". Yeah, he'd been young when he'd had his first taste. Maybe a necessary fix, given the circumstances. His mom had thrown a fit that his dad had given him the beer, until dad had pulled her out of the room and she came back with such grief in her eyes, like something had died inside of her. She hadn't quite looked the same after that day. It was the main reason he'd never even considered the idea of a relationship, or having his own family. Of course it had always been a non-issue before. He'd never allowed himself to get close to anyone until now.

"The Ikovs aren't meant for family life. My father never should have gone that route. It led to his weakness and ultimately to his own death. Had he never gotten married, never had me...well, his life would've lasted a lot longer, and there would be a lot less vampires in the world. And I never forgot that. I was never allowed to forget it. I was a liability. So was mom."

Violet pondered his words. His evasive personality was starting to make a lot more sense to her now.

"After he died I had to take over," Roman said.

"You *had* to? You were a kid, Roman."

"I wasn't a kid, Violet. I had never really been a kid. It was my duty. And besides, they were coming for my uncle, and he was way too old to protect himself at that age, let alone protect me. Knowing my dad was gone left him sitting wide open, and I had to learn fast how to defend us. There were a lot of people who wanted him dead. Me too, just because I was my dad's son."

"Not to be mean, but your parents did you a real disservice. Despite what you say, you were a kid, Roman. You should've been left to worry about kid stuff, not making sure you kept your uncle alive and killing monsters. Your dad should've thought about that before he went off and let himself get killed."

"Well, like I said, my dad made a mistake." He seemed semi-wounded by her criticism, even though he knew it was the truth. During the moments he allowed himself to think about his life he knew it was unfair to expect that shit from a teenager, but it was just life. His parents did the best they could with the hand they'd been dealt. Just like he had.

The waitress brought the pizza and cut the pie, placing large slices on their plates. They thanked the woman and she walked away. Roman picked up a fork, cutting into the food and starting to eat.

"Roman, I didn't mean to offend you." He looked a million miles away and she was worried she'd hurt his feelings butting in where she wasn't really wanted.

"You didn't," he mumbled with his mouth full. "It's not like I haven't thought the same thing a thousand times. Believe me, I was a very angry young man. I didn't ask for this. But it's my life."

"Well, I suppose anger can be constructive in your line of work." She grinned, trying to lighten the mood.

"Yes, rage is a helpful tool."

"Is your uncle still living?" She picked up the gooey pizza and took a bite, scalding the roof of her mouth. "Ouch," she whined, hurriedly chewing. "Hot." She fanned her mouth with her sauce-covered fingers.

He smiled at her. "I'd use a fork with that," he said, handing her a napkin.

"Yeah, thanks," she said, rolling her eyes and wiping her messy digits.

"My uncle died of natural causes a few years ago. So, I'm it, the last of the vampire slayers--well, at least from my family."

"And you're never going to get married, or have kids, or anything?" She took a big drink of her pop and ran her tongue against the roof of her tender, blistering mouth.

"No. Why would I inflict myself on someone else?"

"Inflict yourself? You're an amazing person," she said, kicking him under the table.

He jumped slightly, startled by the sudden jolt. "Yeah, I'm a real charmer."

"Oh, whatever. You're so kind hearted."

"Kind hearted? Ask the people who are headless because of me." The thought that he was "kind hearted" made him laugh.

"They aren't people." Violet scowled, irritated by his tone.

"Yeah, well still, I bring final death to them."

"And that's bad, how? It's not like you're killing innocent people."

"I know what you're saying, V. I just realize I'm as much of a killer as they are. Better at it than they are. And I would rather not involve anyone else in all this. It's bad enough that you know."

"I'm glad I know," she said, cutting off a bite of pizza with her fork and blowing on it.

"I'm not."

"I am. I'd rather know what reality is than go through life blindfolded."

He stopped eating momentarily and pondered her words. She truly would never be able to go back to her previous life. Even if she never saw another vampire the whole of her existence and he disappeared from her life completely--*which was the plan*--she could never be normal again. But he needed to convince himself otherwise because he couldn't, wouldn't, stay with her.

"Besides, I like that you've *inflicted* yourself on me," she said.

She smiled and he wanted to tell her that he was happy about it too, but refrained. The less she knew the easier it would be to move on later.

The waitress stopped by the table and he asked for another drink. She was full, having downed three pieces of garlic bread and a giant piece of gooey pizza. So, she pushed her plate away and leaned back against the wall again.

"I can understand you never wanting to have kids and stuff because of this, but why do you have to be alone?"

"It's just better this way," he said, shrugging his shoulders.

"Is it really? You seem pretty content right now."

He looked at her then. Her eyes were glistening, so beautiful in the candle-light. Her lips looked soft and moist. She was so exquisite, and he realized he was content. For the first time ever, he was content. "It doesn't matter if I'm content. I'm not going to risk your life for selfish needs."

He didn't want to risk her *life*? He had more or less admitted he was content just then. Did that mean that he would contemplate her as someone he would want to settle down with if his life was different? She felt her stomach flutter at the thought.

"Roman, my life was at risk before you entered the picture. You're the one that saved it, remember? I would be dead without you in my life," she said.

He didn't say anything, but her declaration made him look at her differently. She was right. She would be dead right now had he not been there that night. "Lux wouldn't have allowed that," he said, trying to deflect his importance.

"Lux? You have to be kidding, right? Don't you think he would have eventually killed me? Or made me like him? You said it yourself."

His arguments were being shot down left and right. There was nothing he could say to her. She was right, of course. Lux would have eventually done one or the other. He still might.

"If I hadn't died that night when I was out walking, I would have eventually done myself in with drugs or some other stupid nonsense. And even if I hadn't died, I may as well have considering the life I was living with Mark and all that destructive stuff. You saved my life, Roman. *You* saved my life."

145

"Lux saved your life. He's the one that sent me." He refused to acknowledge credit. There was no way he could allow himself to become some sort of false hero to this little girl.

"Why are you fighting me on this?" she asked, furrowing her brow.

"Because, Violet, you're a little girl, and you think I'm something I'm not. I'm not some knight in shining armor, or some hero sent to save you. I do a job because I have to."

She looked down at the table now, fighting the urge to yell or cry or both. She was angry with him, insulted by his words, *little girl* and *job*. She was just another job to him? She wanted to smash his face in and force him to see her for who she was, and not for what he wanted to believe. She looked up and he could see the fire in her eyes.

"Roman, I am not a little girl like you keep trying to convince yourself. I'm not some weak pathetic creature who can't take care of herself. You've seen me at the lowest point of my life. You've seen me make some really stupid mistakes, and you've picked me up a dozen times now. But I am *not* a little girl. Why do you insist on treating me like one? "

He sat silently now. How did this conversation turn so badly? *Because he's socially inept and not worth the effort she was putting into him?* Yes, yet more reasons he was no good for her. He was completely incapable of normal human interaction.

"Lux doesn't think I'm a child, and I'd say he has a few years on you. Are you going to answer me?" she asked and folded her arms across her chest, expecting him to lash out at her.

He didn't say anything, just continued to watch her as her face turned redder and her eyes grew darker, more incensed. She was intent on getting an answer from him. "I'm a lot older than you, Violet."

"And what does that have to do with anything? So, if I was fifty and you were sixty, or whatever, you'd still think I was a little girl?"

"I won't live that long," he said matter-of-factly, looking her directly in the eye. She had no idea just how serious this all was.

That shut her up for a moment. She wanted to tell him how ridiculous his statement was, but maybe it wasn't ridiculous? She felt her eyes tearing up again. The reality of his existence was overwhelming to her in that instant.

"The last thing I need is to bring you further into all this than you need to be. You need to have a normal life. You need to go to school, get married, have kids, and live a normal life. You *can* do that. Once this situation is handled you can go back to living your life. You're on the right track now. You're away from that fucking loser. You don't need more turmoil and danger around you." He paused for a moment, his brow deeply furrowed. "And if I don't convince myself you're too young for me by repeating it over and over and over it will make it much more difficult when it comes time to leave."

He hadn't meant to spill his guts out so thoroughly. He felt his stomach heave as the nervousness of what he'd just divulged took over his brain. Why hadn't he just kept his mouth shut as he always had before? Damn it. Now she had some inkling as to the depth of his feelings, feelings he didn't even fucking understand, or want to understand.

She sat stunned by what he'd said. The look of confusion on his face was startling to her. He'd never looked so uneasy since she'd met him. My god, he looked nervous as hell, completely out of control of his emotions, and not at all his usual demeanor of confidence.

He took a drink and looked down at the table, unsure of how she would react to what he'd just said. She could laugh it off or scream. He had no idea. What he did know was that he was a fool for shooting his mouth off.

"Damn it," he grumbled, taking another drink. "See how stupid I am? I have no social skills whatsoever. I'm meant to be alone and to kill things. *That* is my life. Why the fuck would I involve someone else in this? You should live a normal life. That is what you should do. While you still can, you should live a normal life."

He couldn't look at her now. Maybe he was the child between the two of them? He was the one fumbling with his words and feeling awkward. When it came to relationships she was the one with the experience, even if it was a fucked up experience. He was older than her in years, and years only, when it came to this relationship crap.

She reached over and put her hand on his, he looked at her cautiously. A sweet smile kissed her lips as she looked at him. "Roman, do you honestly think I could ever live a normal life now? Lux denied that for me when I was seven years old. My parents are gone. My grandparents are gone. Vampires are after me. And *you* guaranteed that my life would never be normal when you saved me instead of letting me die like I should have. I will never live a normal life. And why would I want to anyway? I *don't* want to. I want to be with you, and you are most definitely not normal in any way, shape, or form, vampires or not."

ROman exhaled and slowly shook his head. "God, I'm such a fucking moron," he said, resting his head on the back of the booth and covering his mouth with his hand. He looked back down at her and shook his head with a nervous smile. "You know you're going to be the death of me?"

She grinned and squeezed his hand. "Nah, high cholesterol will be the death of you, judging by your diet. Let's go."

What the fuck had just happened? He had never been so laid bare in the whole of his existence. Completely exposed. Vulnerable. Weak.

She had about a thousand questions she wanted to ask him as they walked back to the hotel. And he had about a thousand more he needed to ask himself. Had she seriously blurted out that she wanted to be with him? God, her insides roiled with embarrassment. Yeah, there was a lot she needed to say and to think about. There was a lot he needed to think about too. Like how on earth he would extricate himself from her life. Instead, they both walked quietly and absorbed the night around them.

The sky was crystal clear, the clouds had moved through the city, leaving a windswept clean sky. The air was downright cold and she clutched his arm, huddled beside him as her feet struggled not to trip into his. The height difference was awkward to say the least, but she didn't care. She found walking in step with him to be the easiest way to not get bonked on the head by his shoulder.

This was insane. He had opened something he had no idea how to close without just leaving her high and dry with no real kind of explanation. He could not do that, of course. There was no point in talking to her about any of this. He wouldn't make the same mistake his father and the generations before him had made. No way. It didn't matter how much he liked her. And he did like her, didn't he? He liked her more than he should. No, there was no way in hell he was going to drag anyone down this path. He would teach her to defend herself because she should know that, and then he'd handle the situation with the vampire, and then he'd move on to whatever evil bullshit he had to move onto next. But he would not take her with him, or leave her like his father had always left him and his mother, waiting for him to come home. He had seen firsthand how his mom cried nearly every night, wondering if his dad was still alive. She used to hide behind closed doors, or outside on the porch swing in the middle of the night, but he could always hear her and always see the swollen red eyes in the morning. This girl had already lost her parents, she didn't need to lose anyone else, and the reality was that he would die doing this. It was only a matter of time. And it would be brutal.

"Do you still want to go to a club or something? I got a flier from that store this afternoon," she said, fighting the noise of the traffic and wind.

"If that's what you want," he said stiffly.

She knew he had to be freaked out by the conversation they'd had. How could he not be? She certainly was. It was so strange feeling like she might really be on the verge of an actual relationship with him. It made her giddy and scared to death. He obviously had done some thinking about the possibility, based on the few things he'd said to her. But in all reality he may just really believe what he'd said, that he needed to be alone, that he was a killer meant for nothing more than killing, and maybe he would walk out of her life as quickly as he'd walked into it.

149

The thought devastated her, and her eyes began to sting even thinking about it. She wouldn't push him, but she wouldn't let him off the hook either. It would be far too easy for him to hide behind his walls and walk away, whether he really wanted to or not, unless she let him know just exactly how she felt and what she thought.

What she wanted was to forget all the vampire nonsense and go away with him somewhere and live a normal life. She wanted a small house in the country with a white picket fence and dogs and cats and nothing but the two of them and happiness. Obviously this was not reality and never would be reality for her. It wouldn't be reality for her with anyone. It simply didn't exist in this world now and never did.

"Roman?" she said, stopping suddenly and pulling him up against a building so that others could pass by freely.

"What?" he asked, looking somewhat concerned and afraid of what she might say next.

"So, what are we? It's a stupid question, I know, but I guess I need to know. If you have no intentions of being in my life once you've fulfilled your obligation, then I want to know. I have to know if you feel anything more for me than just some brotherly type instinct or sense of duty."

He smiled, which was unexpected and caught her off guard. "I am definitely not feeling brotherly instincts towards you," he said with an ornery grin on his face as he rubbed his sideburn and looked down the street briefly and back at her. "But honestly, I haven't allowed myself to think for even a moment about anything beyond you being a girl I need to protect. I will say, what little common sense I have tells me you'd be better off with me out of your life once this is over."

Finally, some honesty, some sense that a barrier had come down, even if it was only a little. She looked up at his face. He looked more vampiric in that moment than even Lux had looked to her. His skin glowed as white as the full moon, the street lights reflected in his eyes, like silver halos around his pupils. The loose strands of hair that had escaped the rubber band at the nape of his neck were floating above his head like dancing threads with the wind.

"Common sense is overrated."

The corner of Roman's lip lifted slightly. "Yeah, well, I seriously haven't let myself think too deeply about this and could probably give you a better answer at a later time." As much as he wanted to avoid this whole discussion, he wouldn't do that to her. He liked her too much to treat her with that much disregard.

"Fair enough," she said, and started walking again.

He had successfully dodged committing to anything. But at least he'd given her something.

They got back to the room and she found the flier with her purchases from earlier in the day. "Do you know where this is?" she asked, handing the flier to him which was decorated with intricately drawn gothic art and lettering.

"Yeah, more or less," he said, reading the text. "It's funny to me how much vampire imagery they use in these clubs. You know, they're a haven for the undead." He laughed out loud at himself. "*Undead*, too funny," he said, shaking his head.

"Undead, undead, undead," Violet said, deadpan in her delivery as she quoted the lyrics to a Bauhaus song. Roman just looked at her, completely oblivious. "Ever seen *The Hunger*?"

"I think. Maybe?" His brow was furrowed.

Violet rolled her eyes and laughed. "The band at the beginning?"

He still had no reaction.

She laughed. "Well, what's so funny about them using vampire imagery?" she asked, crinkling her nose. "It makes sense to me."

"Because it sounds so stupid and ridiculous. I've been around this since I was born, and I still find it unbelievable at times, especially when I'm talking about it out loud. It's ludicrous." He took his jacket off and tossed it down on the bed. "We'll take a cab over there. I don't want my car getting fucked up in the street."

"Well, I'm gonna get ready. It's already like ten o'clock. I'm sure by the time we get there things might be hopping."

"Do goth kids hop?"

"Yeah, they hop around like faeries." She snickered and scooped the bags off the floor. "Do faeries hop though?"

"That, I would not know."

Violet laughed.

She took her hair down. It was knotted and curly from having been put up while it was still wet and being whipped by the wind. She decided to just leave it down as it actually looked like she'd want it to anyway. She didn't even have to bust out the teasing comb. Her skin felt greasy from the humid wind and buttery bread and pizza she'd consumed, so she washed her face and brushed her teeth. She sifted through her makeup bag looking for the daffodil scented oil Amber had bought her for her last birthday. It was one of her favorite scents, and it always triggered very good memories of her mom's garden in early spring. There was a sea of yellow, orange, and white on the side of her house every year. She anointed her neck, chest, and arms with the oil and placed it back in the bag. Then she put her makeup on, heavy green and black around the eyes, pale pink cheeks and lips, and then went about the task of deciding which new outfit she would wear.

Roman flipped through the channels not seeing or hearing anything on the screen. His head was spinning, too many thoughts, and too many questions. He had no idea why he hadn't just lied to her and told her "thanks, but no thanks". Granted, he wasn't a liar usually, but it would be for the best for both of them if he just walked away.

She opened the door and tossed the bags back to the floor by her purse. Roman looked up from the television and turned the set off. She wore a floor length emerald green dress that grew darker and faded into black at the bottom. The sleeves were long, her fingertips barely showing beneath the edge. The silver heart rested against her stomach. The fabric was thin and meshy looking and clung to her body. He could see straight through the material and was thankful she was wearing something underneath, well, sort of thankful.

"My God, you're attractive," he said, leaning back on his elbows. He wasn't even trying to compliment her, just stating a fact before he could stop himself. At least his brain had stopped him from saying what he was actually thinking.

"Shut up," she said and rolled her eyes, dismissing his compliment as her cheeks turned bright red.

He didn't say anything but stood up and walked over to her. "I'm serious," he said, lifting her chin with his index finger. Fuck, he had to stop this before he went too far.

She smiled and felt her face warming, amongst other parts of her anatomy, then looked away, bending to pick up the new boots she'd bought. The moment was too intimate. She had to deflect. She sat on the edge of the bed and laced them up while Roman went to the restroom to avoid staring at her more. She picked up her hoodie from the floor and put it on, zipping the front and then sitting on the edge of the bed waiting for him patiently.

"You ready?" he asked, walking back into the room. His hair was loose now and slightly curled on the ends.

"Yep," she said, and stood up as she slid her purse over her shoulder and followed him to the door.

"You do have an I.D. right? They won't let you in if you don't."

"Of course I do, moron," she said, looking cross at him. She hated being talked to like an idiot, which he knew, and was teasing her.

He laughed and shut the door behind them. They walked downstairs and he went to the counter and had the concierge arrange for a car. He was still old school about some things and couldn't be bothered with an app. She watched as he spoke to the man behind the counter. He always seemed so confident. He never appeared awkward or weak in any way. Which was what made that earlier conversation even more bizarre. Seeing him that flustered had been weird. He walked back to her and they went outside to wait for their ride.

And what was the deal back at the room? Would he have kissed her if she'd stood there longer instead of being a nervous dolt and backing away? Ugh, her body wanted his so badly she ached.

10

VELVET BOX

SHE SHOWED HER IDENTIFICATION and they put a fluorescent pink band on her wrist, designating her as "underage". There were so many people there, she scanned the crowd and waited for Roman as he walked to the bar. She leaned against a column that had been wrapped in dark purple fabric and silver ribbon and noticed the way the club had been transformed into a gothic playhouse. Upon further observation you could see beneath the decoration that this place was a sports bar the rest of the week. She applauded the promoters' dedication to their passion but also found it rather amusing.

"These clubs weird me out," he said, handing her the soda and guiding her further into the place.

"Why?" she asked as she took a sip of the Diet Coke.

"Because I'm not a scenester." He leaned against the wall and took a drink of the beer. "I come to these places to hunt, not socialize."

She considered the reality of what he'd just said to her. "I think a lot of these people are hunting, Roman." She grinned and looked up at him.

His hair fell around his face in beautiful loose coils. He almost looked angelic, like he was some dark fallen angel.

"I guess so," he said.

Roman might not be a scenester, but she had no doubt looking the way he did that there were a hundred pairs of eyes sizing him up the moment he stepped through the doors.

Violet looked around the room, and immediately noticed the death rock girl she'd seen the day before with her friends at the Tucson Truck Stop. Annoyance suddenly blossomed in her chest because the morons seemed so arrogant. Was it their behavior that really pissed her off, or the fact that she recognized that she and her friends acted just like them? There wasn't much difference, except that these people had it easy comparatively speaking. Everything was a stone's throw away for them. All the cool clothes and clubs. Violet and her clan had to make their own. The sight of them made her stomach clench. She didn't want to be like this anymore. It was pointless and did nothing but add misery to her life. And she had added her fair share of misery to others' lives. She was so over this.

The snooty girl from the shop was looking over at her and Roman. The bleached blonde guy she was with was looking too. What Violet wanted to do was ask them what the fuck they found so enthralling, but this wasn't her place and it didn't really matter anyway. She looked up at Roman, who seemed uncomfortable as he leaned against the wall, and she wondered if his shoulder still hurt. The nice thing for her to have done was allow the man to lie around the hotel and rest, instead of traipsing out to some lame club that he clearly hated. He was always so quick to give her what she wanted, and she was always too quick to take it.

"Do you want to go?" she asked, fighting the loudness of the obnoxious electronic beat that thumped without variation. The sound system was far too loud, and she had to nearly scream in order for him to hear her.

"I'm fine," he said, smiling at her and then looking back to the crowd. "I see you have admirers," he said, pointing the bottle towards the two.

Violet rolled her eyes. She had comments to make but they weren't worth fighting the noise pollution. Violet saw a table across the room open up and she pulled Roman's arm and quickly dragged him to it. He was taken off guard at first, and almost chipped his tooth as he'd been getting ready to take a drink. She sat on the tall stool, having to lift herself up onto it.

"It's a little quieter back here," he said, leaning over and talking into her ear. The warmth of his breath, and his proximity, made her instinctively lean into him.

She nodded and smiled at him. "Do you see any vampires?" she asked, remembering what he'd said earlier, and wondered if he would kill one right here if there was one lurking about.

"No, but I'm not really looking for them. I don't care tonight. I'm going to go get another drink. You want something?"

She looked down at her nearly full glass and shook her head no. He walked through the middle of the dance floor. He was a head or more taller than most people in this place, except for the few tall men and girls wearing massive heels, but he dwarfed them too. She looked over to see the death rock girl and her friend watching him and then looking back at her. What was their deal?

Violet despised the music this club was playing. She hated all this electro EBM crap. It was destroying an otherwise creative music scene. The consistent beats and stupid sound samples from song to song made her to want to stab her eardrums out. At least at The Cage they played some variety. I guess this place wasn't as "worldly" as she thought it would be. Surely to God there was more to it than *this*.

Roman approached now with two bottles in his hands. She looked at him with a peculiar expression, wondering what was going on with him. He'd had three beers at dinner and now he was drinking at least as much here. It wasn't like this behavior was unusual for her friends, but she hadn't seen him drink this much.

"I don't want to have to keep running back and forth," he said in a dismissive explanation, and took a drink.

She smiled coolly and looked back to the dance floor. He must be feeling strange about this whole situation and wanting to numb himself. It made her a little angry, as she didn't think she should be something that needed numbing.

She watched as the array of gothlings and rivet heads mingled and danced mindlessly to the synthetic rhythms searing the room. She longed for something a little moodier, a little darker, and a little more sensual than this. Maybe she came here on the wrong night? Maybe other nights were better? This couldn't seriously be the best Chicago had to offer?

"I'm going to go request something," she said, leaning against Roman, who was already on to the second drink.

He nodded at her and watched as she made her way to the DJ booth. She seemed to slink across the floor, very feline in her movement. She reminded him of Mylori in that way. He decided he'd be better off never pointing that out to her. Thinking about what her reaction would be to that tidbit brought a vague smirk to his lips.

His head was warm and sleepy, his body relaxed and calm, he needed to be relaxed and calm for more reasons than just the situation he'd created with her. He watched as she leaned against the booth, talking to the black haired guy with the headphones, the apparent person responsible for the noise that penetrated his otherwise calm disposition. Even through darkness, smoke, and colored lights he could see her smiling and flirting as she spoke to the man. She placed her hand on his shoulder as she tilted her head appreciatively and he knew right then that she'd been successful. That was the kind of guy she should be with, not him. The thought made him feel nauseous.

She started back towards him and then stopped, distracted by the girl they'd seen earlier. The pudgy female seemed to initiate the conversation and Roman wondered what it was they were talking about. He imagined it was either some "Oh, I saw you yesterday!" thing or perhaps some sort of "you don't belong here" banter. He decided he didn't care all that much. Besides, she was more than capable of defending herself with words. He probably should intervene on the strangers' behalf because they wouldn't win a verbal sparring match with her if that was the route they were going. He wished he could hear the conversation because he always found it amusing when she took someone down. Unless it was him. She could handle herself. So, he looked down at the table and focused on the black lace tablecloth while drinking the rest of the unsatisfying alcohol.

"Hello Roman," his voice crooned.

Roman grunted with exasperation and turned to see his dear friend Lux standing behind him. "Hello Lux," he said, halfheartedly.

"What? Not excited to see me?"

"Not particularly," Roman said, setting the bottle down and pushing it away from himself.

"I'm not here to cause you any trouble. In fact, I had no idea you'd be here."

"So, why are you here?" Roman said, looking at the man with distaste.

"Why wouldn't I be? Goth girls that want to be vampires are sort of easy pickings."

"Don't tell me. I don't want to know." Roman began peeling the label from one of the bottles.

"I didn't say I actually *make* them vampires, don't worry."

"Yeah, killing them is not much better. Don't want to know, Lux," Roman said, growing more agitated by the second.

"Who says I kill them? Sometimes I just want to fuck and drink. Relax and lighten up for fuck sake."

"What do you want?" Roman turned to look at him again and then back to Violet, who was still talking to the girl and her friend.

"She is beautiful, yeah?" Lux said, leaning an arm against the table. "I liked the red haired friend too," he said, teasing Roman and looking off to the crowd.

"Don't start."

"You really *are* in a foul mood."

"And?"

"And knock it off, stop being such a fucking twat."

Roman took a deep breath. Yeah, he knew he was being an ass and there was no reason for it. No good reason anyway. "I did something really stupid," he said, finally letting his guard down.

"And that's new?"

Roman looked at him, eyes focused and serious, and glared at the vampire.

"I'm sorry, you were saying?" Lux said, stifling his sarcasm for a moment.

"I got too attached to her. So fucking stupid," Roman said, looking briefly at Lux and back to the bottle.

"The stupid thing is that you're acting like a fucking crybaby as if it's the end of the world. So, either leave town or fuck her, what difference does it make?"

Roman was taken aback by that. For some reason this just wasn't the reaction he'd expected, considering Lux's own obvious feelings for Violet.

"Look, I know you think you're this martyr that has to go through life all alone fighting the evil vampires and all that bullshit, but she's not exactly as weak as you think she is. She's not some wilting little flower you need to protect from the big, bad world. She can handle herself. But it's not time. She's just not ready to do it alone yet."

Roman contemplated his words for a minute, his brow lowering over his eyes in a heavy scowl.

"Come on, stupid, you haven't noticed her strength?"

Lux was a little surprised for several reasons. One, that Roman had admitted a weakness. The old Lux would hurt Violet just to fuck with him. She was lucky he liked her and that he was protecting her. And second, that Roman had done seemingly no homework at all and hadn't put any depth of thought into this entire situation. Proof that he'd been preoccupied, and thus weak. This was a revelation.

"What are you talking about?" Roman turned in the seat to look Lux in the eyes now.

"I told you there was more to the story than me being *in love* with her. You think some little girl was going to stop me from killing her just because she looked into my eyes? Roman, I had stared death in the eyes a thousand times, a thousand pairs of sweet innocent eyes. It was seeing it reflected in *her* eyes that made the difference. She's as capable as you are, she just doesn't have years of training behind her."

"What the fuck are you saying? You said there wasn't anything supernatural about her."

"Is there anything supernatural about you?"

"Well, no."

"Then why does she have to be in order to be powerful? Mylori and I are the same creature, we have the same abilities, and I think you know that she's a thousand times more than what I am. Don't be so blinded by her supposed feminine frailty. She's not a helpless child."

"Then why the hell didn't you tell her all this the other night? You made it seem like she was just this sweet little girl who stole your heart with her innocence or some shit. What was that all about?"

"I didn't lie, that was the truth. Everything I said to her was the absolute truth. She doesn't need to know the rest. Yet, or maybe ever. It's not my call."

"You don't make any sense and you're pissing me off."

"Me, piss you off? There's a shock." Lux laughed at him.

Roman was angry and confused. "If you knew she was somehow capable of growing up to be like me, why didn't you kill her then? Why would you let her live?"

"Why not let her live? I thought about killing her through the years, but to be honest, I grew fond of her. She's special. It was fascinating to me, having long since forgotten what it was to be human. And she's special, as I said. Remember, nothing I said to her was a lie. Plus I thought maybe someday I'd turn her into one of us. Oh, Mylori would love that." He laughed, clapping his hands together. "How fun would it be bringing my little baby vampire Violet home with me? I can hear Mylori's screech already." Lux chuckled and raised an eyebrow at Roman. "But back to you, and why I didn't kill her. Why don't I kill you? I have no need to kill you, or her."

"You *can't* kill me." Roman scoffed.

"Oh, Roman, you're so funny." Lux laughed heartily, tossing his head back. "Sure I could. Granted, it would be difficult, and yeah, *maybe* you'd kill me, but we both know I could do it. And you think if I asked Mylori to help we couldn't kill you? Oh, especially now." He laughed, and it was unnerving to Roman.

"Why especially now?"

"Oh, come on. You've got to be kidding me with this denial bullshit."

"What?" Roman had no idea what Lux was blathering about.

"Ah, the stink of it is all over you, my dear old friend." Lux smiled, his teeth glistening like carved ivory.

"What the fuck are you talking about?"

"Seriously, Roman." Lux's tone of voice was patronizing. "Stop hiding." He was laughing hysterically now.

Roman frowned and clenched his fists. He looked down at the bottle in his hands with a remembrance of something Lux had said. "Wait, you said it's not up to you if she dies?"

Lux tipped his head to the side and smiled. "I'm not *god*."

"Who are your friends?" the girl asked, looking over her shoulder to the two men.

Violet turned and was surprised by Lux being there. "Uh, the dark haired one is Roman and the other is Lux," she said, turning back to the girl again.

"So *that's* Lux?" the girl asked, biting her bottom lip. "I've seen him around and heard the name, but never made the connection. And he's *your* friend?" The girl looked Violet up and down skeptically.

Violet made a face at the girl and looked back at the two men. "Something like that."

"Hmm... can you introduce us?" the blonde guy said to her, practically giddy.

"You wouldn't want to meet him. He's not a very nice guy."

"That's okay. We're not very nice either," the girl said with a laugh and leaned into her friend. "What about the other one? I assume he's your boyfriend?" she said, her words dripping condescension.

"Something like that," Violet repeated, crossing her arms and wondering where this line of questioning was going.

"Hmm..." the girl hummed, looking Violet over again.

"If you're just going to be patronizing then why did you even bother to stop me? What's the point of this?"

The girl laughed and looked at her friend who started laughing as well.

"Oh, I get it, because you want to meet them," Violet said in a haughty tone of voice, pointing to Lux and Roman. "I could introduce you. I'm assuming you probably think they'd prefer your company over mine? I mean, after all, the two of you are sooo cool, with your expensive goth clothes your mommy bought for you and your uber cool piercings and tattoos." Violet rolled her eyes and laughed, then leaned forward like she was going to whisper something to them. "The black haired one? See how tall he is? Let me tell you, girls, it's proportionate and he knows exactly how to work it." Violet clutched her chest and smiled like she was remembering a blissful moment. "And the other one? Sweet lord, he's something you can really sink your teeth into."

She laughed at her own idiotic joke. She looked at the two of them and smiled like the cat that ate the canary.

"And I get to take them both home with me. They're *mine*. So think about *that* when you're home alone tonight, watching sparkly vampire videos on YouTube and crying cuz you're so lonely," Violet said with a smile.

The girl stared at her blankly, not knowing what to say as the male friend looked away, not wanting to be involved in the tongue lashing, though hiding a smirk. Apparently he found Violet's snark a little more entertaining than the stupid stuck up bitch he was with. Violet was annoyed with herself for thinking the girl was cool the first time she'd seen her, even as snooty as she had been. Violet was done with stuck up snobs.

"Seriously, get the fuck over yourself," Violet said, and walked away from them and back towards the two men, who looked as though they were in the middle of a serious conversation. Well, at least one of them did, Lux was laughing hysterically.

"Ah, Violet, happy to see you again," Lux said, reaching out and putting his hand on her shoulder as he leaned in to kiss her on the cheek.

Violet wrapped her arms around him and kissed him on the lips, lingering there before turning to Roman to do the same. She was so annoyed by the prior conversation she could spit. She looked across the room at the two goth dorks who were standing there slack jawed, then she sat down beside Roman and put her arm through his. Both men looked at her a bit shocked, but understood what she was doing. Roman was a little dumbstruck.

"Someone feeling territorial?" Lux asked, drawing her attention.

"No, pissed off at having been belittled," she said, her brow furrowing deep into a scowl.

"If you really want to make them mad..." Lux said, one fang showing through his crooked grin.

"No," Roman growled.

Violet laughed as she smiled at Lux. The thought of really taking the two of them home seemed rather appealing at this moment and Lux's brow rose as though he'd read her thoughts. Maybe he had? Her eyes went wide for a moment.

He smiled at her. His eyes looked alive, glittering jewels dancing with light. He was vibrant, nothing dead about him. Were vampires considered dead? She didn't even know. Undead. Oh yeah. *Undead, undead, undead.* His hair was loose and looked stunning beneath the flashing red lights. His skin looked radiant. He looked like a young model in his fashionable suit. The memory of the dream she'd had of him in the club suddenly flashed in her mind and then faded, but not before he smiled, knowing. He picked her hand up and kissed the delicate bones of her fingers, and then brushed a kiss against her temple. The feel of his lips flamed on her skin for a moment and then died. Lux smiled at her, his mouth looking menacing bathed in red light.

She noticed that Roman looked very unhappy and sullen. She looked up at Lux and back to Roman, wondering just what the hell they'd been talking about.

"It's nice to see you too," she said, finally responding to Lux's initial greeting, but looking only at Roman, trying to ascertain if he was okay.

"Who are your friends?" Lux asked, looking beyond her to the people she'd been talking to prior. He was mildly wounded by her obvious disinterest in him as she looked at Roman with such concern.

"They aren't my friends," she said, rolling her eyes. "Ah, but they did want to meet you two." She grinned and elbowed Roman, who didn't react and just kept staring forward at the bottle, continuing to peel the label. "If I knew you'd just fuck them and never call them again I'd introduce you, but I don't want their blood on my hands," she said, looking at Lux and grinning an evil grin.

Roman looked over at her finally and gave her a smirk, having found her statement amusing. She smiled back at him and elbowed his side again and leaned into him.

"Ugh, you two are making me sick," Lux said, and walked away.

She watched as he seemed to disappear, swallowed up into the crowd, and wondered how it was that Roman could let him live knowing that someone here would probably die tonight because of him. And then she remembered what he'd said about it all. *It's not all black and white.* And what difference does it make if someone gets killed by a vampire or killed in a car accident?

The song she requested came through the system, slow and lush. Sultry strings and middle eastern rhythms poured through the speakers and the lull of a breathy female voice moaned seductively.

"This is the song you requested isn't it?" he asked, looking down at her. It was so obviously different from anything else that had played since they'd gotten there.

"Yep," she said, resting her head against him.

"Aren't you going to dance?"

"Nope," she said, looking at the dance floor as it cleared. "These people are lame," she said numbly. "I'll take BFE, Ohio any day of the week."

"I told you there wasn't anything to do in the big cities."

"That's not true and you know it, but let's go home."

Mark came up behind her, whispering something against the back of her neck, and slowly brushed the thick swathe of dark hair that rested there to the side. Cecelia turned around, her eyebrows knit together in question, and looked back at the spider she had been watching build a web in the window.

A while ago he had said something to her about wanting to share her with another.

An hour later he stood beside her dismissing the comment as if it had been a joke. And now his hand crawled through her thick nest of hair, cupping her skull gently, and then he grabbed a fistful and pulled her forward, dangling from his arm like a severed head.

This was okay with her. She liked being dominated. Her life and death had been spent being mistreated. It was her one true power; the ability to take abuse and void out the power men thought they had over her by using her.

"Steven?" she said, looking back at the boy who had been sitting silently for far too long.

"What?" he asked, looking up from the television at her and Mark.

"Come here," she said, turning to face him.

He pulled her hair tighter and sank his teeth into her neck. She fought the urge to collapse beneath the rapture of his kiss.

"What?" Steven asked like a small child who'd been sent to the principal's office.

She pulled the white silk away from her leg and looked down at the cowering boy. She grinned at him and raked her fingernails across the tender white flesh of her inner thigh.

Mark sank his teeth deeper as the anger of seeing Steven bowed down before her built up inside of him.

She reached out and cupped Steven's face with her hand. The blood ran in streams down her thigh dripping to the floor. She smoothed her fingers through the red liquid and smeared it across his lips.

Steven hesitated and then moved forward, lapping the trail of blood from her leg, coaxed along by her cold dead hands.

Mark pulled her head back, tearing further into her muscle and bending her collarbone from the pressure. A little harder and the bone would snap. She closed her eyes, mesmerized by the pain.

Yes, she liked being dominated.

II

TURNING

THEY STOOD AT THE edge of the sidewalk, waiting for a taxi to come by to pick them up. He was being so quiet and she knew by the far off look in his eyes he was slightly buzzed from the alcohol, though he was by no means drunk. It would likely take a case of beer, given his size. He leaned out into the street looking up and down. He hadn't said much since Lux left them upstairs, and it made her wonder what had been said between them before she had joined them at the table. He turned and walked back toward her, throwing his hands up, annoyed by the fact that no cabs were anywhere to be found.

"It's okay. We're in no hurry, right?" she said, trying to ease his obvious tension. "I can just use my phone to..."

"It's annoying," he said as he shoved his hands into his pants pockets. "It's fucking cold out here."

Violet felt uncomfortable. She didn't know how to react to his bad mood, since she hadn't really witnessed this side of his personality before now. She'd seen him angry, but it was always because she had made him so. This was new to her. She didn't say anything but looked at the ground racking her brain trying to figure out what she may have done to piss him off.

He paced back and forth, intermittently walking to the street and looking both ways. "The fucking driver better show."

"Relax Roman," she said in her calmest tone, not wanting to anger him further.

He stopped pacing and looked at her. He knew she was right, this was really no reason to get angry, but he was tired and just wanted to lie down right now. "Aren't you cold?" he asked, almost accusatory in tone. Her clothes were thin, she had to be cold.

"A little, but I'm alright. Don't worry, the car will show up eventually."

He snorted and walked back to the street.

She walked over to him and reached out to grab his jacket to get his attention. "Hey," she uttered, her voice soft and gentle.

He turned and looked down at her. The expression on her face was so very serene. Her eyes reflected the streetlights, giving her that otherworldly look she always got outside in the dark.

"Are you mad at me about something?" she asked, her brow furrowed slightly. The dimple she got in her chin when she was sad glared at him.

"No, kitten." He smiled slightly for her and put his hand on her shoulder. "I'm not mad at you about anything."

"Then why are you so agitated? Did Lux say something to piss you off?"

He exhaled and led her back away from the edge of the street. People randomly walked around them, making him feel awkward. He didn't want to have this conversation around people. Hell, he didn't want to have this conversation at all. "Lux always says something to piss me off. His mere existence pisses me off."

"Well, what were you guys talking about anyway? Whatever it was must have been funny considering I saw him laughing hysterically."

"Yeah, he always laughs at my expense," Roman said with all seriousness. "We didn't talk about anything terribly important."

She could tell by his tone of voice he had no intentions of telling her whatever it was they'd spoken about.

He walked back to the street, hailing the taxi that was driving toward them. It pulled over and they got in, finally shielded from the cold. The heat felt shockingly hot and uncomfortable in comparison to the frigid night air. Roman told the driver where to go and he settled back against the seat, slouching down and resting his head as he closed his eyes.

She looked over at him, wondering what was going on behind those closed lids. Something had gotten him riled up. This whole day had been so strange. A whirlwind of emotion. She looked out the window, watching the buildings and people zip by in silence like a scene from a movie. The glare on the glass from the street lights, tail lights, and neon signs made her think back to Christmas when she was a child. Her parents would take her on rides in the car to see Christmas lights. They would always drive over to Akron, and as a little girl that was like going to a big city. It was so different from where she grew up, surrounded by farm fields and forest, and it seemed so oddly magical. It was always so exciting and such a happy time, seeing the colored strings of lights against the white snow and backdrop of the city. She would always be hot and sleepy in her sweaters and thick fake fur coats, and invariably she'd fall asleep on the way home. Damn, she always loved those drives. She wished she could go back in time.

Roman moved against her, settling down against the seat. She rested her head on his shoulder, content to feel his body against her side. He never moved, never put his arm around her like he normally did when they sat like this in the backseat of a car. She closed her eyes and focused on the sounds of the engine. The way the heat blew through the vents, the sound of the cars whizzing by outside, the tires on the pavement. And then she noticed the song on the radio. Instinctively she wanted to smile or laugh because Def Leppard was one of those bands her and Steve liked to listen to for fun. But then the lyrics hit her and she nearly broke down crying because they just seemed so sad and perfect.

"I don't want to touch you too much, baby. 'Cause making love to you might drive me crazy. I know you think that love is the way you make it. So I don't want to be there when you decide to break it."

Was she really this choked up listening to Def Leppard? Joy Division? Sure. This Mortal Coil? Made sense. The Cure? Naturally. About a dozen other bands she could think of off the top of her head? Definitely. But Def Leppard? What the fuck was wrong with her? And the way Roman shifted beside her made her wonder if he was just as hit in the face as she was. Doubtful, he probably wasn't even listening, but the lyrics really couldn't be more accurate. And that was sad.

They pulled up in front of the hotel and walked to their room. Roman never spoke and barely made eye contact with her. When they got inside the room he walked straight to the bathroom. She walked over to where she'd piled her clothes and began undressing, putting the black t-shirt on, and her hair back up in a haphazard knot on top of her head. She was sleepy. It had been a long day and she wanted to wash her face and crawl into bed and fall asleep pressed against him. She was starting to get anxious to get back home, even though she didn't know what waited for them there. She was humming the song from the car thinking about just how sad those words made her feel. *I don't want to touch you too much, baby. 'Cause making love to you might drive me crazy.* She internally rolled her eyes and sighed.

He walked out of the bathroom and looked at her, pausing as she hummed the song quietly. He blinked his eyes and looked away then bent over, unlaced his boots, and kicked them against the wall with a thud that made Violet jump. He looked at her again and then pulled his shirt over his head and tossed it on the dresser, turning his back to her. He unbuckled his pants, leaving them open, and sat down on the end of the bed. He picked up the road atlas he'd brought with him and began looking through it. This behavior was so unlike his normal orderly and controlled self. He never just tossed anything down. He was obviously upset by something and it made her wonder what Lux had said to him when they'd been apart. It made her anxious to see him acting so unlike the usual.

She looked at his wound, noticing the bruise on his shoulder had lessened some. It was noticeably more healed than it had been in the morning. How was that possible?

She walked to the bathroom to get ready for bed. She brushed her teeth, then picked up the white wash cloth and lathered it up to wash her face. She rinsed the harsh soap from her face and looked at herself in the mirror. The rosy glow of her cheeks and clarity of her eyes made her look healthier than she'd looked in eons. Her mind wanted to go over all this crazy bullshit she'd been through in the last year so badly, but instead she stopped for a moment and looked down at the sink, that damn song still playing in her mind. It was so beautifully sad. And ridiculously cheesy, she knew. She would lose so many cool points if her friends found out she really liked that song, not that it mattered. She didn't give two fucks about being cool. It was just so odd.

The iridescent bubbles looked like dirty sea foam mixed with her makeup and the pearly white suds of the soap. She smoothed her fingers over the bubbles, so soft against the pads of her fingers. Suddenly a prayer came to mind, to whom she was praying she really didn't know, but she needed help. She needed to tell someone about how she wanted to be strong, and she wanted to be good, and she wanted to be there for Roman the way he had been there for her. She looked into the mirror and into her own eyes as if she was talking to someone. She stood there begging with her eyes and the words that flowed ceaselessly, seemingly of their own volition, in her mind. She finally blinked and then cleared her head and went back into the bedroom.

He was lying on his back with the TV on looking at her as she walked into the room. She no longer looked like a girl that was too young for him. That scared the fuck out of him, because if he couldn't see her that way then he'd have to force himself to deal with real emotions, feelings that he had never allowed himself to feel before. Things were getting too convoluted to ignore. Their lives were too entangled at this point to pretend she meant nothing to him anymore. Had she been just another woman he would have never let her leave this room at all the last two days. This getaway would have been about one thing, and one thing only. But he couldn't do that to her. She meant too much to him to just fuck and move on. God, she was soft and supple and beautiful. And if he had been less capable of controlling his mind and body he would have her here now, and as many times and ways possible, before they left, assuming she would want that too. He honestly had no idea what she thought or felt on the matter because there was no way he would talk about it with her if she didn't bring it up. But he couldn't do this. That fucking song said it better than he could. What the hell kind of bullshit was going on with his brain.

She went about her business, unaware he was watching her, or maybe aware and not caring. The lean muscles of her body flexed as she moved. She was toned, and feminine. Soft and strong at the same time. For a moment he remembered Lux's words and he couldn't imagine they could really be true. But then he recalled how much weight she'd been able to lift and how far she could run without any prior conditioning. The proof was there, he knew in his gut that what Lux had said was true. *What is she? What am I?* Human. He felt sickness growing in his gut. It stung like poison that felt like it was expanding and burning its way through his chest cavity and infecting his entire body. *He didn't want this life for her.*

He watched as she folded her stuff. There was a substantial pile of clothes that she'd amassed in the last two days, not including the several things she'd brought with her. She diligently folded and sorted. He'd never been around any woman long enough to really understand the need they had to buy things. That was a cliché, wasn't it? It seemed to make her ecstatic when she'd bought him the plates and blanket, or even a bag of chips at the store. There were all these clichés about women and shopping, apparently they were true? He felt his eyes giving under the weight of sleepiness, alcohol, and nausea. But mostly it was just plain exhaustion. His brain wanted out of this day, and so did his body.

Violet finished folding her things and flipped the light off, walking over to where he was sleeping. He looked distraught even in his sleep tonight and she feared she was the cause of this. She lay down on the bed beside him on her stomach and watched him, her legs bent at the knees, feet in the air like a teenager. She wanted to touch him, to smooth her fingers over his skin, as she listened to the faint rush of air when he inhaled and exhaled through his nose. She watched the rise and fall of his powerfully built chest, the roundness of his shoulders, the carved detail of his biceps, he was simply perfect. His body was, his look, everything about him, was perfect to her.

The throbbing pulse in his neck jumping rhythmically over and over and over struck her with fear as she suddenly realized that pulsing artery was the only thing keeping any of them alive. Life, and everything that she knew it to be, revolved around these pumping organs that no one had any control over. What told their hearts to keep beating, and when would that voice tell them to quit? Panic swept over her, through her, engulfing her, until she forced the thoughts away.

She studied the wound on his shoulder. *He could have died. Stop!* She furrowed her brow and focused again. The bruise was turning that yellowish green and black color, it was ugly, and it seemed to smear around the holes in his skin almost like some hideous tattoo. He looked like he'd been bitten by a dog. A big, vicious dog.

His eyes were closed tightly, brow creased into a scowl. His face was just so... his slightly parted lips, the long straight angle of his nose, those black lashes and brows... he was so beautiful. She felt her heart swell for a quick moment, as though it had beat an extra long time, as she looked him over.

Her fingers crept forward to touch him. His face was prickly with stubble, the dark shadow covering his jawline, around his mouth. She smoothed her fingers across his sideburns and then over his black eyebrows feeling his eyelashes tickle like a paint brush across the pads of her fingers. His eyes opened and he looked at her, surprised by the sudden intimacy. She smiled at him and felt the soft pink of his lips smiling back at her briefly beneath her fingertips. She continued to trace his features as he shut his eyes again and let her.

"Roman?" she said, barely audibly.

"Mmm hmm," he said, his voice a rumble, the deep baritone resonating in her chest.

"You don't have to be afraid of me," she said, placing her palm flat against his cheek.

He opened his eyes and looked at her again, her face so soft and sweet, and in that moment the idea that he could be afraid of her seemed ludicrous. But he was afraid. He was afraid of everything that having her in his life would mean. It was dangerous. Having to always keep her safe would be impossible. He'd have to worry about keeping her alive every second of the day and night.

"There's nothing to worry about," she said sweetly.

"There's a million and one things to worry about," he replied, and rubbed her cheek with his finger.

She closed her eyes and smiled. "Yeah, and there always will be. So, why worry about any of it?"

"I don't understand any of this, and I feel completely inept for the first time in my life. I was so much better off being a loner."

He looked scared to her, like she'd felt a hundred times in the past few weeks. And he looked genuinely confused and sad. "Don't say that," she said, rolling over on her back and staring up at the ceiling. "No one's better off alone." She laid her head on his arm and turned her face towards his, and rested her forehead against his cheek. "You don't have to have all the answers in one day."

"I don't want to leave you hanging because of my inability to think clearly."

"I'm not going anywhere," she said, closing her eyes

Her words were simple and effective. She had made him feel slightly better about the situation. He had been dreading this moment all evening, thinking she would want some sort of revelation from their earlier conversation, and knowing he wasn't capable of giving her anything. His stomach felt sick and overwhelmed. He rolled over on his side and wrapped his arm around her, resting his face against her breast. She was taken by surprise, but overwhelmed by his actions, as she knew that it probably took a lot for him to reach out to her in this way. His hand clutched her arm and she felt his warm breath on her skin. She smoothed his hair and rubbed his back, comforting him and squeezing him occasionally.

He hadn't been comforted by anyone since he was a child. It felt good. "My stomach hurts," he muttered.

"My poor baby," she said with sympathy. She rubbed his back and squeezed him again.

My poor baby. That felt good too.

12

HOME

SHE OPENED HER EYES slowly. The soft morning light was filtering in through the gaudy floral drapes. Roman hadn't moved all night and neither had she. It pained her that she'd have to move him now, because she enjoyed the closeness and hated to disturb him. Slowly she lifted up off the bed, urging him to roll over in his deep sleep. He complied, turning onto his other side and reaching for the blanket and pulling it around his shoulders. She walked quietly to the bathroom, except for the cracking of her ankles as she took each step. Her ankles were stupid. She had never been able to sneak up on anyone because of her cracking ankles. She sat down on the toilet with her eyes still closed, and felt herself falling back asleep. She finished peeing, then washed her hands, and walked back to the bed, crawling in behind him and putting her arm around him. Her still damp hands felt cold against his warm stomach and made his muscles clench. He moved his arm, allowing her to tuck hers beneath his and held onto her hand. He rolled back onto his back and groaned as he wiped his eyes with his other hand.

"I wonder what time it is," he mumbled.

"I don't know," she whispered, not wanting to open her eyes but doing so anyway. She turned her head to look at the digital clock on the side table. "It's nine o'clock."

"Fuck. I guess we should probably get up and get out of here."

"I wish we could sleep for like a month straight," she said, as she pressed her face against his bare shoulder. The truth was neither one of them wanted to get back to reality.

"Yeah, that would be nice, but I guess we're going to have to get up or we're going to have cleaning staff hovering over us soon," he said, sitting up and stretching.

She watched as the muscles of his back bunched and elongated beneath his skin, moving like some sort of serpent trapped beneath the white flesh. She noticed the map of scars, some had clearly been deep.

"I'll go take a shower so you can sleep a little longer," he said.

He looked back at her and then stood up and made his way to the bathroom.

She turned over and looked at the television they hadn't bothered to turn off the night before. The news was on and once again she felt oddly uncomfortable at how weirdly off it seemed. Watching this same basic routine, but with different people, a different set, in a different city, was off-putting for some reason. She wanted to go back to sleep so badly, but she knew he wouldn't be long, and that she probably wouldn't be able to fall asleep anyway. She was looking forward to getting back home, if for nothing more than the familiarity of it, even if she wasn't looking forward to whatever was ahead. But what she did want was to be in her own bed, surrounded by her things, with her friends, in her town. She had enjoyed Chicago, and if she had to move this would be the place, but she realized her home wasn't as bad as she had once thought it was.

She stood up and stretched. Her spine cracked, the shock of which scared her immediately and simultaneously felt unbelievably good. The "killer" shirt was sitting on the dresser and caught her eye. She pulled her t-shirt off and put his shirt on. It came down to her knees and the sleeves were nearly to her wrists. The rest of her clothes were strewn about. Black leggings and socks were what she chose to wear with the *killer* shirt.. She wasn't going to shower. She just wanted to get on the road once he was ready. It took a few minutes to pack up the rest of her stuff and set it by the door. She put her boots on and sat back on the bed staring at the television. Ugh, she was so tired.

Roman stood under the cold water allowing his body to wake up. He felt nauseous, and surmised it was the combination of greasy pizza, alcohol, and tension. He took the tiny bar of soap and washed his body. He stood for a few more minutes, attempting to calm his stomach and wake up a little more, and then got out and dried himself off. He brushed his teeth, towel dried his hair, then pulled it back away from his face. She was laying back on the bed with her eyes closed when he walked back into the room.

"Hey, you're wearing my shirt," he said, kicking her boot with his foot.

She jumped and sat up with a smirk. "Yeah, I figured since it isn't really your style I'd keep it for myself. That way it'll always remind me of you when you take off and leave me." She grinned at him, obviously kidding, but the words hit him like a ton of bricks.

He looked away and found the shirt he'd been wearing for the past two days and pulled it over his head. Ordinarily he would fold his clothes but instead he shoved his things into his duffle bag and zipped it up. He fastened his belt buckle and reached for his boots, which he'd kicked against the wall the night before. He sat down on the foot of the bed, pulling them on and lacing them.

"Hey, I was kidding," she said, leaning against him. He didn't say anything, just continued lacing his boots. "Roman?"

"I know you were kidding," he said, looking over at her briefly, flashing his dark green eyes, and then went back to his task. "It's just not funny."

"Sorry," she said, sarcasm dripping from the words, and stood up and went into the bathroom.

She spent far too much time trying to wash the tiredness from her eyes, stalling from going back to the inevitable uncomfortable conversation that was waiting for her in the other room. She brushed her teeth and then breathed deeply several times, before walking back into the bedroom where he was standing there waiting for her.

"I didn't mean that like it came out," he said, trying to explain his statement. "I just meant, I don't find it funny that I'm going to have to move on after this."

She stared at him for a long moment looking angry with him. He didn't say anything, but took the brunt of her glare.

"Why?" she asked, placing her hands on her hips and jutting one foot forward. She looked like a defiant teenager.

"Why what?"

"Why do you have to move on?"

"It isn't obvious? Vampires won't come running to me, Violet."

"Yeah, well, what does that have to do with *me*? You have to stop being my friend because you have to go hunt down some vampires? Lots of people have to travel with their work, Roman, and lots of them have friends and even, *gasp*, families."

He was befuddled by her ability to make his life seem no different from any other job. *He killed vampires.* That wasn't normal to anyone but him. She didn't seem to take it very seriously at all, almost as if he was just a traveling salesman or some businessman.

"It's not that easy. I'm not selling encyclopedias. I could get myself, or you and your friends, killed."

Violet rolled her eyes. "No one sells encyclopedias anymore."

Roman exhaled. "You know what I meant."

"Yeah, I do."

They stared at each other for a moment.

"So? Women marry marines and cops and lion tamers every day. That crap is dangerous too. So, why do you feel like you can't have friends and family?"

He had never thought of it in that context before. *Lion tamers?* That almost made him snicker. But it didn't matter. "Violet, my mom cried herself to sleep every night wondering if my father was going to come home. Why would I put anyone through that?"

"Obviously your mom didn't mind too much, she stayed, right? So it was hard, I'm sure the good far outweighed the bad. Stop making yourself into such a martyr. I think you enjoy pain and loneliness a little too much and you're looking for excuses to run."

Those comments pissed him off. She knew nothing about his life, or the hell it had been for him or his family. She had no right to offer advice on the subject. "It's not as simple as you're making it out," he said with obvious irritation in his voice.

"You know, you're right, and I'm not going to sit here and beg you, or try to convince you of anything. Obviously it's irrelevant, and so am I." She bent over and picked her bags up and stood by the door turning her back on him. She was fighting tears for the thousandth time in his presence. "Let's just go already," she said, dropping her head and resting her chin against her chest.

He stood still for a few moments, bewildered again as to how these conversations kept turning so ugly. All this angst because of a joke she'd made that he couldn't just laugh about. Instead he had to vilify her and make her the enemy again. Since the "little girl" thing wasn't working anymore he was resorting to making her his adversary. His defense mechanisms were destroying the only friendship he'd ever had. And she had been so kind to him last night, coddling him like *he* was a child. He walked over to her and put his arm around her, pulling her back against his chest.

"I'm sorry," he apologized, squeezing her and tucking his face into her messy hair. She still smelled like the smoke machine fog from the club the night before and the sweet scent of flowers from whatever shampoo she used.

She leaned back against him, accepting his apology and cherishing the feeling of intimacy and warmth his words gave to her. She turned around and wrapped her arms around his waist and hugged him. "Just stop worrying so much, Roman. Don't you think God knows what He's doing?"

"What does God have to do with this?" he said, pulling his face back and looking down at her skeptically. Hadn't she been the one to question all that?

"Well, nothing happens accidentally, right?" she said, looking up at him, resting her chin against his chest.

He looked at her for a long moment. She had changed a thousand different ways since the day they met. He brushed the stray strands of hair away and held her face. "You really are going to be the death of me."

"Well, I am *a killer*, see?" she said, and laughed, referring to the word on her chest.

If she only knew how true those words might be.

"Thanks for taking care of me last night," he said, tightening his arms around her.

"It's about time I returned the favor. Let's go already." She pulled away from him and waited for him to open the door.

He picked his duffle bag up and looked around the room to make sure he hadn't forgotten anything. "Let's go eat free breakfast."

"Good idea."

She had dozed off three times on the drive and hadn't really talked much. It gave him time to think about the things she'd said. Some of it had made sense. He knew that to his mom, his father had meant the world. She had sacrificed any hopes of normalcy for him. And even though she cried a lot, she was happy most of the time. No one's life is ever perfect, right? Maybe it's someone's job that makes them cry, or a disease they never asked for, but no one ever lived a *perfect* life--right? And if she was as Lux said, then wouldn't she be more than capable of defending herself? She could come with him, or stay at home, and he wouldn't have to worry as much about her being able to defend herself like his father had always worried about him and his mom.

It was insane that she had caused such a change in his mindset in such a few short weeks. Never for one moment had he ever wanted a life with someone. When he was twelve years old he had decided that he would never, ever have a wife or a family, and she had caused him to rethink that in just a few short weeks. His problem was that he was always too methodical and calculated. But, of course, that is what had kept him alive to this point. But human beings and their emotions weren't logical. As he looked over at her curled up on the seat beside him he couldn't imagine going back to the world of being completely alone. He didn't want to be alone anymore. It was completely irrational, but he didn't want to be alone. Lux and Mylori had known what he had refused to even allow himself to consider. But it was true. *He loved this woman.*

They were nearly home when he finally decided he better talk to her about what she'd asked him. What were they? He wasn't even entirely sure, but he knew he didn't want to leave her.

She had awakened for the third time and was singing along to some hideously bad country song on the radio, her bare feet resting on the dashboard. She was munching on the chocolate covered peanuts he'd bought at the last rest stop, which she'd slept through.

He was amped from the five cups of coffee he'd consumed since leaving Chicago that morning. His stomach still felt queasy and he was determined to stop eating pizza once and for all, failing to realize it wasn't the pizza that had made him sick, it was all of these strange revelations.

"You need to teach me to fight and stuff when we get back," she said, looking over at him. Her cheeks were still red from sleep and her hair was beyond tangled.

"Yeah, we can start tomorrow," he said, preparing himself for the conversation he wanted to start. How does one just start these conversations? What kind of segue way was appropriate?

I'll teach you to kill vampires. Oh, by the way, will you be my girlfriend?

"Duuuuhhhhh..." he said out loud, laughing at himself.

"Um, okay?" she said, wrinkling up her nose and popping another piece of candy in her mouth.

He looked over at her and laughed. He was thirty one years old and had no idea how to navigate these waters. Sure, if she was a stranger, he could pick her up in a bar, not that he really did that, but that would be easy compared to this. That wasn't much different from hunting vampires.

"You're odd," she said, and sang along with another bad song.

"How do you know all the words to these songs, miss punk rock?"

"Because I used to listen to all this when I was little. My parents listened to it. So there," she said snidely, snubbing her nose at him and taking a drink of the diet pop he had also gotten her.

He looked over at her and smiled and then his face went very straight

"What?" she asked, concerned about the lack of expression on his face.

"Nothing, just..." He looked back at the road, completely at a loss for how to proceed. "You know I'm completely inept in regards to relationships, friendship or otherwise." He looked over at her, pausing for a moment at the stymied look on her face, and then looked back at the road. "I've had more time to think now. Maybe I can give you a proper answer regarding what you asked me yesterday at dinner."

She felt her stomach flip nervously in fearful anticipation about what he might say, fully expecting to hear about how he needed to move on, she was a great girl, blah, blah, blah.

"I think you're probably right. Although, in terms of my actual job, it would realistically be smarter for me to be alone. But I don't want to go back to that." He looked over at her, expecting her to laugh at him or something equally as horrific, but she just smiled at him like a happy girl. "I feel stupid," he said, leaning his head back against the seat.

"Don't feel stupid," she said, sympathetic to his feelings.

She completely understood the awkwardness of initiating such a conversation, as she had been far too shy at one point to ever do such a thing herself. In fact, if

Mark hadn't pursued her she would probably have been single to this very day. Despite the fact that she liked to play it off like she was all that sometimes, in reality it was all a façade. There had never been a time in her life that she believed she was worth much of anything. She was completely insecure and always had been.

"I don't want to lose you. The thought of going back to living alone... I don't want that life anymore. I know it's foolish. You could get killed."

He paused for a moment, trying to convince himself to back away, to make the gravity of the situation more important than his feelings. But he couldn't. He looked at her. He didn't want a life without her. It was terrifying.

"Violet, I am dead serious about that. You would be better off far away from me," he said, hoping she understood the real threat being with him meant for her life. Hoping, maybe, she'd be stronger than he was and would run far away from this.

She looked at him, her brow furrowed slightly, but she reached out and touched his leg in comfort, coaxing him to continue. He looked away from her and back to the road ahead.

"But things aren't how I originally thought they were. Your life isn't what I thought it was," he said, hesitating for a moment before he continued. "I don't know how this will all work. I'm completely inept, and I imagine I will not be very good at making you happy." He looked over at her briefly again and then back at the road. "I envy you for all the relationships you've had with humans."

"There's nothing about my life that should make you feel envious, Roman." *Humans?* Odd that a person would clarify something like that. His life really had been strange. "It's not like I've been so successful. You met Mark."

Roman chuckled. "I meant, humans in general, not boyfriends."

"Besides, you already make me happy. So, just keep doin' what you're doin'."

He looked over at her and shook his head. "I don't know how this will work out, but I don't want to go back to a life without you."

"Aw," she said, cooing like a little girl looking at a basket of kittens. She reached over and squeezed his arm.

"Oh God," he said, wincing and pulling his arm away from her. He felt really stupid and insecure.

"I love you too, puppywuppkins," she said, pinching his cheek.

He grinned at her and looked away. "Okay, I can go back to being a manly-man now that all this emotional crap is straightened out. You know how I feel now, right?"

"Uh huh," she said and popped another candy in her mouth. She reached over and put one in his mouth too. "No need to torture yourself anymore. I know all these girlie emotions and stuff are hard for you big strong macho types."

Violet acted like it was no big deal because she knew just how hard this conversation had to have been for him. Inside she was soaring, but she wasn't going to make a federal case out of the whole thing and scare the shit out of him. Instead, she started singing along with the radio again.

He felt relieved, although he was well aware how pathetic his delivery had been. He was sure she still must have some sort of questions, or something, considering his bumbling. "You'll have to be patient with me, V. I'm not very good at this relationship stuff."

"Obviously I'm not either, dork," she said, giggling.

He smiled at her and reached over and grabbed her hand and held it tightly. It felt different to him now. Like it was *his* hand and he was finally allowed to touch her without having a wall around himself. It was all so strange and awkward and good.

She smiled at him and squeezed him back.

It felt good to be home. She took a deep breath as they walked across the lawn to the backdoor and into the kitchen. Amber and Randy were in the living room watching television. Violet ran into the room squealing like a little girl and tossed the bags down on the floor. Amber stood up and hugged her friend, squeezing her tightly and spinning her around. Roman lumbered behind her, sat down in the red chair, and said hello to Randy. Watching the two girls, so happy to see each other, was yet more proof of how isolated he'd been. No one reacted like that to him.

"I got you guys some cool stuff," Violet said, flopping to the floor and shuffling through the bags. She found the purse and hat she'd gotten them the first day there, and the cool silver ring and leather studded belt she'd bought them, too.

"Cool, thanks, man," Randy said, shoving the hat down over his limp mohawk and standing to wrap the belt around his waist.

"Thanks Vi, I really love this," Amber said, looking at the gifts.

Violet proceeded to tell them all the places they'd gone, and about the interesting shops she'd visited, and how lame the club was they'd been to. "It would have been fun had you guys been there though. We could have at least jumped around like idiots."

"What? Roman wouldn't do that with you?" Randy laughed, knowing there was no way in hell that could have happened. Picturing it was humorous.

Roman laughed and shook his head. "No, I just sat there like a stick in the mud."

"Well, anyway, we had fun," Violet said, looking over at him and then back to her friend.

"Okay, you have to tell me the real story now," Amber said, grabbing Violet's wrist, pulling her up off the floor, and dragging her to the kitchen. "What's going on? You better give me the real details. Spill it, Violet." Amber smiled, not letting go of Violet.

"What?" Violet asked with a smirk on her face, knowing full well what information she was referring to.

187

"Stop it."

"Okay, the truth is I'm not sure what's going on. I know he likes me, but it's complicated, and so we're just going slow or whatever," Violet said, feeling her cheeks warm.

"So, did you guys do it?"

"No. I said going slow!"

"Hey, going slow means different things to different people. Fucking isn't always lumped in with going slow."

"And that is weird," Violet said, as though that was a given. "I haven't even kissed him, you slut."

Amber tilted her head to the side and closed her eyes slightly, sizing up her friend. "So, why did you go to Chicago anyway?"

"It's a really long story, Amber. And I promise I'll tell you everything. But later, okay? I *promise* I'll tell you everything."

"Okay, but you better tell me tonight. I want to know, damnit," Amber scolded, then hugged Violet again.

Yep, it was good to be home with her friends. Violet carried her things up to her room, flipping the light on and looked over at her answering machine. There were several messages blinking. She hit the play button as she started putting her clothes away or tossing them in the hamper. Most of the calls were hang ups and the few that weren't were of someone laughing.

Roman walked into the room. "What's that?" he asked, regarding the maniacal laughter on the machine.

"I don't know, probably Mark or something," she said in dismissal. She didn't want to think too hard about the possibilities or she'd get scared again.

"I'm going to go home, Violet. Are you going to come with me or stay here?"

The thought of him leaving sent a chill through her body, but she rationalized the situation and calmed herself down. "I guess I'll stay home tonight. I want to hang out with those guys and tell them more about the trip and stuff."

"Are you going to tell them why we went to Chicago?"

"I'm not sure if I'll tell them tonight. I know I should probably just get it over with, but I'm so mentally exhausted from the trip. Plus I know they'll freak out about it, and I don't want to scare them. I understand why you tried to hide this from me now," she said, setting the empty bags down and walking towards him.

"I don't want to leave you here alone. Something could happen," he said, putting his hands on her shoulders.

"I'll be alright," she said, trying to reassure him with a smile.

He hugged her tightly, not wanting to let go. He knew he'd worry all night wondering if she was okay. They were going to have to start training. There was a lot for her to learn, and the faster she was able to protect herself, the more relieved he would be, especially when he wasn't around.

"We'll start training tomorrow, okay? The quicker you can protect yourself the better. If you get freaked out at all, or anything weird happens, call me."

"I will, why would I stop running to you for protection now?" She laughed and rubbed her hand across his back.

"This is so weird," he said, not wanting to let go.

"You should stay," she suggested, not really wanting him to leave.

"Yeah, well, I should probably at least look in on the apartment I pay for."

"So, do that and come back." She leaned back away from him and looked up at his face.

"I can do that."

It was odd that wasn't already the plan since they hadn't spent much time apart lately. But somehow now that they were, whatever they were, it seemed less casual, like he couldn't just invite himself into her bed to spend the night.

"It's so nice to finally be able to lust after you." She grinned devilishly.

"What?" he said, startled. It was weird hearing things like that from her now that they were *whatever*.

"Well, you know, before I was supposed to be treating you as a *big brother* or something, and that's just kind of gross. Now that you're--well, whatever it is you are--I can officially look at you differently." She walked away from him and started picking the empty shopping bags up off the floor and putting them in her trash can.

"Yeah, I get what you're saying," he responded.

She looked back at him and grinned and walked over to him. "So, you're going to come back?"

"Yeah, after I do some stuff."

She wanted him to kiss her, but she wasn't about to push her little squirrel at the park by running up on him too quickly.

"I'll see you later," he said, and patted her on the head.

A pat on the head. Nothing said *boyfriend* like a good old grandpa-like pat on the head. "What's next? A Werther's Original?" she said with a chuckle. "Wanna watch the Matlock Marathon tonight when you come back?"

"Huh?"

The perplexed look on his face made her laugh harder.

"Nothing, sweets," she said, following him to the door, quite pleased with her own sense of humor.

She filled the tub with hot water and slid into it, relishing the heat. The contrast from the air in the room to the hot water gave her goosebumps. Her muscles clenched, and then her body acclimated itself to the change. She slid beneath the water, letting her hair soak through and then sat up and leaned against the back of the tub.

Amber knocked on the door. Violet told her it was okay to come in, and she walked over and sat down on the floor and leaned back against the wall.

"So, tell me what all happened. What's going on?" Amber said.

Violet took a deep breath. She was just going to be out with it. She was going to tell her friend the whole truth, as she would need to know eventually anyway.

"Okay, prepare yourself for something really weird," Violet said, tilting her chin down and looking at her friend with raised eyebrows.

"Okay..." Amber said, raising an eyebrow of her own.

"Well, you know that murder that happened last week at the store that Roman and I witnessed?"

"Yeah?" Amber said, drawing out the word with trepidation.

"Geez, this is going to sound insane..."

"What?" Amber asked, fearing she might tell her something like Roman and she had been the murderers, and had to skip town all Bonnie and Clyde style.

"Well, I'm not sure how to tell you this, but the guys who did it were vampires."

Amber's face twisted in confusion, her head jerking back in stunned surprise. "What?"

"Seriously, Amber. I saw it with my own eyes. They attacked us. They had fangs and everything." Amber looked at her friend with skepticism. "You know I wouldn't lie to you, right?"

"Yeah," Amber said, still unsure if her friend was pulling some joke or something. *Vampires?*

"Amber, there's more to it. Roman kills them. That's why he came here."

"To kill vampires?" Amber said, lowering her voice doubt.

"I promise you, Amber. I'm not making this up. There are vampires here. In Mantua. I saw them. Actually, so did you." Violet looked deeply into her friend's eyes, conveying the seriousness of what she was saying.

"What are you talking about?" Amber asked, leaning forward. "I never saw any..."

"Lux and Mylori."

"Lux and Mylori are vampires? Come on," Amber said with a chuckle.

"Amber, I'm not lying to you. You know I'm not lying to you. You had to notice the way you felt when they were here?"

"Yeah, I felt weird, but I just figured it was because I was tired, or drunk, or something."

"We went to see them in Chicago, that's why we had to go," Violet said, trying to convince her friend. She explained all Lux had told her, and all the things she'd seen, in great detail. She also told her Roman's history and how the woman Cecelia was out to get her, and that Roman was going to protect them.

Amber sat in dumbfounded silence, absorbing all that Violet told her. She didn't know whether to laugh or lock every door and window in the house and never go outside after dark again. She could tell by the earnestness of Violet's words she was telling the truth. Plus, her friend had no reason to make up such an outlandish story anyway.

The water had grown lukewarm, and Violet's fingers and toes were pruned. "I need to get out of this bathtub," she said, reaching for the towel beside the tub and standing to wrap it around her torso.

Amber sat perfectly still, looking at the linoleum. How the hell was she supposed to react to this?

"Amber, I can have Roman explain this to you in better detail. I don't really understand much about it myself. He's going to teach me to fight them so that I can protect myself."

"And Lux has been watching you since you were little? That wasn't really a dream you had? The dream about the vampire climbing out your window and the fur and all that...it wasn't a dream?"

"No, weird huh?"

"Um, just a little. Okay, I'm terrified now."

"I know. So am I, but Roman isn't going to let anything happen to us."

"And how the hell could he protect us from freaking vampires? He's just a human being like us? Even if he is all giant muscle mountain man, or whatever. Unless he's one too or something?"

Violet laughed. "Amber, don't be dumb. He's been training since he was a kid. His family has been doing this for, like, centuries and junk."

"Hey, how would I know?"

"Well, for starters, you've seen him outside during the day."

"I guess." Amber was quiet for a long moment. "I'm never going outside after dark again."

"I know how you feel."

"He's coming back over here isn't he?" Panic swept through her as she looked at Violet for safety.

"Yeah."

"Good, because I don't think I want to be here without him considering there's a freaking *vampire* out to get you."

"Yeah, that's pretty much how I feel about it too."

"This is fucked up." Amber's face was turning red and her eyes looked glossy. She was bewildered, and unclear how she should process this information.

"I know, Amber, why do you think I've been so wigged out lately?"

"I just thought, well, with your mom and dad, and then the drama with Mark...I wish you had told me sooner," Amber said, looking up at her friend.

"I know, I just didn't understand it myself and didn't know what to say."

"Can I tell Randy?" she asked, sliding up the wall and back to her feet.

"Of course."

He needed some alone time. After the last couple of days, he'd had no time to really digest it all. The crap with Lux alone was enough to throw him, but the decision to give this relationship a go was just downright mind boggling. He walked in the dark apartment as he'd done thousands of times before. Not this particular apartment necessarily, but a hundred just like it, some better and some far worse. He tossed his keys down on the table and walked to the bedroom. He actually liked this one. He could get comfortable here. He flipped the light on and sat down on the bed, taking in a deep breath and laying back onto the firm mattress. The room still smelled like her. She had a sweet flowery smell, which he thought appropriate given her name.

The last two days had been the most bizarre of his life. A lot had been thrown at him very quickly, most notably the whole revelation about relationships and the insight into Lux's complex and mysterious brain. Lux was the last thing he wanted to be thinking about right now though, so he pushed those thoughts aside and thought about Violet instead. There would be a lot to do in the next few days, or weeks, depending on how long they had. She needed to learn a lot, though he had no doubt she'd excel. He may be physically stronger than her, but her instincts would be better, at least he thought so, for whatever reason. Probably just wishful thinking on his part, but he'd take it. He needed to believe she'd be okay, and that she could defend herself if necessary.

What would they do once this was all over and Cecelia was dead? He couldn't stop. There would never be an end to his duties. And he'd never done anything else. Would she accompany him, or wait behind like his mother always had? He also realized it wouldn't necessarily be up to him to make this decision. She was strong willed and pretty much got what she wanted. Besides, it was her life too and it wasn't right to think he could dictate to her. He wouldn't dictate to her. That was fucked up. How could he refuse her anyway? Even Lux hadn't been able to refuse her.

He pulled himself up off the bed and went and showered. His stomach was rumbling with hunger so he walked to the kitchen and opened the refrigerator. Of course there was nothing available. He called the pizza place, already failing in his attempt to *not eat pizza ever again*, then went and got dressed and waited for the food to arrive. He turned on the television and allowed his brain to become sucked into some inane program regarding home improvement. He now fully understood how to tile a floor and install baseboards, not that this skill would ever come in handy, he supposed. The pizza arrived and he ate.

The house was dark when he pulled in the driveway except for the faint peach colored light which radiated from her room. She'd probably still be awake, perusing some magazine or writing her thoughts down in one of her notebooks. He hadn't realized how seriously she took that until he'd seen the stacks of notebooks piled in haphazard columns beside her dresser the last time he'd been in her room post decluttering. He wished he could pick them up and survey every thought she'd had for the last ten years. What a fascinating read that would be. There were probably passages dedicated to the first time she'd kissed someone, or the first time she'd loved someone. He could only imagine. He was probably better off not knowing.

He saw her silhouette appear like an all-seeing shadow in the window, and then disappear as quickly as it had come. He walked up onto the front porch and waited for her. The lights flashed as she turned them on one by one, making her way towards the front of the house. The door opened and she stood there with a big smile splayed across her tender face, the soft pink velour of her pajamas reflected against the milkiness of her complexion. She took his hand and pulled his body against hers, hugging him fully. This all felt so strange and awkward to him. He hadn't freely received affection in almost twenty years, at least not affection that didn't come at some price. Of course her affection came at a price too. That price was a fear he'd never known before and had always hoped to avoid. There wouldn't be a time from this moment forward that he wouldn't be scared to death of her being killed.

She led him upstairs to her bedroom, neither of them uttering a word. He remembered that first time she'd invited him upstairs and some of the same thoughts were swirling around in his head now that he'd had that night. As suspected, a notebook was open in the middle of her bed, red ink coagulated and skittering across blue lined paper, in the middle of crumpled blankets. She scooped the journal up and tossed it to the floor.

"I told Amber," she said, sitting down on the edge of the bed.

Roman looked down at his soft, pink angel and didn't say anything, knowing she would continue. Her eyes were wide and glossy in the low light of the room, her lips moist looking as she licked them between sentences.

"She didn't believe me at first, I don't think, but I convinced her I was telling the truth. She's pretty freaked out," Violet said.

"Naturally," he said, taking his jacket off and setting it down beside the door.

There was a different look in his eye, a new feeling being conveyed through those dark green orbs. She knew that look with great familiarity, but she'd never seen it in him before now. This was the first time they'd been alone like this since the car ride back from Chicago when he'd finally told her he had real feelings for her and wanted to try to have a relationship. So what would happen now? Would he want to sleep with her right now? Would tonight be the night that something physical happened? It wasn't that she would mind, she'd thought about that a lot, more than she should have been thinking about it actually. But now that Roman really liked her as more than just some random girl he had to protect, would he want to have sex with her? God, she felt nervous and awkward. Like she was on a first date. Which she supposed would make her a slut for even thinking about giving herself to him. She internally rolled her eyes at herself for over analyzing everything. She hated people who looked way too far into everything instead of just letting things be as they were meant to be. Ah, but she couldn't be one of those brainless idiot types, and as she watched him standing there she wondered what was going to happen.

"Is she alright?" he asked, sitting down beside her, his eyes had never left hers since they'd come up to her room. He saw her so completely differently now. It was mind boggling how once he'd allowed himself to open up to the possibility of having her really in his life she no longer looked like some young feeble girl he had to protect. Now she looked like his woman. The person he would kill anyone or anything to protect. Fuck, he was whipped. If vampires feared him before, they should be terrified of him now. He would kill his way through thousands of them if it meant keeping her safe.

"She'll be alright. The fact is she'll probably handle all this better than I did. She's pretty unflappable." She lay back on the bed, placing her feet against his leg.

How could Amber handle anything better than Violet? It hadn't seemed like much for her to accept all the craziness she'd learned in the past week.

He looked down at her little toes curled over the top of his thigh. Her feet were pretty. He'd never been one to think about feet. But hers were cute. The petite silver painted nails sparkled with metallic flecks. Blue veins mapped the surface of her white skin, rising above the thin frail bones of her feet. Her toes were perfectly straight. He found that enthralling for some reason, probably because his were crooked from being broken. He'd never seen a perfect little foot like hers before. Then again, he hadn't looked at anyone's foot before. Why would he?

He looked back at her again thinking about what she'd just said, amazed that she and her friends so easily accepted insanity. Were they so adaptable, or did they just truly not grasp the danger of it all? He supposed it didn't really matter either way. Her mouth drew his attention again, the softness of her lips, the way she nervously bit the bottom one and looked away from him briefly and back again.

It was as if two very separate entities inside of him were operating. One was completely fixed and honed in on her and what she was telling him, and the other was distracted by her beauty. It was truly the first time he'd allowed himself to really look at her completely. There had been fleeting moments prior, but now he'd given himself permission, and looking at her was like giving a glass of water to a dying man in the desert.

"Are you sleepy?" she asked, trying to distract him. She was mildly intimidated by the vibe he was sending. It wasn't because she was afraid of him in any way, but because it was unfamiliar coming from him. Seeing him look at her like that made her feel shy. He was like a stalking panther or something and she had no idea how to handle this.

"I'm sleepy," he said, looking away from her finally and rubbing his eyes. He knew he must have been looking at her like she was a giant steak, and he was starved.

She didn't ask him about removing his clothes to get comfortable this time. Everything was different now and she was unsure how to even act to a degree. It was easier when she had just had a secret crush on him or only thought of him as the "big brother". It's much the same way a girl can act differently around a girl or a gay male friend than she can around a potential boyfriend. It was okay for your friend to grab your tits, not okay for a dude on a first date. Well, no one should be grabbing anyone's tits without permission, but whatever. She internally rolled her eyes. Why the hell were her thoughts rambling like an idiot? Whatever. The point was still valid. She stood up and pulled the covers back. It was getting too cold to sleep without them now. She waited for him to move and crawled beneath the warm quilt, tucking herself in tightly.

Roman stood up and turned his back to her and removed his boots. He pulled his shirt out of his pants and loosened his belt. He had no intention of making this any more awkward than it needed to be. He could tell by her demeanor she was as borderline frightened by what was ahead for them as he was. After all, her road hadn't exactly been easy either. He still hadn't fully accepted that any of this could even be possible, and there was no way he would jump in and screw things up from the start. He flipped the light switch by the door, and crawled across the bed, lying flat on his stomach and snaking his hands beneath the cold pillow. She turned her face towards his and smiled at him. It was going to be hard being a gentleman.

God, he was so hot, his face was so perfect and beautiful. The way his brow creased like he was scowling even when he wasn't, those lush lips, his perfect nose. She wished he would just breach the distance and kiss her. She bit her bottom lip thinking about it and then he smiled the faintest smile at her, the movement just reaching his eyes.

She wished her mom and dad could be here to know him. They would be happy she was spending time with someone so genuinely good and unwaveringly kind to her. They had never seen that in the choices she'd made while they were living. It stung her deeply, thinking back to the times her mom had cried as she'd told her to make better choices and to get rid of the people sucking the life out of her. Her mom had been the one to watch her sit and cry as she'd waited by the phone for one of them to call. How many times had she done that? How many times had she sat there staring out the window waiting for his car to roll up the driveway only to get a call several hours later that he'd forgotten? You don't forget someone you love. And that right there was the answer. There was no love. There was possession and obsession, but no love.

Her mom had always regarded Mark with skepticism, and the only reason she hadn't disliked him completely was because she had a good heart and couldn't totally relegate someone to being "bad". But her father had flat out disliked Mark, because Mark had never been able to look him directly in the eye. Her dad wouldn't trust anyone who couldn't look him in the eye. It was a barometer he had used with everyone and had always been able to catch Violet in her little teenage lies with that trick. Mark had known that her father would have probably broken every bone in his body if he'd known exactly what he was doing to his daughter, and in his own house. So Mark had always avoided her dad if he could.

Her thoughts drifted back and she focused again on Roman, who lay there quietly, doing nothing more than pondering her. He drew the soft contour of her mouth with his eyes concentrating on the arch of her upper lip as it pointed like a little M. Her bottom lip was pouted naturally giving her the appearance that she was always slightly sad even when the rest of her face was smiling and lit up with enthusiasm. Her bangs dusted jaggedly across her forehead, her hair in tangled cords over her shoulders, concealing her neck. He took his hand from beneath the pillow and lifted the hair and let it fall over her shoulder and behind her back so that he could see her features more clearly. His fingers slightly brushing against her skin caused her eyes to close briefly, involuntarily intoxicated by the gentleness of his touch. He smiled at her, cradling her chin with his index finger and thumb.

"Good night," he said.

His voice was low and grumbly. The tone of it moved through her limbs and sat in her chest warmly. She rolled onto her side and lifted her arm from beneath the covers and ran the back of her hand across his cheek and let it rest in the crook of his neck. His pulse gently thumped against her warm hand.

"Good night."

She opened her eyes. It was dark in the room, which felt strange to her. The night light had burned out sometime while they'd been sleeping. She looked at the clock. It was five in the morning. The sun would be rising fairly soon. She looked over at Roman, whose eyes were still tightly closed in perfect rest. He hadn't moved an inch since she'd last looked at him. She wondered how he'd been able to sleep so soundly given her usual rambunctious sleep habits. She peeled the blanket back and tiptoed across the room. She slid her dresser drawers open, finding her tracksuit, a pair of socks, and a bra, and then snuck across the hall to the bathroom. She got ready and pulled her hair back in a knotted up ponytail and walked down the steps to the kitchen. Amber would be getting up soon to get ready for work. Now would be a good time to go running and get back in time to see her, and Roman would never even realize she was gone. She opened the refrigerator and found a bottle of water and drank it as she ate a granola bar. After she finished her breakfast, she found her old sneakers in the laundry room piled in the back of the closet.

She tucked the silver heart into her sweatshirt and grabbed her keys off the table and walked outside. The metal of the chain and pendant acclimated to her body's temperature making it less cold against her still sleep-warmed skin. She needed to figure out a better way of carrying her keys besides tucking them into her bra. It felt annoying against her skin.

The first frost of the season had crystallized the damp ground, covering every surface that had been exposed to the night sky. A thin layer of white dust covered everything reminding her of winter, which would be here very soon. It looked beautiful.

She walked out to the street and started jogging. White clouds puffed from her mouth as she exhaled. She felt nauseous from all the water she'd guzzled and the heaviness of the granola bar, but she knew it would pass as she fell into the rhythm of running.

She wasn't entirely sure why she'd decided she needed to start jogging today, or why she wanted to go alone. It just felt right. Maybe just being back home, the reality of whatever was coming, it made her want this physicality. She needed the time with her own thoughts.

The air was sharp and cold in her lungs, her chest cavity expanding, drawing in big gulps of dry, frigid air. She felt as though some cells in her body were being fed clean oxygen for the very first time. Her body was alive, thrumming with energy, and pumping hot with blood. She understood how this could become addictive. Her muscles warmed as each step took her further and further towards a goal of which she wasn't aware but was compelled towards. She felt alive, burning with it, as her lungs filled with sweet oxygen. Alive. It had been so long since she felt alive.

The streets were still, perfectly silent. She saw a light here and there as without doubt people were rising to get ready for work. She passed her childhood friend Cassie's house. Cassie's parents still lived there, though Cassie herself had moved out of state to go to college to become a certified nurse. It was a job that Cassie would be well suited for, Violet imagined.

She hadn't been her friend in a very long time, though seeing her familiar yard with the swing set and evergreen shrubs they'd used as a fort, gave her a longing to know how her old pal was doing. Maybe she'd walk down some afternoon and talk to her mom. She'd always loved her mother, who had always been so sweet and tender hearted. Violet and Cassie's moms had spent a lot of afternoons together, drinking sweet tea and talking about the girls, or weeding their flower gardens, or traipsing off to yard sales.

Violet had been such an asshole to Cassie. Once she started evolving into the person she was now she had tossed Cassie aside. Yes, they were growing in different directions, but Cassie had always supported her and never judged her, yet Violet couldn't continue their friendship because Cassie simply hadn't been "cool enough" by Violet's new friends' standards.

Cassie had the last laugh though. She'd been a happy, well-adjusted girl, and Violet had spent the last four years in constant agony over one moronic thing after another.

She wondered if her old friend would accept her now or if she'd snub her the way she deserved to be snubbed? She knew the answer. Cassie would accept her with open arms because she was a good person.

Violet stopped and looked at the beautiful blue spruce Cassie's family had planted in their yard in remembrance of her parents. She hoped they'd decorate it with lots of pretty lights this Christmas. For the first time she didn't cry at the memory of her mom and dad, only smiled that someone besides her had loved her parents so much. Her body urged her on and she picked her pace back up again.

Violet ran a good five miles. Her body felt better and stronger now than it had when she'd started earlier. It was like her limbs were mechanical, like she was a machine, and that every part of her body served a purpose and served it well. She could feel her heart and lungs working perfectly together, flowing and pumping and living symbiotically, driving her faster and faster towards that unknown goal.

The sun was already peeking above the treeline, the sky pale purple-gray and she knew by the hue of the overcast sky this would be another gloomy day. She decided that though her body was giving her no signs of slowing she should turn around and get back home before anyone worried about her. Roman would probably panic if he woke up and she was gone without a trace. And really, she should have left some sort of note given the current state of things. Man, she was stupid to go out in the dark. She just figured since it was so close to dawn it would be safe. Maybe it was, maybe it wasn't. She was an idiot. She rounded the block and headed back towards her house.

Amber was in the kitchen when she arrived back home cooking eggs and making a lunch for Randy who was upstairs showering. He was starting his new job at the lawnmower factory today.

"You were jogging?" Amber asked as she flipped the eggs.

"Yes, training, remember?" Violet breathed heavily as she reached into the refrigerator and pulled out the orange juice.

"Shouldn't you be more careful out there?"

"Nah, not that close to sun up," she answered dismissively, knowing full damn well that she shouldn't have gone out. "So, Randy starts his job today? That's exciting eh?"

"Yeah, he's content with it. We need the extra money. We're saving up because we're thinking about getting an apartment eventually. We don't want to take advantage of your place forever."

The statement slammed Violet right in the face like a brick. Where the hell had that come from? "Amber, you aren't taking advantage of this place. It's not like you guys aren't contributing."

Violet was upset to hear this. She had no idea how they could have gotten the idea they were some sort of inconvenience. The thought had never crossed her mind that they were an inconvenience or that they were taking advantage of her. She loved having them here with her, and they actually contributed to the household, unlike that lazy piece of crap Steve. And she hadn't even minded Steve until he turned into an asshole. But the thought of living alone now terrified her.

"I know you don't think so, Violet, it's not even about you. We just think we should have our own place. Plus you and Roman will eventually want your privacy, won't you?"

"I don't even know what's going on with him. Honestly, he may leave once all this is taken care of."

"He's not going to leave," Amber said in exasperation. "He so obviously loves you."

"He will leave, probably, what he does is important." Violet took a swig of the orange juice and put it back in the fridge. "I don't want to be alone," Violet said with tears in her eyes. She hated that everything always had to change.

"Violet, Roman isn't going to leave you. And besides, it wouldn't be for a while anyway, so don't get all sad about it now. I'm sure however it works out it will work out. You won't be alone. And besides, we won't move far even if we do move. One of these days you will want your own space when little baby Romans are running around here."

Violet couldn't help but smile at that, her stomach involuntarily fluttering with butterflies. *Holy crap, little baby Romans.* Amber noticed the grin and smiled in return.

"Think they'd be like 5 feet tall at birth?" Amber asked as she flipped the eggs in the pan.

"God, I hope not," Violet said with a laugh and a pained expression.

Randy bounded down the stairs dressed in his work jeans and a sweatshirt. He was barely awake. "Morning," he mumbled, walking to Amber and kissing her as she handed him his breakfast.

"Good morning, Randy," Violet said, envious of their domestic bliss. "Good luck with the new job."

"It'll be cool," he said half-heartedly.

And she knew it would be okay for him as he always made the best of every situation. She couldn't even recall the last time she'd heard him complain about anything.

"Alright, well, see you guys later. I'm gonna go shower and go back to bed," Violet said.

Violet walked upstairs to the bathroom. She took her sweaty clothes off. They smelled like outside. Then she got in the shower. The thought of her having to be in this house alone suddenly terrified her. If Amber and Randy left there would be no reason to stay. There were too many memories in every square inch of this house. As long as she had friends here taking up the space, she could live without the constant barrage of all she'd lost overwhelming her. But if they were gone, and there was nothing to distract her, she would fall apart.

She finished showering and finally got around to combing the knots from her hair. She braided it and put her pajamas back on and went back to her bedroom. The soft pale sky had lit the room to a pretty light purplish hue. Roman was still in the same position she'd left him, only he'd pulled the blankets over himself. She climbed in beside him and placed her hand against his cheek, rubbing his face gently, moving her thumb across his warm skin. She leaned over and kissed his cheek. He opened his eyes briefly then closed them again, rolling onto his side and putting his arm around her and pulling her close against his body. He rested his face against her, nuzzling her ear. She could feel the moist warmth of his breath, the heat of his body warming her. She closed her eyes and went back to sleep.

13

BLOOD SACRIFICE

SHE DROPPED DOWN FROM the table like a bleeding clot, smearing across the floor in thick bloody strokes. She felt the wood grain piercing her palms and knees in slivers, cursing her pink stained flesh for its weakness. She raked her nails at the floor, punishing her skin for its weakness. As the nail bed detached itself she threw her face against the chair. Had she known the pain she would inflict she may have stopped short of the actual pounding, but she wasn't very bright at times. Pain was good. Pain was life.

She picked herself up from the floor and tugged on the barely attached nail. Wincing, she yanked it bleeding and screaming from its soft pink bed. She would sleep and wake and the pain would still be present. Too young still to heal so fast. Always too young. Cursed weakness. Water even stung. She felt the cold marble now against her dead limbs.

Lux would surely come again, wouldn't he? Yes, he would come with Violet's screaming death. Of course he would come.

"What are you doing, Cecelia?" Mark asked, picking the bloodied woman up from the cracked filthy floor.

"Suffering for God," she murmured, allowing her body to go limp in his strong hands

"Fucking stop it. Quit feeling sorry for yourself. You remind me of *her* when you act this way."

The woman's eyes came alive with fury, piercing through him as though she could light him on fire with her stare. The searing was so intense that he nearly dropped her to the floor. He didn't know what to say to her. She was so unpredictable. He thought it best to say nothing at all when she looked at him this way.

"Don't you ever tell me that again," she said, pulling herself from his arms and standing. "You forget who I am, *child*."

He looked at her body. She had clawed herself to ribbons, linear beads of blood mapping her skin. She almost looked tattooed, like some Maori pattern covered her white skin, textured and smearing. This woman was insane, he knew it. And he loved it.

"Why did you do this to yourself?" he asked, wiping his hand across her chest and placing his fingers in his mouth. Her blood was rich and thick from all the lives she'd taken. He could hear the echoes of the dead in her blood, racing through his veins, entrapped in red blood cells and the very marrow of his bones.

She pulled his face towards her body. Her fingers gripping his skull, causing dull pain at his temples. She would pierce his head like a bowling ball had she not wanted him to fuck her then.

"Don't ask me silly questions," she said, forcing his mouth to her breast.

"So, where are we going to do this?" Violet asked, handing him the sandwich she had made for him.

"I don't know. You know this town better than I do. We need someplace secluded or cops are going to show up for domestic violence," he joked and took a bite. "Thanks for the sandwich" he said with his mouth full.

"Yeah, domestic violence against you since I'll be the one kicking your ass." Violet smirked and bit into her own sandwich.

"No doubt," he said with a grin. "In the woods or something."

"I know where we can go. There's an old baseball diamond out at Harper Farm. It's set way back in the cornfield. No one will be around. I'm not even sure they use the field at all now."

"That sounds good. I hope you're ready to get your ass kicked."

"I hope you're ready to get *your* ass kicked, dork. So am I going to get to use weapons?" she asked with a raised brow.

"Not today, first learn to fight with what you have."

"Piece of cake."

He looked at her, noticing the way her demeanor had changed. She had been so frail only a few weeks prior, and now she seemed fierce and invincible. Almost as though she had discovered who she was meant to be and finally felt comfortable in her own skin.

"Roman, I'm glad you found me. Lux did something right, right?"

"I suppose he did, though don't ever let him know that or you won't hear the end of it." He smirked and drank the last of his water. "I guess we can go."

They drove down Peck Road. It was a winding loose gravel road that snaked through corn fields and over small hills. The gravel pinged the side of his car, making her wince every time she heard it. She could imagine the damage to the paint, though he didn't seem to mind.

"It's not much farther," she said, looking over at Roman who seemed relaxed for the first time in days.

He looked back at her and smiled. "Just tell me where to turn."

She watched closely for the dirt road since she hadn't been there since the seventh grade. That was her last season of softball. Her cousin was the softball star, Violet just did it because her friends did. Penelope had actual awards and titles with her teams. But Violet had loved coming out here. The thick smell of the corn fields and tall grasses seemed comforting even then. Her father had always brought her, carrying her through the tall grasses on his shoulders when she was still small enough to do so. And it was always exciting going for an ice cream cone afterwards, win or lose.

"There it is," she said, pointing to the right side of the road.

He pulled up the jagged path and up over the rise of the field. There the diamond sat, unkempt and empty.

"I used to play shortstop," she said, almost sadly. She certainly mourned her youth, aspects of it anyway.

"Go figure," he grinned and opened the door. He was unsure how to even really start her training, since he had been trained from about the age of eight. His uncle had been very methodical, but he knew they had no time for all the theories and different fighting techniques. He would simply teach her how to keep herself alive and to kill the enemy. They could work on the rest later. *How fucked up.*

She jogged ahead of him out onto where the infield once was and looked from the tree line to the edge of the field. She remembered having to sneak off into those woods to pee during the game. She always hated that. She smiled and closed her eyes, inhaling deeply. She could almost smell the scent of orange kool-aid and juicy fruit gum. Nothing had changed in her mind's eye except that there was no more laughter, and no more daddy watching from a fold up aluminum chair.

Roman reached her, realizing that she was taking in her surroundings, hearkening back to some lost memory, and it was interesting to watch her in this trance-like state. She was so able to stop her body, to pull it out of time and place and to absorb the world around her. This would make her dangerous to them. All she had to do was learn how to focus with intent, and she would be damn near psychic. Honed intuition was a deadly advantage. He could see now that her eyes weren't in the present, she was far off, back to another time, and he would allow her to continue until she was ready.

The black birds cawed from the harvested field beyond the old diamond. Bent golden stalks, jagged and jutting up from the corn soaked ground that fed them, made crunching sounds as they walked over them. She looked at the sun that was diffused through gray skies and a thick blanket of clouds. It was a cold silvery looking orb. The sun and moon had changed places for the day.

She looked at Roman now. He stood still, patiently waiting for her. His long legs were bent slightly, arms hanging loose at his side. If things were different she'd want to move somewhere distant, maybe Nebraska or Wyoming, some place like that. She'd want to live in the middle of some field just like this, surrounded by wheat or corn. And she would have his babies and take care of them all with gratitude. She grinned at the thought. But this simply wasn't reality. It was never going to be reality. She didn't even know who she would be in that context. But in this moment it sounded like the perfect life.

"So, I guess we're ready?" she said.

"If you're ready," he said, walking towards her.

"I guess so. I honestly have no idea what I'm doing."

"You will when I'm through with you," he said, and kicked her feet out from under her.

14

BLOOD LINES

ROMAN WAS SHOCKED AT how quickly she had picked up what he'd shown her. He guessed that what Lux had said really was true. She was born for this. The thought of her having to be in a situation where she would need this training terrified him. But he knew that if she was truly meant for this she could handle herself. It's not as if he hadn't known of other females like himself. He'd met a woman in Germany a few years back who was only slightly bigger than Violet, though not nearly as cute. He figured no one would be nearly as cute to him now. The woman was every bit as skilled as he was, just not nearly as cold, and was lacking the experience he had. But she was deadly. He had enjoyed her company when they'd been together.

His thoughts went back to Violet. Yes, Violet would handle herself just fine. He was sure. He would make it so.

Next he would teach her weaponry. Oh, she was going to love that. Her level of aggression was surprising, and while she'd never knocked him to the ground, he knew he'd have bruises all over from her. It didn't bother him. Sparring with her had been fun.

Roman could hear the phone ringing as he unlocked the door so he hurriedly shoved the door open and walked to the phone.

"How's our girl?"

"Lux, what do you want?"

"Wow, that's very cordial of you," Lux teased with a laugh.

"We're not friends, remember?"

"Okay, let's treat this as business then. How is Violet coming along in her training?" Lux's tone had shifted, and Roman knew he had made him angry.

"She's fine. Why do you want to know?" Roman really didn't want to tell Lux much of anything. He didn't like the idea of him calling to check on her.

"*Because I want to know.* You are aware that I could have just called her myself and asked?" Lux was pissed and tired of Roman being such a dick all the time. Well, more than usual since he got involved with Violet.

"Stay away from her."

"Hmm...staking your territory?" Lux asked, trying to lighten the mood.

"I'll stake *you* if you don't shut up," Roman said, relinquishing the attitude.

"I finally got a laugh out of you. Lighten the fuck up already."

"Yeah, well, she's fine. Doing extremely well actually."

"I told you she would excel, did I not?"

"But Lux, you said she isn't chosen, so how is it that she has these abilities?"

"Chosen. Those are your human words, not mine. No one is *chosen*, some of you are just born with extraordinary abilities...stemming from your bloodlines."

"Bloodlines? What do you mean?" Roman leaned against the wall furrowing his brow and twisting the telephone cord.

"Come on now, Roman. Your uncle didn't tell you the family secret? Your mother certainly knew..."

"Don't talk about my mother." Roman's patience for Lux's inability to get straight to a point was wearing thin as usual. The vampire had a way of annoying him and then turning around and making him laugh a second later. He just wanted answers this time. There was more at stake now besides his own ass.

"Oh yes, settle down Oedipus. I forgot about you human males and your sensitivity towards your mothers." Lux laughed.

"I swear to God, I'm going to fucking kill you the next time I see you."

"Don't bring *God* into this. Seriously, lighten up, Roman. You're extra sensitive now that you have a girlfriend."

"You're really going to resort to high school teasing? Just get to the fucking point. What are you talking about? What family secret, and what does this have to do with Violet?"

"Calm down. You're worse than Mylori when she's in one of her moods."

That got a laugh out of Roman. Mylori was notorious for her moods. She'd wiped out entire villages because of those moods.

"Just imagine if Mylori had menstrual cycles. Can you imagine the havoc she'd cause?"

Roman snickered. "I shudder to think. But get to the point, Lux," he said in a normal tone.

Lux paused briefly. "I feel fairly certain I just stereotyped my sister. We both know hormones, or not, she is a monster."

"And we also both know plenty of men who are worse. But get to the fucking point."

Lux chuckled. "Alright, alright. I guess your uncle never told you about how your family experimented with your dear old auntie?"

"Experimented how?"

"They drained her of her blood and ingested it all those years they kept her locked away. They were ruthless and power hungry and used the poor vampire like she was a milking cow."

"You're lying."

"Why would I lie about such a thing, Roman? Come now, you really are naïve. You think your abilities are natural?" He paused briefly and continued, "Well, they are natural, just not natural to your species. You haven't wondered how it is that your body heals so quickly or how you're far superior to any of the human males you fight? Look in the mirror. Do you look your age?"

"You don't know what you're talking about."

"Roman..." Lux's tone was calm and sympathetic now. He could hear the disgust and anger in Roman's voice, and it wasn't his goal to anger the man, at least not this time. It was clear Roman wouldn't want to hear this truth given his hatred for Lux's kind. "You know I'm telling you the truth."

Roman was quiet for a long moment, taking in the words and mulling them over. His brain was spinning, trying to make sense, trying to look back to the past to understand what he was being told. There had been signs, he remembered hearing his mom and uncle talking late at night, and he'd just assumed what he'd heard were old tales and nothing more.

"How could humans pass down vampire blood? It has been centuries," Roman asked.

"Blood is blood. It flows through veins and into wombs and feeds little growing babies. You understand anatomy, correct?"

"And then they killed her because they were finally finished with her?"

"No, they killed her because someone finally saw that what the family was doing was fucked up and they took pity on her. And that is where your people stem from, the side of the family with sense and morality. Roman, your ancestors were far more brutal and evil than she would have been had she been left to roam free. Her personality was..." he paused for a moment searching for the right words and then continued, "gentle and serene. She would have killed a few humans here and there, but eventually she would have allowed herself to die like so many do. She didn't have the kind of fortitude it takes to survive for centuries. Your ancestors *brought* her humans to sustain her life so that they could use her blood for their own means. They were worse than she would have been had she been left to live her life. It's just lucky for you that someone in your family tree had fallen in love with a woman with an actual soul who saw through what they were doing and ended it. But it didn't stop the blood from flowing through the generations."

"This is just wrong. There's no way any of this is true."

"Look through your books, friend. I have no reason to lie to you. I should have told you sooner, but I thought you must know on some level. I was wrong."

Roman's brow furrowed as he contemplated what he was hearing. He had known on some level, maybe, but he had always denied it. This could not be. It could not. He hated vampires. He would not accept that side of himself. Ever. He switched the focus off of himself.

"And what does this have to do with Violet? Don't tell me she comes from the same sort of thing? Her family was normal," Roman said.

"No, she's another story. A story that I don't know anything about, but somewhere in her family's history something happened."

"And you don't know?" Roman asked, skeptical at the feigned ignorance.

"I don't know, Roman." Lux grew quiet for a moment and Roman wondered if he would continue. "I knew it was true when she was seven years old and I looked into her eyes."

Roman contemplated everything Lux was saying. It made perfect sense, and yet didn't. How could this be true?

"Roman, this is the reason you read us so well. It's why you understand us. It's why you always know where we are and what move we're going to make. Our blood calls to yours. We recognize our own. And that is the reason you are superior to your kind, humans, and even most of mine. It's in your DNA."

Roman said nothing. He knew that what Lux was saying was true and it disgusted him. He wanted no part of who they were, and yet if Lux was telling the truth, then he did have that old blood inside of him. And so did Violet. Somehow.

"Read your books, Roman. I'm sure there's documentation," Lux said.

"My uncle always tried to get me to read the history and I didn't want anything to do with it. I only ever cared about killing you bastards."

"Yes, you're feisty that way," Lux said with a chuff. "You need to tell the girl. Don't let her go through life not knowing. If she finds out the truth on her own, and that you knew and didn't tell her, she'll never forgive you."

"As if she doesn't have enough to worry about." Roman exhaled, wondering how on earth he'd be able to dump yet another terrible revelation on her. This would just lead to more questions to which he would have absolutely no answers.

"You know, Roman, in some ways this makes you superior to us."

"I am superior to you."

That caused Lux to laugh. "Yeah, well, like I was saying... you have some of our strengths without any of our weaknesses. Your human body is stronger in that it can sustain the sun."

"But it can't sustain time."

"No, not forever. But your decaying process is slower than most."

"How the hell am I going to tell her this?"

"I can do it if you want." The amusement in his voice was obvious.

"No," Roman said with force.

"Kidding, geez. You really need to lighten up. Go get laid or something."

Violet waved goodbye to him as he drove away. Her legs were sore and tired, aching like a giant charlie horse. She would have to work hard to get through this, but was happy with how she felt. It was nice to feel alive, like she was accomplishing something. It was strange that she might finally be doing something with her life that actually would matter to someone. Why did it always take something insanely tragic or dangerous to force her to make a change?

The fear of what might happen always lingered like a gray cloud hovering and following just behind her head, but she felt like for the first time in her life she was taking steps to combat the fear. There had always been fear in her life. When she was little she had been afraid to do so many things for fear of getting hurt, or laughed at. She'd spent her preteen years afraid of standing out, and then later afraid of fitting in. And this last year or so had been wrought with fear of Mark and his tantrums, of taking one drug too many and never coming back mentally. And then of course the fear of being completely alone. But now she was moving ahead. Granted it wasn't the usual "safe path" one would take, but it was a path, and it seemed to suit her.

Roman had actually fought her during her training. It didn't seem like he'd taken it easy on her, at least not too easy. Shockingly enough she'd been able to handle him. She knew there was more to defending herself than just punching and kicking a friend could teach. She would have to learn the weapons, and of course there would be natural instinct, intuition, stamina, and the sheer will to live. All of these were skills she could learn and hone. Yeah, she was looking forward to using weapons.

She opened the back door. Randy and Amber were sitting at the kitchen table reading the newspaper. How domestic and strange.

"Hey," Amber said, looking up with a strange, unreadable look on her face. "Did you hear the news?"

"No? What's the news?" Violet asked, setting her stuff down by the door and walking over to the two. There was definitely a somber mood about them.

"They found Gwen in the woods behind Malinda's Grandma's house."

"What?" Violet exclaimed. She pulled out a chair and sat down. "What do you mean by they *found Gwen*? What happened?"

"The newspaper says they speculate she was raped and beaten to death."

"You have to be kidding me?"

"Here," Amber said, sliding the paper towards her.

Randy looked over at Violet, obviously still shaken. His hands were trembling and the look on his face terrified her. She'd never seen him look this way.

"I think it was vampires," he said quietly, unsure he should even speak such nonsense out loud.

Violet looked away from the article to her friend who was so obviously horrified. "Why do you think that?"

"I just do. Who would murder her?" Randy looked down at the table and shrugged his shoulders.

"It could be anyone, Randy. It could have been some trucker coming through town for all we know. Don't jump to conclusions. Anyway, why would a vampire rape her?" Amber wanted to believe there was a perfectly "normal" explanation for this.

"It could be anything. You know, I really didn't like the girl, but I'd never wish death on anyone." Violet felt herself growing sick. Her stomach felt like it wanted to escape her body. What the fuck was happening? Everything in her world was turned upside down.

"I wonder how Steve is taking this?" Amber said, looking over at Randy.

"Probably not very well. I should call him," he said mechanically.

"When's the last time you even saw those guys?" Violet asked, continuing to read the article.

"It's been quite a while. I haven't really seen Mark or Mosley in weeks. They're supposed to come to my gig tomorrow night though, at least that was the plan the last time I talked to Steve."

"Well, I hope Steve's alright. He always had a soft spot for her," Violet said and stood up. "You know, you have a halfway decent day and something like this happens. I shouldn't complain though. I'm alive. I'm going to go soak in a hot bath."

"I'm going to make mac 'n' cheese for dinner, you want some?" Amber asked, standing up and walking towards the cupboards.

"Yeah, thanks," Violet said, despondent.

"Is Roman coming over?" Amber asked.

"I assume so," Violet said, turning back to look at her friend. It was becoming difficult to hide her emotions. She was genuinely saddened and disturbed about the death of someone she never even liked. Every mean thing she'd ever said to Gwen was racing through her head.

"Don't go there," Amber said, knowing exactly what Violet would be thinking.

"Can't help it," Violet mumbled, and walked up the stairs.

Violet sank into the hot water and inhaled the fragrant bubble bath. Her lungs expanded in her chest in a way they never had before, filling her chest cavity to capacity. The exercise was paying off. She closed her eyes, trying to block out her thoughts, hoping she'd be able to take a little nap.

Her mother used to tap on the door to make sure she hadn't fallen asleep and drowned in the tub if she had been in for longer than a half an hour. No one would knock today.

Her mind wandered from subject to subject. There was so much to think about, so many changes she had to adapt to now. And then she thought back over the last time she'd seen Gwen. That smug look on Gwen's face had made Violet want to hurt her. Someone had taken care of that for her.

Her stomach lurched and it took all her strength to keep from throwing up bile. Nausea had always plagued her when she was stressed. She was sick to her stomach a lot actually. It had been sensitive her whole life. But stress got her worked up like nothing else. The morning had been so good too. She and Roman had such a good time, as silly as that seemed considering he was teaching her how to kill vampires. And now she was fretting over something she had no control over. It wasn't her fault Gwen was dead.

But I could have been nicer to her.

She answered the door wearing a long black nightgown. The material was soft and silky against her moist skin. Her body was still red and hot from the bath. Roman wrapped his arms around her, holding her as close as he could to his body. Her warm wet hair smelled so sweet. He pressed his lips to her forehead and let go of her.

Amber was standing at the table spooning heaps of cheesy goodness into bowls. She looked at Roman and grinned, wanting to say "I told you so" to both of them.

"You hungry?" Amber asked, sitting down beside Randy who was already dumping ketchup and black pepper into his food and stirring it.

"I'm always hungry," he answered with a crooked grin on his face.

Violet walked to the table and sat down. She hadn't said a word since he had arrived and he hadn't said anything to her either. His presence was enough to make her feel a little better. She begrudgingly took a bite of the macaroni, her stomach still feeling queasy on and off. She was hoping having food in it would help, but there was never really any rhyme or reason to her body's madness when it came to such matters.

"You sick?" Amber asked, wondering why Violet was picking through her food.

"Just sick to my stomach," she answered, shrugging her shoulders.

Roman looked at her, his eyebrows furrowed with concern.

"Hey, maybe you're pregnant?" Randy laughed and pointed at her with his food laden fork.

Violet's face contorted and Roman laughed nervously. Amber kicked Randy under the table so hard he jumped and looked at her, not understanding what the big deal was.

"Yeah, I don't think so," Violet said, shoving a bite of food into her mouth.

"You could go on Maury to find out who the father is. Would it be the dark and mysterious Roman? Or the piece of shit ex, Mark?" Randy said and laughed.

"Wow, Randy," Amber said, slapping the back of his head.

Violet shot him a look that could kill.

"I was just kidding! Sheesh," Randy said, shrugging his shoulders. "Just trying to lighten the mood a bit."

Roman cleared his throat. "Jokes aside, you guys all seem really somber, what's going on?" Roman asked, changing the subject quickly and looking back and forth between the three of them.

"This girl we know was found dead. None of us really cared for her, but it's sort of freaky, ya know?" Amber explained.

"What happened to her?" Roman asked, leaning back in his chair and chewing the food slowly.

"The paper didn't say much. Basically just that she may have been raped and beaten. I tried calling a couple mutual friends earlier but no one seems to know anything," Amber said.

"I'm sorry to hear that," he said, taking another bite of food.

"I still think it was vampires," Randy mumbled.

Violet looked up from her bowl and shot a look at him. She was still uncomfortable with the subject.

Roman wasn't used to hearing normal people talk so casually about vampires either. "What makes you think that?" he asked.

"Nothing in particular, it's just what I think. Not a whole lot of murders go on in this town, and seeing as how apparently there are vampires running amok, it just seems to make sense to me," Randy said, very matter-of-factly.

Roman appreciated the directness. Randy always said exactly what was on his mind. "It's not out of the realm of possibility," Roman said, looking over at Violet, wondering how she was doing. She had barely eaten a few bites.

"See," Randy said, looking at Amber with a scowl.

"Okay, goody for you, Randy. You solved the mystery," Amber said with sarcasm.

"I'm not saying all that, but it's *not out of the realm of possibility*." Randy smirked triumphantly quoting Roman, The Expert.

"It's something I can check into," Roman responded. "You feeling alright?" he said, turning to Violet with concern over her quiet demeanor.

"I'm alright," she said, giving him a forced smile.

They quietly finished eating and then Roman and Randy went to the living room. The girls stayed in the kitchen and cleaned up the dishes, clearly wanting their space.

"We're so domestic." Amber laughed, elbowing her friend in the side.

"Yeah, who knew?" Violet tried to smile.

"So, *are you pregnant*?" Amber asked, looking at Violet with a devilish grin on her face.

"Amber," Violet said, tilting her head and looking at her with a grin on her face, "not unless it's by some miracle. *Are you?*"

"No, just getting fat." Amber laughed as she scraped the remnants of Violet's plate into the garbage disposal.

"Yeah, I feel the same way." Violet rubbed her stomach.

"Hardly, you actually look normal now. Gasp!"

Violet looked down at her body. She was still a little thin, but her bones weren't jutting through her skin quite as sharply as they had been when she was dating Mark. The fact that she'd gained weight so quickly was proof she'd been starving herself. Mark had always liked her thin, or so he said, until he'd make cracks about her not looking "womanly enough".

Roman never really said anything one way or the other except for being concerned she wasn't eating. It never came across as judgey though, just worried. She didn't even know if he was really attracted to her physically. It was especially confusing to her since she knew he had been with Mylori, and she definitely did not look like her. But Roman never indicated he was attracted to her, that was obvious anyway, and she wouldn't assume.

She thought about Gwen and how well-endowed she had been, and how she and Amber had even teased her about being fat. "We weren't very nice to her, Amber," Violet said, her brow furrowed with deep regret.

"Let it go, Vi. She's dead and there's nothing we can do about it now," Amber said.

"I know, it just bothers me how I behaved. I'm not a very nice person."

"What are you talking about? Of course you are."

"No, Amber, I'm really not, or I wasn't. Think of the mean things we've said and how little respect we give people."

"Most people don't deserve it and you know it. Plenty of people have treated us both like shit. Have we made mistakes, yeah, we fucking have. You're right. But who cares now? We move on and we make better choices, okay? Stop beating yourself up over crap you can't change anyway."

"I guess you're right. I just feel guilty thinking about the damage I've done to people with my words."

"Stop giving yourself so much power. You ain't all that." Amber laughed and wrapped her arm around Violet's waist, giving her a squeeze before wiping off the table.

Violet chuckled and walked into the living room. Amber meant well, but it hadn't changed her feelings. She'd been a bitch to a lot of people and had no doubt messed some of them up somehow. She had probably added a lot of unnecessary insecurity to people who already had enough of their own.

The two men were sitting on the couch with their feet propped up, drinking beer, and watching cartoons. She assumed that was Randy's choice of programming as Roman seemed a little too intense to enjoy cartoons. But what did she know? He did watch crappy old sitcoms. It looked funny to her, but seeing them there made her feel better. It was almost semi-normal. As normal as a vampire slayer and a twenty four year old with a mohawk watching cartoons could look. She snickered and walked over to Roman and sat down on his lap, snuggling down against him and resting her wet head on his shoulder. It felt good to feel normal.

He wasn't expecting the affection. This whole girlfriend thing wasn't something he was used to, never mind this sort of contact with her. This was really the first time he'd ever had a girl in his lap like this. She didn't look like she felt awkward, but it was foreign to him. Still, the silkiness of her gown, and the softness of her skin, felt good to him. The weight of her in his lap felt right. He placed his hand on her stomach, feeling the thin fabric warming to his skin. He rubbed her belly softly with a bit of apprehension.

"You feeling better?" he asked, his voice quiet.

She looked at him with a smile and nodded her head. "A little better now."

"There's got to be something better than this to watch, Randy," Amber said, slapping her boyfriend in the back of the head playfully. She flipped the lights off and grabbed the afghan off the back of the couch and tossed it to the floor so she could lie down. "Find a movie or something."

"Whatever, boss," Randy joked and started flipping through the channels. He stopped on the classic movie station where an old film was just starting, something black and white and musical. "We're watching this," he said, tossing the remote to her.

"That's fine," Amber said, tugging on his foot and pulling his sock partially off. It dangled off the end of his foot.

"I like these old musicals," Violet said, her voice sullen.

"Yeah, me too," Randy said, leaning forward to look at her.

Roman's hand gently resting against her stomach made her happy. It was like having a hot water bottle against her skin. She felt the random, sporadic twitching of his fingers and the soft pats as he moved his palm gently over her. She was comfortable and comforted. Mark had never been this tender with her. She felt the warm swoon come over her. Every time his hand moved, or he shifted his weight, or breathed a little more deeply, her body melted against him further. She wanted to take him upstairs to bed right now, but she wanted things to be different this time. They were barely a couple. She wanted to savor all these first moments, to stretch out each and every moment until she ached with it. She found herself moving her fingers slightly, stretching her pinkie in order to feel his hand against hers, or nestling her head against his shoulder in a way to feel him without being painfully obvious. She wanted to run her fingers over every inch of his beautiful skin. Instead she stared blankly at the television unaware of what she saw and completely consumed by his presence.

Roman finished the beer Randy had given him and then leaned forward, setting it on the coffee table. Randy had already offered another but he'd declined. His last bout with excessive consumption hadn't gone so well, though he was nowhere near excessive consumption now, and hadn't really been then either. It takes a lot to get a horse drunk. Taking in his surroundings, he had to admit to himself that he felt really content here with them. He could get used to this life too easily.

It was about an hour into the film that Randy was completely asleep, having a belly full of carbohydrates and alcohol. Amber had followed shortly thereafter. Both of them got up for work early, so it wasn't uncommon for them to crash out like this watching television. Violet fought her tiredness, not wanting to miss a moment with Roman. His eyes were heavy, his body calm and relaxed.

"Are you still feeling sick to your stomach?" he asked quietly, not wanting to wake the others up.

"Only a little. This happens when I get overly stressed about stuff sometimes," she said, lifting her head from his shoulder.

His shirt was wet where her head had rested and the thick aroma of shampoo was strong and clean smelling. "Are you going to be okay?" he asked.

"Of course," she said without hesitation. "If I could deal with losing mom and dad this is nothing, right?"

Roman pressed a kiss to her forehead. "I need to go out tonight. I've taken too many nights off and I need to find out what's going on with this Cecelia person so I can get rid of her."

"Mmm...Do you have to?" she said, snuggling back against him and wrapping her arms around him.

"Yeah, I have to."

"Why don't I give you a key so you can come back when you're done?"

This was definitely new territory for him. "If you want me to."

"Don't be stupid," she said with an eyeroll and a grin he couldn't see, but he could feel her cheeks moving with her smile against his shoulder.

"I hope you know not to let anyone in your house. Since I've been such a slacker we have no idea what she'd try to pull. Fuck, I don't even know where she is. God, I have really dropped the ball here."

"Eh, sorry for being a distraction," Violet said.

"Well, it's really inexcusable since I was brought here to take care of you."

"And you have been. Think of all the counseling you've given me since you arrived." Violet sat up with a playful grin on her face. "Besides, I can kick her ass now." She held up her dukes and made a joking scowl.

"Well, I would feel more comfortable kicking her ass myself, if you don't object," Roman said and took her balled fists in his hands.

"Oh, if you insist. My hero." Violet batted her lashes and held her fists to her cheeks all swoony-like in jest.

"Dork," Roman said with a laugh. He had never once used that word before he met her and her friends. "I should go, so I can get back sooner," he said, moving his legs and trying to rouse her. He stood up easily with her in his arms and tossed her back down on the couch. She bounced and squealed from the surprise. And still Randy and Amber slept without waking.

Violet hopped off the couch with a giggle and walked toward the kitchen, since he had parked on the street behind the house.

He followed behind, his eyes fixed on her body. Her movements were so fluidly feline, the black silk helped the image of a stalking panther that was rolling around in his brain. Her milk white shoulders were round and soft looking, shoulder blades protruding gently through the fabric. He wanted to plant his mouth between them. God, it was strange having these feelings for her, but his body seemed to have no problem acclimating to the change in relationship status.

She leaned against the counter and looked up at him, not wanting him to leave, but knowing this was their reality and she would have to get used to it. She might be going with him soon, when she was ready. Being on a team with him was exactly what she wanted.

"You think you'll adjust to this?" he asked, hovering over her like a giant.

"Yes, of course, do you?" She was giving him her best *come hither* stare now.

"We'll see I guess," he said, shifting nervously. "You're not going to make it easy for me to go, are you?" He grinned.

She smiled and tilted her head. "I have no idea what you're talking about."

"Yeah, okay," he said, taking one of her hands and pulling it up to look at her small fingers and pretty silver nails. The bones were delicate and he couldn't imagine that such strength was contained in these hands. He had to tell her the full truth of what Lux had told him earlier. Maybe she could even help him read through the books. He felt relieved knowing there might actually be someone to finally share all this chaos with for the first time since his family died. He had people in his life he could have reached out to if he'd wanted to, but it was easier to stay unattached. Until now. He didn't want to be unattached from her and it was terrifying and confusing.

"Have you always had long hair, Roman?" she asked, reaching out with her other hand and gently pulling a handful.

"Yeah, why?"

"I just wondered. I've always had long hair too."

Her hand running through his hair was killing him. It would be so easy to just stay and blow off his hunting another night. But he couldn't. It was imperative he end this threat sooner than later.

"I'm gonna go now," he said, taking her other hand and gripping it, too. His eyes were glossy and sparkly in the dark light of the kitchen. He took his finger and pushed the strap of her nightgown back up onto her shoulder. "Get some sleep," he said, and kissed her forehead. "You'll feel better in the morning."

His warm mouth against her skin felt gentle and so loving. "I forgot I was sick," she said, and tipped her head to the side.

"Good."

"Remember to come back," she said softly, reaching for the keys that she'd thrown on the counter earlier.

"I will, kitten." He kissed her gently on her forehead again and walked outside.

She watched through the curtain as he walked down the path through the yard to his car. She turned the locks and walked back to the living room, not wanting to go upstairs. Despite what she'd told him, she hadn't forgotten about Gwen or all the other madness that was surrounding her. It all still freaked her out, and she was afraid of all that had happened. She would lie down on the couch and watch old happy movies with her blissfully sleeping friends.

15
BLACK HAIR AND VIOLENCE

ROMAN DROVE THE STREETS, trying to decide where to start. There wasn't anything going on in town. All the lights were out. Everyone was asleep, safe inside their houses.

He decided to go to the old standby *cemetery* and take a walk to see if he found anything. Why those moronic creatures hadn't figured out they could live amongst humans fairly easily was beyond him. Indeed, Lux and Mylori had learned centuries prior this was the best option. It was more comfortable and less conspicuous. Hiding in crypts and the like was just stupid. It was like putting a target on themselves that screamed *I am the undead*. It was mind boggling that so many vampires seemed to apparently get their information on how to live from watching cheesy movies. Vampire society had evolved as much as human society had, moreso really. With their superior capabilities they had even made advances that had brought humans forward by default. Vampires were everywhere, in every facet of society. From the upper echelon of the elite, to the gutters.

He turned his lights off and sat in the car silently for a few moments. He put Violet out of his mind so he could focus on what he was here to do, if, in fact, there was anything here to do. No doubt Cecelia was the kind of idiot who would be turning simpleton humans into the kind of dumbfuck vampires that would hang out in the cemetery. Keeping minions unaware and stupid better served a master in their ability to control them. He didn't know Cecelia, didn't know if she was intelligent or not, but didn't suspect she was all that bright given her course of action.

He opened the door and leaned back, grabbing the weapon from the back seat. Driving around with such weapons could be risky, though less so than carrying firearms. It had been years since he was last stopped by any law enforcement and had been able to convince the officers after quite a bit of bullshitting that he'd been practicing martial arts, blood covered sword and all. He drove the speed limit after that night. There was no need in calling extra attention to himself, seeing as how he already looked like trouble to most people.

He closed the door and walked to the grounds. Fuck, he hated cemeteries. There was always a certain stench that emanated from the decay below the ground. His legs always felt tingly, like electric currents ran through his veins, as he stepped over the mounds of dirt and sunken gravesites. He reasoned this came from the decaying bodies below the ground emanating through the soil. It would be too faint to detect with his senses, but not faint enough to escape his spirit. There was a certain unknown variable to all of this. He was sure there were things his body detected that his brain didn't register. The physical would detect the metaphysical in a way that wasn't understood to the conscious brain.

He felt the wet grass beneath his feet and groaned inside. Running in wet grass was a pain in the ass because it was slippery, and he just didn't feel like having to be that good on his feet tonight.

He stopped and looked around the stones and trees, he didn't see anything moving. There was nothing living here. There was nothing dead either.

Roman sat down and leaned against a headstone, sitting perfectly still. He'd learned through the years to slow his breathing and to still his body in order to remain undetected by most but the highly attuned. He half wished Lux was here to keep him company, or to just handle this whole situation, but he also knew Lux would never agree to kill his own kind. He'd explained that it would be akin

230

to Roman killing humans, which was never an option. He knew Lux was lying. The vampire had no real conscience. Still, he wanted all this over with already so he could move on to the next conquest.

Moving on, that would not happen now. He was finally almost content with that idea, though it was just so contrary to the way he had lived his entire life.

There was suddenly a shift in the physicality of the grave yard. He knew there was something near him lurking, watching him even. Roman remained perfectly motionless as he adjusted his vision further to the surrounding darkness. His eyes honed in on the approaching mass of flesh that now moved through the graves effortlessly and without wavering. Roman was the targeted trajectory. He stood up, preparing himself to slaughter what came his way. Whoever it was, they weren't afraid of him. But they would learn to be in moments.

He took his ruined clothes off and tossed them to the floor and stood there in his underwear. He'd throw the clothes out later after he cleaned up. He turned to view the gaping wound across his back. It was a deep gash that started just below his right shoulder blade and curved in towards his spine. Another inch deeper and this could have been serious. He should get it looked at and have it professionally cleaned and stitched. He should, but he wouldn't.

His hair was matted with blood and tangled from the scuffle he'd had with the vampire. Dried crimson cords of hair stuck to his forehead and neck. The vampire had been extremely strong and skilled. Roman was lucky to be standing.

He remembered what Lux had said to him in a prior conversation. He looked in the mirror. *Do you look your age?* No, he didn't.

The memory of Violet's question in the kitchen came back to him. It was time for a change. He bent over, sending a wave of nausea through his body from the pain of the bleeding wound. He had lost a lot of blood. He caught his breath and then opened the cupboard and found the trimmer he used on his face. He plugged it in and held the vibrating machine in his hand. It was loud and shrill in the quiet of his bathroom. He picked up the front of his hair and shaved it off, then continued to shave row after row of his thick matted hair until nothing remained. He turned the clippers off and smoothed his hands across the surface of his scalp. The bristly stubble felt almost sharp against his palms. He saw the scar across the occipital bone that he hadn't seen since it had happened eleven years prior. Now that had been a rough night.

He turned to look at the wound again. Long thin black hairs stuck in the oozing red trail that smeared down his back and had seeped into the fabric of his underwear. He really should have it looked at by a doctor. It had been a while since he'd had a wound this deep, and it was just out of his reach. But instead he peeled the blood soaked underwear off and then got in the shower, letting the water run over the stinging wound until the cold stream finally ran clear around his feet and down the drain. Every move he made sent a sharp pain through him. The cut throbbed as he moved beneath the sharp bite of cold water. He rolled the bar of soap across his body, washing the mud and caked blood from his skin. The open wound stung in the pelting water. He raked his fingers over his scalp, wondering why the hell he hadn't done this sooner. It would be so easy. It felt good to be clean.

He went to the kitchen and brought a garbage bag and a broom to the bathroom. He cleaned the floor up and threw his clothes into the bag with the mass of black hair. Blood was smeared on the tiles where his clothing had been discarded. He took the damp towel from the rack and mopped the blood up. The grout was stained. He'd have to take care of that later.

Roman was still shaken by how strong the vampire had been. He hadn't been as big or tall as Roman, but he had been agile and unpredictable, and had offered no information. He wasn't even sure if the vampire was connected to the threat to Violet at all. Roman had fought with him too long, hoping he'd give something up, and that's what got him hurt. Had he just killed him at the initial attack he would've gotten away unscathed, but he hadn't. In the end, the vampire had given him nothing, but the thing had learned to fear him before meeting its end. It had been a pleasure killing him, the look of surprise and awe coming over the vampire's face had been gratifying. One less threat to Violet. Fuck, he wasn't even sure the vampire had been a threat to Violet. It didn't matter.

He pulled the shirt on, trying to avoid rubbing the fabric over the gash. He needed help covering it because he couldn't reach the wound. It would continue to reopen and bleed until he got it really cleaned out and covered. He wasn't looking forward to that as he was sure there would be debris in the wound that would need to be flushed out. He put a pair of jeans on, then bent over to pull his boots up feeling the lesion tearing and seeping again. He walked to the bathroom grabbing the supplies he always had in abundance, found his keys on the table where he'd thrown them, and headed out the door.

The house was dark, so he knew she'd be sleeping. He got out of the car, feeling the shirt sticking to his back. The pain caused him to wince as he peeled the shirt away from the wound where the fabric had stuck to it. He slipped the key into the lock and walked into the kitchen. The television was on, illuminating the room to a soft bluish hue. He walked in and found her curled up on the sofa. Her hands were resting against her stomach. Her hair fell across her face and shoulders, thick and blue black, reflecting the light of the television. The shiny fabric of her gown caught the electric rays of the screen in morphing wave-like patterns. He didn't want to startle her, and in truth, didn't want to have to deal with comforting her knowing she'd be freaked out by his wound. It was completely unfair she had to deal with any of this shit, all thanks to Lux.

He sat down in the red chair and stared blankly at the screen. He leaned forward, not wanting to put pressure on the wound or get blood on her furniture. His shirt was wet. His head felt so nice and icy cool without the thick hair. He rested his head in his hands, feeling the bumps his skull had developed from years of bashing. He closed his eyes, exhausted.

She stretched her body, her feet falling over the edge of the couch. The cold air felt good. She was hot from being beneath the thick afghan. For a moment she wondered who had covered her up, but then realized it must've been Amber. She rubbed her eyes and opened them focusing on the hunched man in the chair. *Mark!* She sat up, suddenly frightened and absolutely terrified that Mark was in her house. She cleared her eyes, afraid to breathe. She leaned forward as quietly as she could and focused. It was Roman. He was completely asleep in the chair and his head was shaved. She pulled herself off the couch and walked over to him and rubbed the top of his head. The sandpaper surface of his scalp was nice. She smiled as he stirred and looked up at her.

"I like it," she said with a smile.

He smiled in return and took her hand and held it. He was exhausted and just needed her comforting presence. *How times had changed.*

She kneeled before him and leaned her body into his as he wrapped his arms around her and hugged her tightly. He could feel the slit in his back split open and tried not to wince but was unsuccessful.

"You alright?" she asked, looking back up at him.

"I got cut pretty badly," he said bluntly. He wished he didn't have to burden her with this. "I need you to help me."

"Where?" she asked and stood up, eyes filled with concern for him. She knew he usually took these things lightly, so he must really be hurt if he was asking for her help.

"My back," he said, twisting to show her.

The fabric was darker where the blood had seeped through his shirt. She pulled the shirt up. Her eyes opened wide as she saw the fileted skin lying open, gaping and coagulated. "Roman, you need to go to the hospital for this!" she said, looking back at him.

"No, just help me clean it and cover it. It'll be fine," he said, pulling his shirt back down and standing up. "I brought bandages and antiseptic."

"You need stitches," she said, grabbing his arm.

"No, just clean it up. It'll be fine. I promise you." He smiled at her, trying to reassure her with his words. He knew now why he healed so quickly. This would heal too. "Besides, if it doesn't look a little better by tomorrow night I promise I'll go get it looked at, okay?"

"What if it gets infected?"

"If it doesn't look better by tomorrow night I'll go get it looked at, *okay*?"

Her brow furrowed, she wanted him to see a doctor. This wound was bad. "Okay, I guess." She shrugged, grabbing his hand, "Let's go clean it up."

He followed her upstairs to the bathroom. Roman took the shirt off and leaned against the sink. He knew from experience this would probably be excruciating. She was busily opening packages and peeling the safety seal off the peroxide bottle. She grabbed the cotton balls and started soaking one, preparing to start cleaning the insanely deep gash.

"You're too tall for me to reach that high and see what I'm doing," she said, looking at him in the mirror. "It'll be easier if you kneel, if you can."

He crouched down on his knees, resting his arms and head against the cool marble of the countertop. The cold surface felt comforting against his hot forehead.

She looked at the wound, afraid to touch it, not wanting to hurt him. There were small slivers of shaved hair and grass stuck in the injury. "Roman, this is going to hurt," she said with hesitation. "There's hair and stuff in it."

"It's okay, go ahead," he mumbled, not lifting his head, bracing himself for the impending pain. This would be nothing compared to other things he'd gone through, but it still hurt like hell.

The scar across the back of his head, jagged and white, caught her eye and made her brow furrow. There were several bumps on his skull. What had he been through in his life? She re-wet the cotton and started slowly cleaning the dried blood and debris from his skin. The muscles in his back tensed and then relaxed as she removed the cotton.

"Well, the peroxide isn't fizzing, I guess that's a good sign it's not infected yet," she said, tossing the pink and brown cotton ball into the trash. She continued working on the wound until finally it looked clean. She could peel back the skin with her finger like a flap, he'd been sliced open like a fish.

"I still think you should go get stitches," she said, smoothing some antiseptic ointment over the wound. She placed a cotton pad against the wound that she would affix with medical tape.

"If it's not getting better by tomorrow night I will," he said, lifting his head and looking up at her in the mirror.

She secured the gauze and put her hands on his shoulders. He turned around and rested his face against her and wrapped his arms around her waist.

"I'm really tired," he sighed into the soft fabric and her warm body.

"I can imagine," she said, easing him up off the floor.

He flipped the light off and walked to her bedroom. She pulled the blanket back and crawled into bed, waiting for him to get his boots off so he could follow. He unbuckled his belt and pants to make himself more comfortable and slid across the bed on his stomach.

"That wound looks really nasty," she said, quietly rubbing her hand over his shaved head.

"Yeah, it could have been you," he said, focusing intently on her eyes. They glistened in the dark. "Are you sure you want this life?"

"No, but I know I don't want a life without you." She smiled. "Aw, I'm so sappy." She grinned and rustled his used-to-be hair.

"Thanks for taking care of me," he said, reaching his arm over and wrapping it around her.

She leaned over and kissed his eyes shut. "Goodnight, Roman."

"Amber, he got hurt really bad last night," Violet said as she busily went about the task of making french toast and sausage.

"How?" Amber replied while setting the table.

"Killing a vampire, I guess. He didn't tell me what happened, and he was too exhausted, so I didn't ask."

"So, that's just his normal life?" Amber said, half in disbelief.

"Yeah, it's what he's been doing since he was like fifteen or something. Weird huh?" Violet put the food on a platter and walked over to the table.

"Uh, Just a little. Where is he, anyway?" Amber asked, taking her fork and placing some toast onto her plate.

"He's still sleeping. I didn't have the heart to wake him up."

"This fucking freaks me out," Amber said, having difficulty wrapping her mind around it all.

"I know, Amber, and I'm sorry you guys are even involved."

"Yeah, we're sort of in danger by proxy, eh?"

Violet looked at her friend and laughed. "By proxy! It cracks me up when you say that!"

"What's so funny about it?" Amber snickered.

"I don't know? It just sounds funny."

"Um, okay, so anyway..."

"Sorry, yeah, thanks to *yours truly* I guess you guys are in danger, *by proxy*. But try not to worry too much because we're not going to let anything happen."

Randy wandered down the stairs dressed in his work t-shirt and faded jeans. His hair was slicked back away from his face. He tiredly grabbed a plate of food and walked to the living room to watch his morning cartoons without ever saying a word. The two girls watched him as he walked away and looked at each other and grinned.

"So, not to change the subject, but what's going on with you and Roman anyway? Are you officially official or what? You seemed pretty cozy last night." Amber asked, for the hundredth time, looking at her friend with suspicion.

"Nothing, I guess."

"Nothing?" Amber said, setting her fork down and looking at Violet with confusion.

"Yeah, nothing, I don't even know if he's really all that attracted to me to be honest. I mean, yeah, he says he is, or whatever, but he's never even, like, tried to kiss me or anything." It made her uncomfortable and insecure talking about her and Roman. She hadn't been embarrassed by such conversations in years, and here she was stuttering nervously like a twelve year old.

"He finds you attractive, don't be stupid. I've noticed it this whole time, how he has always looked at you, even when you were clueless. And he definitely seems different since you guys got back from Chicago. I mean, that *vibe* wasn't exactly non-obvious last night. He was all patting your stomach and whatever. I'd be shocked if he didn't have a massive boner when you were sitting on his lap."

"Oh my god!" Violet said and laughed as she rolled her eyes with embarrassment.

"What? You're fucking hot, wearing that slinky nightgown and stuff? Please. I get a boner looking at you and I don't roll that way."

Violet laughed and shook her head.

"He so obviously loves you, Vi," Amber said, reaching out and squeezing Violet's wrist.

"You think? " Her voice lilted, hesitant and hopeful. "I know he cares about me, but I'm not quite sure he thinks of me, like, totally that way." Her thoughts always seemed to drift back to feeling inadequate and thinking there was no way anyone could truly love her or really want her. She was never good enough. And Roman was just so extraordinary.

"Violet, come on. Maybe he's just shy?"

"I don't know? I can't picture him being shy with women. He didn't hesitate to tell me about fucking Mylori. He was pretty open about that. I'd think if he was shy he wouldn't talk about that kind of stuff at all? I mean, he's obviously been with other chicks too. Duh. How could he not? And I've been naked around him multiple times, and we've slept in the same bed a lot. So, it's not like it wouldn't have been easy for him if he wanted me."

"He's been with Mylori?" Amber said, her mouth falling open in shock and maybe awe.

Violet shifted her head and scowled.

Amber made an "oops" face and changed the subject back. "Well, don't you think maybe you should ask him about it? It's pretty inconceivable to me that you guys haven't even kissed and yet you've been sleeping in the same bed for weeks now."

"I know, it's kind of odd, but I swear it wasn't like girlfriend/boyfriend stuff until just recently. Like literally the subject didn't come up until we went to Chicago."

"Yeah right, whatever. You could tell yourselves that all you want, but it was painfully obvious to the rest of us. Why do you think Steve moved out?"

"What's Steve got to do with anything?" Violet asked with annoyance.

"He left because he couldn't stand seeing you and Roman making googly eyes at each other. Well, plus Mark nagged him about it nonstop."

Violet rolled her eyes and then looked up towards the stairs. "Let's stop talking about this before Roman wakes up and hears," Violet said, wanting to change the subject. There were far too many issues bobbing about in her head. She didn't want Roman hearing her talking about this with Amber before she even talked to him about it. Besides, there was no way all these people, Mark, Lux, Roman, and apparently Steven, were this obsessed with her. The very idea was ridiculously stupid.

Roman could smell the scent of breakfast wafting beneath the door. He rolled over, feeling a sudden sting in his back. At least the wound felt dry. He stood up and rubbed his eyes. The realization of not feeling hair down his back stunned him momentarily. He hadn't had hair this short since his birth. Actually, he had a full head of hair at birth too, though it wasn't long. He walked across the hall to go to the bathroom. His muscles were beyond sore. He put his hand against the wall and braced himself as he pissed. His arm trembled as it held his weight. He could barely stand. The vampire had given him a good beating. But Roman won the fight. He always won the fight. He washed his hands and looked at himself in the mirror. There was a stranger looking back at him.

There was a lot he needed to do today. He needed to tell her all that Lux had told him first and foremost. She needed to know the truth about everything before he would feel comfortable with her making decisions about the future or continuing on this path. She may discover the truth and want nothing more to do with him. It wouldn't be right to get more involved with her before telling her everything. *Fuck.* He wanted to fuck her. He squeezed his eyes shut disgusted with himself for even thinking about it at this moment. Why did he have to always be so moral? She was going to run for the hills. And that would probably, most definitely, be in her best interest.

He exhaled and shook his head at himself and splashed his face with some cold water. He dried himself on the hand towel.

He also needed to continue training her. It would be difficult with the pain in his body, but it was of absolute necessity now.

He stretched his arms above his head to loosen his sore muscles, then buckled his belt and walked downstairs.

"Good morning," he said, walking over to the girls and pulling a chair out at the table. He hoped the change in his appearance and the giant patch of gauze wouldn't draw too much attention. He hated being the center of attention.

Amber looked up, stunned momentarily by the change. He looked considerably more menacing than he had with his long black hair. Her eyes flicked over his naked torso and then noticed all the bruises around his neck and shoulders. To her credit, she didn't say anything, but offered him a platter of french toast and sausage.

"Thanks," he said with a smile, raking some food onto his plate.

"Are you feeling better?" Violet asked, reaching over and raking her nails gently across the side of his head.

He wanted to close his eyes like a dog and relish the feel of that. No one had ever done this to him. "Yeah, I'm alright," he answered, looking at her and wishing she'd keep rubbing his head. It felt good. Relaxing.

"Dude! Why'd you shave all your hair off? Your hair was awesome. You could have had a killer mohawk, man," Randy said, walking into the kitchen with an empty plate, which he dumped in the sink and then stood beside Amber.

Roman laughed politely and didn't answer.

"Imagine the mullet he could have had," Amber said with a laugh.

"Oh man," Violet said, laughing as well.

"Yeah, but the mohawk? That thing would have been amazing," Randy said.

"Not everyone wants a mohawk, Randy," Violet said, rolling her eyes and smiling.

"Well, just sayin'." Randy laughed and picked his keys up. "Yay, I get to go build tractors now," he said with zero enthusiasm and held the keys up and jingled them.

Amber stood up and followed him to the door.

"See you guys later," Randy said, opening the door and kissing Amber good-bye.

"Bye," Violet and Roman said simultaneously.

"I'm gonna go take a shower," Amber said, scuffling her yellow fuzzy slippers across the tile floor.

"Enjoy," Violet said in response, and then turned back to Roman as she ate the last bit of food on her plate. "So, is your back feeling better?"

"I'm really sore, but it's not bleeding anymore," Roman said, detached from the situation. He'd had a million injuries, this was no different.

Violet looked at him, wondering what was going on with his mood. He was so hard to read at times. And right now he seemed a bit distant. Given the convo she'd just had with Amber it made her worry. She stood up and took her empty plate to the sink and rinsed it off. She then filled the sink with warm, soapy water and piled the dirty dishes into it to soak.

"V, there's a bunch of stuff I need to talk about with you today," Roman said, turning around in his chair to look at her.

She grabbed the dish towel and walked back to where he was seated at the kitchen table as she dried her hands. "Okay, now I'm scared," she said. He could see the dimple in her chin giving her fear away. "Is this where you tell me you love me, you're just not *in* love with me?"

"What?" Roman asked, completely caught off guard. "No, of course not. Why would you think that?"

"I don't know," she said, looking at the floor.

"There must be a reason you'd say that?" He lifted her chin so she'd look at him.

"I don't know, I was just talking to Amber about stuff." She shrugged her shoulders, not sure just how much she should say. He was eventually going to get annoyed with her always having drama, wasn't he? Ugh, she was just going to spill it in her horribly awkward way. "I just...I guess I don't quite know how you feel about me still. I mean, I know you care for me or whatever, but you haven't even kissed me or anything." She felt her face turning red as she fumbled with the dish towel.

She had always been bold with Mark, but she'd surmised it was because she didn't care about him to the same extent she cared for Roman. It's not as frightening to offend someone, or look stupid in front of them, if you don't care if they really love you or not.

Her eyes rose again to meet his. He was taking her in quietly. It hadn't dawned on him how insecure she'd been over this. He had assumed she'd be the confident one when it came to this whole relationship thing. He was the one who should be insecure. How could she not know how she made him feel? He thought it had been painfully obvious from the beginning, though he had been denying it and trying to hide it, so maybe he had actually been successful?

"I just think... maybe you aren't attracted to me *that way*." She shrugged her shoulders slightly, feeling very vulnerable and waiting for him to tell her that he really wasn't attracted to her *that way*. She was prepared for the inevitable.

His eyes seemed to change. They looked at her with softness, so open and so green. He smiled and shook his head.

"What? Don't laugh at me!" she said, forcing her awkward grin back and slapping his arm.

"I'm not laughing, Violet. I just assumed you knew how I felt about you."

"Hello! I'm not a mind reader, and you're impossible to gauge, mister stoic," she said, enunciating each word and raising her eyebrows. She put her hands on her hips and tipped her head to the side.

"I haven't kissed you yet because I didn't want to push anything on you. You've been through a lot and the last thing you need is some guy groping you."

"You're not *some guy*." She rolled her eyes.

Roman exhaled and looked away briefly before looking back at her. "Originally I had no intention of getting you involved in all this chaos."

"Well, I could've been a one night stand," Violet said in jest and rolled her eyes again.

"Yes, you could have been," he said, his voice so deep and rumbly, a look passed through his eyes that made her stomach flip. "The night we met I kicked myself for not taking you up on your invitation to come inside. Believe me, I thought about it all night. Or maybe a few nights."

Violet blushed and bit her bottom lip.

"But then I saw you again, and we became friends."

"And you realized how stupid and gross I am?" she said, half in jest.

"No, *dork*, I realized I liked you too much." He chuckled and she smiled in response. "The plan was to leave. I was going to protect you, finish the job, and then leave, pretending I never met you. You were just a girl I had to protect. Nothing more. I put the idea of us sleeping together out of my mind."

Violet shifted, looking away from him. He reached down and tipped her chin back up. "But then things started to change and I wanted you. I wouldn't let myself entertain the idea of us being together. I couldn't let myself feel what I was feeling." He paused and looked away from her for a moment and then looked back. "Believe me, the thought entered my mind regularly that we could just sleep together. It would have been so easy to give in and just touch you. I wanted to, but I didn't want to be just another asshole that took advantage of you. I had no intention of staying around. So how could I do that to you when I liked you?" He took her arms in his hands and pulled her forward. "You have no idea how difficult it has been."

She grinned, her cheeks flushing pink as she leaned into him, allowing him to wrap his arms around her. She pulled back slightly and took his face in her hands and smiled at him. "I really, really love you," she said quietly.

"I love you too," he said, surprised by his admission, the words coming before he'd had a chance to even think or stop them. But it was true, he did love her. The emotions felt strange and foreign, but good.

They were so close, even in height with him sitting down and she bowed to him. Violet smiled nervously, her hands holding his face. She couldn't believe he had just said that he loved her. He hadn't even kissed her or anything, and he loved her. He had never expected anything of her, or from her, and he loved her.

The pads of her thumbs softly brushed the line of his black eyebrows, dusting over his lashes, his eyes closing as she touched them.

"I can't believe you love me," she said, barely audible, and kissed the tip of his long straight nose, and then his mouth, savoring the softness of his lips.

"I think you're insane for loving me," he muttered, and caught her chin with his teeth, biting gently and then kissing her there.

Violet pressed her lips to his, pausing, apprehensive. Her hands cradling his skull, she moved her mouth against his, kissing him gently, barely touching his lips. His mouth was so warm and soft, his lips so lush. They felt exactly how she had always pictured them feeling and tasting. Roman opened his mouth, sucking her bottom lip, teeth nipping her lightly. His tongue was warm and sweet, tasting of maple syrup and powdered sugar as she licked his tongue and lips delicately. She loved the feel of his angular jaw moving beneath her hands as he kissed her, the stubble of his shaved head and face prickling her palms.

It had been a little startling that she'd kissed him, considering he'd thought about it, and forced himself to stop thinking about her kiss, a thousand times since they'd met. She was so human and soft and delicate and flowery, so completely unlike what he'd experienced before and so completely unlike himself. The other women he'd been with had been like him. Cold, brutal, almost dead inside. A physical act only. She was real and warm and soft. And she loved him. And he loved her. What a marvel she was to him.

Her tongue swirled over his. God, her mouth. He wanted to crawl inside of her. The movement of her tongue was killing him. Her breasts pressed against him, the thin silky gown, and the warmth of her body through the thin fabric... He wanted her more than he had previously understood. And then he remembered what he had to tell her, what she needed to know, and he realized he couldn't allow this to happen until she knew the truth about everything. She needed to know who she was, *what* she was, before he took this to a place where he couldn't stop. He growled and kissed her deeply, giving everything to her.

"Let's go have coffee," he said, pulling his mouth from hers reluctantly.

Her face was flushed pink, her eyes languid and caressing as she looked at him. In that moment he truly wished he could be a bad guy and not tell her the truth. He wanted to take her upstairs for hours, and then run off to some place where she would never have to know the truth. It was so unfair that her future had been written by vampires who didn't give a shit about their actions.

"Coffee? Okay," she said with a smile, having completely forgotten that he had wanted to talk to her about something. She kissed him again, not ready to stop just yet, and he was completely willing. "Mmm..." she murmured as she licked his bottom lip and bit him gently.

"Ugh, come on," Roman groaned, kissing her again and then taking her hands in his and standing up. She looked up at him, smiling as her chin rested against his sternum. "Come on, let's go," he said, bending to kiss her forehead.

Well, apparently he did find her attractive after all. Violet smiled and bit her bottom lip.

Randy's shirt was tight on Roman. She could see the bandage through the fabric as well as every muscle of his upper body. *Very pleasant. Good job, Violet.* She grinned to herself.

"Why didn't you just give me that *killer* t-shirt?" he asked, stretching the bottom of the shirt.

"Because it's dirty. And besides, this looks *much* better."

"It's grass green," he said with distaste.

The dull look on his face made Violet laugh. "Yeah, I know. Pretty funny." She grinned and looped her arm through his. "It brings out the color in your eyes." She winked at him.

"Swell." He looked down at her and made a face. "I get to pick your next outfit then."

"That's fine. Obviously I don't mind going out in public looking like an idiot." She laughed, looking down at her faded and worn jeans and the purple long sleeved t-shirt with The Hamburgler on it.

"Yeah, I guess not," he teased.

She laughed and smacked him. "So, are we going to resume training today?"

"It's obviously going to be hard for me, but we have to do it. There's no time to screw around anymore," he said, opening the door for her.

They walked up to the counter and ordered their drinks and then found a booth back in the corner of the coffee house near a window.

"Roman, it looked better this morning. Last night I could have peeled the thing up and probably stuck half my finger down inside of it. Ew, now that's a pleasant thought," she said sarcastically, wrinkling her nose. "This morning the deeper part was already healed. What gives?" she said, dipping her finger in the caramel coffee and licking the whipped cream away.

"That's what I need to talk to you about," he said with hesitation.

He'd been gathering his thoughts all morning, trying to figure the best way to tell her what Lux had told him. He realized beating around the bush wasn't necessary anymore. She needed answers the same way he needed answers, and being direct was the easiest way to make that happen.

"I spoke to Lux yesterday, and he told me something a bit disturbing about my family," he said, taking a sip of his drink.

Violet looked up from her latte, completely rapt by what he'd said.

"Remember how I told you my family kept my aunt locked away for all those years? It turns out they kept her alive because they were using her blood to transfer the power of the blood to themselves."

"What?" Violet asked, not shocked or disgusted as she didn't know these people and it didn't affect her the way it did him. She was genuinely curious.

"I've known the power of their blood, hell, even their saliva heals to a degree. It makes sense to me why they did it, but it was sick and wrong."

"So, why didn't they become vampires then?"

"That's not how it works. There has to be a mutual exchange in order for that to happen. The blood works almost like some sort of medicine. Honestly, if they bottled the stuff a lot of diseases could probably be cured, but that's not the point. The point is, because they drank the blood, some of the attributes associated with the blood mixed in with their own and made them somewhat immortal themselves."

"So, how did it end?"

"I need to do the research to get the specifics on that, but Lux said my family history books should have the details. How he knows all this I don't know, and I didn't really ask. Fuck, I should ask. But I have a feeling I won't like the answer, and I can only deal with so many fucked up messes at a time. But what I do know is that genetically that blood is in me too."

"So, you're saying you have vampire blood in you?"

"Yes."

He looked away from her and took a sip of his coffee. He wasn't sure how she'd react, but he assumed she'd be calm and probably take this part of the news better than he had, since it didn't really affect her all that much, and she seemed to take crazy news relatively well. It also didn't appear she really had anything against vampires for the most part. Which was odd in and of itself.

"I mean, that's really no big deal, right? It doesn't seem to hurt you in any way. And if it's going to make you heal faster that's awesome. You're like Superman or something." She smiled and kicked him under the table, wanting his attention back. He'd been staring at his cup since he'd told her the news.

He looked up at her with a slight lift to the corner of his lips. She had a way of making things seem so damned innocent and simple. "Your friends are walking this way," he said, looking over her shoulder to the approaching devil dolls.

"Violet!" Malinda said, reaching out and touching Violet on the shoulder.

"Hi girls," Violet said halfheartedly. Damn it, she was in no mood to chit chat with such a conversation hanging in the air.

They seemed more gaunt, more strung out, pale with black smudged eyes. They were dressed identically again, and Violet figured this must be their new thing.

"What happened to your hair?" Malinda gasped at Roman, who sat perfectly still, staring at the two strange girls. He had been around these goth types frequently and he still thought they were generally pretty comical.

"I cut it," he said stoically.

"Ahh...she's trying to make you look like Mark. I see how it is," Malinda said, and winked at Roman and then looked back at Violet. "Just kidding, dear," she said, tapping Violet's arm.

Violet looked up at her with violence in her eyes.

"Are you going to see Randy's band play tonight? We're all going. You should go too," Dory mewed, looking at Roman. Her eyes glistened as they picked up the wet sparkle of raindrops from the window.

"I'm not sure we'll make it, it just depends," Violet said dismissively.

"Wow, you're looking kind of *puffy* or something," Malinda said, whispering the latter half of the sentence and looking at Roman from the corner of her eye.

Violet looked at the girl with a look that could kill. Had she forgotten who she was talking to? "It's called being healthy, Malinda. You might want to see a doctor yourself. You look like a sick cat."

Dory giggled, not at her friend but at Violet, and hid her face behind her hands.

Roman lowered his head, not wanting to get involved in the catty exchange.

"Well anyway, I'm glad to run into you guys. Did you hear about Gwen?" Malinda spoke seductively, her voice uncommonly sweet for the topic. The expression on her face was so composed with absolutely no sign of remorse.

"Yes," Violet said, looking away from her and taking another drink of her coffee. Her eyes glanced towards Roman who was obviously distracted and annoyed by the girls' presence.

"What a shame." Dory giggled behind her fingers.

"Why do you think this is funny?" Violet asked, disgusted with the two.

"Oh, come on, you hated her, Violet. Don't be a hypocrite now," Malinda said, tilting her head to the side and looking down her nose.

"I didn't like her, that's a fact, but I don't think her being left dead and naked in the woods is funny. I wouldn't wish that on anyone and I feel completely disgusted with myself for how I treated her. What the fuck is going on with you guys? What's happened to you? I don't remember you being such little cunts before."

Roman looked up, concerned that Violet might react physically because her tone was so harsh. They were pushing every button and it was clear she was in no mood for it. Not that he blamed her. She was completely accurate in her assessment. The girls were acting like little cunts. Dory giggled again, her eyes looking delirious.

"Nothing's happened to *us,* Violet. It's obvious *you* have sort of gone astray," Malinda said.

Violet didn't respond. She had nothing to say and it was taking all her willpower to keep herself from knocking their teeth down their throats. She didn't know what the fuck was going on with them, but she wasn't interested in dealing with them anymore.

"Walk away, girls," Roman said, looking up at the two of them.

"Hopefully we'll see you tonight." Malinda smiled, syrupy sweet, and every bit as fake as she could be.

"If I'm there I'd suggest staying away from me," Violet warned. Her eyes were sharp and focused on Malinda.

"You don't own the scene anymore, Violet," Malinda said, her tone so condescending even Roman wanted to react. Dory giggled again.

"I never wanted it," Violet growled, not looking away from the girl. "It's all yours, darling. Have at it."

Malinda smiled and reached for Dory's hand, leading her away. She stopped and looked back briefly. "I hope that's fat free." She grinned and turned around and kept walking.

"What the fuck was *that*?" Violet asked, incredulous as she leaned forward stunned.

He shrugged his shoulders. "I have no idea. I don't know these people. Nor do I care to. But it's clear she was trying to get a reaction from you."

"Roman, they were not that way *at all* before. They were the sweetest girls I knew."

"Maybe they're taking drugs?"

"That has to be it. I have no idea, but it's disturbing."

"You know you aren't fat, right?"

"Well, compared to them I am," she said, rolling her eyes.

"And you know they're too skinny, *right*?" he asked, wanting to make sure they hadn't touched some nerve in her. He knew from past experience this was a sensitive subject with her.

"Roman, there is no '*too skinny*' as far as most people are concerned," she said, crossing her arms. "Now where were we?"

He exhaled a slow, deep breath and focused his eyes on her. He couldn't tell if she was being sarcastic, or their words had actually wounded her ego, but she wasn't interested in pursuing that conversation, so he let it drop for the time being. "I'm hoping you'll want to help me go through the family history to find out more details."

"Of course," she said, perking back up. She was fascinated by the possibilities of reading his family history.

"Lux said something else," he said, stopping to take another drink.

"What?" she asked, doing the same.

"You know that you don't have normal strength," he stated calmly.

"Huh? What do you mean?"

"You're stronger than a girl your size should be."

"I guess? I mean, I never thought about it before, cuz I'm just me," she said, shrugging her shoulders and furrowing her brow.

"Lux says somewhere throughout your family's history something like what happened with my family happened to you."

"What? I don't think so!" she scoffed at him, trying to think back through the little history she knew. "I really don't think so?"

Roman stopped himself from pushing the point, not wanting to bombard her. "Something happened somewhere along the line."

"I really don't think so. Did he say what happened? Did he know?"

"He swears he knows nothing, though it's difficult to know with him whether or not he's telling the truth." He tried to gauge her reaction to this conversation. She seemed shocked, but not necessarily freaked out.

"So, what you're telling me is that you and I have this blood in us and it makes us like *vampires*? But I don't see it, other than me being strong? Couldn't that just be some weird coincidence, like how some people are just really good athletes?"

"No, Violet. You can feel them when they're near, right? You feel something different?"

"I guess."

"Lux told me that the vampire blood recognizes what they are. I don't understand the science behind this," he said, lowering his head, annoyed by his lack of answers and inability to explain. "I just know that vampires can sense other vampires. Lux says that's what makes me an exceptional hunter."

"I just don't know how this can be true. My family was completely normal in every way, Roman."

"I don't understand it either, kitten."

She sat quietly, going over each of her family members in her head, looking for some kind of clue. Roman watched her as the wheels turned and knew she was searching for answers or clues within her own history that might now suddenly make sense to her.

"There's nothing," she said. "There's nothing in my life that makes sense in regards to all of this." She sat back in the booth and rested her hands on her lap.

"I wish I could give you more," he said sincerely, and reached across the table, inviting her hands to his.

"Yeah, I wish there were some real answers too. But I mean, I guess it doesn't matter how it happened, right?"

"Not really." He smirked, gripping her hands.

"So, what powers do we have?"

"I don't know if they're considered *powers* or not, V, but it just seems like we're a little stronger than average. We heal faster, age a little slower, and have some sort of sense when it comes to locating them."

"I guess that sounds okay," she said, shrugging her shoulders. "I mean, those aren't *bad* things." She seemed to be somewhat coming to grips with what he'd told her, even if logically it made no sense. She was far better at adapting than he was. "Do you ever crave it?"

"Crave what? *Blood*?"

"Yeah, do you crave it?"

"No," he said, taken aback by the question. "It's revolting to me."

"But maybe that's your brain talking--your sense of right and wrong--and not your body?"

"No, Violet."

"Okay, just asking," she said, raising her eyebrows.

"Do you?"

"I used to think I did, but that was probably just stupid vampire bullshit. You know, goth crap."

"Are you sure?"

"Of course I'm not sure. I know the idea was never *revolting* to me. But you can convince yourself of a lot of things that aren't right when you want to."

"Yeah, I suppose you can," he said, thinking back to how he'd justified the relationship with Mylori as being okay, even though he knew it wasn't right.

"I can't believe how well you're taking this information. I thought for sure you'd either not believe me, think I'm a nut, or you'd run for the hills and tell me to fuck off," he said.

Violet scowled at him playfully. "You ought to know me better than that by now. Besides, I've faced far worse things than finding out I've got super powers. You're not getting rid of me that easily."

Roman squeezed her hand. She was so much more relaxed than he was.

"Anyway, I suppose we should get to work and worry about all this later?" She smiled and squeezed his hand back.

"Yeah."

16

METAL SLIVERS

CECELIA LEANED INTO HIM as she gripped his forearm, biting down into the tendons and muscle. The crunch was audible, the sound satisfying a baser urge, causing her to tear and rip into the muscle harder. She could hear the flow of blood in her ears ringing, dizzy and feral. The muscle jumped between her teeth as he flexed and leaned back into the couch. Mark's fingers channeled through her hair as she fed from his yielded veins.

Malinda and Dory huddled slack jawed and giddy in the corner of the room. They were afraid to get too close for fear she may lash out at them.

There is so much fear in this.

Cecelia's eyes rose towards the girls, watching them as she fed, enjoying the dread and pleasure in their eyes. She relished watching them huddled on their knees together like dirty orphans in a back alley.

They taste so sweet. Their fear and adoration tastes so sweet.

She pulled away from him, leaving his arm to spill out onto the couch. He pressed the wound to his mouth, lapping up the remaining seepage. The smell of her saliva and his own torn flesh aroused him.

She stood and moved towards the girls, lifting her hands towards them, offering them to come to her. She went to her knees and caressed the frail beings, her mouth glistening red and wet, her tongue stained with his blood. She pressed her mouth to Malinda's forehead, leaving a smeared crimson kiss. Malinda's head fell back, offering the woman her neck. Cecelia smiled and lifted the soft fabric of the girl's skirt. Malinda's breath was heavy with anticipation. Cecelia smoothed the back of her hand across Malinda's cheek and caressed Dory's arm as she leaned forward, biting gently into Malinda's thigh. A rivulet of blood flowed over her tongue like sap from an autumn tree, thick and sweet. She would be gentle with them for the time being. They were far too delicate to want to harm them just yet. Her marks would be hidden so that no one would suspect. And one day they would be her children.

Malinda held onto Dory for strength as the woman slowly took her blood.

Mark observed Cecelia manipulating the girls with a smile on his face as he stroked himself. His body was thrumming, frenetic with energy and bloodlust.

Cecelia sat up, grinning seductively at Malinda and then turned to Dory, whose face was sweet and soft. Her pale cheeks were gaunt and more sunken than the other girl's. Cecelia kissed her mouth. Her tongue tasted Dory's, and then she licked her own lips, guiding the girl to follow her. Dory's tongue crept out of her mouth, tasting the metallic blood and saliva Cecelia had left in the wake of her kiss. Gently Cecelia caressed Dory's soft head of curls, guiding her to the open wound between Malinda's thighs.

She sat back as the girls did as she showed them. She stood and walked back to Mark and straddled him, replacing his fondling hand with hers and leaned into him, laughing quietly deep in her throat. He growled and took her neck in his mouth. The pale flesh burst open violently like a gushing piece of fruit. She watched the girls nuzzle each other as he sucked hungrily, his body growing harder in her hands.

"This is really basic. There's no need for anything fancy. The goal is to get it over with the quickest way possible."

He held the sword out toward her, allowing her to take the handle.

"Don't make conversation unless you need information. Don't screw around, because most of them are manipulative and intuitive to a phenomenal degree. Even the stupid ones have instincts they don't even know how to control, but they're there all the same. Go for the neck, it's as simple as that.

She held the blade up and looked at it closely. There were no dents, no nicks out of the metal, just smooth, sharp steel.

He picked the other weapon up from the ground and showed her how to hold it, how to center her body, and how to swing her arms smoothly and evenly. "None of this means anything when it comes down to it. Instinct and the will to survive will take over. The most important thing to know is that they can kill you very easily, so you need to kill them first. I know it sounds stupid, but that's what it all boils down to."

"So, how do I practice this then, really?"

"We'll spar."

"But you're hurt?" she said, slicing through the air and relishing the feel of the blade cutting through the wind.

"They don't always attack you when you're ready, V," he said with a wry grin. "Now charge at me, but obviously don't try to stab me for real."

"You look so fucking hot right now," she purred, a huge smile on her face as she lunged forward, thrusting the blade in his direction. The movement came so swiftly that she was shocked by her own aggression.

Roman jumped back, startled by her sudden attack. "I was thinking the same thing about you," he said, jumping out of the way and pinning her arm behind her back.

"Hey!" she whined, trying to get free.

Roman kissed her on the cheek from behind and spun her loose. She smiled, a fierce determination in her eye, and licked her lips. Yes, she liked the feel of this.

Violet and Roman sat on his bed, leafing through his books and reading his family's history. She had barely made a dent in the book she was reading when her mind began to wander.

"Roman, my dad died instantly in the accident, but my mom stayed alive for a week," she said, looking up at him.

"Did you get to talk to her?"

"No. I mean, I talked to her, but she was gone already. She had brain damage."

"I'm sorry," he said, looking up at her and rubbing his hand against her cheek to push the stray hair away.

She was thankful for his comfort. "But her body," she said and paused, clearly remembering something. "The doctors were surprised by the way her body was healing itself. They said had her brain not been damaged so severely, she would have been able to come through the accident."

Roman's brow creased, unsure of what she was telling him and hesitant to assume.

"Roman, they were *surprised* by it. She had internal bleeding and about a thousand broken bones, but her body was healing."

Her eyes were welling with tears now, thinking back to the day she'd been escorted by the police to the hospital. Her father was already gone and her mother lay in a broken heap, brain dead, and hooked to machines that sustained her. But they had told her she wasn't really alive. He put his arm around her, pulling her closer.

"Roman, what if she was like me? What if I hadn't told them to take her off the machines and her brain could have regenerated itself?"

"I don't think that's possible," he said quietly. "I really don't think it's possible."

It was true, he didn't think the brain could be repaired, but what did he know? He'd never known a vampire who'd sustained brain damage. But he wouldn't allow her to place more guilt upon herself. And besides that, even if her mother had vampire blood in her, she would have still been human.

"But what if it was, and I let her die? She was never sick, Roman. She looked younger than her age too. You saw the pictures of her. Her and my dad were the same age."

"She never said anything about it to you?" he asked.

"No, maybe she didn't know? I would have never known, had you not come along. Maybe it was the same for her, and no living family knew anything about the history? Roman, what if I let her die?" She looked up into his eyes, needing to hear something that would ease her fears.

"I don't think she would have gotten better, V. Maybe she was like you, I guess someone would have had to have been, if what Lux said is true, but you can't blame yourself for doing what was right to do." He wiped her eyes and cradled her face as she cried.

"I'm so tired of everything being so complicated," she sighed, and let him hold her.

"I know," he said, and kissed the top of her head.

"I don't think I'll ever know the truth of how this happened."

"We'll worry about that after all this is settled with this vampire, okay? We'll find out somehow."

They sat there silently for a while. He knew her brain was probably working overtime, questioning her mother's death and everything associated with it. Eventually he handed her another book from the trunk of things he'd carried with him so that she could focus her thoughts on something else. He was thankful he'd dragged these with him on the trip to Ohio. Usually he left only with a small suitcase and his box of mementos. But for some reason this time he'd brought some reading material. Of course it would just be blind luck if they were able to find anything at all in these few books he did have, especially considering he had hundreds of volumes back home and elsewhere. The likelihood there would be any pertinent information in these few journals was slim to none.

He looked over at her to see her perusing each page diligently. It was better for her to be focused on something than to keep rehashing those last moments with her mom. After a long while of running his eyes over skittering words and dulling text he was shocked by what he'd found. He stopped reading and handed the book to her, dumbfounded.

"So, it's true. It's here in black and white," she said, re-reading the passage he'd pointed out to her.

The entry had been fleeting; a casual reference to his aunt, but what had been written was unmistakable. It mentioned her by name and then said that she had been taken care of and would no longer be used as a "fountain of youth". He had read this journal in the past but had never even considered anything strange in what had been written. It was glaringly obvious what it was referring to now, because he knew what he was looking for, but the few years before when he'd read it he hadn't really given it a passing thought.

"I guess so," he sighed and lay back down on the bed. "Fucking weird finding this out. My whole life I've been repulsed by those bastards and now I find out I have their blood in me?"

"Yeah, but it doesn't make you like them, Roman. Actually it makes you better."

"How do you figure?" he asked, sitting up and leaning back on his elbows.

"Well, because you have your human sensibilities and all that junk, but you also have their strength. Really, I think it gives you more strength than them. If you were only human there's no way you could kill one of them. I mean, do you think your average human could really kill them except by some crazy stroke of luck? I doubt it, or they would have been wiped out a long time ago, right? There's been enough people who know about vampires that surely if humans were capable, their existence would have been made known and a war on them would have been waged. You know humans and their quest to kill things."

"I don't even want to rationalize any of this. It is what it is. I guess the question is how do you feel about it?"

"I don't know what to feel, actually. I'm sort of thankful in that it gives me strengths normal people don't have, but I guess I'm confused by how it happened, and why it happened, and what it means in terms of spirituality."

"I don't think it means anything spiritually," he said dismissively.

"How do you know?"

"Because I know." He shrugged his shoulders.

"Okay, that's vague," she said, crinkling her nose and shoving his leg.

"What? Why would it change anything?"

"Well, because vampires are evil or whatever."

"I don't know if they are any more evil than human beings, or dogs, or bears, or butterflies, for that matter. I mean, they can be, but so can people. It's not like they can't control themselves." Roman fell back down on the bed, his arm propping his head up.

"So, then why be on some big crusade to kill them?"

He paused for a moment, thinking about the question. "I don't know, because it's what I've always done, I guess. It's all I've ever known. It's just what Ikov men do."

"Any Ikov women?"

"No. Ikovs are always male."

"That can't be true," she said, laughing.

Roman furrowed his brow and thought back to the family tree. He could only think of a couple female ancestors and they had been born at a time where women were not equal.

"There's only been a few women born in my family, none of which took part in this bullshit. I've always been taught to protect women. I guess that sounds pretty sexist and outdated."

"I don't think it's sexist to want to protect women. I mean, as long as they're not treated like weak little helpless idiots that can't fend for themselves. I would protect anyone. Male or female. If I could."

The corner of Roman's lip turned up slightly. "Same. And I do. I don't only get sent to protect beautiful little girls in rural Ohio."

Violet laughed and rolled her eyes. "Who sends you anyway?"

"Lux sent me here. But I normally just go wherever I am needed. If Lux hears something he calls. Otherwise I go wherever. It's pretty involved. There's a whole network of contacts. I'm not the only one who does this. I'm just the best."

"Humble much?"

Roman shrugged. "It's just the truth. I don't think I'm better as a human being. I'm just better at this."

"Well, I guess we know why now. You're like a vampire, or whatever. That's not a bad thing. Vampires seem like they're not all bad, right? Lux seems okay."

"I guess so." He smirked and reached for her hand. "Stop forcing me to think too deeply about vampires and my existence. When I came here it was simple for me. Vampires are bad, people are good. I kill vampires. Now you have me contemplating the truth of our existence and the morality of humans versus vampires. I've seen so much evil shit my view got a bit skewed one way."

"Sorry," she said, and snickered. "I'm a deep well of contemplation. What can I say? But if vampires aren't all evil, and people aren't all innocent, why is there a line of distinction there, and what makes killing one wrong and not the other?"

Roman considered that for a moment, his brow knit with contemplation. "I suppose it's akin to killing a rabid animal, or a man-eating lion, or something along those lines. It's not really evil that Vampire kill people to survive. They have to eat. Humans take life to survive as well. As do other animals. You wouldn't say a lion is evil for killing a gazelle."

"I guess so." Violet shrugged and thought about that. Maybe humans are evil to kill animals to survive since they have a choice. Lions don't. But humans are predators every bit as much, right?

"Most of them get off on their power and really are evil. They are the apex predator and they know it. And most of them live accordingly. So, I feel no remorse in taking their lives. None."

"How bizarre," she said, lying down beside him. She stared up at the ceiling looking up at the meringue-like spikes.

"It is bizarre, I guess. Because I've only known this life I never stopped to think about it, really. I have a job, and I do it. Why pontificate further? There's sort of no point to it, really. It has to be done, end of story."

"I agree, though I still have questions." She turned her head towards him.

"You need answers and I don't have them," he said, turning to look at her.

"We'll get them though," she said. "Somehow. Maybe my aunt knows something." Her brow was deeply furrowed as she contemplated that. Maybe her aunt was the same? Which would mean her cousins were also like her?

He caressed her cheek with the back of his hand. "It's so weird not having hair," he said, changing the subject as he rubbed his head back and forth across the blanket. She smiled and kissed his hand.

"You look beautiful without hair." She rolled over onto her stomach

"So, are we going to that show tonight?" he said, pinching her bottom lip and not letting go.

"I don't know," she said.

"It would probably be a good idea. We might run into someone." He let go of her and rested his hand on her cheek.

"That's what I'm worried about," she said, rolling her eyes. "Stupid Malinda and Dory. And what if Mark is there?"

"Who cares? Fuck all those people, anyway. Based on their actions it's pretty clear they're not your friends. And Mark is nothing. I broke his jaw once and would gladly do it again. In fact, maybe I'll track him down for the fun of it." That brought a grin to her face, but she didn't say anything, and looked away briefly. "Those girls didn't really bother you, did they?"

He rolled over on his side and pushed the hair back from her face. It felt so strange being this intimate and content with someone. It was so abnormal to be at ease like this, to reach out and touch her as he pleased, to give and feel affection. It was going to take some time to get used to it all. But he wanted this life with her, which was the strangest thing of all.

"Not really, I mean, I guess not. It just seems so weird how much things have changed. Those girls, like, idolized me a few weeks ago, and now they talk down to me like I'm nobody."

"Fuck them, Violet."

"I know it doesn't matter, it's just weird. I guess paybacks are a bitch." She turned over on her side to face him and grabbed his hand and rested her head against it.

He leaned forward and kissed her softly. She closed her eyes, imagining they were some place far off where they had no responsibilities and nothing in the world was wrong. She didn't want to open them again, didn't want to mourn or be afraid anymore. She didn't want to fight. She wanted him and tranquility.

She opened her mouth to touch her tongue to his. God, he was a good kisser, with those full lips and the painfully soft licks and random little nips he gave her. He rolled on top of her, covering her partially with his body, his hands cradling her neck as he kissed her mouth more deeply, then moved to her neck. She couldn't help the little moan that escaped her as he sucked the column of her neck, his teeth raking gently over her pulse.

She felt his body reacting to hers. For the first time she could feel just how much he really did want her physically. All the nervousness and anticipation of this moment, the newness of his body against hers, the revelation of what it was truly like to have this kind of relationship with him, was profound and enveloping. There was nowhere to run off to this time, no reason to stop or hide anything.

He relinquished her neck and rose up on his palms, bracing himself with locked arms. His muscles were tight, flexed. Violet smiled so slightly, shyly. There was nothing mirthful in his expression; he was honed in on her, all seriousness. He hovered over her, staring into her eyes briefly, before lowering his head to kiss her sternum. As he nuzzled the soft skin between her breasts, he lifted the bottom of her shirt with one hand, pushing it up slowly. His fingertips were calloused and rough as they moved gently over the tender flesh of her stomach. The sensation gave her goosebumps. He kissed her breast, and then nipped her through her shirt as his hand found her other breast beneath the cloth, making her arch into him and let out a gasp. She felt his mouth smile with satisfaction at her response.

The shrill sound of the phone in the quiet apartment rang out, causing her to jump and bump her head against his. She laughed at her nervous overreaction and sat up eye to eye with him.

"Seriously?" she said.

Roman let out an exasperated breath and kissed her again. The phone kept ringing. "I'm not answering," he growled, placing a flat palm against her chest, pressing her gently back onto the bed.

Violet complied and the phone stopped ringing. She wrapped her arms around his neck, her legs falling open to accommodate his hips against the cradle of hers. Roman sat up, leaning back on bent legs and peeled his shirt off. Violet came forward, her cheeks flushed pink as she nervously waited for him. She felt virginal, apprehensive, shy, and completely and utterly overwhelmed by him in the best way possible. He reached for the hem of her shirt again, fingertips brushing against her skin, leaning into her to kiss her lips, and the phone blared loud again.

Roman let out an irritated huff and sat back as his head fell back. He looked down at Violet, she was grinning with one finger in her mouth, chewing the nail and looking devilish.

"You should get that," she said as she bent one knee and let it rock back and forth.

"No."

"And how often does your phone ring?"

"Only one person calls me."

"Me?"

Roman growled and balled his fists against his thighs. "Besides you."

"What if it's something important? No one ever calls you unless it's important, right? Besides me."

The phone stopped ringing again and Roman smiled and started reaching for her shirt. Violet laughed and took over, pulling the top over her head. Roman paused, taking in the sight of her. Beautiful black lace against impossibly white skin, the softest hint of pink nipples showing through the fabric.

"You're so beautiful," he said and leaned into her, taking her mouth with his completely and thoroughly.

Violet wrapped her arms around his neck and pulled him down onto the bed. He was so heavy, so solid to hold onto.

"Mmmm..." she murmured as he kissed her neck again.

The phone started ringing again.

"Mother fucker," Roman growled as he pounded his fists into the mattress and bounded from the bed to the kitchen with her tagging along behind, giggling.

She watched his long strides, his tight muscles as he moved quickly down the hall. Her body was still thrumming electrically from his touch. The sooner they finished with this call the sooner they could go back to what they were doing. And looking at those back muscles and shoulders made her absolutely want to get back to what they were doing.

"What?" he said impatiently. There was no politeness in his tone whatsoever, so whoever was on the other end had better be ready.

"Ah, Roman, how are you, old friend?"

"Why are you calling here constantly? I didn't hear from you for six months, and now you're calling me nonstop."

"Catch you at a bad time?" Lux chuckled, very pleased with himself.

"Just get on with it. I'm busy"

She knew by his aggressive reaction it was Lux on the other end. Besides, Lux was the only other person that called him, besides her, according to him. She leaned against the kitchen counter in front of the sink and watched Roman. It was funny to her how much Lux got under his skin. They were almost like demented brothers in some way.

"Yes, I imagine you are." Lux laughed.

"Get to the fucking point," Roman warned.

"The fucking point, clever word selection. I assume the little flower is hovering nearby?"

"Get. To. The. Point. You have three seconds. One, two..." Roman turned and looked at Violet and shook his head, and Violet laughed.

"Alright, alright, settle down. I'm just calling to see how things are going with Cecelia."

"Haven't found her yet."

"Yeah, she's not your typical crypt dweller. I taught her that, at least."

"So, why don't you tell me where she is?"

"Because I don't know, dickhead."

"I almost believe that."

"Roman, I'm offended that you don't believe me. Why would I lie to you?"

"Well, you lie about a lot of things. And since Cecelia is your offspring you know where she is, relatively speaking, at all times." Roman's eyes drifted back to Violet, who was grinning ear to ear, amused at the conversation. She could only imagine what Lux was saying on the other end to goad Roman.

"Do you think I have a GPS tracking system installed in all my little vampires? I knew she was in Ohio, but my Spidey Sense doesn't give me an address. And I never lie. I might omit, but I don't lie." Lux chuckled slyly.

"All your little vampires? So how many of your *little vampires* are out there, Lux? Are you a breeder?" Roman knew Lux was not a breeder, but Violet's facial expression was priceless as he said it. Her eyes grew wide and he could read plainly she was afraid Roman was going to go after Lux next. As much as he hated it, he knew she liked the fucking asshole. "You know how much I love breeders. And omitting is lying, you cunt."

"Roman, you know very well I'm no breeder. It was a joke. I killed them all off myself, long before you ever came around."

"Except for Ilya. And Cecelia. And Mylori. Am I forgetting anyone?"

"Fuck you, like you don't love my sister. And you couldn't kill Ilya with Bea Arthur's stake."

Now that made Roman laugh out loud. Lux's knowledge of popular culture and humor was incredible for a two thousand year old vampire. "Well, I wish you had killed this dumb bitch and saved me the hassle."

"I don't kill my own," Lux said with a casual boredom.

"And yet you just told me you killed all your offspring long before I was born."

"Stop throwing my words back at me. You're making me angry, and you wouldn't like me when I'm angry." Lux was joking, making another reference. "And fuck you. You know I've only sired these three."

"Ilya, I get. Mylori, I get." Violet scowled as he spoke that name, which made him laugh. "But why Cecelia?"

"I honestly don't know. She wasn't even a particularly good fuck. I think I felt sorry for her. She has those big sad puppy dog eyes. Oh, and big tits."

"Big tits gained her immortality? Violet could have died because you liked her tits?" Roman was back to being pissed off again.

"I do like Violet's tits, but I don't see how that alone could cause her death. Well, maybe her un-death," Lux said with a chuckle, knowing Roman would be fuming over that joke, which made it all the more hilarious to him. "No, I was referring to Cecelia's gigantic breasts. They are incredible, and apparently I thought them worthy of immortality. But she's such a boring airhead, even they lost their luster. Wars have been started over less, Roman. And besides, you're there to protect Violet now. Oh, and you can thank me for that little gift any time now. You're welcome."

"Fucking dickhead. If you have nothing to tell me, I'm ending this conversation. I have better things I could be doing."

"Better people you could be doing, you mean." Lux laughed.

"Yes, better people I could be doing," Roman said with a laugh, finally chilling out. His eyes locked on Violet like she was prey.

"Oh my gosh," Violet said in shocked embarrassment, her cheeks flushing as her jaw dropped open. Roman's hungry stare made her bite her lip in shyness and look away.

Lux could hear Violet perfectly. The sound of her voice and reaction made him smile. "Let me talk to her."

"No."

"Come on."

"Why? You've already caused enough trouble in her life."

"I've caused her very little trouble," Lux scoffed. "Ask her if she wants to talk to me. I bet she says yes."

Roman covered the mouth piece of the phone and cocked his head to the side. "You want to talk to this moron?"

"Hey, I heard that," Lux said with a chuckle.

"Sure," Violet said, raising her eyebrow, curious as to what he wanted.

"Do not be an asshole," Roman warned Lux.

"I told you she'd say yes," Lux responded in triumph.

Roman grunted and handed her the phone. She took it warily from him and held it to her ear. "I'm going to go take a shower," Roman said, reaching out and placing his hand on her shoulder. His palm was so warm, his touch making her go all gooey inside again.

"A cold one?" she asked, and grinned at him. Her own cheeks turned red, embarrassed she'd even said it.

"Something like that," he grumbled as he shook his head and leaned over and kissed the side of her neck, then walked away.

"Ugh," she groaned and closed her eyes briefly, then watched as he left the room.

"Hello, Violet," Lux said, interrupting her from her thoughts, having heard the entire exchange. "Roman isn't manhandling you is he?"

"Um, no..." she said, somewhat embarrassed by the question, though she should've known better, considering she'd just teased Roman so openly as she held the phone.

"Good. Don't let him get his big mitts on you." The thought of Roman getting to touch her at all made him sort of sick to his stomach.

Violet said nothing, not sure how to respond. Lux took her silence for the awkward pause it was.

"So, I imagine Roman's news comes as a shock to you?" His voice was smooth and low, almost breathing through the phone. As though he had flipped a switch and dropped his usual cool routine.

"The whole me being a vampire thing? Yes, that was shocking," she said with a nervous giggle. "It makes sense for Roman, but I just always thought I was normal," she answered awkwardly. "Well, relatively speaking."

"I suppose you'll join him now?"

"What do you mean?"

"Follow him around and kill us *evil vampires*?"

"I don't think so, I mean, I don't know. I guess I have to worry about keeping myself alive for the time being. I haven't really had much time to think about killing you *evil vampires*."

Lux smiled dolefully on the other end. "Has anything happened?"

"No, and that's probably bad, right?"

"No. She's a scatterbrain. She may have forgotten by now why she even came to town."

"You know that's not the case, Lux."

"No, it's not the case."

"Why do you lie to me?"

"I don't, Violet."

"But you do. You told me there wasn't anything supernatural to me, and you knew there was."

"What you are is perfectly natural to me."

"You know what we meant. Vampires aren't normal-natural to humans."

"Timing is everything."

"What's that even supposed to mean? Roman's right, you talk in riddles too much."

"Roman," he spat. "Don't quote him to me, Violet. He's a child, and I am an immortal. I answer to no one. I speak when I feel like speaking, and in a manner of my choosing. I will not be dictated to by children."

Violet sighed. She hadn't really meant to start some kind of pissing contest. Nor had she meant to offend him. She just wanted to know and understand what was happening.

"Lux, I like you, okay? I don't care that you're a vampire. My brain can't really grasp the magnitude of your age or what you truly are. You are my friend. At least, I think you're my friend? But you need to stop fucking around and just tell me what I need to know. That is, if you actually care enough about me to keep me safe," she said, hoping he would listen to her.

She heard him chuckling on the other end of the line.

"Wow, look at you being all forceful," he said with a laugh.

"Stop that! Don't be condescending!" She sounded like a child throwing a fit even to herself.

"I'm not, dear. I promise. It's just funny how you speak to me. There's no pretense. You say what you mean."

"What other way is there to be? Being mysterious and talking in riddles is bullshit. So tell me everything, or just fuck off."

Lux laughed again. "Your feistiness will keep you alive."

"You think that's all it takes? I don't think that's all it takes. This is serious, Lux. I think you've forgotten what it means to die, to be so close to death at every second. My life could end in the blink of an eye. From a car," the image of her parent's crumpled car flashed in her brain, "or a heart attack, or a fucking random virus. I can die that easily. So tell me how to save myself from this stupid bitch."

271

She was wrong. He knew more than anyone how easily she could die. He had watched humans wither and die for centuries. Some violently, some going gently into that good night. But all of them die. "You have everything you need, my love. Everything."

"What do I have? I have nothing. Why didn't you just kill Cecelia yourself? You knew she was coming here for me. Why bother sending Roman when you could have just done it yourself?"

"I'm not going to kill one of my own. Why didn't you kill your little boyfriend Mark? You know you wanted to and he deserved it."

"That's different. That's murder."

"And killing Cecelia wouldn't be murder?"

"You kill things all the time," Violet said, impatiently.

"I kill my food, just as you kill yours. Or are you a vegetarian?"

She bit her lip, he had her there. "Well, Mark wasn't trying to kill me."

"Oh really?" Lux said. She could tell by the tone of his voice he was amused.

"Why, what do you know? And how do you even know about Mark anyway?"

"I know everything and I know nothing, sweetheart. I know that he deserved more than a broken jaw. I will kill him myself one day, my love."

"Don't call me that, Lux," she said with a begging tone to her voice.

"Ah...crossing a line I guess?"

She didn't say anything, not wanting to hurt him, and she could tell by the tone of his voice he was already wounded by her rejection, for some bizarre reason.

"Listen to me." His tone had changed now to one of complete seriousness. "I am telling you that you will be okay. *Roman* will take care of you. I sent him to you because he is fully capable of protecting you. It was necessary. There's a broader plan. He is human, but he can protect you as well as most vampires could."

"But we're not exactly *human* are we?" she replied, almost accusing.

"You're more human than any girl I've ever known," he said sadly.

"Okay, now you've confused me. Am I part vampire or what?"

Lux chuckled. "It meant nothing, Violet, just ignore me. I don't know what I'm talking about a good portion of the time. My old mind isn't quite as sharp as it once was."

"I almost believe that," she said, and laughed.

"Ahh, echoing Roman already. You two sound too much alike. It's disturbing and sickening." He chuckled, and then got very quiet. The change was tangible and made Violet go stiff. "Violet, I was sorry to hear about your mother, both your parents. I'm sorry you had to go through all that at such a bad time too."

Violet's eyebrow rose, wondering where this comment had come from. "Thanks," she said.

"You know that I knew them very well from coming to see you."

"How well did you know them?"

"Just from observing, Violet. Don't get paranoid."

"Don't be paranoid? How can I not be paranoid? Look at all that's happened. And I know my mother was just like me, Lux. Did you do it to her?"

"Sweetheart, I was just making a comment, no ulterior motive, no hidden meaning, nothing more than me telling you I am sorry they died."

"Do you know how this happened to me, Lux? Do you know how it happened to my mother? If you know something, you better tell me now. I *will* find out, and if I find out you knew and didn't tell me, we'll kill you."

Violet meant every word she said. He knew it wouldn't take much convincing for Roman to try to kill him, especially if he was hurting her in some way. Roman walked around the corner and caught the tail end of her comment. He was shocked by the statement, as he knew she had a soft spot for Lux and they seemed to share some type of bond, however bizarre or unhealthy it might be. She looked up at him with earnestness in her eyes. She would get an answer.

"Violet..." Lux spoke gently.

"Tell me. If you know something, you better tell me right now. This is your chance to prove to me you are a good person."

"Violet, I don't want to tell you."

"So, you do know?" Violet steeled herself, determined to get the answer she needed from him.

Roman pulled a kitchen chair up and sat down. He was amazed that she seemed to be able to get answers from Lux where he had always had to fight and drag things out of him. And even then, he usually never got the whole story.

"Violet, I don't want to tell you. You won't be happy."

"I'm not happy now, Lux. If it's something you did, then just tell me. I will try not to hold it against you. I know you're evil or whatever. You're excused, okay? Just tell me the fucking truth."

Roman was proud of her for being forceful with him, although he wasn't sure she'd get what she was after. He'd known Lux to disappear completely without a trace in the past, only to show up a year or two later in some hick town where he'd been staying. It wasn't out of the realm of possibility for him to do that again without telling her anything.

"I don't want to talk about this right now."

Lux hung up the phone and stood still for several minutes staring at it. He would have to tell her eventually, although only because he felt some sort of obligation towards her. Why he cared he didn't fully comprehend, but he did. The truth wasn't all his to tell. There was a lot to consider. A lot of pieces to the puzzle and it wasn't all about him or Violet. The time would come, or maybe it wouldn't.

Violet's jaw went slack. She placed the phone back in the receiver and walked over to Roman. "He hung up on me. Call him back right now." she said, trying not to cry. She knew he had the answers she wanted, and she would drag it out of him if she had to tie him up and torture him.

"He won't answer," Roman said, standing to do it anyway. He picked up the phone and dialed. Just as he'd said, there was no answer. "Tell me what he said."

She explained what Lux had told her, and gave him her impression of his tone, and perhaps some speculation as to the meaning behind his tone. She knew he had something to do with her mother having vampire blood based on his refusal to answer her questions. He sounded almost frightened, like he was afraid of her reaction. She wondered if it was because he might fear Roman's revenge for something he'd done, but somehow she knew it had more to do with her own disappointment. He was afraid of alienating her.

She remembered the night in his room. How alone he'd seemed. *A man with the entire world and nothing.* She couldn't hate him. She knew she should, but she couldn't. He seemed almost pitiful to her, like some lost and lonely being without a real friend. She knew Roman would scoff at such an idea, but he hadn't been there with him. *"Let's pretend for a while."* he'd said. Pretend what? Pretend to be human? Pretend to be friends? She was his friend, at least she thought of herself as such.

"Maybe we should just go get something to eat and go to the club? Randy's band goes on at ten." She walked out of the room and over to her stuff, which sat beside the door.

Roman watched her, confused at her constant ability to change moods. One second she was adamant about getting Lux to spill his guts, the very next she wanted to get something to eat and go to a club? She continuously amazed him with her ability to just let things go as if they weren't anything. She always seemed to take everything in stride. He would be on his way to Chicago right now if Lux had important information like this about his life, but she just wanted to forget for a while and go see her friend's bad band play.

"Are you okay?" he asked, wanting to make sure there wasn't some hidden fear, or anger, or *something* behind her mask.

"No, Roman, but I haven't been for months, so what's another night?" She shrugged her shoulders and picked up her bag.

"So, where do you want to go eat?"

"The Oven of course, it's been a while."

"Well, Lux effectively killed the mood earlier," Violet said, and rolled her eyes. They had been on the verge of consummating their relationship before that call from Lux. Violet briefly wondered if that had been his intention. Could Lux know what they were doing somehow? Ugh, whatever.

"Later," Roman said, his voice so growly it made her insides ache. He leveled her with a stare. Violet grinned nervously and bit her bottom lip. Roman's mouth quirked to the side in a grin.

"So, do you think he'll answer the phone if I try to call him later?"

Roman's smile was erased. "Not if he doesn't want to talk. Lux does what Lux wants to do."

"I'll get my answers," Violet said, and dumped some sugar into her coffee.

"You can't possibly be this nonplussed over this whole situation," Roman said, pushing the sticky plastic tri-fold menu aside.

"I don't get it myself. Ordinarily I'd be completely freaked out, but I guess so much has happened lately that I'm just numb to it all. Lux has all the answers to my whole life, and he probably won't tell me, and yet I just really don't care right now. I'll worry about it later. But I will get my answers eventually, even if I have to torture him to get them." Violet sat back, leaning her head against the back of the booth.

"That sounds like a great plan," Roman said with a smile as Violet shrugged. "You're far more easy going than I am. If it was me I would be halfway to Chicago right now."

"Yeah, that's probably a good thing. At least from here Mister Bitey can't suck our blood."

"Mister Bitey?" Roman chuckled.

"Captain Fangman better? Maybe Count Luxula? Nosferluxtu?"

"Nosferluxtu, that's the one," Roman said and laughed. "I think he would probably like that."

Violet saw the waitress approaching the table, and sat up out of politeness. She hadn't always been so polite, but having all this shit going on in her life had forced her to have a new attitude about a lot of things. She ordered breaded mushrooms and a chocolate milkshake. Roman made a face at her, and then ordered his own healthy meal of biscuits and gravy and the essential slice of pie. The waitress walked away and Roman chuckled to himself.

"What's so funny?" Violet asked.

"Well, if there's one good thing about having this blood in our veins, it's that it will probably prolong the inevitable hardening of our arteries."

"Yeah, we probably really should try to eat healthier. We'll start tomorrow." She laughed and rolled her eyes.

Roman talked to her about what they still needed to do in terms of her training. She had pretty much grasped everything almost immediately and thus there wasn't a whole lot more to do but just practice and get her stamina up. It had been the same way for him, only he'd had an uncle that enjoyed forcing "lessons" on him every given moment of the day. Most of which were completely unnecessary, as the only thing that ever kept him alive was his ability to think on his feet and the will to live, and that can't be taught to someone.

He thought about his family briefly. It didn't make any sense why they'd kept the truth hidden from him. Maybe they figured since he was the last of the line there was no reason to worry him? Or maybe they feared it would send him down some wrong path? He certainly could have had the truth had he wanted it. It was all there right beneath his nose, and he'd been uninterested in knowing it. Maybe they figured since he wasn't interested there was no sense in telling him? The most logical explanation is that they wanted to protect him from the truth as they knew how much his hatred of vampires consumed him. After all, it was *vampires* who'd stolen any semblance of a normal life from his family. He may have gone off and done something crazy and reckless with this information at that young of an age. And he had been young when they'd all died. Violet shifted across from him, drawing his eyes.

Her eyes twinkled under the dusty yellow light of the room. Her ability to forget and release her worries was appealing to him. He'd never been able to do that himself. He held onto everything and carried it like a badge. It was an attractive aspect of her personality. But right now he was more preoccupied with her physical attributes. He found himself looking at areas of her body he didn't particularly take notice of before--or rather--didn't allow himself to notice. It was increasingly more difficult to make conversation these last few days. But it was imperative he stay focused on keeping her safe right now and thinking about what it might actually mean to love her only served as a distraction that could prove deadly if he wasn't careful.

"You there?" she asked, tapping the table with her fingernail.

"Sorry, you distract me," he said, snapping out of his breast-induced trance.

"Um, if *I* was distracting you then how come you didn't hear a word I just said?"

"Sorry, it wasn't your voice what was distracting me." He slouched down in the seat, not taking his eyes from hers.

It was strange to hear the obvious flirtation coming from him. He'd been so *brotherly* all this time, she would have sworn he had absolutely no interest in her as a woman even a few days ago, but now things were different. She hadn't felt this bashful around *a boy* since middle school. She rested her arms on the table and clasped her hands together and stared at him deeply.

"So, what about all this, Roman?" she asked.

"What do you mean?" he asked, not breaking his gaze.

"I mean, where is this all going? Lux asked me if I was going to go with you now. I don't even know what *this* is, do you?"

"We can figure out all the details as we go, can't we? Besides, you don't want to leave your home, do you?"

"I've been thinking about that a lot. Amber told me she and Randy are planning to move out. I don't want to be alone in that house full of all those memories."

"I can't really just stop doing this."

"I know you can't and I wouldn't even think of suggesting it. Granted, in a perfect world we could just go off somewhere and not be bothered by anyone, right? But I guess that's pretty unrealistic."

"That would be nice. It would be pretty nice to live a normal life for the first time." Roman had never even considered such a thing.

"Yeah, I don't think that's in the cards at this point, do you?"

"No."

"So, that leaves me having to figure out what I'm going to do."

"You don't have to figure it all out today," Roman said and took another drink of coffee.

"Oh, I know, but I've been thinking about it. I've decided what I think I'm going to do is sell my house once Amber moves out."

"Why would you do that?" Roman asked, concerned by the unexpected idea. He thought the place was important to her, given the loss of her family.

"Well, I'm not going to sit there by myself while you take off for who knows how long, doing whatever it is you do, while putting your life in danger. I won't stay home worried sick all by myself. And my parents aren't there anymore. It's all just things and ghosts of memories. The memories I can take with me, I'd rather not look at the constant reminder anymore. You know how hard it is for me to see the chair my dad sat in every night when he got home from work? The stain he made by dumping a plate of chicken wings while we were watching a baseball game is still there. Memories are everywhere in the house. I won't even go into their bedroom. It's too strange to see Amber and Randy's things in there instead of theirs. Everywhere I look there's a memory. There's the hole my mom accidentally kicked in the wall when I came home drunk when I was fourteen, and the carpet my dad tore dragging a couch across the room. There are scuffs on the linoleum from moving the new washer in, paint drips on the carpet where I knocked over the bucket and dad yelled for thirty minutes. I could go on, and on, and on. Everywhere I look I'm surrounded by these reminders that they're no longer living there. It's like a fucking shrine."

"But what are you going to do? You have to live somewhere."

"I don't know, and it's far enough away that I don't have to bother thinking about it just yet. Who knows, I may change my mind anyway. I may chicken out."

He looked at her, appreciating how much she'd changed in the short time he'd known her. She was almost a different person. No, she was more *herself* than she had been. The first few times he'd talked to her he understood that there was something deeper to her, but she had come across as rather immature and appeared so very young. Now she seemed far more astute than he was in most areas.

"So, we should go back to my place so I can change and then head out to the club."

"Change? What's wrong with what you've got on?" he asked, checking her over.

"Oh please."

She walked in ahead of Roman, who was lagging behind looking through the parking lot. She was sure he must know *something* was going on because he was acting distant, and that wasn't normal for him now. It was a cold night, and the way the sky looked it seemed like it may snow.

She saw Jim immediately. He was the first person she recognized. It seemed as though a lot of new people had made their way into their tiny scene since last she'd been around. Funny how quickly things changed. She smiled at him. She could tell by the half lid condition of his eyes and the limp way in which he stood he was high and probably drunk. It made her sad in the pit of her stomach.

Since she felt sort of insecure about her appearance after seeing Malinda and Dory that last time, she'd decided to get dressed to the nines. It was vanity on her behalf, of course. Having Malinda act all high and mighty and insinuate she was fat had meant more to her than she'd let on to Roman. She finally wore the corset she'd bought in Chicago, with the black and pink skirt, and knee high black leather boots with the thick rubber soles. Normally she would have worn some kind of heels, but there was a vampire after her, and she might have to run. The boots weren't exactly practical for that, but she wasn't about to wear tennis shoes and wreck the look. Granted, it shouldn't matter, but it did matter to her still. It hadn't been so long since she had been the envy of those girls, and now they were talking down to her as if she was nothing. Plus, she wanted to look good for Roman. They'd never been out together as a couple, and she wanted to make him proud. It was silly, because she knew he didn't even care about stuff like that, at least she didn't think he did. And she knew he didn't give a crap at all about the stupid goth scene, so he would've been happy just to see her in jeans and a t-shirt. But again, it shouldn't matter, but it did to her.

Her hair was woven with thin pink velvet ribbon, randomly braided, some thick and some thin, and hanging down her back in tangled ropes. Her eyes were lined thick with black and pink, and her lips were glossed with cherry colored lip gloss.

She walked to the bar and ordered a diet soda and waited for Roman to finally get in the building. Amber should be around there somewhere. Randy was spotted quickly, talking to the rest of his band as they set up their equipment. He was shirtless, baggy shorts hanging off his thin frame, and strapped into a black bass guitar. Amber appeared around the corner from behind the stage with Dory and Malinda, arm in arm, slithering beside her. They looked ghostlike and frail dressed in red velvet doll dresses and white stockings. Their appearance was becoming more and more alarming and disturbing to Violet. Something wasn't right. They were acting too different, their appearance too gaunt, and there had to be more to this than drug use. They all took drugs. They didn't all look like skeletons or characters from a zombie flick, though some of them tried to achieve that look. She chuckled to herself at the thought.

Violet waited for Amber to notice her, not wanting to butt into any conversation, and content to avoid talking to the demon girls for as long as she could manage. She turned her head to the side, seeing Roman walking through the door and toward her. He didn't appear to have any strange expression on his face or look in his eye that might suggest he found something suspicious outside. More than likely he was just being cautious and that's why he was being distant when they'd arrived.

He walked up and smiled at her and sat down on a stool beside her. He ordered a beer and then looked at her. "I'm pretty glad you didn't wear that to see Lux." A sliver of a smile snaked across his face.

"Yeah, not the most appropriate thing to wear to that occasion," she said, looking away from him towards Amber and the girls. "I think something's wrong with them."

"Obviously, in more ways than one," Roman said, rolling eyes.

"No, I mean, they look like they're sick."

"Drugs will do that."

"It's more than that, Roman." She looked back at him, catching his gaze and holding it. "We all took drugs--none of us looked like *that*."

"Violet, you didn't look much different when I met you," he said, not wanting to hurt her feelings. "I'm sorry to tell you that, but it's true."

She looked back at the girls, contemplating what he'd said. She really had slipped far with Mark. "Well, still, I think there's more to it. They look sick."

"Heroin?" Roman said, and took a drink.

Heroin? Could they really be that far gone?

Amber was walking towards them now with a big smile on her face. She was dressed from head to toe in skin tight black leather with six inch stiletto knee high boots to match. She looked unreal. Her perfect body and that outfit made her look so much like a superhero, or a high fashion model. Violet felt so inferior around her when she looked that good. She'd been told a thousand times she was just as pretty, but looking at Amber she knew that just wasn't possible, not with her long legs and perfectly huge breasts. Violet shook her head and smiled at Amber, very glad to see her, though not thrilled with her companions.

"Hey, I'm glad you guys made it!" Amber said, reaching out and hugging Violet and knowing full well what Violet had been shaking her head at. It was a common theme of discussion. "You look hot. I'm going to have to borrow that corset." Amber grinned in satisfaction.

"Yeah, yeah, whatever. How could we miss a performance by yet another Randy bandy?" Violet smirked and rolled her eyes.

"Yeah, I know, they kind of suck, but what can ya do?" Amber grinned and ordered a drink.

"Dude, seriously, that outfit is killer," Violet said, taking a sip of her pop.

"I made it while you were in Chicago. I guess I forgot to show you with all the freaking drama around the house," Amber said with a smirk, and took a swig of her rum and Coke.

"You *made* that? Holy fuck, make me one."

"Sure," Amber said, turning around and leaning against the bar. "Hey, Roman," she said, casually raising her glass to him.

"Hey," he replied, looking at her briefly and going back to scanning the room.

"You'd look killer in this as tiny as you are," Amber continued, taking a cherry from her glass and popping it in her mouth.

"Right, we'd look like Smurfette and Linda Evangelista walking around together," Violet scoffed and laughed.

"Shut the fuck up, you don't have blue skin or blonde hair," Amber said, and shoved Violet with her shoulder. "You're the most fucking beautiful girl I know."

"I agree," Roman interjected casually, looking over at Violet and locking eyes with her briefly before returning to scan the room. It hadn't even seemed like he'd been listening.

Amber and Violet looked at each other and giggled like giddy high schoolers.

Malinda giggled too, drawing their attention. The two girls had been hovering around Amber like a shadow waiting to be invited into the conversation. Their demeanor was different than the last time Violet had spoken with them. They seemed almost submissive and hesitant like they'd been in the past. Roman noticed this too, but looked away from the group and surveyed the room.

"Look, Malinda and Dory are here," Amber said, sliding aside and flaring her nostrils at Violet. This had always been a secret little sign between the two when something was annoying, funny, or suspicious.

"Hi girls," Violet said, looking around Amber to the two of them.

"Hello," they answered in tandem.

"I love your corset," Malinda said, stepping forward and reaching out to touch the leather. Her fingers moved over the soft hide like feathers.

"Thank you. I got it in Chicago," Violet replied, attempting to make conversation. She really didn't have anything to say to these girls.

"Nice." Malinda smiled slightly and looked at Roman. "Glad you came," she purred.

Roman looked at the girl and then looked away again. There was zero desire in him to make small talk, especially after how they'd treated Violet. He watched Randy and his friends as they continued running cables and setting up cheap lighting equipment they'd bought off the internet.

"So, where's Mose and Steve? Aren't they in this band?" Violet asked, looking around the room trying to locate the two.

Dory giggled under her breath and then covered her mouth. Violet and Amber looked at her and rolled their eyes.

"They both quit last week," Amber said, leaning against the bar and watching her boyfriend. "Out of the blue they called and said they didn't want to play anymore."

"So, what's the deal with that?" Violet asked.

"I don't know. Who fucking knows with any of these rat bastards?" Amber said snidely.

"I'm going to go talk to Randy," Roman said to Violet and Amber, then excused himself and walked towards the stage. He wanted to talk to men for a while as these girlie conversations had a tendency of going south really quickly.

"Dear lord, he's fine," Amber said, leaning into her friend. "Seriously, the shaved head thing is working for him."

Violet laughed and agreed with her. "Yeah, look how nice his ass looks in those jeans." She grinned and shoved her friend with her elbow. Roman just happened to look over as she was smirking and shook his head, knowing he was right to leave the hen house.

"Mmm hmm," Amber concurred.

"Seriously, oh my God, Amber, I have to tell you..." Violet began and then stopped, noticing that Malinda and Dory stood perfectly still, focused solely on her, and it was starting to creep her out. "What is up with you two?" she snapped.

"What do you mean?" Malinda asked, taking a step forward.

"Are you guys doing drugs or something? You look really crazy and your personality has changed dramatically."

"We're not taking drugs," Malinda said softly, looking down at the ground. Dory giggled and looked away from the three of them.

"So, what's going on, Malinda?" Violet asked, looking past Malinda to the deranged girl whose eyes were skittering around the room. She could tell they were hiding something. It couldn't be more obvious.

"We're fine," Malinda said, turning around and grabbing Dory's hand and leading her away.

"What the fuck was that?" Amber asked, looking at Violet with a perplexed look on her face.

"I have no idea," Violet replied, shaking her head. "Clearly they have lost it."

"Eh, good for them," Amber said flippantly. "So, what were you going to tell me?" Amber asked, dismissing the previous topic.

"Later," Violet said, with a devious grin as Roman and Randy walked towards them. Randy was quite a bit shorter than Roman, though with the mohawk spiked perfectly he was nearly the same height.

"Those are some foxy boys," Amber said quietly with a giggle.

"Yep," Violet agreed. "Man, we're pathetic, ogling them like construction workers. What's next, cat calls?" She laughed and looked at her friend. They were still laughing when the two men arrived.

"What?" Randy asked skeptically.

"Oh nothing," Amber said, standing and wrapping her arm around him.

Roman looked at Violet with a questioning look on his face and sat back down on the stool beside her. Yes, he was glad he'd missed whatever conversation they'd just had.

"Factory worker by day, rock star by night!" Violet smiled and hugged Randy.

"Yeah, I guess I wear many hats," Randy said, laughing at his cheesy comeback.

"When are you guys going on?" Violet asked, and sat back down. Roman was busy ordering another beer.

"In about fifteen minutes actually. I have little faith the show is gonna be good tonight. The soundman doesn't know his ass from a hole in the ground and Ben's new. So don't expect a whole lot."

"I never do," Violet said, with a wink.

Amber laughed and squeezed Randy.

"So, I guess Steve and those guys probably won't show up?" Violet asked, looking around the room.

"I doubt it. They've been real dicks the last few times I've seen them. I haven't talked to Mark in almost a month. I have no fucking idea what's up," Randy said, scratching the side of his head and taking a swig from his bottle.

"I'm sorry if I caused you any trouble with them," Violet said, taking a drink of her soda.

"It ain't you, man. They're just fucking assholes. They must be smoking crack or something."

"Seems like a lot of that is going on around here?" Violet said, looking at Randy and then to Roman who was scanning the room.

"Yeah, I guess," Randy said, turning to look back at the stage. "I'm gonna go make sure everything's plugged in again. Knowing those fuckwads someone tripped on something and unplugged the mixer. Fucking jackasses." He turned and kissed Amber's cheek. "See y'all after the show," he said, and walked away.

"He's so fucking punk rock," Violet said, with a laugh.

"He gets so worked up before these things he can't sit still," Amber said, taking a swig from her drink.

"Yeah, like the cords are gonna be unplugged. I just watched him plugging them in," Violet said.

"Total spazz," Amber said, and shook her head.

"Looks like a lot of people showed up," Roman said, finally breaking his silence. The little club had been steadily filling since they'd arrived.

"Yeah," Violet replied, looking around the room. Most of these people she had either never seen before, or were only casual acquaintances from her days of hanging in the punk scene. She'd drifted away from that after she started seeing Mark. He hadn't allowed her to go out much without him, and he'd always hated these people. The truth was these people all hated him.

"Why are you being so quiet?" Amber asked Roman. She walked around and stood in front of the two of them.

"Am I usually really talkative?" he said and smirked, then took another swallow from his bottle.

"Ya got me there," Amber said with a grin. "So, are there any of *them* here?" Amber asked, turning to look at the crowd behind her.

"Not yet, that I can tell," Roman answered. Talking about this situation so openly was still so weird to him. "What about you, Violet? See anything?" He wanted to know if she'd be able to discern these things as well as he could.

"No, I don't think so. Although Malinda and Dory definitely have some sort of vibe going on."

"So, you think they're vampires?" Roman asked, raising an eyebrow.

"No, I didn't say that. I just think maybe something is going on. They had some strange odor, or something, wafting off of them."

"You're probably smelling the meth on their skin," Amber said sarcastically.

"You think they're on meth? They seemed sort of calm for that?" Violet asked, not catching her sarcasm.

"I was kidding, Vi," Amber said, bugging her eyes out.

"Oh," Violet said half-heartedly as she watched the two girls huddled together close to the stage.

Violet felt her body tingling. It was an unsettling feeling, like the feeling she usually had before an anxiety attack. She leaned against the bar, trying to calm herself, not wanting to go into an attack right now. The last time she'd had one was the night before her parents' accident, ironically enough. The idea that she'd start having them again was terrifying. It was crippling to live like that, not knowing when she was going to have another one, being afraid of never coming back from one. She would usually go months without having an attack, and then out of nowhere she'd start getting them again and it would last for a few months and then they'd go away again. Sometimes she'd even wake up with red blotches on her skin. The doctor had said they were stress induced hives, but that didn't make her fear of them go away.

"You alright?" Roman asked, leaning into her.

"Uh huh," she said hoarsely, leaning her weight into him.

"You feel it too," he said, knowing.

She looked up at him, thankful he was experiencing the same feeling.

"What's going on?" Amber asked, concerned by the sudden change in demeanor in the two of them.

"Nothing," Violet said, smiling at her friend with reassurance. "Just promise me you and Randy will stay within sight tonight.

"*What is going on?*" Amber asked again, demanding an answer.

"Violet, stay with Amber, I'm going to go look around." Roman stood up, squeezing Violet's arm tightly and then letting go. "Be alert," he said, looking at her and then Amber and then walking away.

"Tell me what's going on!" Amber said near panic.

"Amber, there's something here. I thought I was having another anxiety attack, but it's them, there's one here somewhere."

"Holy fuck! We need to get out of here!" Amber said with wide eyes, clutching Violet's arm.

"No, we'll be okay. Just stay with me."

Violet had to trust that everything would be okay, that they were safe. Roman never would have left her alone otherwise. Besides, she was training for this. She had to trust herself and her instincts. She grabbed Amber's arm and held onto her hand.

Roman walked through the club, eyeing everyone he passed. The band had just started playing and everyone was focused on the stage. All these people were friends, or at least acquaintances of Randy and his band mates. There was nothing *vampire* about any of them. He walked towards the stage and stood there momentarily looking for other rooms or side bars and noticed a door that led backstage. That's where he needed to go, a wave of energy blasted him as it always did when he felt them. He walked forward ignoring the man who sat on the stool beside the door who followed behind Roman insisting he not go back there. A woman stood with her back to him. Her long dark hair fell beautifully over milk white shoulders and down the back of a vibrant red dress. She turned to look at Roman now, her lips were smeared with magenta colored blood, shiny wet. Her fingers looked dipped in crimson and glistened against her pale pink tongue as she licked them clean. Malinda and Dory were on the floor looking up at him, one with fear, the other some sick joy. Their legs were askew, panties lowered to their knees beneath their doll-like dresses. The three of them looked like some twisted family portrait, mother and daughters gone horribly sick and wrong.

"The nice thing about women, Roman, is that you can taste them without even having to bite them." She smiled and slid her finger across her curled tongue. "Isn't that right, *Killer*?" she asked, turning back to the girls.

The bouncer ran up behind Roman and saw the two girls on the ground, legs open, and the woman hovering over them. "Get back here, mother fucker... What the fuck? This is some sick shit," he said, stopping in his tracks at the scene before him. He grabbed Roman by the shoulder, taking a fistful of his jacket and shoving him back towards the door. "All you sick mothers are going to have to get the fuck out of here."

"Come on," Roman said to Cecelia. His voice was a guttural command, low and deep, and almost demonic sounding in tone.

"Mmm... I like a man who's forceful," she said, turning to look at him.

"Get out of here," Roman ordered the two girls on the floor. Malinda stood up, quickly fixing her clothes and pulling Dory up from the ground where she was still sprawled and giggling. She tugged on the girl until she got her up on shaky legs.

"You can leave, dolls," the woman said, turning to the girls and lifting her hand. They stood up straight and scurried out of the room as if compelled.

"I mean it, man, this sick shit ain't happening in my club. Get out!" the bouncer growled, waving his heavy flashlight at the two. "I'm all for girl on girl, but this shit is warped."

"Come, *Killer*, let's you and I take a walk," Cecelia purred, walking towards him and extending her arm to him. She tried to take Roman's hand but he pulled it away from her.

"Oh, don't be such a grump," she said with a pout.

Roman walked with the woman back out into the club, gripping the vampire's elbow.

"Ya'll lucky I didn't call the police," the bouncer said as he slammed the door behind them and sat back down on his stool.

"We weren't doing anything illegal," Cecelia purred and placed a wet kiss on the man's cheek.

The guard wiped his face and scowled. "Get out of here. Now."

Cecelia smiled at the bouncer and looped her arm through Roman's as though he were escorting her on a date.

Violet watched Dory and Malinda as the one pulled the other across the room to the door. She thought it was peculiar how Malinda seemed panicked and Dory had her head tipped back laughing uncontrollably. She felt her heart leap in her chest as she looked over and saw Roman standing with Cecelia moments later. The woman looked across the room at her and smiled and then held onto Roman's arm. It reminded her of the dream she'd had when Mylori had been with Roman across the club smiling at her. Violet stood up and walked towards the two. Amber followed behind terrified to be alone. Cecelia's lips were blood red and glistening. The vampire had been drinking Malinda and Dory's blood.

That's why the girls look so sickly.

Cecelia's eyes glowed as Violet approached her. They looked like an animal's eyes at night when they caught the light, all silvery and luminescent. She wanted to fly across the room and snap the girl's neck and drain every blessed bloody drop from her veins. It would feel thick and rich and sickly sweet running down the back of her throat and sitting like milk in her stomach. Yes, she could smell *his* blood on her, all over her. She was Lux's.

"Roman, have you fucked her yet?" she asked, tilting her head and resting it against him. "Have you?" she asked, lifting her head and looking at him. "I assume you have. I've heard she's a little slut." She knew taunting him by saying such things about his girlfriend would piss him off, and a pissed off human was a stupid human. He was legendary for his violence and abilities. Though he still was only human, or maybe not? What was that scent?

Roman shoved her off of his arm. It took all his energy not to kill her right there. He couldn't though. It wasn't the way things were done. No one in the room even noticed the fiasco. They were focused on squealing guitars and thundering bass. But he knew they'd notice him decapitate a woman in the middle of the bar. Could he pull that off as theatrics? No.

"Mmm...I bet she tastes like strawberries, Roman. I *know* she tastes like Lux. I can smell him all over her. My blood sings being near her. My body lusts to touch what is his." Cecelia grinned and looked at Roman out of the corner of her eye.

He wanted to rip her head off. Literally take her neck in his hands and pull her head out by the root.

"Cat got your tongue?" she asked, taking her finger and wiping the remainder of the blood from her lips and placing the finger in her mouth. "Ah, tender young womb." She smiled at him knowing how the anger raged in his blood.

Violet walked up, stopping abruptly. Her eyes were blue flames piercing through the cigarette smoke and the multicolored lights of the stage.

"Hello Violet," Cecelia said, a cheery lilt to her voice.

Amber stood behind Violet gripping onto her arm. She had no idea what was going on and was terrified.

Violet felt her blood swirling. She was transfixed by the wet lips and brilliant blue eyes of the woman. Roman stood beside her looking down at Violet wanting her to remain calm. It wouldn't take much to send this psychotic vampire into a frenzy and she could easily kill a half dozen before they'd be able to stop her. He had weapons on him, concealed, but nothing large enough to be effective here inside the club. Besides, it would look like a massacre. There would be no way to cover it up with so many people present.

Violet said nothing but stared at the woman. She felt the blood in her veins pulling towards the vampire. It was terrifying and exhilarating standing before her enemy. She had no idea why this woman even really hated her. Could it all be solely based on jealousy? It wasn't even as if she and Lux had any real relationship. She had barely even met Lux but a few weeks prior.

"You feel his blood calling yours," Cecelia said as she leveled her with a stare.

"I feel something stirring inside, yes," Violet responded, showing nothing.

"His blood recognizes his blood," Cecelia said, starting to reach for Violet's perfectly pouted lips. The draw of her mouth was inevitable. Those beautiful little lips of hers.

"Why don't you come outside with us, Cecelia?" Roman said, stepping between the two, shielding Violet completely from her view. He looked down at Cecelia with a slight grin on his face. He was itching to kill her, fists clenched, muscles taut and burning with lactic acid. His blood was screaming too. Like recognized like. It was the vampire in him. It all made so much sense now.

"You don't really think I'm that stupid do you?" She smiled and tilted her head to the side looking around the mountain of a human to view Violet again.

"Lux said you were," Violet taunted as she stepped around Roman.

Roman shook his head and grinned and put his arm across Violet's chest from behind, pulling her back against his own. To anyone who was looking it appeared he was holding his girlfriend. But that was not what was going on at all. She was antagonizing Cecelia, trying to draw her outside for a fight, and he was holding Violet back in protection. Not only couldn't they start a fight inside, and he knew Violet was perfectly capable of doing that, but he also wanted to protect her in case Cecelia lashed out, and he knew Cecelia was perfectly capable of that.

"I'm not a child, *human*. You aren't going to hurt my feelings or make me jealous by saying things like that," the vampire spat.

"You say that and yet here we are. What's the purpose of your little visit to town anyway? You don't even know who I am," Violet said with a roll of her eyes.

"*You* don't know who you are!" Cecelia seethed.

"I know exactly who I am. And I know that I won't be the one dying here." Violet said haughtily, a slow smile spreading across her face.

Cecelia looked down at the girl taking in every detail of her face. That perfect lush little mouth, the thin arch of black eyebrows over endless blue pools, small fragile nose, creamy skin touched pink in the cheeks. It would be so sweet when she bit into her like a ripe peach. Her blood mingled with her Sire's, screaming down her throat, and spilling everywhere. Cecelia shook her head, steadied her gaze again.

"Hmm... It wasn't enough to kill them off. Weren't you supposed to be with them that night?" Cecelia asked, running her finger over her lips. Her eyes inflamed, that iridescence catching the lights of the room like broken mirrors catching reflections. "Should've killed three birds with one stone."

Amber was terrified. She wanted to run away but knew that being with Roman was the safest place she could be right now. She looked at the stage, Randy was safe there. Playing his music completely unaware there was a freaking vampire only a few feet away. How the heck did she get involved in this? *By proxy*, the words echoed in her head and calmed her somehow. Yes, by proxy, as they had laughed about before. She was with her friend, her best friend, and she would stand with her, even if it got her killed.

"Don't try to take credit for things you had no part in," Roman growled, knowing what the woman was insinuating.

"Really? I had no part?" Cecelia said.

"No, you really didn't, and pretending otherwise isn't going to get under her skin. You are going to die. Come along quietly," he said, taking the woman's elbow in his hand. His fingers clamped onto her bony arm, crushing, he could feel the bones bending in his grip.

"Come along quietly, ironic that statement coming from you." She laughed and jerked her arm from his grip.

Inside Cecelia was disturbed by the strength in his hand. He was no mere human. She could smell the vampire wafting off of him now so strongly it was near suffocating. Old, old blood. Something far beyond any of their comprehension. *If* she had to breathe, and she didn't, she would be gasping for air. She made every attempt to get under his skin. She knew Lux had a soft spot for this *human* and fucking with him was bringing her such delight.

"What are you referring to exactly?" Roman said, stepping forward. His own eyes were ablaze with anger as he towered over her.

"Come on now, Roman, I was there. Why don't you tell your little girlfriend about your escapades?"

"I don't know what you're talking about," Roman said, looking down at Violet who had never taken her eyes off the vampire.

"Yeah, he fucked Mylori, big deal. Maybe they were loud? I don't know and don't care," Violet said with abruptness. "Not a revelation and not bothering me." She rolled her eyes and crossed her arms over her chest. "And like you were there. If you had been he would remember you because he's not one to forget details. Seriously? If that's all you got for game you have failed miserably." She looked up at Roman and rolled her eyes again. "It doesn't surprise me you had no idea what she was referring to because you're not a snarky little catty bitch. Take it from an expert. Her game is weak. You're out of your league, Titsy." That even provoked a little laugh from Amber which drew Violet's eyes. "Seriously, she's an amateur."

Amber nodded with a grin until she noticed Cecelia scowling and looking as though she may rip her throat out.

Roman felt a sudden pain in his stomach like he'd been knifed only the pain was purely emotional. Fuck, he was never going to live his moment of weakness down. Well, it had been more than a moment, but whatever. Mylori would haunt him forever.

"You're a funny girl, Violet. I will give you that. And not without your physical attributes. If I didn't want you dead so much I'd keep you for myself," Cecelia said.

"Thanks for the offer but I think I'll decline," Violet said, rolling her eyes. "I've had better offers from better vampires."

At that Roman definitely felt like he was going to erupt.

"Just curious, how do you think doing all this will gain you favor with Lux anyway? He thinks you're pathetic. He said, what was it?" she asked as she looked up at Roman, who just looked at her bemused and on guard. "Oh yes, that you were a dumb girl with huge tits, but that even they weren't enough to bother saving," Violet said with great satisfaction at the look of hurt that quickly flashed on the vampire's face before disappearing.

"Damn," Amber said as she gripped Violet's arm.

"Yeah, I know right? He's cold even for a vampire," Violet said and shook her head in amusement. "I would feel genuinely sorry for the way he disregards you, if you weren't threatening to kill me. But as it stands, I find it completely hilarious." Violet said with a shrug of her shoulders and a look of "oh well" on her face.

"You're awfully bold for someone who's going to suffer an astonishing amount of pain." Cecelia's head lowered slightly, her eyes bore into Violet with such malevolence Roman stepped between them again.

"So, what is it, Cecelia? All of this boils down to jealousy?" Violet said, stepping around Roman who was really getting anxious to move this outside. Violet was doing a good job of antagonizing Cecelia and he wasn't sure how much more the vampire would take before snapping. Stupid or not, she was still a vampire and was still dangerous.

"Well, yeah, so what?" Cecelia responded flippantly and looked at her nail polish, which was dried menstrual blood. Roman snarled. "Lux hurt me, and I'm going to hurt you. You have a problem with that? It makes perfect sense to me. And he doesn't even care enough about you to stop me."

Violet guffawed and looked up at Roman with a bewildered expression. "Can you believe this? If you think Lux doesn't care about me then why do you? If you really think he doesn't care enough to stop you from killing me then *why are you even here*? And furthermore, he doesn't care enough about *you* to stop Roman from killing you. Who do you think sent him to this town to protect me, my dear?"

Cecelia was suddenly roused by Violet's words knowing they were true. Lux had sent Roman to kill her. How had she not put that together before? The look of enlightenment was evident on her face. Had she really not put this together before this moment?

"Wow, you *are* stupid. I thought Lux was just being mean. I mean, the Killer, who happens to be friends with Lux, shows up to protect me at the same time you arrive in town? Seems like simple 2 + 2 math to me, and I suck at math," Violet said.

Amber stood perfectly still not wanting to garner any attention from the vampire who peered down at her intermittently. She clutched the back of Roman's shirt terrified to move. For once she wished Violet would keep her sarcasm to a minimum, even if she was serving it up pretty brilliantly.

"This is getting old," Violet said, turning to walk away. "Come outside and kill me already." Roman turned and watched as she walked towards the door.

"Aren't you going to stop her?" Amber asked quietly, looking up at Roman in terror.

"Come on, Cecelia. Let's go outside." Roman smirked. He was surprised by Violet's boldness and courage. Perhaps it was just naiveté, not really understanding what she was dealing with in regards to vampires, but it was amusing. Stupid or not, Cecelia was a vampire, and her strength and the danger she represented was beyond anything Violet could comprehend just yet. But Roman knew what it meant to fight a vampire. This was not anything to ever take lightly.

Cecelia said nothing but began walking towards the door.

"You should stay inside," Roman said quietly to Amber as he took her hand from his shirt and held it briefly. "You'll be okay. There are no vampires inside. Stay near Randy. You'll be okay, I promise." He looked into her eyes reassuring her she'd be safe and then followed the vampire outside.

"Please don't let her hurt Violet," Amber said, her eyes glistening with tears.

"Nothing is ever going to hurt Violet." Roman squeezed her shoulder and then followed Violet and the vampire outside.

The parking lot was dark and quiet. Violet had no idea why she'd suggested this. She had been safe as long as she was inside that building. Cecelia wouldn't have dared to start something in front of all those people. Vampire or not, an angry mob would have torn her limb from limb, or at the very least, the police would be called and no vampire wants that kind of attention, she assumed. Violet leaned against a truck that was parked close to the door. Roman and Cecelia walked out only moments after she got there.

"Cecelia, this is seriously stupid and so very anticlimactic. I thought you'd have this really good reason for wanting me dead, some diabolical scheme so intense and terrifying that I would have a nervous breakdown when we finally came face to face. But this is it? I mean, really? You came here obviously wanting to get caught. So what is it? Lux doesn't want you, but you're mad at me because Lux expressed some mild interest in me? Really? I knew nothing of it. I had no idea who Lux even was until a few months ago and the only reason he and I ever met was because you drew him here with your threat to me. Typical." Violet huffed incredulously and looked at Roman. "It's like those women on Jerry Springer who always get mad at the mistress instead of the cheating husband." She looked back at Cecelia, disgust clearly present on her face. "Lux is your problem, not me. But if you insist on all this drama, then I guess we'll just have to deal with it."

"You think this is all there is to this? You are a stupid little girl! You have no clue what all this entails." She looked at Roman. "Are you going to attack me here in the parking lot? I am just a poor, defenseless woman and there are security guards all over that place. Do you want to go to jail and leave Little Miss Violet all alone and unprotected?"

"You don't have to die right now, but you will die very soon," Roman answered, absolute vehemence dripping from his tone.

"So you both keep saying." She grinned, tossing her long hair over her shoulder. "You don't even know where I'm staying. If you did, you would have come calling already. Lazy. Lux dropped the ball if he thought you were going to protect her from me."

She was right and Roman seethed with anger at himself. He'd been so wrapped up in Violet that he'd gotten lazy.

"Hey, what's going on out here?" the security guard said, flashing the light in their eyes. Violet winced and covered her face trying to regain her vision.

"Nothing," Roman said, walking forward and taking Violet's hand. He turned around and noticed Cecelia was already gone. She had vanished as though she'd never been there.

"Either get back inside or leave," the man said, motioning towards the door. "Go get a room. There's no loitering outside."

Violet turned to survey the parking lot. She saw no trace of the woman and knew she was nowhere near as the nervousness in her blood had quieted.

"Come on, V," Roman said, bending down to her and urging her to go back in the building.

She looked around again for some sign of the vampire but saw nothing.

"The mistake we made was talking to her," Roman said, ordering another drink and leaning against the bar.

"What else could we do?" Violet asked.

"Nothing," Roman said and took a drink. Her eyes were watery and the dimple in her chin was evident. "Don't worry," he said, smiling and tapping her nose. "This is a cakewalk."

"I hope you're right."

"I know what I'm talking about. Lux is afraid of me, Violet. I have killed a lot scarier beings than some psychotic little waif. If she's not scared shitless right now then she truly is stupid. She talks a good game, but did you notice her only recourse was to make ridiculous barbs? Do you think any vampire worth their salt wouldn't have just attacked both of us, or at least tried?"

"Lux is afraid of you?" Violet asked, distracted by the statement.

"Why do you think I'm still alive?"

Violet pondered his words. It made sense. She'd noticed the way Lux acted around Roman. There was a quiet respect. "Is he the oldest vampire alive?"

Roman snickered. "No, but he's the oldest I personally know. I have killed older vampires though."

"That kind of seems like a shame. I mean, to survive all those years and then WHAM!"

"Yeah, well, ask all the lives they stole what a shame it was when I took their heads off."

"Yikes," Violet said, pondering the power of the man standing next to her.

"Speaking of yikes, remind me to never get into a catfight with you," Roman said with a smirk.

"Hey, it's what I do. You've got a sword and I've got a vicious tongue," Violet said with a casual shrug.

"Oh really?"

Violet's eyes bugged out realizing the obviously innuendo she'd accidentally stumbled into. "Um..."

Roman laughed and took another drink.

Amber walked up to the two of them, still obviously shaken. "Did you get her?"

"No," Roman and Violet said in tandem.

"What happened?" Amber asked with fear in her eyes.

"She got away this time. Don't worry," Roman said, smiling at the girl and taking a drink.

"Easy for you to say, mister vampire killer," Amber said, trying to grin and shirk her fear.

"I'm serious, Amber, don't worry," Roman spoke in a measured tone with purpose, slowing his words and reassuring the girl. "I couldn't kill her here, but she'll be dead before morning."

"Are they almost done?" Violet asked Amber, motioning towards the band.

"Yeah, like one more song," Amber answered, turning to look at the stage.

"Good, we need to get out of here and get back home. We'll wait for you guys. I don't trust what Cecelia might do," Violet said, looking at Amber and then to Roman.

"Speaking of which, I wonder where those two girls went? You were right, Violet. I should have listened to you. She's been using them," Roman said. "You knew something was off and I dismissed it. I'm not usually so lazy. I'm sorry."

Violet smiled half heartedly. "It's okay. I didn't know what was going on, just that something was different. I wonder if she's giving them her blood too?"

"I doubt it judging by their appearance. They would look robust if they were consuming vampire blood," Roman said.

The band finally ended their set and Roman and Violet helped Randy carry his equipment to his car. Amber was sitting inside warming it up. The sky was crystal clear and the temperature had dropped another five degrees.

"I think it'll snow soon," Violet said, looking up at the night sky. She was freezing standing there with no jacket on, covered in goosebumps, senses heightened.

"Take my jacket," Roman said, removing it and handing it to her.

"I'm fine." She was enjoying the cold sensation and the way it made her feel fully alert.

"So, see you guys back at the house?" Randy asked, tucking his hands into his pockets.

"Yeah, go straight there, Randy," Violet said and took Roman's hand. She finally acquiesced and took his jacket. It dwarfed her.

Roman and Violet loaded themselves into his car.

"Lux is the one who brought the blood into your family," Roman said, cranking the heat so Violet could warm up.

"I know," Violet said, looking out the side window. "But how do you know?"

"She made reference to it," he said with derision.

"Roman, do you think she caused my parents' accident?" Violet said, suddenly looking at him with panic in her eyes.

"No, I don't. She was just saying that to hurt you."

"But how do you know?"

"Because she didn't. Lux wouldn't have allowed that, I don't think."

"What a great guy," Violet said with sarcasm and looking back out the window.

"Besides, how could she cause someone to run a red light?"

"I know you're right. Just... hearing that made me..."

"Violet, I promise you by this weekend all of this will be over."

"How can you be sure?"

"Because I'm going to find her tonight."

"Roman, don't go out tonight," she pleaded with him. She had acted as though she was in control and strong, but she was terrified. She'd been able to put on a good front, but the power that the vampire had over her own blood had scared her to death. It was only by some miracle that she'd been able to stand up to her. What she didn't know was that it was Lux's blood that gave her that strength, combined with her own will.

"What if she comes to the house?" Violet asked, turning sideways in the seat looking at Roman who was always so strong. His skin glowed white in the dark car and his eyes sparkled as the street lights caught their surface.

He looked over at her sensing her fear. It was palpable. Her scent filled the car as her pulse raced, body temperature rising. He took her hand and squeezed it tightly. "Don't you think the sooner we find her the better?"

"I'm really freaked out," she said, trying to be as strong as she could and failing. "I felt so totally under her command."

"Maybe you felt that way, but you weren't. You can't go off of your emotions with vampires because they can make you feel things. You stood up to her, V. I'm impressed. You had the upper hand," he said, tipping his head to the side. His voice was low and rumbling.

"But that's also why I want to put an end to this tonight. Violet, you're strong. You're strong enough to take care of yourself and the others. I'll only be gone a few hours. Trust me, killing her will be easy. I have killed hundreds of vampires and I know what I'm talking about. She's weak. I am being honest with you, I would tell you otherwise. I wouldn't leave you alone if I was confident." He squeezed her hand, reassuring her.

They pulled into the driveway. Roman got out and opened the trunk pulling out several swords and handed them to her. "Keep these with you. She's not going to come here, but if she does, be prepared. Randy and Amber can protect themselves too. Swing a big sword around and eventually you'll hit something vital. No training required," he said and gave her a wink.

Amber stood beside Violet huddled against her in the cold air, trembling. Randy was busy hauling his equipment into the house.

"If anything comes at you, swing this at its head. It's that simple," Roman said, looking at Amber directly. "I won't be gone long," he said, looking back at Violet.

Amber jogged to the house frightened by the prospects. She helped Randy with the final load of equipment and went into the house flipping all the lights on as she went.

Violet looked at Roman and watched as he took a long blade from the back of the car and placed it on the front seat. She took his jacket off and handed it back to him. He pulled it on and zipped it up.

"I *promise* I won't be long." He smiled slightly and rubbed her bare arms with his hands.

She felt the rush of blood to the surface of her skin as his hands touched her. She wanted to tell him not to leave, to come inside and help her pack her things so that they could go away somewhere and not worry about this, but instead she smiled sadly and laid her head against his chest. He wrapped his arms around her and hugged her tight.

"You should go in, you're freezing," he said quietly.

"Promise me again you'll be back soon," she said, looking up at him.

He took her face in his hands and kissed her deeply, making her forget all fear for a moment. "I'll see you in a little bit, kitten" he said and sat down in the car. He looked at her for a long moment then started the engine. The car roared to life.

She turned and started to walk towards the house hesitantly then stopped and turned around fearing this might be the last time she'd see him.

"Stop worrying, V. This is just another vampire in a long line of vampires I've killed. Now get inside before you make yourself sick." He smirked at her and closed the door.

Violet looked at him again and then turned and walked up to the house. She watched him pull away, terrified she'd never see him again. And what would she do then? What if he never came back? *Help him, please.*

She and Amber had both waited in the bathroom as the other showered because they were both too creeped out and scared to be alone.

Like the typical boy he was, Randy sat downstairs looking at the swords, feeling the weight of them in his hand, slicing through air. Violet had warned him how sharp they were, but that hadn't stopped him from running his thumb along the edge and slicing it open. The television was loud and every light was on in the house. They'd made sure each window and door had been locked tight and even the outdoor lights still glared in the darkness.

Violet waited at Amber's door as she put on pajamas. Amber did the same for Violet. They grabbed their blankets and pillows and jogged down the stairs. Randy had made sandwiches for three and poured pop into plastic tumblers. Violet sat on the floor in front of the couch and covered her legs with her thick quilt. She bit into the sandwich and took a drink of the soda. Her stomach was too queasy to eat. She couldn't help worrying about Roman. He had warned her about this. He'd warned her that getting involved with him would mean she'd have this fear night after night.

Amber and Randy made jokes about the sitcom they watched hoping to ease all their minds a bit. The presence of the swords in the chair beside the couch was enough of a distraction to stop that from happening. Violet had made it clear she didn't want to talk about any of this just yet. She'd be able to talk more easily during the day, or once Roman was home. She didn't want to freak herself out any more than she already was.

"Maybe we should turn the lights out?" Randy asked. He was exhausted having worked all day and having played an hour long set earlier.

Violet sat up and looked at him. She was afraid of the dark. They all knew she was afraid of the dark.

"Come on, Violet, don't you think having all these lights on only makes it easier for them to see us? If the lights are out they won't know where we are in the house," Amber said, nudging her friend with her foot.

"They can see in total darkness. The difference is we can't," Violet said, lying back on the floor.

Amber and Randy shut up after that.

Randy and Amber had fallen asleep an hour prior and Roman still wasn't back. She had walked back and forth from the front door to the back door a hundred times. It didn't bring him home any quicker. Where the hell could he be? The sun wasn't too terribly far from rising, maybe two hours tops. She wanted him here safe with her. She sat back down on the floor and slid back into the pile of pillows and stared at the television until her brain finally gave out and forced her to sleep.

She walked around the corner and saw him sitting there. His lush hair fell over his face. She knew he was hiding his face from her. Reaching out, she brushed it aside, lifting his chin so that he would look at her.

"Where are we?" she asked, kneeling before him and resting her hands on his knees.

His eyes went soft and a smile came to his lips. "It doesn't matter where we are." *he said softly and touched her cheek with his hand.*

His eyes seemed on the verge of tears, or so full of emotion they pulsated.

She looked around the room. This place was familiar. She'd seen it before. She noticed the white curtains flecked with small yellow rosebuds billowing softly as the air breathed in gentle flutters. The walls were soft yellow and there was a bassinet sitting crooked in the corner of the room.

This was her mother's nursery at her grandparents house. She'd seen it in the family albums. Of course when she'd been there while they were alive it had looked completely different.

"Why did you bring me here?" she asked, standing and walking to the crib. "I already know it was you." She turned to look at him again, his head lowered.

"I wanted to tell you the story," he said, turning to look at her. "Come here."

She walked over to him and kneeled before him as he took her small hands in his and ran his thumbs across them gently.

"I found your mother there in the corner after I crawled through the window. Her parents were downstairs listening to the radio and eating cake and drinking coffee. You know they did that every evening?"

She nodded her head. This was something they had done every night of their lives together and she had taken part in the nightly ritual many times herself. Cake and coffee every evening before bed.

"She was so quiet and soft lying there looking up at me and completely unafraid. She smiled at me, a soft bubble forming on her lips as she cooed and wiggled her feet and hands. I took my finger and popped the bubble and felt her little wet mouth. Violet, I didn't lie to you when I said you made me feel what it was to be human for an instant. It was the same with your mother. I loved her the moment she smiled at me."

"Then why did you do it to her?" Violet asked.

He sat quietly for a moment. His eyebrows knit together, his lips pursed slightly as he surveyed his thoughts. "Selfish reasons," he answered, brushing the hair away from her face.

"What do you mean?"

"I can never be human, Violet. I will never be anything but this thing. I wanted to know what it felt like to give birth to something human. I wanted to watch her grow and become something I could never be."

"But you could have done that without giving her the blood, Lux," Violet said, slightly perturbed with his answer.

"I told you I am selfish. I couldn't leave her with nothing of me. Besides, it made her stronger. It connected us."

"Why didn't you just make her a vampire?"

"She was a baby!" he said, seemingly appalled by the idea.

"When she got older, duh!" Violet answered crossly.

"Because I wouldn't wish this on a creature as gentle as she was. Besides, I want all vampires dead besides Mylori."

"What?" Violet said, standing up and turning her back towards him. She looked around the room in fascination, never having seen it with her own eyes.

"Violet, why do you think I help Roman? Some good will gesture? No, I want them all dead. They pollute the earth."

"You make no sense to me," she said, looking back over her shoulder.

"I know I don't. That's a good thing," he said, standing up and walking to the window. He rested his hands against the frame, feeling the edge of the wood pressing into his palms and leaving a deep cleft. "I came through this window and walked over to her bed and let her drink from the tip of my finger. She was so trusting, cooing the whole time she fed. I watched her little cheeks flush pink, her eyes grew brighter. Her little legs kicked with happiness." He shook his head as if erasing the memory. "I watched her year after year, growing older, never sick, and never unhappy. Your grandparents were good to her."

"They loved her," Violet said, walking towards him.

"I loved her too, in my own way," he said, looking down at her.

"Did she ever know you?" Violet asked, and sat down on the side of the bed.

"I saw her in public a few times as she got older. She always looked at me with some knowing glance but in passing. Almost like she recognized me from somewhere *she couldn't place. But I never spoke to her." Violet didn't need to know the truth of their relationship. There was so much more to this story.*

"What did you expect from her? That she would grow up and be like Roman? That she would become some warrior or something?"

"No, I never thought anything beyond how beautiful she was in that tiny crib looking up at me in the dark." He turned and looked at her. A sad smile came to his lips. "Much the same way you looked at me."

"You came looking for her that night didn't you?"

"Yes, and to my surprise I found her beautiful daughter," he smiled and then sat beside her. "Violet, I should have never come to this place. I make no excuses for my actions, but I can't regret what I've done. I don't regret who I am. Sometimes I wish I knew what it felt to be human again, but I don't regret who I am anymore."

Violet sat quietly. She wasn't angry with him. She knew she should be repulsed by him, but there was such a melancholy way about him that she just felt sad for him. "I don't understand why you felt the need to watch over me all these years. My mom and I were just normal people. There are thousands of normal people you could have been obsessed with. So what made us any different than the ones you kill?"

"I don't know," he answered, tilting his head to the side and looking her in the eye. "Yes, your mother was normal, but you were anything but normal. You were born with my blood already in your veins."

She looked down at her hands and contemplated what he'd told her. There was no answer good enough to explain any of this.

"Just don't hate me," he said, looking at her. His eyes burned with sadness.

"I can't hate you." She smiled gently at him--a soft smile spreading sweetly on her lips that warmed his heart. "But Lux, why didn't you come and save my mom? You could have saved her after the accident."

Lux got very still. It was unnerving. His body simply stopped as though he was dead. Violet watched intently, trying to detect any movement, any sign that would show life in him, and saw nothing. Finally he moved, his head bowing for a moment before he looked up at her again. It startled her to the point that she jumped. He placed his hand against her cheek and looked at her with great sadness.

"I came too late. I felt something was wrong. Violet, I was always able to feel your mother, just as I am able to feel you. All I have to do is think about you and I'm with you. Don't let that frighten you. I don't take advantage of it often, only when I feel pain of some kind. It makes me curious. And I felt such grief that it was crippling. I was in Madrid when it shot through me and I knew something was terribly wrong because I couldn't connect with her. But I knew she still lived. By the time I got here she was gone, but I saw her beautiful daughter sitting beside the bed. The machines had long stopped, yet you remained."

Violet remembered that night. She had been forced to make the decision to turn the machines off and she sat there for hours after her mom drew her last breath, unable to move from her side. She remembered feeling a warmth come over her, some feeling of comfort that finally let her get up and leave.

"It was you?" Violet said, raising her eyes to his.

Lux said nothing but wiped away a tear that had fallen from her eye. "I was too late and it killed me when I saw you and felt your grief. So, I stayed around making sure you were okay. I saw your friends come to you and I knew that you would be alright, so I left. Unfortunately only a few short days later I found out about Cecelia. She is my child so I knew immediately what she was up to and why she was here. I hadn't thought of her in years really, but for some reason I felt the inclination to check in with her. I was probably feeling wistful because of your situation. I did what I knew I had to, and that was protecting you."

"So, you sent Roman instead of coming yourself?"

"Yes, she is my child, as I said. We don't kill our own. And while I have no qualms about what Roman will do to her, because she deserves what comes her way a thousand times over, I couldn't bring her death.

"Roman is so lonely, was so lonely, and so were you. And he is nothing if not loyal. He is even loyal to me and he despises me." Lux smiled without any mirth reaching his eyes.

"He doesn't despise you," Violet said, rolling her eyes.

He stopped again, completely motionless. All movement halted. He looked like a statue. It was so unnerving. And then he exhaled. "Well, nevertheless, I knew that he would keep you safe... and so he has."

"I'm worried about Roman," she said, her eyes now filled with darkness. "He's been gone a long time."

"Yes, Roman," Lux said, standing up and walking back to the window. "He'll be back very soon. He's accomplished what he set out to accomplish a few moments ago."

"How do you know that?" she asked, standing beside him.

"Because, Violet, he always does. And because I just felt her light go out."

17

HAPPY ENDING

DESPITE THE FACT THAT Roman had really been slacking off he had done more investigating than he'd let on to Violet. She didn't need to know the magnitude of Cecelia's threat. He had been going out when he told her he was going home to shower or running out for various errands. What she didn't know wouldn't hurt her, but what she did know could have since she would have been terrified. So, he'd kept it to himself.

Roman had killed four vampires in the last few days and had left one particular vampire knowing that eventually Cecelia would show up to give orders. The four he had previously killed had been dolts. They were the typical sort that hung out in cemeteries and had no clue how to use their abilities. They were newly turned and easy to kill. He hadn't even received a single bruise or scratch in the fights. Of course, there had been no fight. It was a slaying, pure and simple. The newbies hadn't even seen him coming.

He had found the one he kept alive easily enough by following his instincts and surveying the woods close to town. There was an old shack in a clearing near the woods just off the river downtown behind an old mill. The building had been out of use for decades. He had half expected to find Cecelia there, but he hadn't located her resting ground just yet. It didn't matter though, she would come to him and he knew it, especially after their run in earlier. He knew tonight would be the night she'd strike. Her pathetic ego couldn't sustain the blow it had taken tonight without retaliation.

He watched from a tall oak tree about fifty yards away from the shack as Cecelia strode through the trees. The fact that they didn't even sense Roman was laughable. He shook his head and couldn't help his smirk as he watched Cecelia dispense her orders. A third vampire stomped up, this one larger than the other, nearly Roman's height and bulky with thick muscles. Cecelia kissed him, obviously some gift for his loyalty. She was attractive enough, some would even think she was beautiful. Lux surely wouldn't turn someone he found unattractive, and he had good taste, from what Roman had always seen. But selling your soul to someone in order to enact their vengeance was pitiful. What humans will give up for immortality, or maybe just pussy. Men are stupid.

As the vampires were distracted with each other and hanging on Cecelia's words, Roman dropped soundlessly from the tree. He unsheathed the sword from its holder and walked straight towards the trio. Cecelia saw him first and smiled like a lioness. She really was an idiot, so far out of her league.

"Delivered on a silver platter, boys," she said to her pride of kittens and raised her hand elegantly in Roman's direction.

Roman picked up his speed as the two males ran towards him. The smaller one arrived first. Roman sliced through the neck with one blow, the body dropping to the ground as Roman kept going towards the others without so much as a pause. He heard Cecelia gasp. Three steps behind the larger vampire paused and Roman separated his head from all that bulk with one smooth swing of his arm. He paused briefly looking down at the giant vampire and looked up at Cecelia. She was only a few feet away, her hands over her mouth, stunned and frozen in place. Roman smiled, eyes focused so vehemently. He tightened his grip and stepped over the dead vampire.

"Roman, this has all been a tragic misunderstanding," Cecelia begged, her voice wavering in fear. "It was Lux, he told me he loved me and then tossed me aside for her. He's coming for her, Roman. I swear to you, he's coming. I've been foolish, jealous and foolish."

The words came so fast, so soaked in desperation, and Roman knew there was no truth to any of it. At least not the way she was telling it. Lux hadn't seen Cecelia in years, he knew that. Was Lux coming for Violet? Probably, that wouldn't surprise him. But there was no way Lux had shared his plans with her. There was more to this story, but he didn't care. Whatever the story was, it didn't matter because Cecelia was about to die.

"Ro..."

He took her head off before she even had a chance to finish his name. Her eyes blinked in confusion as her head fell to the ground, eyebrows drawn down in confusion briefly before final death came to her.

Roman looked down at her. Satisfied. More gratified than he'd ever been before over a death. This kill felt good.

He swiped the blade across his pant leg, cleaning the blood off. He hated when the blood dried on the steel as it made the cleaning much more difficult. He looked down at the dead vampire, a faint glimmer of hate passed through him and then much needed calmness took over. Months of threat gone. He should have just taken care of this weeks ago. But Violet had been very, very distracting. He thought about how she was waiting for him and felt his body come alive. He took his boot and shoved Cecelia's shoulder forcing the body onto its back. The other corpses were within a few feet of each other. All of them would burn up the moment the sun lit the sky. No trace they had ever existed would be left behind. Forgotten forever. No one was immortal.

Roman walked back to his car, his thoughts going back over the killing. Cecelia had literally offered no fight. The other two had been even worse, at least she had begged for her life. The fact that she hadn't tried to at least fight for herself had been a surprise given the tough act she put on prior. But he'd known from the start she would stand no chance against him. He had fought vampires that were old as dirt and she was just a baby. And she wasn't clever. Still, he'd at least expected some kind of fight from her. He had expected her to have more vampires with her. Six wasn't very many, especially since she knew who he was and of what he was capable of. Maybe she did have more, or maybe they decided to take off. He did have a reputation that scared off a lot of lower level vamps, though how the young ones always seemed to find out who he was was a mystery. Was there some sort of email news group they all belonged to? A subreddit perhaps? The thought was ludicrous, but in this day and age it was possible. Or maybe they sensed something about him?

Whatever the case, Cecelia was now dead. One slash of that blade and it was over. Cecelia was dead and Violet was safe. For now.

Violet was right, how anticlimactic.

He walked up to his car and hesitated. Months of distraction, months of buildup, and now it was all over. Where was he going next? Was he going anywhere at all? Would Violet come with him?

He was exhausted.

He opened the trunk and put the weapon back in the leather sheath and grabbed an oily cloth and wiped the blood from his hands and forearms. He ran the rag over his sweaty neck and then tossed the smelly thing back in the trunk. A bloody rag would be suspicious if he was ever pulled over. He told himself to remember to get rid of it in the morning. He closed the trunk and walked to the driver's side and got in, taking a nice deep breath and exhaling slowly. It would be so nice to not have to worry anymore, at least not for the time being. He headed for his place wanting to take a shower and get cleaned up before going back to hers. She would no doubt be worried about where he was, but the last thing she needed was for him to come in soaked in blood and sweat, and he didn't want to call because it was late, and he hoped she was able to sleep. It would be worth the extra moments away from her to get cleaned up so that he could crawl into bed with her and sleep in finally knowing she was safe. Crawling into bed with her, what a pleasant thought.

It had only taken him fifteen minutes to shower, dress, and eat a couple slices of cold pizza. She was curled up on the floor like a cat when he got there, her body was completely motionless, her breath so shallow it was nearly impossible to see the rise of her chest. There was no color in her face, even her lips were pale. She was so still it seemed as though she wasn't in her body, and then he realized she probably wasn't.

Amber and Randy were on the couch in a knot. It made him happy she had friends like them. He only wished he'd had a single friend when he was their age.

Wow, he'd never wished that before.

He leaned back in the red chair and closed his eyes content enough that she was near and that she was finally safe.

Amber stretched in her sleep rousing Randy. It caused him to jump with a start still freaked out by what was going on around them. Amber was safe and sound asleep and Roman was now back as well. It scared him that Roman had actually gotten into the house without even waking any of them up. Some protector Randy was. Or maybe Roman was just that stealth, yeah, that was it. But since Roman was back and obviously unharmed that had to mean everything was okay. Or at least that they'd be safe in their house now. He shook Amber and whispered for her to follow him back to their room.

"Time for you to go," Lux said, taking her hand and kissing it.

"Thank you for telling me the truth," she said, standing up as if she could walk back to her body.

"I don't regret what I did, Violet, but I'm terribly sad that I was too late to save your mother. I loved her too. And you have so much more to discover about who you are."

She felt her body as she entered into it. The cold vessel felt hard on the outside and mushy inside like a piece of stale bread soaked in hot soup as she settled back into her flesh. The warmth of her insides was shocking. She blinked her eyes open allowing the pupils to dilate and focus on the blanket and floor until they steadied. She lifted her head from the soft down pillow and saw Roman sitting upright in the chair as he slept. Her heart sighed heavily, so happy to know he was home safe. She sat up and rubbed her eyes and yawned then looked down at his boots and noticed the faint semblance of dried blood and mud. He didn't appear to be hurt. Thank God. Crawling across the floor, she kneeled before him and rubbed her hands up his thighs and torso then fell into him resting her head against his stomach. She closed her eyes, happy to hear the never-ending thump of his heart pounding over and over in his chest. His arm lifted, lying heavy across her body, as his huge hand gently rubbed her back.

"I'm glad you're okay," she said, peaceful, not moving or opening her eyes.

"I'm glad you're okay," he answered in the same manner. "She's dead, Violet."

"Good," Violet answered, a shudder running through her that sped up her body evoking the tears from her eyes. It was so wrong to be glad someone was dead, wasn't it? But she was. As her body released weeks of built-up tension, waves of emotion, so overwhelming she couldn't contain it any longer, poured out of her. She cried heavily, her body heaving, her fingers clutching him as she buried her face in his lap.

"Hey," he said, sitting forward slowly and wiping her face. "It's all over now, you should be happy."

"I am," she whimpered, not wanting him to look at her contorting face anymore.

"Yeah, I can tell," he teased and hugged her, allowing her to hide herself against him again.

She laughed between cries and then settled in against him. "I guess I didn't realize just how stressed out and scared I've been until now that it's all over."

"Well, she is dead," he said with authority and pushed her hair over her shoulder and down her back. "No more worries." He knew there was so much more behind her outburst than just the Cecelia issue. So much had happened in her life between her parents, Mark, Lux, Cecelia, even him.

Her sobbing relented and she continued to lean against him comforted by the sound of his heart and deep, slow breathing. Roman was always so patient with her. He had never once chided her for crying, something Mark had always made fun of her for or gotten angry with her about.

"Roman, it's over now, right?"

"Yes," he said, eyes closed and exhausted. The sun would be rising shortly. It had been a long night.

"So, I can finally move on with my life?"

"Mmm hmm," he replied, nearly asleep.

She pulled herself away from him and wiped her face. His eyes were still closed, his stubbly head resting against the back of the chair. She smiled. Finally she could get on with her life, whatever that meant.

She leaned forward nestling between his legs and kissed his mouth. "I love you," she said, just a whisper.

He cracked his eyes open and looked down at her, a smile spreading sleepily across his face, "I love you, too." He kissed her back.

His mouth was warm and soft, his raspy tongue gentle as he parted her lips. It seemed like she'd waited a thousand years for someone this perfect. No one had ever been so good to her. He had saved her. And he had kept her from dying.

In the past her boyfriends had been indifferent, or downright cruel, especially in Mark's case. They either expected her to play the part of dutiful sycophant, or they were so weak-willed she ended up treating them like shit because she just had no respect for that kind of placating weakness. Though her experience wasn't all that vast, a lot had been packed into those few relationships, especially with

Mark. After all the mental mindfuck abuse she'd experienced with him, having Roman was unreal. *And why am I thinking about Mark right now?*

"Because I'm a dumbass," she said, cracking a grin.

"What?" he asked, pulling back and looking down at her.

"Nothing," she said with a giggle and pulled him down onto the floor.

He hovered over her like a giant god. He seriously looked god-like to her. He had saved her life how many times now? More than that, he had comforted her, had been her friend, had allowed her to grieve, and even let her be a total dick to him. And he had remained patient through all of it. And now he loved her too. *He loves me.* It was a revelation.

"You're my hero," Violet said and batted her eyelashes like a dork because being overly emotional usually made her feel uncomfortable. Probably because the aforementioned exes made her feel stupid anytime she expressed herself.

"Weirdo," he said and shook his head. He was on his hands and knees above her looking down at her like she was prey.

She loved the way his muscles bunched at his shoulders, his forearms taut, veins raised to the surface. She turned her head, not breaking their eye contact and grinned devilishly as she licked his arm.

"You're so strange," he smiled and tickled her cheek with his finger trailing to her wet lips.

She turned her head the other way, not taking her eyes from his, and kissed his wrist. Black hair fanned out around her head like living vines coiling with every movement. He saw her in the field then, ghostlike, illuminated by the moon, her hair winding in the wind like vines finding the sun. It was such a clear and profound vision that they were there momentarily, until she lifted his hand and took his thumb into her warm mouth, the pad of his finger pressing against the ridge of her teeth.

The silver heart he'd given her fell to her side. It caught his eye. She'd worn it nearly every day since he'd given it to her, only taking it off during her relapse with Mark. The words had stung him when she'd spoken of their relationship and divulged all the things Mark made her do. Roman had really been kidding himself that this necklace meant nothing to him, that he was only giving the gift as a friend. But he'd known better even then, deep down. One didn't give up family heirlooms to just anybody. God, he had loved her early on and hadn't even realized it. He picked the heart up and set it in the center of her belly, resting it in her navel.

She reached for it and took it in her hands, never letting her eyes leave his. "You can't imagine how much this meant to me."

"I know," he said, leaning down and kissing her again.

His mouth moved over her face and neck, hot and hungry as he lowered himself down on top of her. The weight of his body felt wonderful, so solid and strong. His hand cradled her head as he kissed her mouth again, devouring her like he was starving. She was surprised by his passion as he had been very apprehensive about touching her up until now. Maybe the gravity of the situation had weighed more heavily on him than he'd let on, and maybe he felt as free as she did now? He lifted himself back onto all fours and looked down at her again, eyes shining and ravenous. She licked her lips, tasting his kiss, her arm snaking up to his neck and pulling herself up to force his mouth to hers again. She moaned at the taste and feel of his mouth.

"This probably isn't the best place for this," he whispered between kisses.

"Mmm... probably not," she said, her voice a breath, not wanting him to stop. She reached beneath his shirt feeling the warmth of his stomach, tight and muscled, the back of her hand brushing against the soft hair that trailed below his navel. Her fingers sank into the top of his jeans, clutching the waistband as she grabbed a fist full of denim and pulling him back down.

He fell into her and kissed her mouth again. He could die in her mouth. Die curled up beneath her tongue for as long as she would keep him there. "We really shouldn't do this here," he said again, visions of Amber tripping downstairs flashed in the back of his head. He didn't want an audience for what he wanted to do to her.

"Mmm... probably not," she answered again, not letting him go, fingers gripping him to her.

He kissed her deeply, his hands roving of their own volition. Violet gave a little sigh as his hand covered her breast. Roman moved to her side slightly and reached between their bodies, his fingers brushing the soft cotton of her panties. Violet tilted her hips against his palm as his finger slid the soft fabric to the side and felt the velvety soft skin there. He growled at the feel of her, so hot and wet.

The moment his fingers found her she just about burst out of her skin. Being touched by him like this was overwhelming. Instinctively she reached for him, finding him through his pants. She had felt him pressed against her before, but she had never touched him like this. Roman kissed her, a hungry growl rumbled in his throat that reverberated against her chest as his fingers moved inside her. The heaviness of his body and the warmth of his mouth made Violet melt completely. She growled herself and fumbled with his belt, unable to unhook it.

Violet sighed in exasperation and then laughed. "I'm not very good at this."

"I disagree," he answered and sat up. Violet whined a little, protesting the loss of his body. Roman looked down at her, a look of reverence on his face. Her lips were rosy red and kiss-swollen, her cheeks flushed, and she looked more beautiful than he could ever remember seeing her. He took her hand and held it and then stood up, urging her to follow him. She complied, feeling almost dizzy, her body thrumming and aching for him.

She stood up and bent over to pick up the quilt and pillows as he waited for her. She walked towards him with her arms loaded with the bundle and looked up with a smile at the gorgeous man looking down at her. He bent down and kissed her again, holding her face in his hands and pulling her up onto tiptoes. He took the pillows and blanket and tossed them back on the floor.

Violet's lip quirked into a smile, but Roman wasn't smiling. He was completely serious, focused. She sat back down on the pile on the floor, smoothing the blanket out around her and fell back.

Fuck, he's hot. Violet looked up at him as the words went through her head causing herself to grin. It was so absolutely something she would've said to Amber about him, and that made her laugh.

Roman shook his head and peeled his shirt off and came down to his knees in front of her. She sat up, her fingers deftly moving across his chest and winding towards the back of his neck. As he lowered his lips to hers her hands slid down his body to work on his belt, getting it unfastened this time. She looked down to see the button and zipper, him nuzzling her neck as his breath tickled over her skin. She bit her bottom lip in mild embarrassment as his pants opened. She could feel the heat in her cheeks. She forgot he didn't usually wear underwear and for some reason this made her feel silly and shy.

Roman leaned into her, forcing her to sit. He crawled towards her moving her onto her back as he kissed her. "I hope your friends don't come down here," he muttered between kisses. "Because they're going to get a show."

She snickered nervously, his words sending electricity through her. She closed her eyes as he nipped her neck, his whiskers tickling her and making her squeal.

"Ticklish?" he asked, doing it again, resulting in more squirming.

She reached down into his open pants and he jumped a little. "Ticklish?" she asked and pushed her hand in farther.

Roman sucked in a breath and closed his eyes. He leaned into her, kissing her thoroughly. He was pressed against her core, locked in place by her legs which she had wrapped around his waist. He moved back slightly and reached between their bodies pushing her shirt up, and then leaned into her, skin to skin. He sucked one of her nipples into his mouth, his hand teasing over her panties again. Kissing a trail down her body, over her ribs, circling her navel with his hot tongue...

A faint knock came at the door. Roman stopped what he was doing, came up on all fours and lowered his head in exasperation. "Seriously?" he growled.

"Let's ignore it. Maybe they'll go away," Violet said, reaching for a belt loop and pulling his hips forward.

"They're not going to go away. It's almost dawn. Who would be knocking on your door at dawn?" He was so thoroughly pissed off they were interrupted yet again.

"Vampires?" Violet said, suddenly filled with dread. She sat up and pulled her shirt down.

"Vampires wouldn't knock," he said and kissed her again, his tongue filling her mouth. He leaned forward, Violet fell back to the floor slowly. Another soft knock.

"I am going to fucking *kill* whoever that is," Roman said and sat back on his heels reaching for his shirt. "If that's not a vampire, they're dead."

"Shouldn't you kill them if it *is* a vampire?" Violet said with a snicker and tossed his shirt to him.

"Stop being logical," he said and stood up.

"Your brain doesn't have enough blood to think logically right now," Violet said and laughed.

Roman said nothing but shook his head. He zipped his pants up leaving them unbuttoned and his belt unfastened, and started for the door.

"Roman?" she said timidly.

"What's wrong?" he asked, coming back to her and taking her hand. She had the other one across her chest protectively.

"What if it is another vampire?"

"Then I'll kill it," he said and started for the door again.

"Roman?" she asked again, voice soft and uneasy.

"Yeah?" he said, turning back to look at her, her tone giving him pause.

"Shouldn't you take a weapon with you?"

"My rage is sufficient," he said with a smirk. "These hands are registered weapons in the state of Nevada."

"Dork," Violet said and rolled her eyes, getting the reference.

Violet followed behind him, gripping a belt loop of his waistband. He was still shirtless, belt unbuckled and pants undone. Were they cursed or something? Every time they tried this something always interrupted. They crossed the kitchen and Roman pulled the curtain back and saw that Malinda and Dory stood huddled together peering in through the door at him, eyes black and sunken, glistening in the fading night.

18

SO MUCH FOR THAT

VIOLET FELT HER HEART sink as she opened the door for the girls. Go figure, her happiness couldn't last longer than a few moments, now could it? And what the hell? Every single time she and Roman even remotely got physical something always interrupted.

Malinda walked in ahead of Dory, who stood behind her clutching her coat with her head down. They both looked sickly and ragged.

"Come in," Violet said with kindness and concern, stepping aside and looking out at the yard behind them to make sure no one else was lurking there. "Wait, you're not vampires are you"

The girls looked up at her, terror in their eyes.

"What's going on?" she asked.

Violet locked the door and then looked up at Roman who seemed more than annoyed by their presence even though he was almost always sympathetic. He knew by their appearance they weren't well and he understood why better than anyone would.

"Dory's not doing well. We couldn't go home because we've been gone a few days and they would just think we were strung out."

"Sit down," Violet said, walking to the kitchen table and pulling out a chair.

"I don't know what's wrong, Violet. We couldn't find her, and we just feel so sick... and Dory's not right," Malinda said in a rush.

"You're not going to find her. She's dead," Roman said, lacking any tact whatsoever. "And what's wrong is that you're anemic due to blood loss." Roman walked behind the girls and sat down at the opposite side of the table. "You need to go to the hospital."

"No! We can't! How would we explain this?" Malinda said, sitting down and guiding Dory to do the same.

"That's not really my concern," Roman said with aggravation.

Violet looked at Roman wanting to laugh at his tone as she walked to the refrigerator to get the girls something to drink.

"When's the last time you ate something, and did she give you her blood?" Roman asked, peering across the table at the two girls. They were so tiny compared to him, so frail he could crush them.

"It's been a few days. She didn't really give us any. She said she had to wait until the right time."

"That's bullshit. She would have given it to you if she was going to," Roman said with a scoff. "Count your fucking blessings she didn't."

Malinda looked up at him with hurt in her eyes and then took the water from Violet. "Yeah, well, anyway, I don't know what's wrong with Dory."

"She needs psychological help," Roman said bluntly. He had little patience for these girls given the fact that they did this shit to themselves. "And she needs her blood count to go back to normal. Then maybe she'll be alright."

Violet smirked at Roman, not feeling particularly patient either, and then looked at Malinda. "Why did you do this?" Violet asked, sitting beside the girl. "Didn't you understand the danger involved?"

"I just thought she was cool. I know that sounds really stupid now, but it's true," Malinda said, looking at Dory, knowing why Dory had deteriorated so quickly. Seeing the things Cecelia had done with the others had traumatized her. The only reason she was coping was because she had to, because she was stronger, and hadn't been abused her whole life like Dory had been. "Will she be alright?"

"I don't know, physically maybe, but I don't know anything about psychology," Roman answered, finally relinquishing some of his annoyance. "You should go to the hospital. I'll take you."

"No, please don't make us go. Really, what would we say?" Malinda said with tears in her eyes.

"You need to go," Violet said, leaning forward. Seeing the pain in her eyes and the utter fear and desperation in Malinda's voice made her feel sorry for them. She couldn't let her irritation at being interrupted with Roman cause her to be a callous bitch. Violet knew how seductive this vampire imagery was to the girls and they'd been sucked in, so to speak, by the glamour of it.

"Can we wait until the morning? Maybe we can sleep here and see how things are in the morning?" Malinda said, looking up at Roman and then Violet.

"That's fine." Violet smiled. "Maybe drink some juice or something? Don't they give that to people in the hospital?" Violet asked, looking at Roman for some sort of confirmation.

"Sure," Roman said, shrugging his shoulders. He wasn't normally so dismissive to people in need, but these stupid girls had put themselves in this situation. He wasn't in the mood to father them, nor was it his job. He also wanted Violet. Now.

Violet stood up and walked to the fridge with Roman following behind her. "I think if they get some sleep and eat regular food for a few days they should recover. They're still functioning, so we'll wait and see in the morning. If they're no better they really should go to the hospital. One of them is going to need mental help." Roman spoke quietly, looking back at the girls, and hoping they didn't hear his comments. Truthfully, he didn't honestly mind a whole lot if they did.

"I have to take care of them. I can't just throw them out. They're good girls, Roman," Violet said.

All he could remember was how rudely they had treated her, but she always said that was out of character. And no doubt Cecelia had been poisoning their

326

minds. "Do what you need to do," he said, smiling at her and thinking it was sweet of her to want to take care of them given how they had treated her.

Violet stood on her tiptoes, hand resting on his shoulder to steady herself, and kissed him. She stepped away evoking a growl from Roman. He gripped her wrist and pulled her back and kissed her again. Violet smiled against his warm lips and stepped away, a little stunned by the PDA. She hadn't taken him for someone who would kiss her in front of others for some reason.

"Here," Violet said, handing the juice to the girls. "I'm going to go fix the guest room for you." She walked upstairs scooping the pillows and blanket up from the floor.

Roman sat down and watched the two girls, worried that they might be more sick than he could tell. As disinterested as he wanted to be at the moment he couldn't help but care. The smart thing would be to force them to go to the hospital, although he understood that their condition would lead to a lot of questions and probably get them into trouble with their parents, but he didn't care so much about that. Their health was more important than them being scolded. What a completely stupid situation. He couldn't imagine willingly sacrificing himself to a vampire.

"I'm so ashamed of myself," Malinda said quietly, her voice choking in her throat.

"You should be," Roman responded with coldness.

"I hope she gets better," Malinda said as she took a drink of the juice and looked at Dory. "She hardly said a word all day."

"She's going to need help," Roman said, not mincing words.

Malinda looked at him, her eyes were such wells of sadness he felt guilt for being so abrupt with her.

Violet opened the door to the room Steve had previously inhabited. He'd done a fair job of cleaning it up after he left, due largely in part to Randy nagging him. The bed was stripped bare except for the folded old blanket that sat neatly at the foot of the bed. She walked to the linen closet and back to the room and began making the bed. She heard a rustle at the door and looked up as Amber stood there rubbing her eyes. Her hair was mussed and her flannel pajamas hung off her body as if she was wearing the clothes of a giant.

"What's going on?" she asked, walking in and leaning against the chest of drawers.

"Malinda and Dory are downstairs. They aren't doing well. I'm going to let them stay tonight because they're afraid to go home," Violet said as she went about her task.

"What the fuck? Are they okay?"

"I think so, but Dory's a total nutcase. Like some serious PTSD or something."

"Wow, this is all really fucked up. It totally makes me reevaluate my life."

Violet furrowed her brow and stopped folding down the sheet for a moment. "Like how?"

"Like all the shit we're into. It's so fucked up the amount of drugs and junk we take, all that vampire and occult bullshit we played around with thinking it was fun. It's not fun. I can't believe it's all real."

The look on Amber's face was a mix of fear, shock, and regret. Violet understood it all too well as she had been feeling that way for weeks now, longer if she really thought through the past, and that was before learning that monsters exist.

"Yeah, I'm never going to be the same after what I've seen and all I know," Violet said, smoothing the pillow cases and unfolding the thick blanket at the foot of the bed.

"Well, you're a fucking vampire, so, technically I guess I'm still messing around with the occult." Amber laughed, trying to make a joke.

"I'm more human than I am a vampire, and I don't think that has anything to do with the occult? More like biology? Cryptozoology maybe?"

"I don't even know what that means. What time is it anyway?" Amber yawned and stretched.

"I don't know, but I think the sun will be up soon," Violet said, looking out the window beside the bed.

"I am so not going to work today. I need a sick day," Amber grumbled.

"You never call off," Violet said, raising her eyebrows.

"First time in three years. I even went back to work the day I broke my wrist there, remember?"

Violet chuckled. "Yeah, I remember. I picked you up and took you to the med center to get checked, you got a cast, and you made me take you back to work after. You're a hardcore motherfucker."

"Gotta make that coin," Amber said with a smirk.

"Well, you took off when my parents..."

"Doesn't count, Vi."

Violet smiled sadly and nodded her head.

"But fuck that noise today. I think vampire drama qualifies me for a day off. Besides, Jill can function without me for a day."

"Get some rest, mama," Violet said.

"You too," Amber said, looking back at her as she walked across the hall.

"Yeah," Violet muttered, knowing she wouldn't be sleeping anytime soon. Not with Roman all growly and in her bed.

She finished straightening the blanket and then walked downstairs, finding the three of her houseguests sitting quietly. The girls had finished the juice she'd given them and Roman looked utterly exhausted. He sat slouched down in the chair staring blankly forward.

"All set," Violet said, startling them. "Sorry." She laughed as they all jumped.

Roman stood up and walked over to her. He looked down at her, his body encroaching her space. "I'm going to bed." He grinned sleepily and patted her on the top of the head, messing up her already disheveled hair.

"I'll be in shortly," she said, noticing how much she sounded like her mom when she said it. That was a phrase she'd heard her mother say a thousand times in her life. She reached out and grabbed his thick wrist halting him from leaving and planted a kiss to his sternum.

His eyes burned as they bore into her. "Hurry."

Violet blushed and let go of his wrist to allow him to go upstairs.

She gathered some more water and juice for the girls and led them to their room. She told them to sleep as long as they wanted and to help themselves to the fridge.

"Thanks Violet," Malinda said as she took her coat and shoes off.

"It's okay, Malinda," Violet said and smiled.

"No, we were really mean to you and I'm sorry."

"It's not like I haven't been mean to my fair share of people. Don't worry about it."

"But not us and it wasn't right. You've always been nice to us," Malinda said. "She just... she got in our head. I just wanted an escape from my life and..."

Malinda's eyes were filled with tears and Dory wrapped her arms around Malinda from behind, clinging to her like she was the only thing keeping her upright. Maybe she was.

"It's okay. I'm fine and you're fine," Violet said, reaching out and squeezing Malinda's wrist. We're here and we're fine. "Try to get some sleep. Things will look better tomorrow."

Violet smiled and shut the door behind her as she left the two girls huddled there together. She needed to get away from the emotions. It was too much, stirred up too much.

She was so used to being taken care of lately herself and it felt sort of nice taking care of someone else for a change, like she wasn't as weak as she'd felt. Violet walked over to the bathroom and washed her hands. She looked up at herself in the mirror and noticed the dark circles that had formed under her eyes. She hadn't realized how exhausted she really was. Splashing some water on her face refreshed her a little, but she was still so tired. She went to her room. Roman was on his stomach stretched across the bed with his shirt and boots off, feet dangling over the edge. Ugh, he was so freaking hot. It was never going to not be amazing to her that he was really that good looking. Sure, maybe he didn't look that beautiful to everyone else. But to her he was utter perfection. And now she could touch him whenever she wanted. She didn't have to maintain some kind of barrier between them out of insecurity. He said he loved her. She loved him.

Violet smiled and slid down beside him remembering how good it felt to kiss him. His body was so damn perfect, his muscles so huge and strong. Everything about him screamed comfort and protection. She settled against him, snuggling up to him. He had saved her tonight. He had taken out her enemy and saved her. Again. He let out a soft groan acknowledging her presence and then opened an eye slightly to look at her.

"I am so tired," he said, his voice a dry rumble.

"Me too," she said and rubbed her hand across his stubbly head.

He lifted his arm and laid it over her wanting her to come closer. He rolled over onto his back so she could rest her head on his chest.

"I'm sorry we got interrupted," Violet said, closing her eyes and nestling against his chest. She kissed his warm skin, taking in a deep breath, and filling her lungs with his scent. He always smelled so good. It used to be coconut shampoo in his hair, now it was whatever manly smelling soap he used. And why was she thinking about his soap?

Roman kissed the top of her head, nuzzling the soft tresses and pulling her closer.

They heard Malinda and Dory rustling around in the room beside them. One of them was crying, the other one mumbling words of comfort.

Roman internally groaned in frustration and laid his head back into the pillow. They were going to have to go somewhere no other humans existed if he ever expected to get anywhere physically with her. Then again, some bear would probably knock on the door, or aliens would land. Something would happen. *Fuck.* He groaned out loud. He was tired anyway. Not exactly the best circumstance for a first time together. Not to mention her twin bed wasn't roomy, though he could make it work regardless. The thought was almost amusing.

He rolled over on his side and lifted her chin so she would look at him. It was so dark in the room he could barely make out her features. He kissed her, his tongue slipping between her lips and touching hers. There was another burst of tears on the other side of the wall. Roman sighed and closed his eyes, giving up on the idea of getting anywhere with her tonight.

"I'm sorry," Violet said, frustration evident in her own voice.

"We've got time," he said, kissing the top of her head. "We're both exhausted anyway."

"This is all my fault," Violet said as though a light bulb had just gone off, her voice a soft lilt filled with grief and regret. "All these people are dead. Gwen. Those vampires Cecelia made. And then whatever is going on with Dory and Malinda. It's all my fault."

"No, this is all Cecelia's fault."

"Who came to town because of me."

"Because of Lux."

"Whatever," Violet said, and rested her head back against his chest, wrapping her arm around him.

"I'm not going to let you blame yourself for this, Violet."

"Let's just go to sleep," she said and snuggled against him.

"I love you," he said, his voice a deep, groggy rumble.

Violet smiled despite her sadness and tilted her head back so that he would kiss her. "I love you too," she said and kissed him, licking his bottom lip, and then wrapped her fingers around his thick neck.

"Mmm... go to sleep," he whispered against her lips, breaking the kiss. "We've got time. And I would kind of like to be coherent enough to do the job properly."

Violet giggled. "As if that would be a problem, but okay. I guess I am tired too. I mean, I can make it work. Just saying."

Roman grumbled and kissed her again, sucking her bottom lip into his mouth and chewing softly on it. "I really wish we were at my place right now."

Violet giggled and moved against him, her eyes no longer wanting to stay open despite how badly she wanted them to. "Yeah," she said, her tongue licking his lips as she wrapped her arm around his chest.

"Mmm..." he mumbled against her lips. Rustling on the other side of the wall and muffled cries permeated the silence again. "Fuck," he growled.

Violet laughed, kissing him one last time before finally acquiescing to the fact that they just weren't going to get what they wanted tonight.

The silver halo around the moon pulsed to some hidden rhythm of heart and stream and wind. Snowflakes fell lightly, landing on the golden crushed wheat of the field. The cold air felt clean and pure as it entered her body and permeated her limbs.

She looked down and saw the pinkness of her fingers. Her nails were luminescent as the flesh around them flushed red for warmth.

The cold touched her but didn't invade.

She walked through the field towards the orangey flame in the distance. The tongues licked the night sky, orange and red and yellow. They danced in time to the breath of the clouds, reflecting off alabaster flesh. She knew his flesh.

And she wondered how it was that they always came here? She had always come here, and now so did he. She thought she remembered him vaguely once before, a faint shadow in the woods, maybe standing in the stream or beneath the yellow oak. But now he really was here interacting with her.

As she approached he looked up at her. He had known she was coming. The look in his eyes and the expression on his face told her he knew. He'd been waiting.

The flakes fell the size of quarters and slowly dusted the ground around them. It snowed for her. She had wanted the snow.

She smiled and circled around the fire towards him. He was sitting on the ground and glowing yellowy orange, his face as peaceful as she'd ever seen. He was strong, everything he'd been built to be.

"You came here once when I was young," she said, sitting beside him. The white silk of her gown was wet at the hem. Her bare feet peaked beneath the edge of the fabric, cold and wet from the melting snow on the ground.

"Yes, I saw you too," he answered and tucked the blue jay feather behind her ear. "But I didn't remember until just now. Where is this place?"

She leaned back into the grass and spread her arms as if making a snow angel and sighed.

"The field beside my grandparent's farm," she said, looking up at him. "See beyond the edge of the trees? There it is." She pointed her pink finger in the direction of the tree line. "But why were you here?" Her hair felt wet from the melting snow.

Warm and cold and wet and warm and cold and wet.

"I don't know." He smiled as he looked at the hidden outline of the farmhouse and thought he caught a glimpse of something, someone familiar, haloed by the faint light emanating from a window. And then he looked back to the woman who sat beside him. "I knew you'd be here though."

"We're awake aren't we?" she asked, sitting up and pulling her knees into her chest. She finally understood that these dreams weren't dreams at all. They were real. Her spirit was truly here.

"Yes," he answered, brushing the dried grain from the moist skin on her shoulder.

She reached towards his face and felt the outline of his jaw, the cut of his cheekbone, the long, straight ridge of his nose, and then she smiled. "It can always be this way."

"Yes, this, or somewhere else," he said, catching her hand and rubbing her rosy fingers. "You said it would snow soon." He looked up at the sky, a snowflake landing on his face and melting in his eye, then blinked and looked back at her.

The fire snapped and popped as the logs smoldered red and orange and blue. It looked like velvet waves as it moved over the surface of the cracked wood.

He leaned forward kissing her yellow-gold cheek and then her lips. The cold sweetness of his mouth was overwhelming. She could see herself not bothering to ever wake up again. What would be the point after all this?

Falling back onto warm, cold, wet ground could be everything. There were no monsters here. Only the moon and wheat and trees and water. And him.

"Violet," Amber said, rapping the door with her knuckle.

Violet opened her eyes groggily and groaned as she wasn't ready to wake up. Fuck, they couldn't even touch each other in dreams without someone interrupting. Her body felt detached from itself still. Roman grunted and rolled over refusing to wake just yet. She pulled herself off the bed and opened the door.

"Huh?" she asked, not having yet opened her eyes.

"It's two o'clock in the afternoon. I was just wondering if you were gonna get up anytime soon?" Amber was wearing an apron and Violet could tell from the warm fragrant air that followed her that she'd been baking.

"Wow, I guess I was tired," Violet said, finally cracking her eyes open. "What'd you make?" Violet asked, walking out and closing the door behind her. She didn't want Roman to wake up if he didn't want to yet.

"Peanut butter cookies. There's some leftover chili too."

"Mmm... peanut butter cookies and chili. Right on." Violet scuffled across the hall to the bathroom with Amber right behind her. "I was having a good dream when you woke me," Violet said, sitting down to go to the bathroom. Amber looked at herself in the mirror, wiping a smear of red lipstick and smoothing her sleek hair.

"Yeah, I can imagine," Amber said with a grin. "So... you and Roman?"

"No, and stop asking. That's embarrassing," Violet said, standing and turning on the faucet.

"Since when is *that* embarrassing to you?"

"I don't know. But let me tell you, I would probably have a different answer for you had the girls not shown up last night. Um, it was on like Donkey Kong until they knocked."

"Downstairs?" Amber said and laughed.

"Um, yeah. Roman kept trying to get me to go upstairs but ya know, I have no patience."

"Like a spoiled child?"

"Something like that. I mean, he played coy for a long time."

"Coy," Amber said and laughed.

"Well, he did!" Violet said and laughed. "Anyway, I swear the universe is plotting against us."

"Maybe someone put a curse on your love life? Are witches real too?"

"Who fucking knows? It wouldn't surprise me at this point. It was funny though. I've never seen Roman act that impatient with anyone. He was so not having it with Dory and Malinda."

"He's probably suffering from blue balls," Amber said with a laugh. She turned around and leaned against the counter.

"Gross!" Violet said and giggled.

"I'm just sayin', weeks of built up tension and many near misses with your girl parts? It's bound to leave a guy frustrated."

Violet rolled her eyes with embarrassment. "Yeah, well, maybe something will actually happen within the next millennia. If this place wasn't Grand Central Station maybe we could get some alone time."

"Go to his place, dumbfuck," Amber said with snark. "Duh."

"*Duh*, even there we get interrupted. Lux called and broke up our last little attempt."

"Geez, maybe you are cursed," Amber said and laughed.

"Well, at least maybe things can settle down once Malinda and Dory get out of here. Speaking of which?" Violet asked, waiting for a potential update.

Amber looked at Violet and then back at herself in the mirror. "Yeah, they came down briefly a few hours ago. I made them eat something and take some vitamins and then I sent them back off to bed."

"I think they're going to need a lot of rest. Did they seem okay?"

"Not really. I mean, Malinda's pretty coherent and basically just seems traumatized and looks like she has the flu or something, minus the snot. But Dory is pretty out there. She doesn't even seem capable of conversation. I can't imagine what they must've seen to get that fucked up."

"She's probably scarred for life. It's one thing to think vampires are cool and to pretend to be one, but it's another to know the reality. Some people can't handle that sort of information. I mean, I was totally freaked out by it at first. And you saw how scary it was yourself. The vampires at the store were terrifying, but Lux is not like them, as you know. And neither is Mylori, I guess, she's just a royal bitch. But the girls were around Cecelia. Who knows what they saw or what she actually did to them? What if they saw what she did to Gwen, Amber?"

"We don't even know if she did anything to Gwen, right?"

Violet looked at her with a look on her face that said 'stop being naïve'.

"Well anyway, I hope they can both pull through this and go back to some semblance of normalcy. I guess they were the perfect candidates for her to manipulate. They were so sweet and innocent and pliable. Look how they were around us, always following whatever trend we were fucking with any given week. Remember when we discovered hardcore industrial? Nothing about us changed, but they showed up to the club the following week looking like metal chicks after being into synthpop the week before. It's like they don't really know who they are."

"I think that's normal for young people, isn't it? I know I've changed a ton in the last five years, and even the last few months."

"Yeah, I guess you're right. Young people are just pliable. I guess it makes sense. You and I both did the same thing. I'm just glad we're over all that trying to be cool bullshit."

Violet smirked, wondering if that was entirely accurate. "I just hope they're alright. I think they will be once the shock of this wears off and they're feeling better. Roman wants them to go to the hospital."

"They probably should."

"Yeah, I know." Violet dried her hands and leaned against the counter.

"So, you gonna wake him up and come downstairs or what? I want to hear what happened last night."

"I suppose," Violet said with a smirk. "I may have to find a creative way of waking him up."

Amber laughed as Violet crossed the wall to her bedroom.

Roman was curled on his side facing the wall. She noticed the large scar across his back that had been open and bleeding just a few days prior. So much had changed in her life. She had learned a lot in these last few days. How she wasn't a complete basket case with everything she'd been though stunned even her. Seeing Malinda and Dory made it even more glaringly apparent why her friends had been so worried about her after her parents' death, and then the bullshit with Mark, and then the vampires. It was no wonder they'd all walked on eggshells around her.

She walked to the bed and crawled in beside Roman, wrapping her arm around him. His arm moved and he grasped her hand. She kissed the back of his neck causing him to stir and roll over onto his back.

"You awake?" she asked, resting her head against his arm.

"Not much fun without you there," he grumbled and forced one eye open.

"Weird huh?"

"Yeah, I guess it is," he said, looking down at her. "When I got home last night you weren't here were you?" he asked, pressing his finger to the center of her chest.

"No," she answered with hesitation. She was unsure how he might feel about that.

"You were with Lux?"

"Yes," she said, looking up at him, "does that bother you?"

"It doesn't give me the most content feeling in the world, but I trust you."

"He told me everything, Roman. He told me that he gave my mom blood when she was just a baby. He said that he hates being what he is and that he wants all vampires dead besides Mylori and that's why he helps you. He said that he has watched me all my life because I was born with his blood."

"He doesn't hate what he is. He loves what he is."

"I don't know, Roman, he seemed really sad. He's different around me than he is with you."

"Of course he is, Violet," Roman said and looked her in the eye. His brow furrowed slightly. "How do you not hate him knowing what he did to you and your mom?"

"Because he's a vampire, he's supposed to be evil, right?"

"You are far more forgiving than I would be towards him. He would be dead now if I found out he was the one who did this to me."

She didn't say anything and was very still. She understood his anger but she just didn't share it. Lux had said he didn't regret his actions. He'd said he enjoyed what he was. But there was always something lying just beneath the surface of his words that she detected. He was a contradiction. It was only a hunch, but she just knew he wasn't as evil or selfish as he tried to come off.

"He tells you what he thinks you want to hear." He hated the way she made excuses for Lux. He knew Lux. Lux would absolutely destroy her life if Roman wasn't with her to protect her from him.

"I don't think so," she said softly and looked up at him again. "Um, why are we talking about him anyway? Let's go get something to eat. I'm starving."

"Starving," he repeated, a dark glint shining in his eyes, and he kissed her.

Instantly she was right back where they were the night before when he'd touched her like this. Pushing herself against him she forced him all the way onto his back. His fingers tunneled through her thick hair, gripping her head as they kissed. Their tongues tasted each other hungrily. His mouth was so soft, his tongue undulating against hers in the most erotic way. All that warm skin was begging to be kissed and licked but she could not stop kissing his mouth.

Roman let go of her and slipped her nightgown up forcing her to relinquish his kiss as he pulled it up and over her head. She pressed her body to his flat against him, sinking into the heat of his body.

"Mmm..." she murmured, snuggling against him like a cat, eyes closed, smoothing her cheek across his collarbone before rising up a little and finding his neck with her lips. Roman growled with approval as her tongue swept over his skin, sucking hard where his artery pulsed against the flatness of her tongue. She bit down. Instinctively she mimicked the actions of a vampire, though completely unaware that was what she was doing. He cradled her to him and pushed his head back giving her greater access. She sucked and bit down again, this time harder making him jump from the surprise and pain of it.

"Sorry," Violet said with a soft giggle and kissed the spot delicately before swirling her tongue over it and repeating what she had just done a little more gently.

Roman took his hand and guided her back to his mouth, kissing her thoroughly. He rose up, his mouth never leaving hers, and led her onto her back. He hovered over her on his arms and knees, bulky muscles bunching as he looked down at her. The afternoon sun was muted as it was sifted through the lacy curtains, lighting the room with hues of peach and rose that softened his harsh features. The contrast of the black stubble on his head and face, jet black eyebrows, and his white skin seemed less extreme in this lighting.

Roman took her in, the flush of pink in her cheeks, her glistening lips, and cascade of lush hair surrounding her porcelain face. She was so beautiful, eyes sparkling, lips rose red and wet from his kiss. Violet reached up and caressed his cheek, stubble prickling her palm as she held his face, eyes locked. Her other hand reached to cradle his other cheek then slid down his neck, over his strong shoulder and arm, then underneath to his chest, the soft hair tickling the back of her hand. Roman dipped his head, finding her breast and suckling her as Violet's hand explored the hard lines of his body. His tongue swirled around her nipple, his raspy tongue teasing the little peak before sucking it into the warmth of his mouth.

Violet arched into him, her knees rising to press into his outer thighs, her body instinctively inviting him to fall into her. She stretched her neck, her mouth needing to find something of him to latch onto. She bit into his sinewy wrist, the bone giving her something solid to bite down on. Roman smiled against her breast and bit her gently in response. Violet squirmed from the ticklish sensation that shot electricity to her core and sat up, leaning back on one arm to brace herself, his face so close to hers. She kissed him as her other hand smoothed over his muscled stomach and dipped into his open jeans. She stroked the velvety soft skin there, her fingers exploring all of him, the first time she had ever touched him like this. Roman sucked in a breath and found her neck and bit and sucked the skin there as her hand continued moving over his sensitive skin.

She had felt him pressed against her before and knew his size was substantial, but actually feeling him in her hand was astounding. All soft and hard at the same time, larger than she could have imagined. Mark hadn't been small, but Roman was... a giant, and proportional. Her hand gripped him tightly. He continued kissing her, his mouth roving over her neck, returning to one breast, then the other.

Violet mewed as he suckled her and his hand dipped between her legs. He felt her through the thin cotton, felt the soft fold, his finger tracing delicately. He was so gentle it was painful, teasing through the thin fabric.

"Take your pants off," Violet whispered, her hand still sunk into his jeans and moving over every inch.

He didn't want to stop touching her just then even to undress. He kissed her again, his fingers slipping into her panties, finding her body so hot and wet.

Violet's eyes closed as a purr of approval reverberated from deep in her throat. She released her hold on him and lifted her hips off the bed pulling her panties down for him.

"Your turn," she said, looking at him with a timid grin.

Roman pushed off the foot of the bed, looking down at her like a predator. She pushed her panties the rest of the way down and pulled them off, tossing them to the floor. She lay back onto the bed, her knees together demurely. This part always made her so anxious. Perhaps it was her low self-esteem, but having someone's eyes on her like this, just staring, waiting, always made her feel self-conscious.

"You're beautiful," Roman said, his voice whisper-soft, as though he knew what she was thinking.

"So are you," she replied and grinned.

He pushed his pants down over his hips and bent to pull them the rest of the way off, his eyes never leaving her gaze. When he stood back up Violet couldn't help but look at his body. He was massive in every way. So tall and so strong. His body was muscled in the way superheroes are drawn in comics. He could be Bruce Wayne standing there. The corner of her lip lifted thinking about it. In many ways he was a comic book hero. He had a secret identity, The Killer, and he had super powers, though vampiric in nature. Every powerful inch of him was hard, wrapped in velvet soft skin. He stood there a moment letting her look him over. It was clear that's what she wanted and it felt good to see her eyes taking him in this way.

He took the opportunity to look at her too. Though he had seen her naked before those were entirely different circumstances and he hadn't really allowed himself to look. She was mythical, like the Violet he saw in that golden field in the dreams all those years prior. Some moon goddess lit with lunar light from the within. Her thick black hair fanned out around her head like curling tentacles or winding vines, her smallish breasts still round and supple, and her hips dipping perfectly into the v between her legs.

"Come here," she said, a delicate request.

Roman placed his knee on the bed, crawling forward on hands and knees. His left knee parted her legs and he hovered above her and kissed her deeply. One of her hands moved up his chest and cradled his neck as her tongue pushed into his mouth. The other hand found the hard length of him and began stroking him again, her fingertips tickling the sensitive hair and skin beneath before sliding back up.

Roman growled as her fingers deftly moved over him. The sound made her ache and she kissed him more forcefully, her hands moving to his backside, fingers digging into his skin, forcing him to fall into her body. Roman collapsed onto her gently wrapping his arms around her. He was pressed into her, every inch of his body flattened against hers. He was so heavy, so all-encompassing. She moved against him, wrapping one arm around his neck as he kissed her, the other gripping his solid muscled arm. Her legs fell further open making more room for his hips. Feeling him pressed like that against her was driving her crazy.

Roman ground his hips against hers, his arms bracing his weight, not wanting to crush her. He didn't want to rush into this after waiting for so long, but he could barely stand feeling her sliding against his groin without just pushing into her. He pulled his hips back, she protested with a little whine. He smirked at her, dipping his head and kissing her sternum, a sweep of his tongue causing goosebumps. He kissed each breast and then moved down, trailing kisses and nips over her ribcage. She writhed around at the feel of his mouth roving over her body, the stubble tickling her as his chin gently brushed against her skin. As his teeth raked over her hipbone Violet arched spreading her legs and begging him to kiss her there and relieve the torture of his mouth.

A loud cracking sound erupted and the foot of the bed hit the floor.

"What the fuck?" Violet said, her heart leaping out of her chest as she gripped the mattress. "Oh my god!" She started laughing hysterically. "We broke the bed!"

Roman sat back on his heels, balled up fists on his thighs. He was off balance and fell back on the floor from the crooked angle of the bed. His expression was bewildered and that made Violet laugh harder.

"Not funny," he said with a scowl, but not with anger towards her.

"Aww...come here," Violet babied, holding her arms out.

"Seriously, someone somewhere is watching this and laughing their fucking ass off. Lux probably has cameras installed in my place and yours along with boobie traps."

"Boobie traps," Violet repeated and laughed. "Come here," she implored, holding her arms out to him as he crawled across the ruined pile. One side of the bed was on the floor, the other still up on its legs.

Roman collapsed into her arms and she smoothed her hands across his back.

"As much as I want to fuck you right now it's not going to work like this."

Wow, those words got her blood pumping again. The gruffness and demand in his voice sent a rush through her making her ache all over. "It's okay," she said, kissing his cheek, her hands trailing lightly over his skin.

He returned her kiss, gentle, slow strokes of his tongue against hers. Violet shoved him gently over onto his back. The angle of the bed was ridiculous for having sex, but she could still take care of him.

Violet laughed. "This is not funny," Roman said, suppressing a smirk.

"We're on a pile of rubble," she said and giggled.

"We are going to my place later and I will rip the phone off the goddamned wall and board up the door and windows."

"Of course then the fire alarm will probably go off, or a UFO will land on the roof."

Violet grinned and leaned on her elbow, resting her head in her hand, and ran her finger over his skin. The black hair on his chest was soft and fine. It was strange because her other boyfriends had been so boyish in comparison. Well, Mark hadn't been boyish really, but he had no chest hair and could go a few days between shaves without having much of a scruff. *Get out of my head.* She finger-teased one nipple, her head dipping to nibble the other.

Roman reached around and grabbed the blanket pulling it over them. "So, I suppose we should just surrender and get up?"

"We have nowhere we need to be today." Her breath blowing across his tongue-wet skin caused an urgent ache in his groin.

Violet pulled the blanket up around her chest and leaned into him. His body was so warm, like he was on fire. She licked his chest and nibbled his nipple again. Roman's fingers snaked into her mass of hair and pulled her mouth to his. They kissed for a long time, slowly, their bodies thrumming, pulling tighter and tighter. She slid her hand down his body, over well-defined abs, feeling the soft hair below his navel, trailing down further.

His skin was so soft, soft and hard. Everything about him was that way. Always gentle with her, yet last night he had killed three living beings. All he had known was death and darkness. His whole life had been filled with blood and grief. The fact that his only friend was a vampire he acted as though he hated spoke volumes.

"We can wait 'til later," Roman said, breathless against her ear even as his own hands explored her. He wanted to do this right, and thoroughly.

Violet responded by taking him in her hand and feeling the length of him as she kissed his neck. His body tightened with every stroke and she remembered the conversation she and Amber had earlier and it made her smile as she held in a giggle.

"What?" Roman asked, his voice so deep it was guttural.

"We're making out like teenagers," she answered and latched back on to his neck.

"I've never made out like a teenager," he responded with amusement, putting his hand against her cheek and looking into her eyes.

"Well, then, you're in for a treat, mister." Violet kissed him again, her hand exploring him further. Roman's breath became more labored, so she knew she was giving him what he wanted. His hand gripped her neck as he bit into her, sucking her skin into his mouth, tongue licking the delicate spot near her collarbone. That alone almost made her come, her neck had always been so sensitive.

Roman shifted his weight, wanting greater access to her body. He wanted all of her in his mouth. The things she was doing with her hand were unbelievable. But he wanted to touch her too. His hands explored her as she continued sliding her hands over the hard length of him. She felt powerful seeing how much what she was doing affected him. Her fingers tickled the soft hair and then her fingers tightened around him again. Roman's body tensed up, muscles bunching and contracting. He tucked his face into the crook of her neck, the sweet scent of her hair filling his nose as he came. He moaned and kissed her deeply, her hair in the way, tangling with his tongue, and he didn't care.

Violet released her grip on him and leaned farther into him and returned his kiss. Sharing this moment with him was unbelievable and she wished they had given in sooner. All that alone time had been wasted in Chicago and at his apartment all those times prior. Roman put his hand behind her knee, pulling her leg up over his hips and slipped his hand between thighs. Violet moaned the moment he touched her and started moving to his exploration. His big hands were skilled, his tongue writhing against hers. She was so wet, the feel of it on his fingers made him want her in his mouth. He wanted to taste her.

He broke their kiss and sat up leaning on his hand briefly, looking down at her, her cheeks all rosy red, her lips swollen from kissing. He slid down her body, the angle of the broken bed was awkward. His knees were on the floor, he gripped her hips pulling her towards him. His head was lowered, eyes looking up at her. She thought he looked more vampire than human as he stared with those intense green eyes. As soon as her hips were near he lowered his head to her and kissed her there, sweeping his tongue and swirling it around. Violet couldn't help the keening moan that escaped. She normally wasn't one to make any sounds, but her vocal chords acted of their own volition, and with what he was doing she couldn't control it. His tongue was doing things to her she had never felt. Mark was never like this.

He deepened his kiss, suckling the most sensitive part of her. She wasn't going to last long, yet she didn't want this to end. Her hands held his head to her body and she moved against his mouth, long sweeping licks, and sucking, his teeth grazing her sensitive skin. One last time and she shattered apart. The longest orgasm she had ever had rolled through her as he continued devouring her. When she finally stopped writhing around and her breath slowed, Roman raised his gaze to her. His mouth and chin glistened, a satisfied grin on his face.

"You made out like this in high school?" he asked, licking his bottom lip.

"No," Violet answered with a look of disbelief at how good that had felt. If messing around was this awesome, what was it going to be like to have *sex* sex with him? "No, I definitely did not." She sat up and cradled his face with her hands and kissed him gently.

Roman nipped her bottom lip and released her, pressing his hands against the crooked bed frame to stand up. As his weight bore down on the frame the other leg collapsed making another loud crack. Violet let out a shriek of laughter as she fell with the bed. Roman laughed and held his hand out to help her up.

"I guess I owe you a bed," he said and smoothed his thumb across her bottom lip.

"I guess I'll just have to spend the night at your place tonight."

"Prepare yourself," Roman said with a dark glint in his eyes.

"Oh my," Violet said, feeling a very pleasant shudder run through her.

"You alright?" they heard Amber asking from the hall.

Violet laughed and answered yes. Roman was sifting through the wreckage for his pants and shirt. He found them and dressed as Violet went to her closet.

"Going to the bathroom," he said and opened the door, which revealed a bewildered Amber standing a few feet away.

"There was a loud crash?" she said with a worried expression, and then noticed his disheveled look.

Roman raised his hand towards Violet's partially opened door and slipped across the hall to the bathroom. Amber stuck her head in first seeing Violet standing in panties and nothing else and then immediately followed to the bed.

"Wow," Amber said, both eyebrows rose in disbelief.

Violet laughed and pulled a t-shirt from her dresser. "Not quite what you think."

"So, he *didn't* just fuck you so hard the bed collapsed? Cuz that's what I think."

"Oh my gosh, Amber." Violet laughed and grabbed a pair of black and purple striped leggings. "No, um, we were in the process then wham, the bed collapsed"

"I heard two crashes."

"Yeah, well, look at him. Does he look like he's made to sleep in a twin bed?"

"You are so not going to give me the details, are you?"

"Oh, I will, just not with him within earshot."

Violet and Amber both laughed.

"Good?" Amber asked as she bent over to examine the bedframe and then stood back up.

"Amber," Violet said to draw her friend's attention back to her. Amber looked up and Violet bugged her eyes out.

"Really? Wow," Amber said.

"Wow, indeed." A lot could be conveyed with a look. "More to come later," Violet said, as Roman slipped back into the room. He took up the entire doorway.

"No pun intended," Amber said with a laugh, triggering Violet to laugh as well.

"Okay," Roman said sheepishly, raking his nails across the back of his skull. "I hear there's something to eat?"

Violet laughed again, which made Amber start laughing.

"Freaking girls," Roman said and backed out of the room shaking his head.

19

SNOW

"I CAN'T BELIEVE HOW hungry I am. It's like I haven't eaten in a month," Roman said, as he shoveled the chili into his mouth.

Violet laughed naughtily as Roman looked up and smirked with a shake of his head.

"Don't think I didn't catch that," Amber said, sitting down at the table.

"What? He's just hungry, Amber," Violet said and laughed.

"Hey, growing boys need to eat," Amber said as she pushed a plate of cornbread towards Roman.

"My God, I hope he doesn't grow anymore." Violet laughed and waggled her eyebrows.

Roman looked up at her and smirked, one side of his mouth rising higher than the other. He looked like he'd devour her.

"God, get a room, you two. Oh wait, you did that already and destroyed the bed." Amber laughed and snagged a piece of cornbread.

"Do you guys always talk so openly about everything?" Roman said with an amused annoyance in his tone.

"Yes," they answered simultaneously.

"Are you vampires now?" Amber asked, her eyebrows drawn down, playful smirk on her lips.

"Um, no, why?" Violet answered, looking from Amber to Roman and back.

"Well, both of you have giant red bite marks on your neck," Amber answered and laughed.

Roman looked at Violet and she looked at him. It was true. They both had giant red bite marks on their necks.

"We made out like teenagers," Roman said in a deadpan voice and filled his mouth with another spoonful of chili causing both of the girls to erupt with laughter.

"Clearly. Hickies are so 9th grade," Amber joked.

Okay, it was a little weird that they both had actual bite marks on their necks. Violet couldn't remember biting him *that* hard. And the mark on his neck was quite something. "Yeah, to change the subject," Violet started as she picked at a cookie.

"Thank God," Roman grumbled and put another spoonful of chili into his mouth. Amber and Violet both laughed again.

"Yeah, so, have Malinda and Dory been back downstairs since the last time?" Violet turned to Amber and asked. "I haven't done a very good job of babysitting. For all I know they're dead up there."

"Fuck! Morbid much?" Amber said and curled her lip. "I was checking in on them. I heard one of them go to the bathroom a little while ago, but no, they haven't been back downstairs. They're not fucking dead, geez."

"You should probably check in on them. I still think they need to go to the hospital," Roman interjected.

"I will when I'm done eating. Amber told me earlier that they came down and she made them eat and take vitamins. So at least they've eaten."

"And apparently peeing," Amber added.

"That's a positive sign," Roman grumbled. He was still disgusted by their whole involvement with Cecelia.

"So, yeah, anyway, Steve called a little while ago and wants to hang out with us tonight," Amber said.

"Really? That's weird," Violet said with a curious expression on her face.

"He told Randy he's been busy moving and settling in and junk. Whatever, ya know? I told him we'd meet him at The Oven like around nine or so. You guys coming?"

"I don't know," Violet said with skepticism. "I don't know that I have much to say to the guy. And we kind of have plans," Violet said, smiling at Roman.

"Oh, gag. You can do that afterwards. Come on, he's an old friend and you guys need to bury the stupid hatchet already," Amber pleaded.

"Is the stupid hatchet different from the regular hatchet?" Violet asked and laughed.

"Shut up," Amber said and rolled her eyes. "Dork."

"I'm not going. I need to go home and clean my apartment. I've been throwing laundry on the floor since we got back from Chicago. Besides, I really don't know the guy and don't really have the desire to get to know him to be honest with you," Roman said, wiping his mouth with a paper towel and picking up a hunk of cornbread. "I don't see me hanging out with him going very well."

Violet laughed at that. "Yeah, you haven't really seen a good side of him."

"There's a good side?" Roman asked with a lift of a brow causing Violet and Amber both to laugh.

"Buried there somewhere," Violet said with a smirk.

"You don't have to go," Amber said, looking back at Violet. "But you should. What else do you have going besides fucking his brains out now that the hubbub is over?"

"Oh my gosh, Amber!" Violet exclaimed and smacked her arm with the back of her hand.

Roman laughed from the shock of the brusqueness of the statement.

"God, I'm just kidding," Amber said and laughed. Amber and Violet lived to make shocking statements to throw eachother off. "So, come on, hang out with me for like two hours and then you can go at it like rabbits the rest of the night. Seriously, just bury the hatchet with Steve. We'll have fun like the old days."

"You're such a punk," Violet said, shaking her head. "You are right though, I need to make things cool with him. I mean, I don't know why I care, but I guess I miss the guy who I used to be friends with."

"Does that guy exist anymore?" Roman asked, looking at her for a long moment before taking another bite of food.

"Hopefully," Violet muttered. "But who knows. I guess I'll find out. Alright, I'll go." Violet looked at Amber. "Besides, I should fill you in on stuff anyway."

"Stuff like what? No more scary stuff, right?" Amber said, flashing fear for a moment.

Roman looked at Violet wondering what she wanted to fill Amber in on as well.

"I just wanted to tell you I'm pregnant," Violet said with all seriousness.

Roman choked on the cookie he was eating and reached casually for the glass of water trying to cover his surprise at her statement.

Violet laughed out loud and Amber looked at her with confusion. "I'm kidding, you dorks. How the fuck would that happen?" She shook her head and laughed.

"Who knows?" Amber said, still recovering from the shock of Violet's words. "Who would believe there were vampires running around either? You could spawn a Sasquatch via Immaculate Conception and it would just be another day around here."

Violet laughed at that. "Well, that's true I guess." Violet shrugged and smirked at Roman who was still trying to clear his throat. "You okay?"

"I'm fine," he said hoarsely and took another bite of the cookie.

"Anyway, I just wanted to tell you what I found out from Lux," Violet said, finally being serious.

"Like I can wait to hear that? Tell me now," Amber said, scrunching her nose and rolling her eyes.

Violet looked up at Roman and grinned. "Well, to make a long story short, you know how Roman has vampire blood in him, right?"

"Um, *what*?" Amber squawked and looked from Violet to Roman.

Roman leaned back in his chair, still very uncomfortable at the way she talked so casually about all this. It wasn't that he minded the open discussion, it was just weird.

"I think I'm going to go watch TV in the other room," Roman said and stood up. He grabbed a couple cookies and stopped behind Violet. "Thanks for the dinner." He smiled at Amber as he put his hand on Violet's shoulder and squeezed then walked out of the room.

Amber was shocked by what she was being told, unable to process the information. "What do you mean *he has vampire blood in him*?!" Amber asked, leaning forward.

"I guess I never told you, did I?"

"Um, *no*!" Amber said snidely.

"Roman found out that he has vampire blood in him. It's a long story that I'll tell you all about later. But basically at one point his family, like old family way back, drank the blood of his aunt who was a vampire and it passed through the family line. It's why he's so freaking strong and stuff. And I found out from Lux that it's the same with me and it was the same with my mom."

"What? What the fuck? Please explain this to me. *You're* a vampire? I was just kidding about the marks on your necks!"

"No, I'm *not* a vampire," Violet said and laughed. "Lux gave my mom his blood when she was a baby and I have his blood in me because it came through her. We're not vampires, we just have some natural abilities because of having their blood in us."

"Whoa. This is insane. I mean, like my logical brain doesn't want to accept what you're telling me."

"I know, believe me, I know. But it's the truth. You know how my mom was, she'd never been sick a day in her life. You know how young she looked and how she even seemed to know everything that went on with me without me ever telling her."

"So, if she's a vampire, how did she die?"

"Because we're still mostly human, we're just a little *enhanced*, I guess." Violet shrugged her shoulders realizing how utterly ridiculous this all must sound.

"And Roman is this way too?"

"Yeah."

"So, what does this mean? I guess I don't understand how you can walk around during the day and all that kind of junk."

"Because we're still mostly human. But you know I've always been better at night than during the day. Even my mom used to stay up most of the night, remember?"

"Yeah, I guess so. What the fuck. This blows my mind," Amber said, her eyes wide as she tried to go over it all in her head.

"Me too, believe me."

"And Lux knew your mom when she was a baby? How bizarre is that? He only looks maybe a couple years older than us. How old is he anyway?"

"I don't even know, but it's old. Like *old*, old."

"This is mind blowing," Amber said, looking down at the table trying to sort it all out.

"Very."

"Are you scared?" Amber looked up, her brows drawn together.

"I was at first because I didn't really understand what it all meant. I was afraid it made me evil, or damned, or something, but Roman assures me that's not the case."

"You don't believe in all that crap anyway."

"I didn't," Violet said, looking down at the table cloth contemplating her own words. She wasn't so sure what she believed anymore.

"So, you believe in God and all that now?" Amber said somewhat incredulously.

"I'm not sure what I believe, Amber. Roman does, and I trust him. He's seen things we can't comprehend. And I didn't believe vampires were real until recently, so who knows? I just don't know what to think or believe. We don't have all the answers, so how can I just blithely discount anything anymore? The supreme arrogance it takes to think we have all the answers to anything is indefensible at this point. And things have been so chaotic I haven't even had time to process all of this."

"This is in*sane*," Amber emphasized.

"No kidding, I know it is. But are *you* afraid?"

"Well kind of, I mean, if you guys have *vampire* in you, what's to stop you from becoming full-fledged?"

"I don't really know," Violet said. Her eyebrows drew together as she looked up at her friend. "I don't understand a lot about this."

"Wow, this is insane."

"I know."

Violet slowly cracked the door open and looked in on the girls. They were both sleeping, curled together like children beneath the thick blanket. It was dark, save the faint light from the street light outside that drifted through the half open shade of the window beside the bed.

"Violet?" a voice whispered quietly.

"Yes?" Violet answered, walking slowly into the room.

"Am I going to be okay?" It was Dory who spoke, her voice so weak she sounded broken.

The girl sat up and Violet could see the paleness of her face reflecting the soft white-blue light through the window.

Violet walked forward and sat on the edge of the bed. "Are you feeling any better?" Violet reached forward and pushed the girl's hair away from her face.

Even though she was seventeen years old she looked so much younger at that moment.

"I think so. I'm just so tired."

"I think you'll be fine, Dory. But you need to rest and keep eating and drinking lots of water."

"I thought she was going to make us like her," Dory said with trepidation in her voice. "I couldn't stop myself. I've always been so weak and afraid. I just wanted..." She choked back her tears and panic. "But she lied."

"It's okay, Dory, it wasn't your fault. Vampires can control our minds and emotions," Violet said, trying to ease some of the guilt Dory was clearly feeling.

"She was never going to make us like her. I heard her say she hates girls." Dory looked away, her eyes haunted, clearly looking back at a memory.

"She doesn't hate anyone now. She's dead," Violet said, and couldn't help the anger that infused the words.

Dory's head dropped, her chin resting on her bony chest. "I don't know if I'll ever forget what I saw."

"You probably won't, but you can move beyond it. Try not to worry so much right now. It's all too fresh still, but it'll get easier every day. You lived, Dory. You faced a vampire and lived."

Dory nestled back against the blankets and stared blankly at Violet's glimmering eyes. She looked ghastly.

"Try to rest. I'm going to call your house and let your mom know you're alright."

"She's going to wonder why I'm not calling, if she even cares that I've been gone."

"I'll think of something." Violet felt sick because she knew how much her mother always had disregarded Dory. That was probably some of the reason Dory had clung to Cecelia. Violet stood up and walked back to the door. "When you feel better, come downstairs and get something more to eat. I'll bring some water up for you, okay?"

Violet walked downstairs and sat down beside Roman on the couch. "Dory's talking finally,"

"What did she say?" Roman asked, taking Violet's hand in his. The warmth seemed to expand from his hand up her arm and through her body.

"She asked me if she was going to be okay."

"And your answer?" he said, looking down at her.

"I told her that she'll be okay."

"It's nice to be optimistic," Roman said and put his arm around her. He had his doubts given the girl's demeanor.

"I need to think of something to tell their parents. If someone doesn't call soon they'll file a missing person report," Violet said.

"Sweetie, neither one of their parents cares," Amber said, lowering her gaze on Violet.

"That's not true, I'm sure they care to some extent," Violet said, looking at Amber for confirmation.

"No, they really don't," Amber said, disheartened. "You know they don't care. Both of them have stayed at my house for a week and their parents never even knew where they were."

"Well, they should care," Violet said sadly. She couldn't imagine a family not caring at all about their child.

"Well, Malinda's grandma cares, but I don't have her number, and besides, there's no reason to worry the old lady," Amber said with a shrug.

"Just say they're here and wanted you to call cuz they couldn't or something stupid like that," Randy interjected.

"Why don't you call?" Violet said, hoping he'd take her suggestion.

"I'll call. What do I care," Randy said, starting to stand up.

"*I'll* call, both their mom's know me already," Amber said, standing up and walking to the kitchen. "Besides, Dory's mom doesn't like you," she said to Violet.

Violet screwed up her face and looked at Roman. "I don't know why, I'm super nice," she said and rolled her eyes. Roman just smirked at her.

"Terrible influence," Randy teased as Violet walked by on her way to the kitchen with Amber.

Her friends' parents never liked her. Amber's mom liked her sometimes. But only sometimes. And she thought it was probably because it came across like she corrupted their kids. One day they were dressed normal and complacent to being abused, the next they were dressing like Siouxsie Sioux and telling their parents to fuck off depending on the parental situation. Of course that was Violet's influence. Violet always encouraged her friends not to put up with being treated like shit. They learned by example. So, was Violet a bad influence? Only if one cares about how someone looks, or thinks kids should be seen and not heard and subservient to authority. If that made Violet a bad influence, then she'd gladly accept the mantle.

Amber called Malinda's mom first explaining that the girls had stayed over and were scared to call home for fear of being reprimanded. Which was stupid considering they were always staying away anyway, but she had to come up with something. Malinda's mother didn't seem to care. Amber knew from being at Malinda's house that her mother cared more about whatever current man she was sleeping with than her daughter. It was one of the reasons Malinda had been so easily taken in by Violet and Amber in the first place. She'd found family, however dysfunctional, in the small group of rejects.

Dory's parents were a little different. Her mother was strict. She was some sort of religious zealot who didn't believe in wearing deodorant or pants. And her father was completely detached and beaten down by his wife's constant judgment and henpecking. Dory had always been an outcast because her mother had forced her to wear old hand me down dresses that were twenty years behind the current style. Her mother had pretty much given up on her though having long since written her off as a "sinner". It was no wonder she'd wanted to fit in with Cecelia.

She was already used to coldness, so Cecelia's lack of nurturing would have been normal to Dory.

"Well, what did she say?" Violet asked, picking up another cookie.

"Dory's mom said she'd pray for us and to tell Dory not to come home until she was ready to repent. And Malinda's mom said 'I figured she must be staying with a friend'. She tried to act like she cared, but we both know better."

"She must've had a new dude over. You know, she had to put on the good mom routine," Randy said snidely. "You know she hit on me once?"

"Ew, gross," Violet said.

"Thanks," Randy said and laughed.

"Dude, you're young enough to be her kid," Violet said as Roman snickered at the exchange.

"Yeah, but I'm all man down south," Randy said, smirking and nodding his head.

"Ew," Violet said with a sneer.

"Thanks again," Randy said.

Violet laughed. "Well, tell the story. Don't leave me hanging."

"She left me hanging," Randy said and smirked at his own joke.

Roman shook his head and quietly laughed at the kid. He always found Randy amusing.

"Alright, enough," Amber said and shook her head. "Malinda's mom's lack of giving a fuck is pretty fucking creepy considering Gwen was just murdered. You'd think a missing child would cause some anxiety at least," Amber said with disgust.

"That is actually sad," Roman said, surprising everyone. They all looked at him like he'd said something weird. They all viewed him as detached, but caring about people wasn't out of character for him, but they didn't know that. "What? It is," he said with a shrug.

"It's beyond sad, and fucked up on all accounts," Violet said, sharing Amber's disgust. "But everything seems okay though? No suspicions and they're free to stay here until they recover?"

"And until Dory decides to repent," Randy said and chuckled.

Roman laughed too, making Randy beam a little.

"Yeah, I guess they just think the girls have been partying or something. I mean, I'm sure they'll both be in trouble when they get home, but at least they'll be alive," Amber said.

Roman stood up and took Violet's hand pulling her up to her feet. "I'm going to go home now," he said, looking at her and then Amber. "Thanks again for the food."

"No problem, I like feeding everyone," Amber said with a smile. "Hey, we gotta leave soon to meet Steve," she said to Violet as she and Roman walked out of the room to the kitchen.

"Yeah, yeah," Violet called over her shoulder. "And Randy, I want to hear that story about Malinda's mom trying to bang you."

"Don't encourage him," Amber said with a chuckle.

"I kind of want to hear that too," Roman said, with a smirk.

"Later, man," Randy said with a wide smile.

Roman nodded his head and led Violet out through the kitchen towards the back door. Violet stood in front of Roman, looking up into his dark green eyes. She held both of his hands in hers, relishing the strength and warmth. In some ways it still seemed so foreign that this man cared for her. How could she be so fortunate? She had been left all alone by her parents and she'd managed to find the one man in the world who would keep her safe. And he loved her.

"So, you're going to do laundry?" she asked.

"Yeah, I need to get that done. I can't stand the place messed up like it is. Plus I'm running out of clothes."

"You want me to come over later?" she asked, batting her eyelashes at him involuntarily.

"Do you want to?"

"What do you think?" she smiled, doing her best seductive routine hoping he wouldn't want to leave.

"Well, how long do I have to wait?" he asked.

"Probably only a couple hours at the most."

"Good, I'll have the place clean by then," Roman said and smiled. "Not that it really matters."

"Nope, not that it really matters," she repeated and brought his hand to her mouth to kiss. "Make sure you launder your bed sheets," she teased and laughed. "Though maybe that would make more sense to put off until tomorrow."

The corner of his mouth lifted into a smile. "Do not be out long," Roman growled, his eyes flashing with a predatory gleam.

"God, I really don't want to go. I just want to go to your place with you right now."

"Come with me then," he said, leaning down and curling her toes with the most luscious kiss. His voice made her melt with the promise of what would transpire if she just went with him.

She broke the kiss with a disgruntled groan. "Ugh, I promised I'd go with Amber. I will so not be staying very long."

"Good," Roman said, lifting her chin with his finger and running his thumb over her moist bottom lip.

"This is strange," Violet said with a bemused smile on her face.

"Yes, it is."

"Well, I guess I'll see you later then," Violet said with a devilish grin.

"Yep," he said, bending down and kissing her again.

"Mmmm..." Violet moaned as she broke the kiss. "Go before I change my mind and blow off my friends for the thousandth time."

"Be careful," Roman said, letting go of her hands and kissing the top of her head.

"I always am," Violet with a smirk.

"Yeah, right. So, what time?"

"Elevenish," Violet said, holding the door as he walked out. He bent to kiss her again and Violet swatted him on the butt playfully to get him to leave.

"Ten," Roman said, as he walked down the path towards his car, not turning to look back.

"Eleven," she corrected and smiled.

Roman grunted and kept walking.

"Love you," Violet called after him.

He turned around and looked at her. "Love you too, V"

Violet slipped out of her night gown and stepped into the shower melting in the steam. The hot water saturated her hair and warmed her all over, so smooth and calming to her sore muscles. She had been so tense for so many weeks and she was just now feeling it since the drama had died down. In actuality, she had been stressed out for years, though it had always been a subtle tension until recently. She was so happy and relieved the danger was finally over. Once Malinda and Dory were on their own again she'd be free to move on from this nightmare completely. Well, not completely, some of the things she'd learned would be with her forever.

She couldn't dilly-dally as it was already seven thirty and they were supposed to meet Steve at nine. She didn't particularly want to go as she was fearful that Mark would show up, or that it would just be too awkward, but she hoped for the best. It would be nice for things to be like they had been back before all the drama. She and Steven had been very good friends at one point. She'd even considered Steven a best friend while she and Amber had been on the outs over something stupid and trivial and hadn't spoken for a few months. *Stupid girls and their emotions.* Maybe tonight they could finally put all the shit to rest and get back on track.

Violet finished washing her hair and then got out of the shower and dried herself off and wrapped her hair in a towel. She put her faded out jeans and Siouxsie & the Banshees t-shirt on and walked back to her bedroom deciding she'd give Roman a call despite the fact that he'd only left a short while before getting into the shower. Not talking to him was torture.

"Hey," she said, rolling over onto her stomach and kicking her feet up in the air. Her bed was still collapsed but Randy had assured her he could fix it with a couple of 2x4s.

"Hi," Roman answered.

She could tell by the bend in his words that he was smiling. "Whatcha doin'?" she asked.

"Sheets," he answered.

"Ooooh," Violet said and couldn't help the bashful grin that followed.

"What are you doing?" he asked.

"Getting ready to leave in a little bit I guess. I'd rather be folding your laundry."

"I'd rather you were folding my laundry too. Or dirtying some."

Violet gasped from the bold shock of the statement and then giggled. "Roman, are you really sure about all this? Like, with me and stuff?" Her voice was softened by the question, almost musical in its lilt, and definitely self-conscious.

"Why do you ask?" The seemingly random question was cause for concern. Had he thrown out some vibe of disinterest in her, or was she now questioning their relationship? Because he thought he had been pretty upfront with his intentions. Perhaps she was regretting everything now that they had sort of moved to some next level. It wouldn't be something he'd blame her for if that were the case, but he hoped it wasn't considering he'd finally wrapped his own head around it.

Or was it a man's job to constantly reassure a woman where she stood and what he was feeling at all times? If he had a clue how romantic relationships worked it would be helpful. Did all women need some kind of constant reassurance? He sincerely didn't know. Mylori had simply found him whenever she wanted to fuck and then left without a word. There had never been any conversation regarding any of it, feelings or otherwise. But then, that wasn't any real type of relationship at all. Maybe women that weren't dead required constant reassurance and definitive answers all the time? God, he was inept.

"I just wonder because you were so adamant about not being involved with anyone. I just don't want to push myself on you and have you regret it later," she said.

"No, I had never intended to have someone in my life. It changes everything. I don't know where it's all going. There's so much to consider."

He realized he had probably just said something really stupid. It wasn't his intent, but he knew he was coming off evasive. He really didn't know how their situation was all going to work. Would she go with him on the road? Would he give it all up and settle down here with her? And if that was the case, would he move in with her, or would they get their own place? Hell, maybe they'd leave and go to one of his homes? He had no idea and hadn't had a chance to think about any of it.

"Oh," she responded, not quite sure how to take what he'd said.

It wasn't as if he'd said he was against the idea of *them* at all, but surely he wasn't completely comfortable either? This wasn't some kind of business venture, they were starting a relationship. What was there to consider? She just wasn't used to thinking about 'how it would work' when it came to being in love with someone. It just simply was. But then, maybe that had always been her problem. Still...

"We aren't trying to start a business together. I'm not an investor," she said dishearteningly.

"What?" he asked, wondering where that came from.

"Nothing," she said, resigned.

"It's not you, I swear."

"Oh no, not the 'it's not you, it's me' speech please," Violet said with dread.

"No, that's not what I meant by that at all. I just want you to know that I'm not sure I'm even capable of the normal relationship that you deserve."

Violet didn't say anything. She knew a brush off when she heard one. She'd called him just to talk briefly, to hear his voice for a few moments before she went out to meet Steve and Mosley and now she'd opened this can of worms that made her feel very uneasy. He was done protecting her, Cecelia was dead, and maybe this was him setting it up for his exit?

"You there?" he asked

"Mmm hmm," she said without inflection.

"You're being awfully quiet."

"I'm sorry, I don't mean to be. I guess I'm just preoccupied with getting ready to leave. I still need to dry my hair."

Violet rolled her eyes at herself, so frustrated with her own nonsense. What she wanted to do was tell him she just needed to know he cared about her, but she couldn't bring herself to say it. Why was she so fucking insecure about this? Things had been perfectly perfect when he left a few hours ago. Now she was picking at things.

"Okay," Roman said, knowing she wasn't telling him the full truth but completely in the dark as to how to respond.

"Well, really I just wanted to call and say hi before I left. I have to go now."

"So, are you still going to stop by later?" He asked, completely bewildered at the turn the conversation had taken.

Obviously he had said something wrong. This mood was something he had never experienced with her previously. He felt like a blind man trying to find his way.

"Oh, yeah, probably later." Violet was the one being aloof now. Her voice was soft and monotone.

"You alright?"

"Yeah, I'm fine," she said, closing her eyes tightly annoyed by her own passivity. What she wanted was for him to tell her that YES he was in love with her, and YES he wanted to spend the rest of his life with her. But he'd only offered her non-answers and she wasn't up for the task of pulling it out of him at the moment.

"Okay, well, have fun and I'll see you later, I guess," Roman said, very concerned by her lack of emotion.

"Okay, I'll see you later," she said and hung up the phone abruptly, closing her eyes tightly and sighing in exasperation.

She was reading way too much into what he'd said, but she was overly sensitive at the moment, no doubt due to all the drama. Leave it to her to make trouble now that everything else was finally settled.

What the fuck was wrong with her? They'd had such a good afternoon. I mean, they broke her fucking bed fooling around! They had fun even after that. And she had to go and get weirdly moody?

But maybe he would still leave her? Maybe trying to figure out where she fit into his very established lifestyle would be more than he'd want to bother with eventually? The thought that he may still take off cut her to the core. He'd said he wasn't sure he was capable of giving her the "normal" relationship she needed. This might be his excuse to leave. After all, she was safe now. What reason was there to stick around? There was no desperate need for him to stay.

Or maybe now that she was safe and he didn't have to play the hero, and they settled into a normal routine, he would grow bored with her and move on to the next damsel? Or what if she was just too boring now that the excitement was over? He had dated Mylori before, a freaking exotic modelesque vampire. Okay, maybe dated was inaccurate for their situation. But who knows, maybe he had downplayed that whole thing with Mylori? She did seem pretty into him. Maybe he wasn't telling the full truth about it? Regardless, what could she give him that would compare to that freaking gorgeous bitch? She was a boring, uneducated, weirdo from nowhere.

Damnit! She should have just left things well enough alone, but she'd just had to pick at it.

Why did she always do this? She always questioned the motives of every person in her life, never content to just accept any situation at face value. They had been happy the last few days given the extreme circumstance, and yet she couldn't just leave things alone. Tonight was supposed to be their night, now there was this weird crappy cloud hanging overhead.

She picked up her hair dryer, which was always plugged in, and started drying her hair. Her dad had told her that was a fire hazard a thousand times. She could hear his voice in her head as she turned it on. She felt numb and unemotional. It was uncomfortable and she wondered what exactly was triggering these feelings. Maybe she was just on overload? Maybe it was PMS? Maybe she just wouldn't allow herself to be happy?

"Stop thinking," she said out loud to herself, staring directly into her own eyes as she stood in front of the mirror.

She finished drying her hair and yanked the cord from the outlet. Dad would be happy. Then she put her socks and boots on and found her leather jacket in the closet and walked downstairs. There was no need to get dressed up tonight, or to even bother to wear makeup. There was truthfully really no need for any of that ever. Who really cared what she looked like? Anyone who did care about her wouldn't give a shit about her clothes or makeup anyway.

She suddenly felt very guilty for having called Roman the way she had and forcing him to prove himself. She could hear in his voice that he'd been relaxed, maybe even happy, and she'd stolen that from him with her needling. He had sounded confused and just as lost in the conversation as she had been. Of course she still wanted answers, she wanted to know the logistics of their relationship, but she had ambushed him. It would probably be wise to just call him right now and talk about it and fix it, saving them both a lot of confusion, but there wasn't time. Amber was calling her name to hurry her up.

Oh well, she would make it up to him later. A thrill ran through her at the prospects of that, and she also felt nervous. Hmm, maybe she should've bothered getting a little more dressed up after all? Then again, she wouldn't be wearing anything for long. She hoped, anyway.

"I guess he's not here yet?" Violet said, scooting across the bench so that she could lean against the wall.

"He'll be here," Randy said, picking up the menu.

"Everything seems so different," Amber said, looking over at Violet. "I mean, none of this seems very relevant considering what we've all just been through. Fuck, Violet, you have *vampire blood* in you."

Hearing that out loud sounded ridiculous.

"I know, try not to think about it. It's embarrassing and weird or something. Besides, I mean, in the grand scheme it doesn't make any difference. I'm the same person I've always been. Nothing has changed," she said with a shrug.

"Whoa, deep," Randy said with a smirk, looking up over the menu.

Violet grinned at him and then raised her head as Steve walked through the door. He looked vibrant, full of *some kind* of radiant energy. He also looked like he'd lost fifteen pounds, which meant he no longer looked doughy. Mose followed behind glaring at her lustfully. It was freaky, like she was a steak and he was a starving dog. Neither of the men looked particularly unpleasant really, only focused. It was unnerving. Violet lifted her hand and waved at them. The two sat down at the table taking particular interest in her. It wasn't so obvious that Amber or Randy seemed to notice, but she sure as fuck did. Hmm... Maybe those vampire senses were kicking in? But it was there for sure, their preoccupation with her, Mark's influence again no doubt. This was clearly some sort of fact finding mission for him. Sonofabitch. So much for making amends.

The two of them engaged in idle conversation with Randy and Amber, but intermittently they would look at Violet as though studying her. It was almost as if she was some strange new creature they had just discovered. Were her vampire attributes showing now for some strange reason and Amber and Randy were immune to it because they saw her all the time? That didn't make any sense though, nothing had changed. *Fucking weirdos.*

Mosley had paid particular attention to her, handing her sugar and cream for her coffee, then a spoon to stir, and napkins. That never happened. And she kept feeling Steven's eyes on her, so she would look and they would lock eyes for long moments before he would look away. What the hell? It wasn't because she looked good either, she had definitely dressed down.

"So, what have you guys been up to anyway? It seems like a billion years since we last saw you," Amber asked as she mixed the cream into her murky coffee.

"Just getting settled into the new place," Mosley answered. He too had an almost otherworldly glow about him. His dark skin was radiant, lush, and rich in tone like emollient dark chocolate. His hair, which was normally long and snarled, was in perfect black dreads.

"So you moved again?" Randy asked.

"Yeah, we're living over here behind the trailer park now," Steve responded, looking at Violet for some sort of reaction. He waited for the crack about being *white trash,* as all the homes in this area were quite run down.

"Oh, so you guys are walking distance then?" she said, actually happy to hear they'd found a permanent place to stay as both of them had mainly spent the last few years moving from one friend's home to another.

"Yes, we're walking distance," Steve answered, looking away from her.

"Most things are in this town," Randy joked.

"Yeah, I guess so," Mosley responded. "You should come over and see the place."

"Okay," Randy said, looking at the two girls. "You guys want to go?"

"Yeah, sure," Amber said, looking at Violet and then realizing that she probably wanted to spend less time than visiting their place would take.

"Sure," Violet said, trying to cover her lack of enthusiasm.

She was kicking herself because what she wanted was to go to Roman right now and fix that stupid conversation they'd had earlier. She could send him a text message, but she didn't want to talk via texting. That was fucking lame.

Roman gathered the clothes from the washer and put them in the dryer. Life would be so much easier if he just wore the same thing every day and never had to wash anything. Yeah, that would go over well with Violet. He stopped for a moment considering what she'd said to him earlier. Obviously she had just wanted some type of reassurance and instead he probably confused her even more. They weren't trying to form a business? The statement had been confusing. He'd had a difficult time even figuring out how it applied to what he'd said. Yes, he was thinking far too logically about all of this. But then, if he truly was thinking logically he never would have gotten involved in the first place. She would grow tired of his ineptitude at some point.

He turned the dryer on then walked back into the living room. There was a half empty bottle of beer he finished before walking it to the kitchen to throw it away. The counter was littered with empty fast food bags and a half eaten pizza that had been sitting there a few days. He threw them in the trash and wiped down the counter and sink. It wasn't that he enjoyed cleaning, he just enjoyed cleanliness. More than likely it had something to do with the chaos of his world. Having order in his home at least gave him control over something. It didn't matter. Once he was finished tidying up he went back to the living room and sat down on the couch picking up the remote control and flipping through the channels.

He scrolled to the guide to check the time. Ten o'clock. Maybe she'd come over earlier than planned. Hopefully their weird conversation hadn't fucked anything up.

It wasn't long before his thoughts drifted. If it hadn't been for shoddy construction things would have turned out a lot different earlier, but as it was he couldn't complain. The feel of her body against his, her hands, her taste...no, he couldn't complain. Why the fuck had he not pursued her earlier? Any normal male would have in this situation. It was clear she was attracted to him, even being as doltish and in denial as he had been it was clear. Everyone else seemed to know. So, what had stopped him from just being a pig and fucking her before? It's not like he had always been such an angel previously. Eh, he had liked her, respected her, that's why. Strange. So strange. No, it wasn't strange. He always respected women, but he had straight up denied any feelings for her at all, sexual or otherwise. That was odd.

God, the way she felt, so warm and alive. Her body seemed to rise to meet his touch, magnetic skin drawn to his. She had melded to him, her hand teasing over his flesh, her mouth as she bit into him, the taste and feel of her against his tongue. He grew hard thinking about it. His eyes focused again on the television. Two minutes had gone by. He closed his eyes hoping sleep would take him until she arrived.

The lot of them walked across the street to the trailer park leaving Violet's car at The Oven. There was trash strewn along the roadside which disgusted Violet. How hard was it for people to throw something in a garbage can? She kicked an empty cup cursing how filthy her fellow human beings could be. Seriously, what the fuck was wrong with people? It's not like she was some hippy save the world type, but it was just common sense. And seriously? This was what her brain decided to fixate on after all that had happened earlier?

"Hey, you're not mad are you?" Amber asked as they lagged behind the men.

"No, why?" Violet said, looking up at her friend.

"I just know you would probably rather be home right now."

"So would you," Violet said with a laugh.

"Well, yeah," Amber chuffed. "Man, this pace is trashy. I haven't been back here since I spent the night at Connie Pinnelli's in the fifth grade. It wasn't this run down back then."

"You spent the night at Connie's house? Why don't I remember that?"

"Because I wasn't talking to you that week because you cut my Barbie's hair." Amber laughed

"What? She needed a mohawk," Violet said with a smirk and shrugged her shoulders.

"Yeah, the day right after Christmas after I had begged for that doll for months?"

"Whatever. You got over it. I think?" Violet said and laughed.

"She did look cooler." Amber paused for a second and continued. "So, you going to Roman's later?"

"Yeah," Violet said, suddenly reminded of their stupid conversation earlier. "I'm such an idiot sometimes."

"What did you do now?" Amber joked.

Violet smirked and shook her head. "I dunno, I just always want him to give me something he can't give."

"By the looks of your bed he gave it to you pretty well."

"Shut up," Violet said and rolled her eyes. "I mean emotionally. I can't just let things be, I always have to push him for more."

"So, knock it off," Amber said.

"Yeah, I'm going to. He isn't like us. He didn't grow up under relatively normal circumstances surrounded by friends who cared about him. He hasn't had any normal relationships and I just pushed him too far or something. I'm just so afraid of losing him. I can't lose him, Amber."

"You're not going to lose him. Just let things develop. Yeah, he hasn't lived like us, but he's a good guy. Like a genuinely good guy. Let him handle defining things and all that. You haven't even given yourselves a chance to get used to the idea of being a couple. Just enjoy the fun for a while. You can make plans and all that crap later."

"I know you're right. Ugh, can we just get this stupid visit over with so I can go fix things?" Violet smiled and kicked a big rock.

"And by fixing things you mean give him a BJ for his trouble, right?"

"Oh my god, Amber!" Violet said and smacked her arm.

"I'm just kidding, geez," Amber said and rubbed her bicep where she'd been slugged.

"Besides, I'd have to unhinge my jaw like a boa constrictor," Violet said just to throw in her own shocker.

Amber looked at Violet and bugged her eyes out. "Seriously?"

"Seriously."

"Damn."

"Not to say it won't happen, but ya know, I might need to train for that."

"Starting eating lots of footlong hot dogs?"

Both of the girls started laughing. Amber continued talking about random things like her sewing projects, some recipe she saw on Food Network she planned to try out, stupid shit Randy had done recently that Violet had been blissfully unaware of until now. She let her thoughts drift, only half listening as Amber told her stories.

Violet looked around, it was an old trailer park. These weren't nice modern modular homes. They were trashy, beat up trailers that clearly hadn't been taken care of by their occupants. She noted the rotten wooden decks and dented up aluminum of nearly every trailer they passed. There were cars on blocks, tipped over lawn furniture, rotted out couches, and scrawny, pitiful dogs chained and barking in several yards. It was an absolute stereotypical nightmare.

The darkness and glowing street lamps hid most of the dirt from them, but even at night this place was disgusting. Not to mention dangerous, more than likely. But what could some redneck do to her that vampires hadn't been able to previously? Roman had seen to it that she could protect herself. Worst case scenario she could always run.

Violet felt her heart heave as she looked into the eyes of an old yellow retriever as they walked by it. The dog was so listless and resigned it barely lifted its head as they passed. She stopped and bent down to scratch the dog's bony chin. His chestnut eyes looked into hers, glossy and wet and filled with utter sadness. His tail thumped the ground as she held his face in her hand. *This is no life for a dog.* She wondered if this was the only kindness he'd been shown.

"What are you doing?" Amber asked, stopping to check on Violet who'd fallen quite far behind the rest.

"Nothing," she said in detached resignation. She patted the dog's head and followed.

Steve turned to look back at the girls and smiled.

She walked towards him. Her face was hidden by the tree shadow which obscured the moon's light from touching her skin. Something was askew about her face, her mouth too pale, her eyes too dry, but he didn't pay any attention to that. He was more concerned with why she was even here. She didn't speak, just stood perfectly still looking into his eyes with such desolate sadness.

"What's wrong?" he asked, reaching forward to try to elicit a reaction from her.

Still she didn't speak, only stared more deeply. Her mouth turned down as her chin dimpled. Even her hair was dull and lifeless.

He didn't look away from her.

Over her shoulder he saw Lux and Mylori rising over the bent stalks of wheat. Like mythical creatures they were, luminescent and vibrant as they came forward.

He could feel more than see the look of disinterest on Mylori's face, perfectly placid and white. Her eyes were so black and fixed as they bore into him.

He didn't look away from Violet.

The wind was blowing her black hair around, cutting like ribbons across her milky neck. Red lines lacerating her skin, his heart pounding with arousal.

He had lied to her when he'd said he never craved it. He always craved it.

She blinked, her eyes wetting them briefly before drying and going dull again.

"Where are you, Roman?" Lux asked and placed his hands on Violet's shoulders. Mylori leaned against a tree, the jagged edge of the bark cutting into her flesh.

Roman looked at Lux and then back to Violet. She had no reaction.

"Where are you?" Lux asked again.

"Sleeping," he answered without speaking out loud.

"Sleeping? I told you to watch," Lux said, squeezing the girl's arms and pressing his face into the back of her hair. He took in deep breaths, his dead lungs filling with her scent and exhaling it back into her hair. "You know she's mine," he said wistfully.

"Not yours," Roman said, taking his eyes from her unblinking eyes briefly and looking at him with anger.

"Yes--my blood, Roman. Not yours," Lux said, rubbing his index finger against the cold artery of her neck.

"But she's not yours."

"No, but she's my child. I told you to watch after her, Roman." Lux's brow furrowed deeply, his eyes so dark and filled with dread. "You have no idea how much trouble awaits you if you fail to keep her safe. From Me. From others."

"I am watching, something's wrong with her. What's wrong with her?"

"I told you to watch, Roman!" Lux's voice was a guttural growl that shook Roman to his core. "I didn't send you here to sleep." The vampire's eyes were pools of moving black tar, like black water rippling with swimming black fish.

"What's wrong with her?" Roman said, noticing the graying color of her skin. The veins were turning turquoise beneath the surface and retracting. Her lips were dried and cracking.

"Wake up, Roman!" Mylori demanded, stomping her foot and clenching her fists at her side. "Wake the fuck up!"

Roman jumped and clutched his chest, his heart pounding in the cavern of his body. Both his cellphone and the phone on the wall were ringing. The tone was so shrill and loud it was momentarily discombobulating. He reached for his cellphone.

"What?" he said, looking up at the television still set on the TV guide channel. It was eleven thirty. As soon as he answered the cellphone the wall phone stopped ringing.

"Where are you?" Lux's voice growled through the phone.

"I'm at home," he answered, rubbing his eyes.

11:30. He shouldn't panic. She had said she would come around eleven, and the last time they talked she had sounded unsure she'd even stop by. Thirty minutes was nothing. She was probably still hanging out with her friends.

"Something is wrong with her. Do not fail to protect her or life as we both know it will end. Find her," Lux demanded and hung up the phone.

He looked down at his cell and dialed Violet's house. The phone rang five times and no one answered. She was probably just still with her friends. That had to be it. Next he tried her cellphone, it went straight to voicemail. She had finally remembered to turn the ringer off. *Fuck*. Nothing was wrong. Cecelia was dead. Panic swept through him.

Something is terribly wrong.

He ran to his bedroom to dress so he could get over to her house as quickly as possible. If something happened to her now he would kill anything and everything in his path before turning the knife on himself. He had never been this lazy in the whole of his existence, and if his lack of diligence caused her pain he would never forgive himself. He picked up his keys and ran out the door heading for her house.

They had walked through the trailer park onto the gravel street behind the park. This was an area she didn't even know existed, which was strange given how small the town was. But there had never been an occasion to wander in this area. The moon drew her eyes, the giant orb haloed in a silvery mist. It took her breath away. She exhaled and watched the cloud of breath rise like smoke into the black night.

"Hurry up," Amber said, turning around to look at her lagging friend.

"Sorry," Violet grinned and jogged to catch up with her.

"What's your deal? You seem spaced out," Amber said, looking over at her curiously.

"I don't know, just looking forward to clearing some things up with Roman."

"Like what? You never really said what you did that was stupid."

"I just said some stupid stuff to him earlier. I just want to clear everything up and let him know I don't need all the answers now, or ever really. I've just been so lost and hurt for so long I guess I just wanted some kind of guarantee he was going to be around."

"Of course you want answers, Vi. There's nothing wrong with that. Expecting to know where you stand with someone isn't asking too much."

"I know, I just think I should leave well enough alone for a while. It's not like we need to get married tomorrow or something. I think I want too much from him too early, especially given his history. It's like you said, just have fun and enjoy it."

Violet looked over at Amber hoping she'd have some sort of insight on the situation, but knew she wouldn't as she didn't know much about Roman.

"Well, I think it's pretty natural that you'd want some stability considering all that you've been through in the last few months. Stop beating yourself up over it. If he didn't care about you he wouldn't be bothering to stick around, right? So just chill and enjoy that massive..."

"Amber!" Violet said and laughed as she rolled her eyes. "You're right, I know, it just concerns me because he is such a loner and he swore up and down to himself he'd never get emotionally involved with anyone. So, I'm finding it hard not to latch onto him with both hands."

"We can't always control our feelings can we? Roman might not be super open with his, but the fact that he let you in as much as he has should tell you something."

"You're right. Thanks for not scolding me." Violet half grinned and looked ahead at the boys.

"Why would I scold you, stupid? Relationships are hard."

"Says the woman who has a more stable situation than anyone I know."

"Yeah, well, it didn't start off this way. I just broke him. And it's not like everything is perfect."

Violet chuckled until she noticed the serious expression on Amber's face. "What's not perfect?" she asked.

"I'm just saying. Life isn't easy, but everything is fine. No worries." Amber looked at Violet and smiled, though Violet could tell she wasn't as unbothered as she was trying to pull off.

Violet dropped the subject because it was clear Amber wasn't interested in talking about it more. She smiled and looked ahead at the guys. "Where the hell are we going?" she asked, noticing a small house sitting back away from the street.

It was tucked behind a grove of trees which rose from either side of the house enveloping the small shack like embracing arms. She'd never even known this house existed. Steve and Mose led them towards it walking down the muddy driveway. The place was old. The paint was chipped off, and it was clearly abandoned. No doubt they were squatting as she couldn't imagine this home even being habitable. How would there even be electricity in such a hovel? Soft dark smoke wafted from the chimney. The scent of smoldering paper and something far more sinister polluted the night air. Violet suddenly felt her body lock as if every cell was on alert and searching the air around her. She stopped and grabbed Amber's arm and then released it.

"Boy, this place is a shithole," Amber said with a snicker and looked at Violet. Violet had turned ghostly white, her face reflecting the little moonlight that sifted through the slumbering trees. "What's wrong?" Amber asked, stopping with a look of worry in her face.

"Nothing, I'm sure," Violet said, watching the men disappear into the house. Clearly she was just being overly cautious and creeped out because of recent events. Not to mention this place looked like a haunted house with its overgrown landscape and busted front porch.

She stepped onto the creaking boards of the porch and followed them as Amber clutched her arm having sensed her dread. The room was lit by a heavy white candle which sat in the middle of a wooden crate. The only other light came from the crackling flames of the fireplace, and from somewhere in the back of the house.

There was a smoldering scent beneath the smell of mold and old furniture that was nearly suffocating to Violet. Amber wrinkled her nose and covered her face clearly smelling the stench too.

"What the fuck is that smell?" Amber asked and stepped through the front door.

"Ah, it's just the smell of death," Steve said and laughed as he waved the girls into the house.

Randy stood still, watching as the two girls crossed the threshold. He had an uneasy feeling about the place. Something wasn't quite right.

"So, you guys really live here?" Randy asked, looking around the room.

The windows were blacked out with black paint, duct tape covering cracks in the glass. The furniture was sparse and beaten up with springs poking through the cushions and dry rot in the fabric. It was as though some family had left in haste decades ago and just left their stuff behind.

"Sit down," Mose offered, extending his hand towards the dilapidated couch.

Randy walked over and sat down reluctantly. The couch was lumpy, the fabric feeling almost waxy against his skin. Amber walked forward hesitantly and sat beside him and up at Violet for some sort of comfort she couldn't give. Violet smelled the odor again as it rose from the heavy woven fabric of the couch. It made her uncomfortable, like she wanted to peel out of her skin and get the hell out of this place.

Steve and Mosley smiled at them and chatted about how they'd found this place one night and decided they could live there without paying anything.

"Do you even have indoor plumbing and electricity? What are you going to do when it gets really cold out?" Randy asked, looking around the room.

"Who needs electricity? And as you see, there's a fire place," Steve said, motioning towards the flaming hearth. "We can save our money for music equipment instead of wasting it on rent and shit."

Violet felt her skin come alive, the scent was heavier now and ripening as their body heat warmed the material of the furniture. She shifted uncomfortably.

Mose stared at her, his eyes dancing deep within his skull. His black skin was darker in the low light of the room. He looked shiny, obsidian. He was so oddly beautiful. Mosely had always been beautiful, but he looked otherworldly, almost

380

fae. He stared at each of them, his eyes never wavering as they bore into one person, then the next. He stared at Violet for the longest amount of time. Her skin crawled looking at his glistening eyes. Violet occasionally caught whiffs of a familiar scent she couldn't place. Then it dawned on her, Cecelia. Yes, the vampire had been here at some point, she was sure of it. She didn't know how she knew, but she knew.

Steve crouched down in front of the hearth. His eyes were glazed over by some hidden force, his lips open and glistening wet. The look of hunger on his face was clearly evident.

"So what's going on? You guys are acting weird," Randy said, leaning forward.

"You're fucking vampires," Violet growled. standing up and shoving her hands on her hips.

"Ding, ding, ding! Violet gets the prize," Steve said as he stood up, his face going smooth and still as he leaned forward.

Roman looked through the back window, the house was mostly dark. His stomach was clenched as tight as any fist he'd ever made knowing something was terribly wrong. He found the key she'd given him and slid it into the door, unlocking it and slipping inside. The thick smell of peanut butter cookies and chili powder still filled the air. He walked into the living room, the house felt so still and dead without them here to fill it up. Violet's aversion to being here alone made perfect sense to him now. He turned and walked towards the stairs hearing small footsteps descending. He peered around the corner and saw the gleaming dark eyes of Dory as she crept towards him, a faint smile peeling across her ghost-like face.

"Violet's not home yet?" he asked, moving aside to let her pass.

"No, I guess not. I didn't even know they left," she said, walking to the sink and turning on the faucet. She cupped her hand and took a drink from her bone-pale palm. She turned and looked at him.

He could see by the look in her eye that she was considering something. "Are you feeling better?" he asked and leaned against the wall.

"Much better, I think," she said, walking to the table and picking up a cookie. "Though I don't know how really, there's no reason for me to even still be living."

"Why do you say that?"

"Because she would have killed us by now. I knew she wasn't going to change us."

Roman considered her words carefully, mulling them over for nuance. "And why would you say that?"

"Because she doesn't like girls. I knew that from the start."

"Then why did you keep going there?"

"Because I have no reason to live. Better to die like that then get stuck in this miserable life forever," she said, shrugging her shoulders with a wistful look in her eyes as she took a bite of the cookie.

"Don't say things like that," Roman said, unsure how to console her and not really sure he should bother. What did he care about some teenager with a death wish anyway? Stupid little girls got themselves into the mess all on their own. So, what was it to him?

"Why shouldn't I say things like that? My mother had been telling me I was dead as a sinner my whole life. So why not just die for real? It's how I felt."

"Past tense?" he said, considering her words again. He couldn't imagine any parent being so callous toward their child. "And how do you feel now?"

"I'm glad the bitch is dead." Dory's eyes flickered with some sort of satisfaction, her smile still sad around the edges.

Roman couldn't help but feel there was something inherently evil about the girl. The way her eyes glistened, the crooked way her mouth smiled, even the tone of her voice was too sickly sweet for him. No one was that sweet.

"You killed her, didn't you?" Her eyes were lit with sick fascination.

"Yes," he answered, not really wanting the conversation to go in this direction. He needed to find Violet.

"Good," she said, snapping out of whatever spell she'd been under. "So, where are the others anyway?"

"I guess they went to hang out with Steve. Violet said she would stop by my place at 11 o'clock, but I can't get a hold of her."

"Steve?" Dory asked, suddenly perking up.

"Yeah," Roman answered, aware of her shift.

"He's one of them now," Dory remarked casually. Her eyes widened as though she'd suddenly come alive with bloodlust.

"One of them, *what*?" Roman asked, pacing towards her, his boots falling like heavy weights on the floor.

"A vampire, Roman. She made all of them vampires, well, *all the boys*."

"And you didn't think to tell us this until now? Where are they?" Roman said, forcefully taking the frail girl's arms in his hands and shaking her once. He knew her arms would be bruised, he didn't care. If Violet was hurt he would kill this little bitch and her pathetic friend.

Dory shrunk away from him in fear that he would hit her, the look of terror in her eyes caused him to loosen his grip. Clearly this girl had been abused her whole life, he had no right to add to it.

"Back behind the trailer park on Route 44."

"Why didn't you tell them this?" His eyes were ablaze with anger.

"I--I didn't know they were going to meet them. I didn't think..." she stuttered.

He turned and flew out the door slamming it behind him. There was no way she could protect herself against them. Dory had said "all of them". How many was all? God he hoped Mark wasn't counted amongst them. He got in the car and sped towards the trailer park, his heart racing and hungry for violence.

"You've *got* to be kidding me," Violet said, slapping her leg with her hands. "Un-fucking-believable. ," she said, turning to Amber and Randy as she set her feet soundly on the ground.

Amber was terrified, frozen with fear.

"I'm not leaving you!" Randy said, standing up and moving towards Violet and shielding Amber behind him.

"Come on, there's no reason to be afraid, you guys. It's great," Steve said, walking towards the three of them.

"Stay away from us!" Violet warned, coming between her friends and the vampire. "Get out of here," she said, turning briefly to look at Amber and Randy. "I can handle this."

"Oh, Violet, you can't handle anything," Steve said, dismissing her and walking closer.

Violet scanned the room for something to fight with, making a mental note of the metal poker in front of the fire. It had no doubt been there for a decade or more. She had to get her friends out of here.

"*You* killed her, Violet," Mosley said, coming up behind Steve. His eyes were filled with boiling blackness.

"Not technically," Violet said, nonchalantly and smiled. Her plan was to distract Steven and Mosley long enough to get Amber and Randy out of the house and to maneuver herself towards the fire.

"Why are you fighting this? You like vampires, remember?" Steve asked, looking from Violet to the others.

"She *is* a vampire, you stupid fuck," Amber said, suddenly shooting up from the couch.

"Vampire? I don't think so. I can smell the stench of humanity all over her," Steve said and rolled his eyes.

Violet turned and looked at her friend. "Get the fuck out of here and find Roman, Amber." Violet's eyes fixed on Amber's. "Go with her Randy."

"You aren't going anywhere." Steve grinned and opened his arms.

"I'm not leaving you alone, Violet," Randy said, lunging towards Steve.

Steve grabbed Randy by the neck and threw him to the ground without any effort. There was no way he could have done that if he was still human as Randy was way stronger than Steve. Amber screamed as Violet ran to the poker, the powerful blood flowing in her veins, old blood more potent than theirs, making her even more swift than the full blooded vampires. She swung the iron at Mose's back and knocked him to the ground. The vampire snarled and rolled over onto his back glaring up at her. Death was clearly visible in his eyes as he glowered. She would only have a second to react before he came flying at her.

"I'm sorry," she said, her heart heavy as she heaved the weapon into his throat, severing his head partially from his body.

Amber screamed as Randy pulled himself up from the floor. Steve was staring at Mosley's writhing body as his eyes stared frantically at him, seeming to beg for help.

"Run," Violet screamed with ferocity, twisting the poker and yanking it from the gaping neck of the beast below her on the floor. *This is not my friend. Not my friend. Not my friend.* The mantra burned in her mind. Over and over and over.

Amber grabbed Randy's arm and pulled him towards the door. "We'll find Roman," Randy screamed.

"I'm sorry," Violet said, choking back tears as she looked at the stunned vampire who stood before her. She couldn't believe she'd just torn through the neck of someone she'd considered a true friend with a fire poker. Steve dropped to his knees and lifted the arm of his trembling best friend and then looked up at her. The body hadn't died yet. It writhed nearly headless on the dank floor.

"Why did you do this? We didn't want you dead like she did. We wanted things to go back to the way they were before *he* came."

"Things changed long before Roman came, Steven," Violet said with as much tenderness as she could muster through her fear, truly heartbroken.

"Well, *I* want you dead." She heard Mark's voice snarling behind her.

She spun around to find Mark was standing in the doorway to the back room. She gripped the iron poker and stepped towards the fireplace so that the wall would be to her back.

"Go after them, Steven," Mark ordered through clenched teeth.

Steve stood up and headed for the door. "This could have been different," he cried, glaring at Violet with bloody tears in his eyes.

Mark stepped forward and ripped the iron from her stunned hands. Seeing him there, his eyes glazed over, his skin deathly white, froze her to the core.

"Yes, I want you dead," he seethed

He shoved her down on top of the thrashing vampire on the ground. Mosley's hands clutched at her as though her living flesh would give him life. Violet screamed as Mark's thick, meaty hands pulled her from the floor, dragging her as she kicked against him.

Roman ran down the muddy path--blade in hand--towards the faint light of the decrepit house. Amber and Randy ran towards him as Steve, the vampire, followed behind catching them quickly.

"Roman! She's still in there!" Amber yelled, thankful to see him.

Steve began running faster towards them with burning eyes, the adrenalin so strong Roman could smell it. He would destroy this creature like no other he'd ever destroyed. Roman growled, his heart exploding in his chest as he relished the coming violence.

"Get to the car and stay put," Roman said, walking past them towards the vampire that was rushing towards him, his eyes fixed wholly on his target.

"I have to help you," Randy yelled, following Roman.

"Protect Amber. Get to the car and protect Amber," Roman growled over his shoulder.

Randy shrank back and wrapped his arms around Amber. Roman's eyes scared the shit out of him at that moment. He was scarier than their friends, the vampires.

Mark dragged her to the back room, the scent of death growing so much stronger it was suffocating. Violet fought against him, kicking against his body and ripping at his arms with her fingers. No matter how much stronger she was from all the training Roman had given her, she had been so taken by such surprise by Mark's presence that she'd faltered.

"Why are you doing this?" she said, raking her nails across his skin and drawing blood.

"Because I hate you" he said, throwing her onto the soiled mattress across the room.

Her head slammed into the wall as she landed, blood splattering like a sick bloom. She looked around the room and saw bodies broken in a heap. She gasped, her hand going to her mouth to keep herself from puking. Her breaths were staccato with shock, her brain a dizzying mass of confusion.

"What's wrong, Violet? Never seen a dead body before?" He smiled and walked towards the lifeless form. "Looks a bit like your mom, doesn't she?" He picked the dead woman up by the arm and dragged it towards her.

Violet closed her eyes and tried to control her own body. She was trembling, paralyzed by fear and the shock of the situation, but she tried to steady her breathing. She had to keep it together long enough to get out of here. If she didn't get her wits together she was going to die. *Please help me.*

"Stupid girl thought we were going to have a good time together. Boy was she surprised when I ripped her throat out." He threw the body down on top of Violet.

The noxious stench was suffocating as she was trapped beneath the weight of the rotting corpse. The cold swollen flesh was doughy and reeked, the coldness seeping into her. She opened her eyes. The bruised, bloated carcass was more than she could bear. Death felt like no other feeling. Her thoughts flashed to her mother's hand, her father's cheek. She closed her eyes tightly and began to sob. Violet felt herself closing down, just like all of those other times he had verbally abused her. There was no doubt he knew he had her completely under his control. This revelation made him a thousand times more dangerous. Like a shark that smelled blood, he was ready. She closed her eyes, her teeth clenched to keep them from chattering. Underneath the decaying weight of the dead, bloated girl, Violet kid, just waiting to die.

"Come now, baby, I know you aren't this weak," Mark said, shoving her foot with his, wanting a fight from her. It wasn't going to be much fun if she didn't cry and beg for her life.

Violet jumped at his touch and clutched her eyes to keep them closed. The girl slid across her, still broken in her lap.

Mark kneeled down beside her and pushed the dead body off of her. He smoothed the hair away from her face and ran his thumb over her cheek, wiping the tears away.

"It makes me so angry when you get like this," he said quietly. "I never hurt you, Violet. I never hit you once. All I ever did was love you. And you always acted like I abused you. You're cowering now as if I've beaten you. I hate when you get like this. I *hate* when you get like this. *I hate when you get like this.*"

He gripped her face in his hand, squeezing hard and pushing his face into hers.

"Things could have been so much different," He said, his tone near frantic, pleading. He clenched his teeth, his spit spraying her face, and then let go, shoving her away as her head slammed into the wall again.

"Things could have been so different!" he seethed, elevating his voice. He began to pace the room. "You already have the blood in you, Violet. She would have let you stay with us. God, I smell her blood all over you. Once she knew you had the blood she would have let you stay with us. It could have been different. We could've traveled the world wreaking havoc everywhere we went like Bonnie and Clyde."

He was a madman now, circling her, growing more agitated with every step and every word he spewed. His thick muscles clenched as tight as they could, his face turning red as his jaw tightened with rage.

Violet was angry with herself for shutting down. Why couldn't she break this goddamned spell of abuse and leap up and fight him? This wasn't like her!

"Why won't you talk to me? *Talk to me!*" he said, hovering over her, her head cracking against the wall again. "I didn't do anything to you!" he said, dropping to his knees. He took her face in his hands again, forcing her to look at him. "Talk to me! Talk! To! Me!"

Violet's lip trembled. "Wh-what do you want me to say?" she cried.

He smiled briefly and wiped his grimy hands over her face and leaned back onto his heels. "I don't even know why she wanted you dead, Violet. She wouldn't tell me." Tears streaked down his contorted face. "No one talks to me. She wouldn't tell me," he said, rubbing her face more forcefully, her skin roughly sliding with the forceful pull of his palm. He looked down into Violet's terrified eyes.

She could feel the dead body leaning against her arm and leg, the coldness of death creeping into her. She needed to force her courage to the surface. Roman didn't know where she was to save her this time. Amber and Randy didn't even know how to find him. If she didn't get her courage to rise up she was going to die.

"I didn't want it to be like this," Mark said, focusing on her throbbing neck. "If she would have known you had our blood she would have let you live and everything would have been okay. She was just jealous because I love you." He said the words before he could even stop them. "But if she'd known you had vampire blood in you, maybe it would have been different."

"No," Violet said, the words barely audible. "She knew."

Mark looked at her shocked that she spoke. "She didn't know that you had our blood. She was never around you. But I can smell it in you. I can smell her in you."

Mark thought all vampire blood smelled as theirs did, but what he smelled was Lux. They all shared Lux's blood.

"I don't have your blood in me, Mark. I have my parents' blood, and I have Lux's blood. That's why she wanted me dead." Her courage was slowly building. If she could just get angry enough, rattle him enough to catch him off guard, maybe she could get away.

Mark's eyebrows drew together, his eyes closing briefly before refocusing on hers. His face knotted in confusion.

"Didn't know about Lux?" she asked.

He didn't answer. It was clear by his reaction he had no idea who she was talking about.

"No, she never did tell you anything, did she?" Violet goaded.

Mark growled, his eyes narrowing.

"Lux is her sire, and he is my sire, sort of," she added with a shrug.

"What the fuck are you?" Mark said, anger coursing through him so forcefully it came off of him in waves of power.

"I don't know, but I'm not all human and not all vampire. Mark, she didn't want you. She was using you to get back at Lux. She thought she could hurt Lux by killing me. This was never about you," Violet said.

Something snapped inside of her. The fear she felt had dissipated. She no longer felt crippled and in that moment she wondered if this was what Roman meant about God. Strength flowed through her from somewhere, calmness and clarity seemed to flow through her veins. Violet sat up, pulling herself away from the oily viscera stained mattress. His eyes followed her as she moved, never having seen this strength in her before. There was some power emanating from her he'd never witnessed, it wasn't from the vampiric blood, the scent of which was now wafting heavily from her skin, but from the human heart that beat wildly in her chest.

"You thought she was going to kill me as a gift to you, didn't you?" she teased.

"I told you, I don't know why she wanted you dead," Mark said with a furrowed brow.

That was bullshit and she knew it. There was zero doubt in her mind Mark had wanted to kill her. And there was zero doubt he had wanted Cecelia, his new girlfriend, to be the one to do it.

"She wasn't doing you a favor--she was getting back at her old boyfriend."

Her eyes were dry now, no more tears, her face vivid pink and swollen with life. He hated the way she looked at him as though she were superior. She looked so smug, so untouchable.

"It doesn't matter why she wanted you to die," he said through gritted teeth and fell against her, pinning her to the wall.

His body towered over her, the full length of his fangs shone in the dark like daggers. He was terrifying. He threw her back down on the mattress and straddled her. She was pinned between thick, iron thighs. The weight of his hips and groin against her pelvis was painful, as though her bones would be crushed. Her arms were locked above her head, one of his hands wrapped around both wrists like an iron clamp.

"I never noticed how strong you are before," Mark said and smiled, pressing her down harder as she struggled against him. He was going to rape and kill her. She knew it as clearly as she knew her own name.

"I never noticed it either," she said and pulled her arm away from him, ripping the skin on his face as she raked him with her nails.

The motion temporarily stunned him but he caught her arm and pinned her again, his weight was too heavy, his strength too much for her.

"Come on, stop fighting, it'll make this a lot easier," he said and leaned forward, kissing his own blood that had dripped on her face. "Ah, the things I could do to you now." He ground his hips against hers, as she struggled to get away.

"Please don't do this, Mark," she begged through quivering lips. That earlier strength was fading quickly. Her eyes filled with tears as she pleaded with him. Maybe the man who had once loved her was still in there somewhere.

He smiled and licked her face as he ran his free hand over her body, stopping to clutch the silver heart. He yanked on it, breaking the chain, and held it up as he studied it. Oblivious to the meaning of the gift. He didn't even know where she'd gotten it, only that she had been wearing it every time he'd seen her since they broke up. He threw it away, the heavy metal clanking on the floor as it landed.

"Fuck your heart" he growled and crushed his lips to hers.

Violet turned her head away from him enraging him even more. He squeezed her wrists tighter, Violet felt the bones snap as she screamed, and he pulled at her shirt, lifting it up. She struggled against him knowing this was it. If she didn't fight back right now with everything she had in her he was going to do horrible things to her body. His fangs sank into her shoulder pinning her in place, the pain searing her as he reached beneath her shirt feeling the soft skin of her belly.

"Please," she begged as his hands sank into her jeans, ripping the button and zipper as he tore them open.

"It makes me even harder when you beg for it," he growled, looking into her eyes. His hands moved to hold both her broken wrists as he sank his teeth into her neck, immobilizing her and forcing himself between her legs.

She couldn't let this happen. She would rather die than let him inside of her again. She ripped her hands away from him with a screech and shoved him back, kicking him as hard as she could. He flew back onto the floor stunned by her sudden burst of strength. He smiled and pulled himself up as Violet moved quickly to her feet.

"You know I like it violent, Violet."

Roman ran towards Steve as if he were some sort of animal fixed on prey. Amber and Randy stood there clutching each other where Roman had left them, paralyzed by fear, unable to do what he'd told them to do. They watched as the vampire leapt on Roman, knocking him back briefly and throwing him off balance. Roman lifted his arm, catching Steve mid-air, and throwing him to the ground with a loud crack. Steve's spine was crooked as Roman lifted the sword, plunging it into the man's chest. The cavity took the blade easily making a sucking sound. He twisted the blade and pulled it out again. Roman was a man possessed. Had Amber not known him she would have been more terrified of him than the vampire that was broken and helpless on the ground as he towered over.

This thing had been their friend.

"You're too late to save her." The vampire grinned as his hands went to the gaping hole in its chest, a smile slipping from its lips.

Roman lifted the sword again and thrust it into the neck of the demon, severing the head. He pulled the blade out and walked towards the house, not hesitating or looking back. Amber collapsed to the ground as she clutched Randy's leg. She couldn't bear the sight of their dead friend lying on the ground. Her mind flashed the scene repeatedly, desperate to make sense of it all.

"I've got to go help him!" Randy said, reaching down for Amber's arm to pull her up.

"Don't leave me! I can't be here alone!" Amber cried, clutching onto him, her fingers digging into him frantically.

Roman walked onto the creaking porch and into the dimly lit front room of the house. He saw the wounded vampire on the floor. His blood had spilled onto the carpet surrounding it in black-red goo. It still lived, its hands blindly reaching at the dark air around it. He sliced through the remaining flesh of the neck without hesitation as he headed for the room in the back of the house. He could smell death, he could smell Violet's fear.

She kicked Mark again, sending him back into the wall.

"Feisty! I like it!" Mark growled, lowering his head as he came towards her. "We should have fought like this when we were together. Violence gets me so hard."

Violet kicked him again, sending him stumbling.

"You are strong, girl, I'll give you that," he said, leaping in the air and landing on top of her as he held her shoulders.

The seeping blood felt hot and sticky beneath his hands as he pulled her forward and sank his teeth into her neck again. She fought against him, tearing at his flesh with her fingers and trying to pull herself away from him. Her head was going dizzy as he sucked the blood from her body, her heart pounded slowly in her ears. Blackness loomed in her peripheral vision as her eyes closed. Her body was failing her, legs collapsing beneath her. *At least he won't touch me again.*

Roman's voice growled through the darkness of the room. Mark spun around quickly, dropping Violet to the floor. Her body made a thud as it hit the ground hard.

"Too late," Mark said, wiping his mouth with his finger and placing it in his mouth.

"You are going to die now," Roman said, his voice void of emotion as he lunged forward, slicing Mark's chest wide open. Blood gushed from the wound in a spray that speckled everything around.

"Ouch," Mark said, looking down at the wound and then back to Roman who was advancing, towering over him like an ominous shadow. Mark leapt forward grabbing Roman's shirt, trying to pull him to the ground to no avail.

Roman laughed, a sound so cruel and demonic. He was still far superior and stronger than Mark. He'd been trained for this his entire life. Roman was more vampire than this weak, pathetic abomination could ever be.

"What are you?" Mark managed to say before Roman grabbed him by the neck.

Roman forced Mark against the wall with one hand, his powerful grip like a vice as Mark struggled to keep from falling. His strength had increased exponentially, almost as if he was imbued with someone else's power, perhaps borrowing energy from the actual air around him.

Roman said nothing but lifted the blade, locking eyes with Mark, whose expression was bewildered and pleading. Roman relished that look, knowing Mark understood now what it felt like to be weak and the reality that he was going to die now. He lifted his hand, pinning Mark by the jaw. Mark fought, his arms swinging wildly. His legs kicked out, landing and hitting a solid, impenetrable wall of muscle and bone. Roman never flinched, the blows completely ineffectual. Mark's eyes were wide with terror, as if he was looking Death straight in the eyes and understanding there was nothing he could do now to save himself.

The blade slid easily into the thick meat of Mark's neck as his hands pulled at Roman's arm, trying desperately to release his vice-like grip. His throat gurgled as blood bubbled from his mouth and from the slit the sword made. Roman felt the neck peeling away from the body as the steel sliced through the muscle and bone. He dropped the body to the floor and watched as the black-red blood burbled onto the stained carpet. The body twitched, electricity still firing in the muscles. Mark was dead.

His death had come so easily. There was no contest, Roman's breathing was not even labored. Had he been here with her Mark wouldn't have been able to put a single finger on her. These vampires were so weak he would have been able to kill all three with no effort whatsoever. Just as he'd done countless times before.

He bent over Violet and went to his knees. He lifted her head and then cradled her limp body in his arms. Her head fell back, the gaping wound oozing bright red. He held his hand over the wound trying to stop the bleeding, his eyes blurred with fury and grief.

"Hang in there," he whispered, pressing his face to her neck.

She felt cool against his lips. He lifted her in his arms and walked through the house. He needed to get her help immediately in order to save her, and even then it may be too late. He cursed himself for not being with her. If only he'd stayed with her. Had his chores really been more important than spending time with her? What the fuck had he been thinking? He should have known better. Had he not been so preoccupied he would have known her friends were turned. It couldn't have been more obvious in retrospect. If she died it would be over for him. And he was fine with that. It would be easy. It would be easy to let everything go.

Just like it had been for his father when his mom died. Only that hadn't been his dad's fault. Cancer couldn't be fought with steel. It hadn't been his dad's fault his mom died. But Violet's death would be on his hands.

He ran with her in his arms to where he had left Amber and Randy. They were still clutching onto one another as they had been the last time he'd seen them. Amber looked up and saw him coming towards them with Violet in his arms. Her body was limp, draped in his arms like the pieta, as if roles had been reversed and the scene was all wrong. Violet looked dead. And Roman looked like a broken monster.

Amber stood up, her adrenalin kicking her into gear, the need to know if Violet was alright taking over everything. As Roman got closer she could see the blood soaked shirt and crimson staining of her milk white skin. Amber wanted to collapse again, the sickness rising from her stomach until it expelled onto the ground. Randy ran to Roman, panicked but ready to act.

"Get her to a hospital," Roman ordered, walking to his car as he held Violet to his chest.

Randy jogged beside him to keep up with Roman's long strides. "Is she gonna be alright?" he asked frantically.

"If you get her to a hospital. Hold her neck, try to stop the bleeding," Roman said, looking at the man. His eyes were filled with fear. "This is my fault. I never should have left her alone."

"No!" Amber said, straightening her spine and wiping her face on her sleeve. "I was the one who pushed her to come with us." She opened the door so that Roman could slide Violet into the car.

"We don't have time for this," Roman said gently, looking at Amber and locking eyes with her. "Keep her alive, Amber," Roman said, terrified at the thought of her dying.

Quick flashes of begging Lux for his blood to keep her alive flashed in his head and were rejected. Lux could never get there in time.

"I will," Amber promised, sliding in behind Violet. She pulled her sleeve down over her hand and pressed it into the seeping wound.

"Say she got bit by a dog," Roman said, standing still, not taking his eyes from Violet's still form in the car. There wasn't any life in her and it made her not look real. She was simply a painting come to life. A horrific image from a nightmare.

"Aren't you coming?" Randy said, taking the keys from Roman's hand.

"Not yet. I need to take care of this," Roman said, despondent. His life was seeping out of him with every drop of blood she lost. Fuck, he should just leave these bodies to rot and be found. What difference did it make? Who cared about protocol? Who cared if all of it was exposed?

"She'll be okay," Randy said, standing in front of Roman, gripping his arms and shaking him to get his attention.

Roman looked into Randy's eyes briefly, acknowledging his earnest statement, then Randy ran to the driver's side and started the car.

"She's going to be okay," Randy repeated to himself as he steeled himself.

"Keep her alive," Roman begged Amber. He looked at Violet's still face one more time and shut the door to the car and then watched it pull away.

The sky was paling, a silvery purple hue lit up the horizon. The barren trees were like black veins against the darkened sky. He walked towards the house, stepping over Steven's dead body, which was already beginning to smolder. It would burn up in the coming light. Poor stupid kid got involved with shit he couldn't control or understand. Roman spat on him as he walked over, kicking the dead body.

He felt nothing. His body was numb. His thoughts, quiet. Walking onto the porch, he stopped briefly, taking in a deep breath. The stench of death suffocated him. His stomach churned, his legs weak, as he held onto the door frame, bracing himself before he continued into the house.

He dragged Mosley to the front door by the arm and tossed him out onto the porch, shoving the lifeless corpse with his foot and watching as it rolled onto the muddy ground. The body made a sucking sound as it landed in the mud. Another stupid kid. Of the three Mosely had seemed the most likable, though Roman had spent virtually no time with him. But he had always been polite.

He returned to the room and lifted the head by the hair and tossed it out the door. The heaviness of the thing felt sick in his hand. Death felt like nothing else, and if she didn't live, he would make as many as he could understand its feel--human devil or otherwise--until he finally allowed it to claim him as well. He would take out as many evil beings as he could until he finally let Death catch him.

He walked to the back room where he knew Mark's body would be, broken and discarded on the stained carpet. It absently dawned on Roman that this had been someone's home at one point, and now it was a house of death, a horror scene from a twisted movie.

He looked around the room and noticed the two dead women, anonymous, naked and thrown aside like unwanted garbage. Someone's child, someone's sister, maybe even someone's mother. Dead and discarded as though they had no value whatsoever. Anger burned in him.

He lifted the body of one of the women and carried it to the mattress, gently placing it down beside the body of the other woman. He pushed the first woman over onto her back as though she were merely sleeping. The gaping mouths and rotting eyes made him sick. He was used to seeing dead vampires, and he'd seen many dead humans, but something about what all this meant was more than he could handle. Mark had used these women to hurt Violet. Roman retched, expelling the contents of his stomach onto the floor. He shook his head, squeezed his eyes shut tightly to focus himself, and stood up. He hesitated for a moment, regaining his balance. He needed to hurry and get this business taken care of so he could get to Violet. Had he been avoiding that situation by taking his time here, afraid to face Violet's death? If he didn't know, she wouldn't be dead. He could leave right now, never knowing if she survived or died. He could still delude himself into believing she had survived, and that he was protecting her from this violent life he lived. No. He had to know. He couldn't leave her. He didn't want to leave her. He would never let her go.

He lifted his dizzy, heavy head slowly and looked across the room at Mark's body and was thoroughly enraged, wanting to kill him all over again. He should've killed him when he was still human, that night he'd broken his jaw all those weeks prior. It would have been easy to hunt him down and kill him that night. How many lives would have been saved if he had just done that. Who cared that he was human? The man was a sick and twisted human that had only caused pain to everyone around him. Who cared why? Who cared what had caused him to be such a broken, vile, piece of shit? He could have killed him before any of her friends died, before she had been tortured again and again and again.

Roman walked quickly across the room and pulled the body up from the ground and then carried it through the house to the front door and threw it out into the yard with one heave. The body cracked, the back at an unnatural angle, as it hit the ground with such force.

Roman turned and walked back and picked the head up. He stared at Mark's ruddy face, fangs and chin still stained with Violet's blood. The eyes were open, dull, blankly staring forward. Roman gripped the head in his hands and felt the bones give way, fingers digging into the meat of the flesh, bones crunching as his fingers pierced through the dead man's skin. He threw it through the doorway, smashing into the frame of the door as it landed in the yard with a rolling thud. It sounded like a watermelon being heaved from the top of a building. He would never forget the sound.

He walked back into the house, surveying the room for more bodies, thankful not to find any. The sludgy stain where Mose had died caught his eye. Violet had gotten one of them. The corner of his lip lifted with slight satisfaction at that knowledge before disappearing. His face returned to the stoic mask he always wore prior to knowing her. He never smiled before her.

He kicked the candle over and watched as the old carpet began to smolder before catching flame. He turned and walked out the front door. He stopped beside Mark's body. So much hate burned inside of him for so many reasons. He lifted his foot, bringing it down with such force upon the body that the chest cracked open, his boot sinking into the flesh to the ground beneath. He pulled his foot out of the chest cavity, his boot making a sucking sound before he kicked Mark with his steel toed boot. He felt the bones and insides gushing upon contact. He would never forget the sound or the feel of that either.

He looked up at the paling sky, took in a deep breath to center himself, and started running as fast as he could, his body propelling him faster and faster as he willed it. He needed to get to her car, which was left at the diner across the street. Then he could get to her. It felt like hours had passed, but in reality it had only been moments. If he was too late to say goodbye it would kill him.

She had to live. She *had* to live. She could not die, *would* not die. His mind raced, begging God, the universe, anyone who could hear his thoughts, to save her. He ran through the trailer park, moving so fast he was nearly a blur. Even the dogs didn't stir when he passed them as by the time his scent and sound hit them he was gone. Soon the house would be in flames and he knew as young as the three vampires were, they would almost be gone even by now. The sun was peeking above the horizon, the sky the palest violet-grey. Fitting. The house would be in full blaze soon and the fire department would arrive. He intended to be long gone by then. Just like those three vampires would be long gone in moments.

He found her car where he'd seen it prior and climbed in, immediately working on the wires in the steering column. The car came to life and he threw it into reverse. It was a damn good thing he knew how to steal a car. At least she hadn't locked it, because busting out a window would be pretty damn suspicious and he knew someone would witness that through the windows of the restaurant. Already there were people eating breakfast before their workday started.

Roman found his phone in his jacket and called Lux. No answer. *Motherfucker*. He could get here in a matter of hours if he was still in Chicago. He needed to get his ass here and heal Violet.

"Get here," he growled into the phone, leaving a message he hoped would be heard.

Ten minutes away from the hospital. He fucking hoped Randy had been able to get her there in time.

20

BETTER THINGS TO COME

HIS CAR WAS PARKED in front of the emergency room door, a red handprint on the glass entryway that led into the hospital was a marker he recognized. He had taken far too long to clean up the mess. If she was gone and he'd missed saying goodbye...

Roman waited for the door to slide open and walked into the lobby, scanning the crowd. Randy was sitting by himself, his head supported by blood covered hands. Roman stood in front of him and Randy looked up the moment his shadow loomed over him. His eyes swollen with tears, his face broken by emotion.

"You made it," Roman said, putting his hand on Randy's trembling shoulder.

"She's back there. They're working on her," Randy said, the words choked in his throat as he tried to regain his composure. "They won't let anyone go back. Amber had to lie and say she was her sister."

"Is she going to be okay?" Roman asked, hoping the news would be good.

"I think so. They're giving her blood and trying to close the wound I guess."

"So, she's going to be okay?" Roman said, needing desperately for it to be true.

"They wouldn't really tell me much, just told me to wait out here. Amber hasn't been back out. I don't know what the fuck is going on back there. No one will tell me shit," Randy said, glaring towards the woman at the front desk.

Roman followed Randy's line of vision and then walked up to the desk and leaned forward to get the attention of the older lady who sat at the desk working on a computer. She looked up and was clearly perturbed by his presence.

"Yes?" she asked, looking up briefly from the monitor and then back.

"I need to know how a patient is doing," Roman said, growing agitated by the woman's seeming complete lack of empathy.

"Name?" the woman asked tersely.

"Violet Roby," he answered, hoping to God the news was good.

"Hold on," she said, typing something and looking at the stack of clipboards which sat next to her desk. "Yes, she's here."

"I know she's here. I need to get back there to see her."

"Are you related?"

Roman looked at the woman stunned by her complete lack of compassion. Had this job so numbed her emotions she had no ability to feel anymore? "Yes, I'm her fiancé," Roman said gruffly.

"Let me see if you can go back," the woman huffed and stood up, leaving him standing there.

Roman turned to look at Randy who had his head in his hands again. He turned back around and watched the women approaching with a doctor in-tow. The man was young, maybe only thirty five, and very well dressed.

"You're her fiancé?" the doctor asked, reaching his hand towards him.

Roman held his blood covered hand out. The doctor looked down and retracted his own apologetically. Roman had no time for idle banter. He wanted, *needed*, to know how Violet was doing.

"Maybe you can answer some questions for us?" the man said, leading Roman through the wooden doors to the back.

"What's going on? Is she okay?"

"She's okay, yes, but there are some anomalies. That must have been some dog. She has several bite wounds and both her wrists are broken. One bite to her shoulder and two to her neck. The shoulder is minor, but her throat wound is severe. She's receiving a transfusion and we have cleaned the wounds and stitched them, but she will likely need plastic surgery to repair the neck."

"So, she's going to be okay?" Roman asked, wanting a definitive answer. He was growing impatient.

"We think so, but again, I have some questions I'm hoping you can answer." The man held a curtain back.

Roman saw Amber sitting in a vinyl chair with her head resting against the edge of the bed, clearly emotionally exhausted. He had no idea how these people would ever return to their normal lives after enduring all they had just been through. The thought that they had watched their friends being killed, their dead bodies continuing to writhe around even after death, how would they get beyond that? Amber looked up, a faint smile touching her lips. She was relieved Roman had made it. She stood up and wrapped her arms around him. It startled him at first, but then he hugged her as she clutched onto him and collapsed in tears. He lifted her and held her up as she hid her face against his chest. Her fingers dug into him and he knew there would be bruises from her grip.

The doctor pulled a chart off the foot of the bed and flipped through some papers. "Does Violet have any conditions that you're aware of?" he asked Roman, his brow deeply furrowed as he studied something in the pages.

Roman looked away from the man to Violet who was so motionless. Her face was more ghostly than he'd ever seen it. Her eyes began twitching beneath the surface of her thin blue lids. White gauze was wrapped around her neck and she was attached to wires and IVs. Both her wrists were bound by casts. She looked so frail, so small and helpless.

"No," Roman answered, taking his eyes off of her and looking at the doctor.

No, she had no illness in her body, thanks to her heritage. Amber still held onto him as though at any moment she would collapse if he let go. Roman moved slowly hoping she would pry herself off of him.

"Well, we're finding an anomaly in her blood tests. Whatever it is it doesn't appear to be harmful as she is physically healthier than even the average person.

In fact she is already healing dramatically. Her blood counts are doubling by the minute. It makes no sense scientifically, but we haven't been unable to determine what these extra enzymes and platelets are in her blood."

Roman considered his words knowing it was the vampire blood that healed her. He had to get her out of the hospital once he knew she would be okay. If he didn't they would give her endless tests and would want to study her like she was a lab rat. Not to mention if the Vampire found out she was being tested it would be a death sentence for her.

"Tell me absolutely, is she going to be alright?" Roman asked.

"Yes, she appears to be fine," the doctor said as he wrote something on the chart and set it back in the rack at the foot of the bed. "We're going to want to keep her for testing for the next few days given the trauma and the irregularities in her blood work. We need to figure out what is wrong with her blood, and we will also need to schedule cosmetic surgery to repair the damage to her neck."

Roman nodded. "Thank you for saving her," Roman said, his voicing gruff in his throat with sincerity. He would shake the man's hand, but his own were covered in blood.

"You're welcome, though a big part of it appears to be her will to live. For someone so small, she is clearly a fighter." The man smiled and patted Violet's foot gently. "I'll leave you to sit with her. We'll be moving her upstairs as soon as they get a bed ready." The doctor smiled and pulled the curtain back. "Your girl has been through a lot tonight. You should be very thankful she made it through."

Roman felt like puking. The whole manic drive to the hospital he'd thought he'd lost her. Thank God for Randy and Amber, and for that damned vampire blood in her veins.

Amber relinquished her grip on him enough to look up at Roman. "I could not have handled her dying," she said, wiping her eyes and finally letting go.

"I know," Roman said, putting his hand on her shoulder. "You should go home and rest. Take Randy home and get cleaned up and try to get some sleep. It's been a long, traumatic evening."

"She's going to be okay," Amber said, leaning against Roman. He hugged her tight for a long moment, Amber not wanting to let go again. "I can't believe they tried to kill us." Her voice was muffled against his shirt.

"They're all gone," Roman said without emotion.

Amber started to cry again, she sniffled and wiped her eyes and nose on her sleeve. "You need to fill out her paperwork, Roman. We got here in such a rush there was no time. I don't know her information like social security and insurance and all that. I did my best, but I don't know it and I didn't know who to call. She has an aunt nearby, but I don't know how to reach her."

"I don't either," Roman exhaled and raked his fingernails over his scalp and down his cheek in frustration. "Is her bag in her car?"

"Yeah, she brought it last night. I'll get it for you and then we'll go home. I can't see her like this anymore."

"Thanks," Roman said, squeezing her shoulder. "Go home and try to sleep. She's going to be okay now. You're all safe now. You can rest without fear." He looked away from her and shook his head once. "I fucked up, Amber."

Amber burst into tears and wrapped her arms around him again. "No, it wasn't your fault."

"It was," he said, knowing every bit of this was his fault. "Please go home and get some rest."

She backed away and looked up at him. Her eyes were glistening pools filled with grief. "It wasn't your fault. And the only reason I'm listening to you and going home is because I don't want to stress you out more than you already are."

Roman tried to smile for her but failed.

Amber squeezed his wrist and then slipped through the striped curtain and walked to the lobby to find Randy. She was relieved that Roman was with Violet. Violet was safe now. She knew after having seen Roman in action that no one could harm her as long as he was by her side. He had been terrifying, a cold killer, but he had saved Violet and probably her and Randy too.

Roman stood at the foot of the bed looking down at his sleeping angel. She was alive. The pink was coming back to her cheeks slowly, too slight for most to detect, but he had studied her face so much that he could see the variance in her pale pallor. Her breathing sounded less strained. He could smell the scent of her blood warming and churning, electric and vibrational, as it renewed her body. She had to be twice as strong as he was. It was the old blood. His aunt hadn't been a vampire even two hundred years, but Lux was one of the ancients. Violet would likely be ready to leave here by evening. As it was she was merely resting from the ordeal as her body knitted itself back together.

"What have you done, little one?" Lux asked as he kissed her forehead.

"I didn't do anything," Violet answered and rubbed her eyes. She looked around the room. They were in his bedroom again, reclining side by side on the thick down comforter on top of his massive bed.

"You almost got yourself killed," Lux said and pulled her against him so that she was resting her head against his chest. She smelled like lilies and warm summer rain.

"It wasn't intentional. I didn't know they were vampires." She nestled against him and closed her eyes. She was so tired.

"Roman should have known," Lux said, darkness creeping into his tone.

"It wasn't his fault. I am a distraction."

"Yes, you are at that," he said with a chuckle and kissed the top of her head.

"I was dying and you came to me," she said, nearly asleep.

"I will always come for you if I can, but you must learn to be more careful."

"I said I didn't know," Violet said, trying to be angry, her brow furrowed like a petulant child.

"I gave Roman to you to keep you safe."

"You gave me to Roman," she corrected and snuggled against him.

Lux smiled sadly and enveloped her in his arms. "Nevertheless, do not go anywhere without him again."

"I won't," she said and yawned. "Lux, when I was dying you came to me."

"Yes, we already discussed this, love."

"I had given up."

"I know. You can never give up," he said against her soft, warm hair.

"I didn't want to give up. I couldn't help it," she said, her eyes now closed.

"I know," Lux said, his voice a soft breath. "Sleep now, rest, and then run along to him."

He sat in the chair beside the bed, the vinyl of the seat felt hot to him as it stuck to his bare arms. He looked up periodically, wanting desperately for her to open her eyes. Right now all he wanted more than anything was to look into those big blue eyes. At least they'd given her a private room and no one was there trying to make small talk or coughing next to her.

He reached into his jacket. He felt the blue jay feather tucked into his pocket right behind the picture she had given him. He pulled out the photo and looked at it. Such big blue eyes. A cute toothless grin. He loved this photo. She was then what she is now. Completely irresistible. It wasn't hard to imagine her having everyone wrapped around those tiny little fingers.

He closed his eyes and tried to relax. His heart was still pounding with fear and anger. He needed to get it together before she woke up.

The television in the corner of the room was on at a low level, some infomercial about knives. It was ironic, maybe. Annoying, definitely. But he didn't have the energy to bother changing channels or turning it off. Besides, it was kind of good to have the noise drowning out the beeping of medical equipment and sporadic announcements over the loudspeaker.

He idly noticed that every so often nurses would walk by the room and peer in at him, some even smiling at him as he looked up. They weren't looking at Violet, they were looking at him. He'd even thought he had noticed them taking pictures of him with their cellphones. There was no reason he could imagine for them to be taking pictures of him, so he thought he must just be paranoid. This wasn't the first time this had happened in the last several years though. He had even had people follow him, but it was something he always assumed was either some women trying to hit on him for whatever reason, or it was related to his *profession*. He didn't want to be bothered right now, and he definitely didn't want Violet to be disturbed, so he got up and pulled the curtain around her bed and slid his chair out of view.

God he was exhausted. He wished he could sleep but he couldn't afford to fall asleep. It was bad enough he was being ogled, but they had also been coming in every hour or so and drawing more blood from her as they tried to figure out what was wrong. Watching the needle pierce her vein as it rose to the surface pained him. Bruises blossomed beneath her skin, like blue-purple petals just beneath the surface. *Violent violets beneath the surface of her skin.*

Seeing the blood brought an unexpected pang to his stomach. He swallowed hard and looked away briefly and then back to her serene face. He'd lied to her about craving it, but he'd also lied to himself. It was unforgivable. A point of pride for him was that he'd always been honest. She may have been asking him because she craved it herself and was confused or scared. As soon as they were out of here he was going to tell her the truth. There was no point in running from it anymore. Regardless of his feelings towards vampires it didn't change their reality. Roman reached out and took her little hand in his. The warmth of her body was seductive. He'd spent too much time with dead things. He rested his head on the edge of the bed and closed his eyes again.

He walked towards the house. Pink petals like snow fell from the sky, dusting the ground, landing on his hair and skin. The air smelled sweet like cotton candy, maybe some flower he didn't know. Lights like fireflies danced all around him, touching him and then fluttering away. They were soft, almost oddly caressing. How strange. He looked all around, spinning in a slow circle. He couldn't see anything beyond the border of the house. The fields, the woods, all gone, drowned by darkness. He turned back to the house. The light upstairs illuminated the yard like a small moon, no other light anywhere, blackness all around, causing him to shield his eyes as he stepped onto the porch. The screen door screeched as he opened it, startling him. It was the first time he'd been to the farmhouse. Again, how strange.

He walked into the living room which was lit by the pink glow of rose scented candles. The house was old but clean and everything was perfectly in place. It was her grandma's house. He knew this because she had told him.

His gaze moved over every object as he walked into the kitchen. The faint scent of some cleaner filled the room, the white cupboards and tile floors were so clean they glistened. Blue gingham curtains moved as the night air breathed through the open windows.

It was always night here, he recalled.

Walking towards the oak staircase he followed the scent of Violet's blood knowing that Lux was here, hovering somewhere near, as always.

When he got to the top of the stairs he went towards the room with the soft oil lamp glow. She was sleeping on the bed beneath a snow white quilt of lace and velvet. Lux stood in the corner partially concealed by shadow. His face was lit, his expression drawn. He said nothing, just moved slightly swaying with the wafting air that blew through the windows.

Roman walked to the bed and sat down. She didn't move, asleep, perfectly still. He'd expected her to be awake here. She should be smiling as she only really ever smiled here. Her real face never seemed to be as peaceful in the waking world, the glint in her eyes never as sparkly in real life. Roman turned to Lux who was motionless.

"You saved her," Roman said as he lifted her fingers in his hand and held them.

"No, you saved her," Lux spoke, barely moving his mouth.

Roman leaned forward resting his head on her chest like he had done in the field. The steady rhythm lulled him. The insistent sound of her blood as it swooshed through the cavern of her heart was intoxicating. He turned his head and pressed his face to her breast.

Lux watched, envious of the intimacy of the moment, propelled to leave but unable to move. He had seen human tenderness a thousand times a thousand times, and yet this was more perfect than any single kiss he'd witnessed.

Her hand moved against Roman's, rousing him. Violet lifted her hand slowly caressing the back of his head. The prickle of his hair sent little electric jolts from her fingertips to low in her belly. His head rose, his eyes finding hers, smiling.

"Let's wake up, Roman. They're going to stab me again," she said wistfully.

"You're awake, little girl. I didn't expect to see your eyes open so soon. You had quite a little accident." The nurse said with a wide smile as she wrapped the rubber band around Violet's arm.

She was a kindly woman, she seemed motherly in every way. The nurse smelled of lavender hand lotion and antiseptic. She had a slight smile as she went about her tasks. Violet felt comfortable with her immediately. She had felt the woman's presence around her, even in sleep, since they'd brought her up to this floor.

Violet smiled and squeezed Roman's hand as he lifted his head from the bed.

"Did you bring her in?" the nurse asked Roman, looking down at the hand that held Violet's.

"No, I pulled the dog off of her." Roman followed the woman's quick gaze and looked down at his hands. They were caked with dried blood. Mark's blood.

"You should wash those hands, they're awfully dirty," the woman said with a sympathetic smile.

Yes. Violet didn't need any reminders. He tried to let go so he could go wash up in the sink but she gripped his hand and grabbed his wrist with her other hand holding him to her.

"When can I go home?" Violet asked, barely able to get her voice to work.

"Rest, honey, you'll be here a few more days. You're healing fast though." The nurse winked and pressed her finger to the vein that rose to the surface and then slid the needle into her skin.

Violet winced and looked away. Roman held her hand tightly and smiled at her.

"Okay, all done for now. Try to relax and don't start talking too much. Your throat's got to be sore. And wash those hands," the nurse scolded Roman with a smile and carried the tray out of the room.

Violet tilted her head and looked up at Roman. His expression was dark, his eyes bloodshot and weary looking. "You saved me," she said, awestruck.

Roman smiled at her not wanting to say anything. Had he only been a few moments later she would have died. It haunted him.

"Are Amber and Randy okay?" Panic swept over Violet and she sat up ready to tear her IV out and head for the door.

"They're fine, kitten. I sent them both home to rest," Roman said, guiding her back down to the bed.

"Did they find you? Is that how you found me?"

"No, Dory told me about Steve and where they were staying."

He finally let go of her hand and walked across the room to the bathroom and scrubbed his hands as best he could. There was blood and other gunk under his nails, no doubt remnants of Mark's skin. She didn't need this shit touching her.

412

He re-lathered and scrubbed some more then wet a wash cloth and brought it to her to wash off her hands.

Violet held her hands up and let him wash her fingers that peaked out of the casts. He was so gentle and careful with her. She looked up at him, her brow furrowed.

"I can't believe they didn't tell us about them being vampires," she said with a frown. "You would think that would be top of the list to tell us?"

"I know." Roman's voice dropped in register.

"Well, they were nearly dead themselves." Violet shrugged, reaching for the heart around her neck and not finding it. "I lost your necklace," she said, starting to cry. She covered her eyes with her damp hands.

"It's just a necklace," Roman comforted, taking her hands away from her face and wiping her eyes with his fingertips.

"No," she said, allowing herself to cry. "It's not just a necklace."

"We'll go back and find it later," he said, wiping her eyes again. He cradled her face with his palm. "We need to get you home. Surprising, I know, but they found something strange with your blood and they want to keep you around for a few days for testing." Roman leaned forward and kissed her cheek savoring the softness of her skin against his lips.

"I want to go home. I'm better now," she said, trying to sit up. Her head spun wildly and forced her back down on the bed.

"Rest a little while longer," he said, kissing her again and standing up. "I'm going to go get something to drink."

He walked down the hall and took his cellphone out of his jacket. Amber answered halfway through the first ring.

"Hello?" she said, sounding anxious but exhausted, no doubt she was completely fried from all the drama.

"Hey Amber. I'm going to get Violet out of here once it gets dark. They're testing her because of her blood coming back abnormal and they're never going to figure out what's wrong with her. We need to just get her home. They think something is wrong with her and are considering surgery to fix her neck. They're not going to just release her."

"Is she safe to come home? Is it safe this soon?" Amber was surprised Roman would be so quick to get her out of there seeing as how she'd nearly died.

"Yes, she's surprisingly well, just still tired and weak. But she'll be fine with a few days of rest. You know that I wouldn't risk her life?" he asked, knowing that Amber was probably concerned he was doing just that.

"I know," she said in earnest. "Yeah, I know that," she repeated, perhaps to reiterate it to herself. "What do you need us to do?"

"I need you to bring her some clothes so I can get her out of here without being obvious."

"Okay, I'll be there."

Roman looked up at the clock. It was five o'clock and already getting dark out. Amber should be here soon. He stood up and walked to the window and opened the curtains. It looked like it would snow. She would like that.

"I brought her clothes," Amber said softly, trying not to wake Violet as she entered the room and handed him a bag.

Roman took it from her and sat it down on the edge of the bed. He gently pushed Violet's arm urging her to wake up. She had been sleeping most of the day, only waking briefly here and there. She opened her eyes slowly, focusing on her surroundings. She was glad to see Amber standing beside Roman.

"Randy's downstairs with your car," Amber said to Roman and sat down in the chair beside the bed.

"Violet, we're taking you home. Do you think you're okay enough to leave?" Roman asked, pulling the clothes out of the bag for her.

"Yes," she said, lifting herself up. She got a slight head rush and closed her eyes waiting for the feeling to pass as her blood pounded in her ears. She pulled at the gown they'd tied her into. "We need to take these wires and things out," she said, peeling the tape back away from the needle in her hand.

"We need to turn the machine off first or an alarm will go off and the nurses will come running." Roman flipped the switch on the machine and helped slide the needle from her hand, rubbing the spot gently with his thumb.

Amber stood up and undid the ties of the gown and helped Violet out of it. She held the sweatshirt up and put it over Violet's head, helping her to maneuver into it. Roman turned his head looking away as Amber dressed her. Amber had brought her pink sweatshirt with the bunny on it. Violet smiled when she saw it.

"I thought you'd want the bunny shirt." Amber winked, knowing Violet's emotional attachment to the shirt. Her grandma had gotten it for her for Easter when she was a little girl. She'd gotten one for all the grandkids in the family. She guessed she was the only one who still fit in it though.

Violet slid her legs to the side of the bed and waited as Amber helped her pull the sweatpants up to her knees.

"Can you stand?" Amber asked, holding Violet's arms to help steady her.

"Yes," Violet said, gripping Amber and pulling herself up from the bed. Her head spun again briefly so she closed her eyes to right herself.

Roman walked around the bed and took Violet by the arm. "Check the hall," he said, motioning to Amber. "Are you sure you're okay?" he asked, wanting to make damn sure Violet was okay to leave. He'd been watching her vitals all morning and knew her blood pressure and pulse were fine.

"Yeah, just a little lightheaded is all," she answered and held onto him. "But I think it's just trauma, you know, nearly dying and stuff?"

Violet smirked but Roman didn't see the humor in it.

"I'm kidding, Roman. I'm okay, just tired. And maybe a little traumatized," she said, smiling again.

"Stop," Roman said softly and shook his head.

He wrapped an arm around her, holding her against his body as he supported her weight.

Amber walked to the door and peered out into the hall. The nurses were busy going over charts at the desk a ways down the hall at their station.

"Come quickly," Amber said, ducking back in the room.

Roman nearly lifted Violet off the ground as he helped her to walk. They walked quickly down the hallway and onto the elevator, Violet collapsed against him, tired from the exertion.

"You *sure* you're alright?" he asked again, looking down at her.

"Yeah, I'm just tired. Seriously, I'm okay. I have felt worse after a night of partying."

Amber laughed. "Randy cleaned your car, Roman. He didn't think you needed the reminder of what happened and he needed something to make himself feel useful," Amber said.

"Thanks," he said, feeling uncomfortable that the kid had to clean up his friend's blood. No one should have to do that. But he was thankful it was taken care of anyway.

"You're welcome. It helped him," Amber said, pushing Violet's hair back away from her face as Roman cradled her.

The doors opened and Roman lifted Violet into his arms and carried her towards the front door. Randy had pulled up in the patient loading area. Amber jogged forward and opened the door quickly as Roman slid Violet onto the back seat and followed in beside her.

"Thanks for coming," Roman said to Randy, looking around to see if anyone from the hospital had followed them out.

"No prob," Randy said, nodding at Roman from the driver's seat. Once everyone was inside he pulled out and drove off towards Mantua.

"We better go to Roman's," Amber said, turning around from the front seat to look at him. "They know where she lives. When they figure out she's gone they may send the cops to look for her or something. I have no idea if you're just allowed to leave the hospital or what?"

"Would they do that?" Randy asked, cocking his head.

"I don't know, but they might, right? I don't know?" Amber said, looking at Roman for confirmation.

"Patients can check themselves out of the hospital against doctor's orders, but given the anomaly in her blood, I just didn't want to get stopped by someone and have to deal with them trying to convince her to stay. But yes, let's go to my place," Roman said, remembering her broken bed.

Fuck, it had only been a few hours ago that they'd broken her bed, and now she had almost died, and two of her friends, and one ex, were dead.

"I really have no clue how that shit works, but I can't fathom them just allowing someone to leave without doing any follow up. Especially considering her bloodwork," Roman added.

The truth was that he was more concerned about vampires than the hospital. With all the networks and shit now involved in the underground he had no idea how connected it all was. They may very well know all about her and would come to cover it all up.

Violet looked out the window. The sky was flaming with amber and fuchsia as the sun plummeted towards the horizon. "The sky makes such pretty colors." She smiled sleepily, looking over at Roman and closing her eyes as he rubbed her cheek and wrapped his arm around her, cradling her to his chest.

Roman carried Violet up the metal stairs to his apartment as Randy went ahead of them to unlock the door. She was still sleeping on and off which gave Roman some relief. She needed to rest so her body could heal. He noticed the dressing on her neck was starting to saturate with blood, a small spot blossoming in the center of the bandage. He would clean her wound and redress it as soon as she was resting on his bed.

"Do you need anything?" Amber asked, walking into his bedroom.

"I don't think so, not that I can't think of any way," he said, turning to look at her.

"Do you want us to stay and help?" Amber asked, not really wanting to be away from her friend.

"I don't need help, but it's up to you, Amber. I know you're worried." Roman turned back around and looked down at Violet.

She opened her eyes and was immediately comforted to be in his home. The familiar scent of his soap and fabric softener made her feel content. She wasn't in any pain. They'd doped her up good at the hospital, but she felt detached from her body, as though her spirit was resting somewhere above them all.

"Amber," she said, focusing on the bright red hair as her vision blurred, "I want you to go and make sure the girls are okay."

"I don't really care about them right now, Vi," Amber said, tipping her head to the side and bending down on one knee.

"I know, but you should go and take care of them. They're sick and they need someone to make sure they're okay. Roman's not going to let anything happen to me."

"I'd rather stay here with you and know you're okay," Amber said.

"I'll be fine. I'm high as fuck right now from the painkillers," she said, laughing a little and causing the others to chuckle. "Besides, what's going to happen to me with him here? Look at him." She smiled as she looked up at him and then at Amber. "I have a hot nurse with a giant needle." Violet giggled and grinned sleepily, her eyes closing again of their own volition.

"Oh geez," Amber said, shaking her head and laughing. "She is clearly doped up." Amber looked at Roman and snickered.

"Clearly." Roman fidgeted and raked his nails across the back of his head.

"Maybe you can go pick up her car at the hospital," he said, remembering that he'd left it there and was happy for a subject change. "The keys are in her bag. Don't mind the wires hanging below the steering column."

"See, all taken care of," Violet said, trying to open her eyes but failing. "I'm gonna be sleeping. Go home and take care of yourselves," she slurred and snuggled into his pillow, falling asleep again.

Amber walked out into the living room and Roman followed her. "I promise I'll call if anything happens," Roman said, placing his hand on Amber's shoulder.

She almost shied away from his touch, flashes of him killing Steve replaying in her mind. The look of absolute hatred and ferocity in him had been so terrifying. Fuck, the whole night had been terrifying. It was confusing because the man she'd seen last night didn't relate to how kind and mellow Roman always was otherwise. Even when he'd fought with Mark when they first met him he had been calm and controlled. Last night was a completely different story. If Amber didn't know the situation she would have thought Steven was the victim and Roman was the evil vampire.

Roman took his hand back sensing her unease and it made him uncomfortable. This was why he didn't have friends. Anyone who saw his true nature wouldn't be able to look at him as anything but a killer. He couldn't blame Amber for being repulsed, though he hoped for Violet's sake that Amber would learn to deal with it. Because he wasn't leaving Violet. He had finally rectified his mind to that.

"We'll bring your car back and drop the keys off after we get her car," Randy said, grabbing the door.

"Make sure nothing happens to her," Amber said, looking up at Roman.

"She'll be fine. I'm not going to let anything happen to her ever again."

Amber smiled up at him and nodded her head. If she was safe anywhere, it was here with him. Who could ever hurt Violet with him protecting her?

After Violet's friends left he exhaled and went to gather his supplies. Her bandages needed to be changed, so he cleaned her up, noting how horrific the wound still looked. It didn't look infected though, and there were definite signs of healing. The bite mark on her shoulder was bruised pretty badly but the puncture marks were already mostly closed. Her throat was a mess, but it didn't look nearly as bad as he thought it might. Truth be told, he still expected her to need surgery, but if she did need it he'd take her somewhere accustomed to dealing with this kind of injury. It paid to know professionals.

He exhaled and paced the room, circling back and forth around the bed, watching her as she slept. She looked peaceful.

The sweatshirt reflected on her pale skin making her look newborn-pink. She was lying curled in a small half-moon, her hands tucked beneath her face, her breathing slow and relaxed. She seemed more peaceful now than she had most of the time he'd known her. He looked at the two casts on her arms. At some point those would have to come off. He sighed, completely stressed. This was all his fault. He had failed like he'd never failed before. It mattered now more than ever, and he'd failed. His legs wobbled and he reached out to steady himself, placing his hand against the dresser. He felt like he might collapse. His brain was buzzing from sleep deprivation and the trauma of thinking she was going to die. His skin felt cold and tingling, little pinpricks of electricity zapping over his skin. He closed his eyes. Whispers, voices he didn't recognize spun in his brain. *Where are you?* He pounded the side of his head with his fists, willing the voices to quiet. The voices got louder and then went silent.

He opened his eyes, staring down at Violet again. He was too tired. That's what was wrong. *I should take a shower.*

He walked to the bathroom and peeled his clothes off, crunchy with dried blood and mud and sweat, and tossed them to the floor. He climbed into the shower and turned the cold water on, relishing the feel of the cold water. He watched the stream of blood ribbon down the drain. He soaped himself multiple times, those voices whispering again, imploring him to come to them. He shook his head.

"Stop it!" he growled, pounding his fist to the side of his head again. He had never experienced this before.

He lathered his body again, wanting the cold water to wake him up, wanting the burst of adrenaline and clarity it normally gave him. It didn't wake him up, it only tortured him. He couldn't leave her alone too long. He rinsed and turned the water off then climbed out. He quickly dried off, wrapping a towel around his waist. It was nice not to have a trail of thick wet hair to contend with anymore.

Feeling clean again, he walked back to his bedroom to find Violet hadn't stirred. He opened the dresser and retrieved his flannel pajama bottoms and pulled them up over his damp legs. Maybe they'd sleep for a week straight. God, he hoped so.

He walked to the far side of the bed and pulled the blankets back and slid down beside her. It felt so good to finally relax. His brain was still buzzing, but the voices had quieted. What the fuck had that been about? He needed to shut down. He needed to sleep. He looked over at her, barely able to keep his eyes open, and ran his finger gently across her cheek, and then fell asleep.

It was midday when he woke up, his eyes opening slowly. He took in a deep breath aware of his surroundings again. The television was chattering from down the hall. He sat up and rubbed the sleep from his eyes and put his feet down onto the cold floor. He stood up then walked to the bathroom. He relieved himself, then washed his hands and face. He actually, oddly, felt rested. He brushed his teeth and then walked down the hall to find Violet curled up like a cat on the couch covered in the blanket she'd given him and watching soap operas.

She turned her head and smiled. "You know, this woman here, Kim, she's been on this soap opera for as long as I can remember. She's got the sweet life." Her face was alight with happiness. It was good to see her looking normal, though strange given all that had happened.

Roman walked towards her and sat down in the chair across from the couch. "You feeling better?"

"Yeah, I feel better."

"Back to normal, better?"

"No, my neck is sore, and it kinda stings and burns when I turn my head, but I'm better," she said, placing her hand over the white bandage. "Thank God for Lux's blood I guess." She shrugged with a grin.

Roman returned her smile and nodded his head. "Yeah, I guess so. At least he's good for something." He understood how much more powerful Lux's blood would be than the blood in his own veins. He was thankful for it because she'd be dead otherwise.

"I think he did something to me when I was out."

Roman leaned forward in the chair resting his forearms on his thighs. "*Who* did what?" He wasn't sure he wanted the answer. If Mark had done something more he didn't know how the fuck he'd process that. He couldn't kill the mother fucker again.

"Oh, I meant Lux. I think he did something. Like to help me heal, or whatever. Is that possible? Because I was gone, Roman. *Gone* gone."

Roman leaned back into the chair and rubbed his face brusquely. Could Lux have healed her somehow? No. Not possible. "I don't think so."

"I saw him though. When I was out, I mean. And I felt his strength when Mark was..." Her eyes trailed away. "I don't even know what happened after I blacked out."

Roman took a deep breath. "Do you want to know?"

"Roman, he was so...full of hate. How could I have ever loved him?"

Roman stood up and walked around the coffee table and sat down beside her. She leaned into him resting her head against his arm. "You're better off not knowing everything."

"You took care of him? Of everyone?" She turned her head, pressing her face against his warm arm.

"I took care of it." Flashes of what had happened replayed in his mind making him feel sick.

Violet kissed his arm and then scooted down to rest her head in his lap. Roman placed his hand on her stomach. It was comforting feeling her steady breaths, in and out, in and out.

"I thought I lost you," he said, his voice a tortured whisper.

Violet rolled over so that she was facing him, her face tucked against his stomach. He could feel her hot tears against his skin. He rubbed her back, his own eyes swelling with unshed tears. He blinked them away and cleared his throat.

"But here you are, my little fighter," he said.

Violet sniffled, clearing her nose and then she laughed. She pulled some of his pajama bottoms to her eyes and wiped them, sitting up grinning sheepishly.

"Let's go to my house," she said.

Roman placed his hands on the sides of her head and pulled her in for a kiss. His lips were so warm and soft, reverent. He pulled back, looking into her eyes for a moment, cherishing the fact that she was here with him. He kissed her again and then released her.

They walked in through the kitchen. Amber was busy cooking something that smelled italian. Randy sat splayed in front of the television, watching some movie with Malinda and Dory, who appeared to be alright. Roman and Violet said their hellos and then proceeded upstairs to her room after Amber had officially given Violet the once over. She looked around the house taking it all in as she went. She was flooded with memories and emotions. Happiness came over her.

She had survived. Roman had survived. They had all survived. Death had come to claim them and they won. *Well, not all of them.*

She pushed those memories somewhere far back into her subconscious, not allowing guilt to come over her today. She would not allow all that had happened that night to control her right now. One day she would emotionally have to deal with it, and the memory of how it felt to shove a fire iron through her friend's neck would no doubt haunt her dreams, but she wouldn't let it take her today. Today she was happy to be alive.

She turned and looked at Roman who stood only inches away from her now. She had been afraid of him in the beginning, stupid and afraid. All she saw now was the man who'd saved her a thousand times since they'd met.

"What?" Roman asked, walking in and sitting down on the bed, which Randy had apparently fixed.

"Nothing." She grinned and stood in front of him.

He took her hands in his as she leaned into him.

"Let's go somewhere far away from here," she said, taking her hands back and holding his face with her fingertips.

"Where do you want to go?" he asked with a raised brow.

"Vegas," she said as a smile spread across her face.

"Vegas? Why there?" He laughed at the seeming randomness.

"I don't know," she said, her brow furrowed in thought briefly. "Maybe cuz it couldn't be more different than this place?"

Roman shrugged slightly. "If that's what you want?"

"Yeah, let's go now," she said and kissed him.

The thought of *Vegas* was exciting. They could just have fun there. There'd be nothing dramatic, nothing dark and ominous over their heads to distract them for the very first time since they'd known each other.

What if all they had was darkness? Maybe she'd get to know him as the *normal guy* and be completely disinterested? She may be one of those girls that needed some sort of danger in her life to stay interested.

Granted, there would always be danger in his life, and her life now too, but he was really pretty average and boring when it came right down to it. They had nothing in common besides their blood and this experience.

He pushed the thoughts to the back of his mind. What did it matter anyway? *Stop thinking so much.* It had taken him weeks to finally acquiesce to the idea of them being together, and now that they were, he wanted more than just her friendship. Even friendship had seemed too much at times, but it wasn't enough now. The idea that there would be no more distractions was appealing.

"So, are we gonna go?" she asked, backing away from him a few inches.

"Are you sure you're feeling alright?" he asked, studying the way she looked for signs she wasn't as well as she claimed.

"Well, not right as rain, but good enough to lie around in a fancy hotel and order room service."

"We gotta get there first," he reminded her.

"Easy peasy compared to what's been going on around here." Violet shrugged and her eyes lit up with the possibility of the adventure.

"Very true," he said and stood up. "When do you want to leave?"

"No time like the present." She grinned and looked like she'd come out of her skin with excitement. Her eyes were radiant, like they were in their dreams.

Roman tilted his head slightly and walked to the door. "Get packing. I guess I'm going to need to figure out something with my apartment."

"Let Randy and Amber watch it for you," Violet said, going to her closet and digging through the pile of shoes to find her duffle bag. She began stuffing random pieces of clothing into the bag.

"How long do you want to stay?" he asked.

"I don't know. Let's not worry about that now," she said, pulling her dresser drawer open and dumping socks and bras and panties into the luggage.

"Okay?" he said, eyebrows raised quizzically.

Violet stilled herself and looked at him. "Roman, I just can't be here for a while. This place holds too many memories. I just really cannot be here now," she repeated for emphasis.

"I understand. You don't need to give me explanations. I get it," he said, leaning against the door frame.

She finished packing the bag, which was stuffed completely, and walked over to him. She stopped in front of him, looking up into his dark green eyes. "Did you ever know that you're my hero?" she said with a wry grin.

"Oh man, let's go." He laughed, placing his hand on top of her head and giving it a shake before guiding her out of the room.

"Seriously, you're everything I would like to be."

"Please stop," he said and laughed as he rested one arm across her shoulders and took her bag with the other. "What's in here? Rocks?"

"Just the essentials," she said, smiling.

They walked downstairs to the living room where her roommates were watching television. Malinda and Dory were nodding off on the floor in a pile of afghans.

"Where you going?" Amber asked, looking up from the television.

"Vegas," Violet said with a huge smile of excitement spreading across her face.

"What?" Amber said, pushing Randy's feet from her lap and standing in a blur.

"Yeah, I want to go. I need to get away from this place for a while," Violet said, hoping Amber would understand.

Amber's face looked solemn. She had not recovered from anything they'd been through, Violet had just nearly died, and now she was leaving?

"Don't be sad. Be happy for me. Please? This is a good thing, and it's not like we're not coming back," Violet pleaded her case, looking to her friend for some sort of support.

"But all this shit just happened. You almost died, like, what, yesterday?" Amber said, looking from Violet to Roman, who just shrugged in response.

"Two days ago, I think?" Violet said with a smirk.

"Violet, you can't be better yet?" Amber said, her brow deeply furrowed with concern as she looked from Violet up to Roman, who just shrugged his shoulders again.

"I feel fine. I mean, not one-hundy, but good enough. I've had worse period cramps than how I feel now," Violet said and chuckled.

"Dude!" Randy said, grunting, as all the girls laughed.

Roman scratched the back of his head as he looked at Randy and shook his head with a smirk on his face.

"Okay, fine, I guess. Just don't stay gone for long," Amber said, walking over and pulling Violet into her arms into a death grip hug.

"Dude, you guys should get married by Elvis," Randy said, standing up to get his farewell hug.

"Oh my God!" Violet exclaimed, laughing with the usual embarrassment from his candid remarks.

Amber laughed and shoved Randy. "Yeah, seriously, you totally should. That would be hilarious," Amber said.

"Um, *hilarity* is not really the point of a wedding is it?" Violet said, smiling awkwardly.

"So, anyway, can you keep an eye on my place for me?" Roman interjected, wanting to change the subject post haste.

Ordinarily he had someone who handled this sort of thing for him, but since he'd been distracted and hadn't expected to stay long he'd never bothered setting it up with Håvard. He was actually going to trust someone other than himself or Håvard for the first time in his life. He should at least let the man know what was going on, but not today.

Amber laughed out loud seeing how uncomfortable this subject made both of them. "You're such complete and total dorks! You'll be married within three days. Mark my words." She laughed and turned to look at Randy, who was also laughing. "Of course we'll keep an eye on your apartment. I'm glad that we finally know where you live. Way to invite us over sooner, Roman."

"Yeah, sorry about that. I'm not really the invite people over type. Spend all the time you want there now though."

"Like how he invites us over now that he won't be there?" she said with a laugh, looking at Randy.

Roman shrugged. "Sorry. I kill things. I'm not really known for my social skills," he said dully.

Amber blanched at that and gripped Randy's hand.

"Thank God you kill things," Randy said in earnest.

"Yeah, okay. Can we not take a trip down that memory lane right now? Come on, let's go," Violet said, bouncing up and down like a child. Her face was lit up like a Christmas tree.

She hugged her friends again, holding onto each a little tighter than usual. Roman left keys and instructions for anything that might come up. He wasn't expecting to be gone that long, so it shouldn't entail much on their part. Malinda and Dory woke up with the commotion, so Violet said goodbye to them as well, offering them to stay as long as they wanted. Violet looked at Amber again. They had been through so much together and both girls were on the verge of tears. Both of them also realized there was no need for such dramatics since Violet and Roman would be coming back. But something felt so different and oddly final. A chapter was ending and a new one was beginning.

Violet looked around the house one last time, this place would never be the same again.

Roman didn't spend much time throwing a few of his things into a bag. He was used to leaving on the fly. Anything he might need could be bought. He made sure everything was turned off and locked up as he headed for the door, stopping to scoop up the blanket she'd given him. He looped it over his shoulder and turned around, pulling the door closed behind him.

She sat on the top step outside staring into the waning sunlight. It would be dark in an hour. She loved the darkness now. It was her home in a way that it had never been before.

"You ready?" he asked, reaching down and messing up her hair. He understood that there was much more to her leaving than just going on a vacation. She needed to escape this place and everything it represented and he was happy to oblige the request.

"Yep," she said and smiled as she pulled herself up. "Ready as I'll ever be."

They walked to the car and she got in, watching Roman in the side mirror as he loaded their things into the back. My God he was beautiful. She would never get used to that. And she would never forget that he had saved her life. Multiple times. Her savior, in so many ways.

He backed out of the driveway and pulled into the street and started driving away. Violet watched as physical memories passed her by, the friend's house, the convenient store, her high school, all just memories of a time that no longer existed. It hadn't really existed at all. All of it had been an illusion. There'd been a secret bubbling beneath the surface of her skin since the day she was born.

She was finally living.

Roman looked over at her intermittently watching as her eyes moved over the surface of every place they drove by. He loved the way she was capable of taking in a thousand things at once, every single detail seemed crystalline. He saw the sign coming up on the right, "all u can eat fish", and he pulled down the street to the trailer park across the street.

"Why are you going down here?" Violet asked, looking at him with concern on her face. Her eyes were so glossy-wet and reflective as they caught the retreating sun.

"I told you we'd go back for it," he said, stopping the car.

She smiled in understanding at what he meant and opened the car door. She walked towards the house on a mission. She knew exactly where it would be, right where Mark had thrown it down. Her brain flashed images, her skin crawling with the memories. She winced, remembering every blow that had landed. *Close your eyes and go. Close your eyes and go.* She inhaled deeply, the smell of charred wood stinging her nose.

He followed behind her and watched as she took each step determined to keep her from ever experiencing another night like the one she'd had here. Even seeing this place made him feel desperate to keep her safe again, taking him right back to that frantic night and all the terror of it.

The building was gutted, charred black, and empty inside. The local news had reported that the abandoned building had likely been caught on fire by hooligans. Apparently law enforcement had been watching the place because reports had been coming in of suspicious activity going on there late at night. It was doubtful anyone had taken it too seriously, as there was a lot of drug activity in the vicinity. Mark, Steven, and Mosely had been reported as suspects and on the run. They would never be found. No closure for any of their families ever. It was sad, but there was nothing that could be done about it.

She walked through the front room and straight to the back where Mark had assaulted her. She was careful not to look at anything but the object she sought. Thoughts flashed, memories replaying themselves like brief snippets of someone else's life. This would haunt her at some point, just not now. She wouldn't allow it to steal her joy today.

Some other day I will grieve. Not today.

She looked down and there beside the heap of blackened cotton and metal coils lay the heart, perfect and silver, untouched by flame or horror. She picked it up and held it in her hand. It was so cool in her palm.

"The chain is broken," she said and frowned as she held it up.

"We can fix it," he said gently as she turned to look at him.

He wondered about all the thoughts behind her pretty eyes. She looked so haunted. They had a long ride ahead of them and he had every intention of learning every last detail that he could. He wanted to know everything about her that he could know.

She walked over to him and took his hand. "Let's leave this place."

Roman's lips lifted at the corner slightly. He turned and led her back to the car. He opened the door for her and she plunged down onto cold leather seats, heart in hand, and felt relief for the first time in what felt like her whole life.

He backed out and began to go back towards the highway as Violet looked out the window, still transfixed by the rusted trailers, the messy yards, and beat up cars which littered this park. There was a whole world back here she had been blissfully unaware of before the night she almost died. Her mouth turned down as she swallowed the lump in her throat. She looked over and saw the old yellow dog sitting upright staring at them as they approached. The soulful brown eyes were so sad in their resignation. She related a little too much to the look in those eyes.

"Stop," Violet said, sitting forward and putting her hand on the dashboard.

Roman stopped the car startled by her abruptness. She quickly opened the door and ran to the dog. She patted the dog on the head, scratching the dirtied yellow fir as its thick muddy tail beat the ground with timid happiness.

"Do you want to come with me?" she asked, scratching his chin. The dog looked at her and licked her hand. She smiled and unhooked the dog and led him quickly to the car.

Roman watched in confusion as Violet stole the dog. He shook his head and smiled.

"That's no life for a dog," she said, leaning over and looking at Roman as the dog jumped up into the car. It licked his nose before he'd even had a chance to react. "Come on, let's go before someone sees."

Roman pulled away quickly and back onto the main highway. She looked in the rearview mirror as she watched her town and the sun fading into the distance.

And the snow began to fall.

ABOUT THE AUTHOR

Tara Vanflower is best known for her work with the darkwave band Lycia. She is currently living in Arizona with her husband Mike and their son Dirk Alrik and a couple of retired racing greyhounds.

ABOUT THE COVER ARTIST

Daniele Serra is a professional illustrator. His work has been published in Europe, Australia, United States and Japan, and displayed at various exhibits across the U.S. and Europe. He has worked for DC Comics, Image Comics, Cemetery Dance, Weird Tales magazine, PS Publishing and other publications. Winner of the British Fantasy Award.

If you enjoyed this book please share it.

www.ingramcontent.com/pod-product-compliance
Lightning Source LLC
Chambersburg PA
CBHW030539260626
47157CB00006B/2100